P9-CME-842

THE BLACKBIRD PAPERS

DOUBLEDAY

New York   London   Toronto

Sydney   Auckland

THE BLACKBIRD PAPERS

Ian Smith

PUBLISHED BY DOUBLEDAY
a division of Random House, Inc.

DOUBLEDAY and the portrayal of an anchor with a dolphin
are registered trademarks of Random House, Inc.

Book design by Nicola Ferguson

This book is a work of fiction. Names, characters, businesses, organizations, places, events, and incidents either are the product of the author's imagination or are used fictitiously. Any resemblance to actual persons, living or dead, events, or locales is entirely coincidental.

Grateful acknowledgment is made to the following for permission to reprint previously published material: "The Peace of Wild Things" from *Selected Poems of Wendell Berry* by Berry, Wendell. Copyright 1999 by Perseus Books Group. Reproduced with permission of Perseus Books Group in the format Trade Book via Copyright Clearance Center.

Library of Congress Cataloging-in-Publication Data
Smith, Ian, 1969–
The blackbird papers / Ian Smith.— 1st ed.
p.   cm.
1. African American college teachers—Fiction. 2. Government investigators—Fiction.
3. African American men—Fiction. 4. Hanover (N.H.)—Fiction.
5. Nobel Prizes—Fiction. 6. Brothers—Fiction. I. Title.

PS3619.M588B58 2004

813'6—dc22   2003068804

ISBN 0-385-51136-1

PRINTED IN THE UNITED STATES OF AMERICA

July 2004

FIRST EDITION
1   3   5   7   9   10   8   6   4   2

To Tristé . . . Forever . . . Unconditionally

THE BLACKBIRD PAPERS

1

rofessor Wilson Augustus Bledsoe's car glided along the dark narrow roads of Hanover, New Hampshire, then crossed Ledyard Bridge into the vast wilderness of Vermont. The rain had started slowly at first, but now heavy drops danced staccato across the windshield of his old Mercedes. He felt relieved to be heading home, away from the noisy party still in full swing back at the president's mansion. The celebration was in his honor, yet he had been the first to leave. It wasn't that he was ungrateful. Bledsoe simply felt uncomfortable in large crowds, especially ones convened in his behalf, as they were these days with increasing frequency. What most of the guests didn't know was that but for his wife's insistence, he wouldn't even have gone. He had much more pressing matters to see to in his lab.

Bledsoe was no ordinary professor. He had just been awarded the twenty-third Devonshire, the most lucrative prize in science and second only to the Nobel in prestige. Winning it was no small feat, even for a full professor at Dartmouth College, which boasted more academic luminaries than universities four times its size. That's why Wallace Mortimer III, the college's revered president, and his wife, Serena, had spared no expense in celebrating their most acclaimed—and certainly their most acclaimed African American—faculty member.

It was clear to all who had gathered this evening that they were celebrating not just the Devonshire but a career that had been filled with a remarkably long list of achievements. Having won a Nobel five years earlier, Bledsoe had trumped his own legend, now becoming the first American to claim the world's two largest science awards. As his colleagues congratulated him on the Devonshire tonight, they teased him about the lavish treatment he'd receive when he and Kay took their complimentary trip to England and were feted at an elaborate ceremony hosted by the Queen. Everyone wanted to know what he was going to do with the $2 million prize money. "Whatever Kay decides," was the most that he was willing to share.

Bledsoe picked up his cell phone and called home. "I'm on my way, Curly," he said. He only called Kay that in private. It was a nickname he'd given her back when they were students together at the University of Chicago. On their first date, flustered and eager, he had mixed up the time and shown up an hour early. Kay, who had just gotten out of the shower, had opened the door expecting to find one of her girlfriends, and instead had found an equally surprised Wilson. She was horrified. Her customarily straightened hair was a mass of unruly curls. He laughed and she almost cried, but an intimacy and candor had been established between them that had only grown through their marriage.

"How was it?" Kay asked.

"Wally and Serena were excessive as always. I'm embarrassed to think how much they spent."

"Who was there?"

"Faces I haven't seen in years. Laurence Wilcox even came up from Harvard."

"Laurence? He hates you."

"Wally and Serena pulled out all the stops."

The Mortimers had evidently been determined to make this a bash to remember, assembling many of the foremost scientists in the academic community, humbling Bledsoe when he stood on the balcony of the mansion during the toast and looked at the crowd gathered below. The first person he had recognized was Yuri Mandryka, perhaps the greatest anatomist the Soviet Union had ever produced, stooped over his cane and raising his glass of bubbly. Laurence Wilcox, chairman of Harvard's biology department, had made the trek up from Boston and was standing with Olson Bulger, the precocious MIT mathematician who already had a calculus theorem named after him before he notched thirty. Wilcox hadn't spoken to Bledsoe since he'd turned down Wilcox's generous invitation to join the Harvard faculty. Wilcox was a giant in the field of evolutionary biology and admired around the world for his numerous publications and prolific laboratory. He chaired the most important meetings and sat on the boards of the most respected scientific institutions. No one had ever said no to an offer from Laurence Wilcox except for Wilson Bledsoe, who simply wrote, "Thanks for your offer, but Kay and I are happy tucked away in these quiet mountains. I'm afraid I'm captive to the indescribable peace just outside my back door."

"Can you believe Garrett flew in all the way from Stanford?" Bledsoe said. "You'd figure he'd have a lot more important things to do than attend a damn party on the other side of the country." Garrett Templeton was the acclaimed chemist from Stanford, who, despite winning a Nobel of his own, was most famous for twice being offered the presidency of Yale and twice turning it down. Like Bledsoe, he had already found the perfect place, a small plot of land on a cliff overlooking the Pacific.

"Well, I'm not surprised at all that Garrett showed," Kay said. "Maybe it'll finally hit home for you that the Devonshire is a big deal, sweetie. Everyone else seems to get that but you."

"Just another reason to throw a party in that old mansion," Bledsoe huffed.

"And I'm proud that you stayed as long as you did," Kay laughed. She knew how much he would rather be toiling away in his laboratory than making small talk at a cocktail party.

"An hour was more than enough," Bledsoe said. "Oh, but there was something very funny."

"Yeah?"

"When I left, a student parking cars asked me to autograph one of my textbooks."

"What did you write?"

"I didn't. I'm not some rock star, Curly. I'm a scientist."

"Wilson, whether you like it or not, you're a star and an inspiration to many people."

"Maybe so," Bledsoe said, relenting. "But like my father said, 'The minute you start believing your own headlines is the minute you stop earning them.' "

Kay chuckled. She'd heard that one many times. "Did you save your appetite?"

"You betchya. I only had one shrimp all night."

"Well, dinner will be ready when you get here."

"See ya soon, honey."

"Love ya." Kay made a loud kissing sound before the line went dead.

Bledsoe pictured the grilled salmon, mashed potatoes, and cucumbers she had waiting for him. It was his favorite meal, had been since he was a kid. His mother always made it for him on special occasions—bringing home a good report card or winning a chess competition. He pushed the old red Mercedes. He had a lot to get done. Right after dinner he planned on returning to the lab—his paper was finally ready to be submitted to *Science*. He could have waited until the next morning, but he had worked on this paper for almost a year, the longest it had ever taken him to publish a manuscript. Even with hundreds of articles to his credit, he still enjoyed that shot of adrenaline when the paper finally left his desk.

Bledsoe thought about the pleasantries he and President Mortimer had exchanged minutes earlier as Mortimer walked him to the door.

"We're very proud of you, Wilson," he had said in his clipped New England accent. "You've done well by Dartmouth and I'm personally grateful for that."

"The college has done well by Kay and me," Bledsoe said. "And the best is yet to come, I hope."

"You've got the Nobel and the Devonshire," Mortimer said. "It doesn't get better than that."

"I'm not talking awards, Wally. I'm talking about research. I've still got some good years left in me."

"You sound like you're on to something."

"The scent is getting stronger."

"Care to share with an old friend?"

"It'll be ready later tonight," Bledsoe said. "I'm still hammering out the final details." Like most researchers on the trail of something important, he didn't care to share his work before he was ready.

"You're looking a little tired, Wilson," Mortimer said. He had put his arm around Bledsoe's shoulders. "I know how tough the grind can be. Don't do what I did and miss out on many of life's opportunities while you're young. Take a semester off and travel the world with Kay."

"I've been giving that some serious thought," Bledsoe said. "We've never been to Asia."

"Enjoy yourselves. You have enough money. Go as long as you want. You'll always have a home here at Dartmouth."·

"Thanks, Wally. Kay and I have been grateful for the friendship we've shared with you and Serena all these years."

"Where are you going now?"

"Home," Bledsoe said. "Kay is holding dinner for me."

"Send her my best," Mortimer said.

Then Wallace Mortimer III, perfectly groomed in a stiff navy blazer and a forest green bow tie, did something he had never done in their twenty-year friendship. He reached out and hugged Wilson Bledsoe. Firmly.

The image of that hug lingered in Bledsoe's mind as he turned onto River Road and switched to high beams. The darkness in these mountain towns was overwhelming, especially on the small dirt roads. Drivers were left to find their way with the moon's reflection and a good dose of intuition.

The car careened down River Road, the longest in the Upper Valley, stretching along the embankment of the Connecticut River and snaking its way into the wooded mountainside. This road was always a challenge, one that students often drove for the sheer pleasure of its difficult terrain and unexpected turns. Bledsoe had narrowly missed several deer since moving out here and tonight's darkness, rain, and wet leaves made a perfect combination for disaster. So despite the temptation to test the engine of his beloved machine, he drove the blind curves carefully, keeping the car positioned as close to the middle of the road as possible, on the alert for any darting animals. Kay had already amassed a small collection of nicks and scratches on the grill of her station wagon, and he was not about to do the same with the Mercedes.

Just as Bledsoe turned into Dead Man's Curve, a sharp uphill bend that had claimed more than thirty lives, something caught his eye. It was difficult to make it out, with the rain beating against his windshield and the stubborn wipers leaving more water on the window than they cleared. But as he got closer, he finally saw a pair of blinking hazard lights a hundred or so yards down the road. They were high off the ground. Bledsoe thought they might belong to a truck. He inched closer, finally getting a better view of an ancient rust-colored pickup with a wobbly pair of wood side railings that rose a few feet above the cabin. The front hood was propped up, and what looked like a man's legs jutted out from underneath the back of the truck. A flat tire or a dead engine, he thought.

Bledsoe slowed to a crawl. A heavily bearded man wearing a pale green jacket stood by the side of the truck, frantically waving his arms. His coat hung open over his ample girth. It was difficult to make out details in the darkness, but Bledsoe could see what looked like a large black grease stain on the stranger's front right pants pocket. He tried to look at the man's face, but it was obscured by a crushed hunter's cap. He could see the heavy beard; that was all. Debating whether to stop, he continued inching forward. The entrance to his property was only a little over a mile away, and he was hungry and Kay was waiting. In just a couple of minutes, he could be home out of the rain and sitting down to a hot plate of salmon. Kay hadn't mentioned it, but he was sure that she planned on surprising him with one of her homemade double-chocolate cakes.

Bledsoe let his car roll by. He was thinking now of how glad he would be to pull up to his house, a massive structure of stone and brick. It was their dream house, not far from the river, buried deep in the woods, hidden on more than a hundred acres of rambling trees and rocky ravines. He felt bad about leaving the two men, but there was still the business of the manuscript in his computer back at the lab. He was determined to e-mail the second draft to the journal tonight, regardless of how long it took him to finish. Stopping would only make his long night longer.

But then he looked in his rearview mirror at the waving man and called home.

"I'm gonna be a little late, Curly," he said, shifting his car into reverse. "A couple of guys are stranded with a broken-down truck here on River Road."

"Don't be too long," Kay sighed. "I don't want the food to get cold."

"I won't," Bledsoe said. He backed up the car until he almost reached the bearded man. "I'll be home soon, sweetie," he said.

"Be careful out there," Kay warned. "It's dark and the rain doesn't make it any better. Make sure you're far enough off to the side so other cars can still pass."

Always the protector, Bledsoe thought to himself. Kay was a great wife and an even better friend. After twenty-five years, he still felt that way.

He suddenly felt the urge to tell her about Mortimer's embrace. "Something else strange happened tonight," Bledsoe said.

"What's that?"

"When I was leaving, Wally asked me where I was going. I told him you had dinner waiting for me."

"That sounds normal to me."

"Yeah, but then he hugged me."

"So?"

"No, he really hugged me. Tight. He's never done that before. I've never seen Wally hug anyone."

"You men are all alike," Kay said. "A little affection is cause for alarm. It's perfectly normal for the two of you to share a hug on a night as big as this."

"If you say so," Bledsoe said, still not convinced.

"Now hurry and see what those men want and get home."

"I'll be there before you turn off the stove."

Bledsoe pulled his car to a stop in front of the truck and cracked the window. "What's the problem?" he asked the stout man. Wilson could barely see the man's eyes under the hat's visor. The rain had matted his already mangy beard.

"I think the engine finally died on me," he said. "She's been making noises for the last couple of weeks. Just didn't have time to take her in."

"I don't know much about cars," Bledsoe said, getting out and moving under the hood. He couldn't make out much in the dark, just rusted metal and black pipes. Even if he could see better under the hood, it wouldn't make a difference. Except for the windshield-wiper-fluid dispenser that he noticed immediately, it was all one big mystery to him.

Bledsoe heard another set of footsteps approach. It must have been the man who'd been under the truck. He approached from the other side of the truck. He stopped next to the fender, then flashed a light on the engine and battery. He didn't come any closer.

"I'm sorry, but this is out of my league," Bledsoe said, still looking under the hood. "There's a service station a couple of miles back on the other side of the bridge. I can call and get someone over here. Where you guys heading?"

"All the way up to Fisherman's Creek," the big man replied. His voice was heavy and slow, as if smothered by his face full of unruly hair. "We're late for a delivery."

"I'd give you a lift, but I only have room for one more," Bledsoe said. He didn't exactly relish the idea of a soaking wet body in his car. Antiques could be temperamental. "Let me get back in and call for some help."

Bledsoe turned toward the second man but found himself looking into the long steel barrel of a shotgun. "What the hell!" he yelled, falling back against the truck's grille. "Put that down!"

"We need to take a little ride," the gunman said. Bledsoe couldn't make out much of his face either, but he noticed all the dark spaces in his mouth where there once had been teeth. The man stepped closer and pressed the gun hard into his chest. Bledsoe moved and the dim hazards flashed some light across the gunman's face. Evil burned in his eyes. They were small and dark and there was a scar that ran across his left cheek from the corner of his mouth to his earlobe. An ugly creature, Bledsoe thought to himself, a judgment that he didn't pass often.

"If it's my car you want, the keys are in it," Bledsoe said.

"Git in the truck," the bearded man growled. "We don't want your car, and don't even bother offering your money, 'cause we don't want that neither."

"Then what do you want?"

"Move it," the big man said, pushing him from behind. "There'll be plenty of time later to ask questions."

The gunman slid the shotgun across Bledsoe's chest and jammed it in his shoulder. He made a grunting sound, then spat on the ground. It was the sound horses make when they're angry. "Git going!" he shouted. "I've been waiting out in this goddamn rain long enough."

An image of Kay in her apron standing at the sink floated through Bledsoe's mind. Why had he stopped?

"In the car, Professor," the toothless man yelled, nudging Bledsoe even harder with the gun's barrel. "It's getting late."

The man had called him Professor. But Bledsoe had never met the man before—at least he didn't think he had.

The bearded man lowered the hood and slammed it shut. Wilson made his way around to the passenger side of the truck, taking his time in the hope that another car would be making its way up the long, dark road. Escape plans raced through his mind, but all of them revolved around his being a lot more athletic and agile than he was. If it had been ten years ago, when he was thirty pounds lighter and jogging three miles a day, he would have tried to overpower them. Instead, he was standing in a suit and wet dress shoes, badly out of shape and trying to hold his bladder.

The bearded man walked around to the other side of the truck, which sank as he settled his heft into the driver's seat. Bledsoe reached for the handle of the passenger door, still feeling the gun planted firmly in the middle of his back. He started to pull the door open, then stepped quickly to the side and yanked the door until it crashed into the gunman. A blast cracked the silence and echoed through the vast darkness. Bledsoe ran to the back of the truck, peeling off his topcoat and suit jacket. Thanks to his grandfather, who occasionally took him hunting on the weekends when he was a teenager, he had immediately recognized the Browning 28-gauge Citori Over and Under, a favorite among skeet shooters. He took off down the road knowing Toothless had only one bullet left in the chamber. If Bledsoe could survive the next shot, he'd have more time to escape while Toothless reloaded the gun.

The second blast came shortly, and Bledsoe felt a rush of hot air across the left side of his face. He ran his hand along his cheek. It had missed. He found his way to the middle of the dirt road, where he could get the most traction, then ran as hard as his tired legs would carry him. He now knew that it was true what people say about what happens when you're facing death. Your life passes through your mind, and in no particular order. He thought about Mr. Crouch, his high-school physics teacher, the smartest man he had ever met, who addressed all his students by the title of mister or missus. Then he thought about the little green swing set his father had erected in their tiny backyard. It seemed like he spent half his childhood pumping his legs until the swing wouldn't go any higher. Then there was the issue of that overdue book. Surely the library would be sending him another annoying reminder soon.

He wondered if old Nel Potter might have heard the blasts. Her house was the nearest one. If he was even luckier, Heidi, her companion, might have heard the commotion.

2

Bledsoe's labored breathing punctured the still night air. He hadn't run more than seventy-five yards and already his lungs felt like someone was holding a match to them.

Fear boosted his hearing, making every sound seem only a foot away. He heard the truck's cranky engine start, then the impatient squeal of old rubber spinning in wet dirt. They would be on him soon. He thought of a plan, but it meant making it into the woods before they caught him. Out among the trees and darkness, land familiar to him, it would be much easier to escape and hide. The bearded man wouldn't be much of a threat, judging by his enormous size, but Toothless could be a real challenge. He had the shotgun, and he was skinny enough to slide through the dense forest without much difficulty. But what troubled Wilson most was his own stamina. Would his already weary legs have enough endurance to outlast them?

Another blast exploded and ricocheted off the distant mountains, finally dying in the blanket of darkness. Bledsoe turned around for the first time since fleeing the truck. He saw Toothless hanging out of the passenger window, steadying the gun for another shot.

"Willlson!" Toothless yelled, then let out a bone-rattling laugh.

Bledsoe ran even harder as he negotiated Dead Man's Curve. He knew that if he could make it down the hill before they caught him, he'd be able to duck into the woods. He knew exactly where the trees would let him pass, but until he reached that point, the snarled vegetation and unforgiving thorns were too dense to penetrate.

The truck gained ground quickly—he could hear the tires eating up the dirt and kicking rocks in the air. The steep decline proved to be even more dangerous on foot than it had been in a car. Bledsoe slid and stumbled, almost falling several times before finally making it to level ground.

A flash of light made him turn back to see the truck weaving down Dead Man's Curve, its brakes and engine screaming. Bledsoe breathed a little easier as he reached the entry point. Two large twin maples marked the spot. He darted between them, hoping his pursuers missed his move.

Complete darkness engulfed him inside the woods, though here and there moonlight broke through the clouds and treetops, giving just enough of a glow to relieve his blindness. Even then, he could barely see objects less than a foot away. Most people would have immediately been lost, but Bledsoe had walked the woods in this area for the last ten years, tracking animals and filling his notebooks with detailed observations. He was fond of what he called his "night scouts," where he studied the mating patterns of owls and other nocturnals with a high-tech infrared camera. Numerous times he had pitched a tent and spent the night recording animal noises, hoping to distinguish the calls of aggression from those of seduction. He would choose the most interesting and distinct, then play the sounds for his class. He challenged the students to guess the animal and the significance of the calls. Professor Bledsoe might not know a damn thing about fixing cars, but he knew these woods as well as anyone could. He stood still for a moment and listened.

The truck's engine had fallen silent. One door creaked open, then another. There were voices, but Bledsoe couldn't make out the words. It sounded like the two men were arguing. Bledsoe raced through a thicket of evergreens and slid between the posts of an ancient wood fence, catching his right pants leg on something sharp. The pain was immediate, followed by a small trickle of warm blood down his thigh. He knew the cut was deep because the cold, wet air stung his exposed muscle.

He stopped for a moment and tensed his leg, then formed a cuff around it with his open hand, trying to stanch the bleeding. He could still hear their voices behind him. They were laughing and calling out to him, taunting him in the dark.

Bledsoe started running. The blood now flowed freely down his leg. For the first time, his fear turned to anger. What the hell did these men want from him so badly that they were willing to chase him into the woods? Maybe they were drunk, a couple of rednecks out to have some fun. But

they knew his name. They also knew that he was a professor. And Toothless had said, "I've been waiting out in this goddamn rain long enough."
Bledsoe continued the arduous run, slashing his way through brush, losing
his balance on uneven rocks and dead tree limbs. He had always wondered
how he would die—having a heart attack in front of his class, say, or
succumbing to the prostate cancer that had squeezed the life out of his
father. But one possibility that had never entered his mind was being
hunted down like a wounded animal.

Bledsoe was on familiar land, and once the clouds slid past the full
moon, its dim glow cast enough light that he could make out some of the
landmarks. He spotted the big old wooden wagon which, according to one
of his neighbors, had once been used to carry supplies on the large farm
and haul the children around the property on the weekends once it had
been filled with hay. Then he reached the tiny ravine that carved its
way through the mountains and around the border of the Potter property.
Normally, he crossed it farther down, balancing himself on a chain of rocks
that stuck out of the foot-high water. But in the dark there was no chance
that he would find the spot. Nor did he have the time. Instead he ran
directly into the chilling water, knowing that if he kept moving in a
straight line, it would take only seconds to reach the other side.

Another hundred yards and he found his first real stepping-stone to
safety. Potter's pond sat in the southern portion of the farm, but most importantly it marked the halfway point between River Road and Bledsoe's
property. With a renewed sense of a hope, he ran hard along the edge of the
water, which he knew was a little more than a mile around. Reaching the
other side, he rested momentarily and gave his burning lungs a break. This
was his favorite place to watch blackbirds dive into the wetlands for food.
It was also where he had once spotted a black bear bathing across the pond.
He had approached it with his camera rolling and come within twenty
yards of it before the bear heard a branch snap under his feet and took off.

The loss of blood started to affect his right leg, numbness and tingling
extending down to the sole of his foot. He could no longer lift the leg, and
as he moved forward, it dragged behind him.

The pain forced him against a tree, where he tore the split pants leg
wider so he could see the wound. It was difficult to make out in the dark,
but he could feel the blood sprouting to the rhythm of his heartbeat. He

pulled a handkerchief from his back pocket and tied it tightly above the wound like a tourniquet. The bleeding didn't completely stop, but it at least slowed.

Wilson heard his name echo in the darkness and jumped to his feet. The two goons weren't going to let the wilderness deter them from their pursuit.

He limped to a clearing fifty yards north of the pond. There was an old barn not too far away. He needed rest and the barn would be a place to hide and sit out the pounding rain. Throbbing with pain, he felt a kind of resentful pity for himself. Here he was, running for his life—tired, hurt, and scared—on a night he should have been celebrating with Kay, sitting at his kitchen table finishing his favorite dinner.

Animal cries rang out in the distance. He immediately recognized the drawn-out whoo-oo-oo raccoons make when fighting with each other, a sound similar to the call of a screech owl.

Bledsoe's breathing had finally settled, but the acid still burned his lungs. He took a deep, controlled breath and headed for the barn. Looking through the tree limbs, he read what few stars weren't covered by the clouds to get a sense of his positioning. He trudged another hundred yards through wet marshy ground before peering up and tracing the jagged mountaintops in the distance. There was a perfect V where two peaks overlapped—another landmark. It meant that he was standing on the path that led directly to the barn.

The high-pitched screech of bats sailed overhead. He fell to the ground twice before finally reaching the high grass. He was cold and hungry and terrified. A few more yards and he cleared the heavy trees. Tears slid down his face as he finally spotted the outline of the decaying barn. Its weathered wood slats threatened to collapse at any minute, the wild vines strangling what remained of the roof.

He slipped into the barn and found a dry spot in the corner. He grabbed a couple of dry-rotted beams and placed them by his side. If he was going to fight two men he would need some type of weapon, though he knew he stood almost no chance against a shotgun.

Time passed, but dazed by his fatigue and fear, he wasn't sure how much. He moved his hands blindly. He touched his face first, then his drenched clothes and his aching thigh. In less than an hour he had gone from champagne toasts to a desperate run for his life. For the first time, he contemplated what it would mean not to be with Kay or his students. The thought conjured more anger than it did fear. There was so much he wanted to accomplish, so many things he had yet to discover. It just didn't seem right for it all to end in this way and in this place.

The rain continued to beat heavily against the ancient barn, pouring through the holes in the deteriorated roof. He finally summoned his strength and stood to assess the damage to his thigh. Some feeling had returned to the leg, but it was stiff and lifting it still required great effort. He stretched his arms, then his back, then chose the board that fit most comfortably in his hand. He limped to what remained of the door and peered out. He couldn't see much in the darkness, but there were no signs or sounds of his attackers. He bowed his head and said a small prayer, then slipped through the missing beams.

He reminded himself that if he could make it across the two hundred yards that remained of the Potter property, he'd be on his own land and only minutes from the safety of his house.

He never saw the swing of the gun. It landed across the left side of his head and instantly sent him into an even greater darkness. A pair of powerful hands gripped his throat. With what little energy remained in his body, he threw his hands wildly, punching and scratching, doing anything he could to relieve the pressure around his neck. He dipped in and out of consciousness. His efforts only weakened him further, making his blows as ineffective as those of a child. He knew that he was growing more helpless against his attackers and that soon he would die.

He thought about the article. He needed to add so little. Now the answer would be lost forever. He had one last chance to save everything. He turned his head and opened his mouth, then with tremendous force, bit one of the hands around his neck. The attacker screamed in pain and fell back, freeing him. He crawled a few feet and took a grading marker from his back pocket. Pulling up his pants leg, he rolled down his sock and rubbed his skin until it was almost dry. Just above his right ankle he scribbled a word, then let the marker fall. Ready now, he turned back toward his attackers. They cracked him against the side of his face with the gun, then those hands were around his throat again. He threw one punch, but it missed badly. He didn't have the energy to throw another.

Kay's smiling face was the last image he saw. She was beckoning him to come to her. He wanted to call out, but his lips wouldn't move. He saw a bright flash of light, then black. Then his life slipped out of his body and into the darkness of the land that once was his paradise and now would be his grave.

3

The sound of a phone pierced the room's silence, causing the serpentine tangle of honey-colored legs and arms to unwrap. Sterling Bledsoe killed the racket in the middle of the third ring.

"It's five o'clock in the morning," he grumbled into the phone. "This better be good."

"Wilson," was all that the woman's voice could muster before dissolving into sobs.

"Kay?" Sterling whispered, now sitting up in the bed. "Is that you?" There was a muffled response. "I can't understand what you're saying," he said.

There was a pause before a man's voice took over. "Sterling Bledsoe?" The voice was official and in charge. "Are you the brother of Professor Wilson Bledsoe?"

"Yes," Sterling said. "What the hell is going on?"

"This is Detective Paul Hanlon of the Hanover Police Department," the man replied. "Sorry to wake you so early in the morning, sir, but your brother is missing."

"Wilson, missing?" Sterling asked, unable to make any sense of the words. "What the hell do you mean, Wilson's missing? Where's Kay?"

"She's right here," Hanlon said. "One of the other officers is trying to comfort her, but I don't think she's in any condition to talk right now."

Sterling looked at Veronica, back asleep under the covers. He left the bedroom and walked down the hall until he reached the kitchen. "What happened to Wilson?" Sterling demanded. His voice had quickly gone from confusion to anger.

"We're still trying to piece together all the information we have," Hanlon answered. He chose his words carefully.

"Skip the bullshit," Sterling shouted into the phone. Sterling Bledsoe knew a lot about police evasions—he was an FBI agent. He had spent the better part of ten years in the National Center for the Analysis of Violent Crime in Quantico, Virginia, where as a supervisory special agent he led an elite team of investigators that handled only the most difficult and highest-profile cases. "Tell me what the hell happened to my brother."

"Please calm down, Mr. Bledsoe," Hanlon said a little edgily.

"Calm down? You wake me up at some ungodly hour, tell me that my brother is suddenly missing, then you want me to calm down. I want some answers, dammit!"

"We don't really have many right now," Hanlon said. "Your brother was heading home last night after a party at the president's mansion. He spoke to his wife twice and said he'd be home shortly for dinner. No one has seen him or heard from him since."

"What time was the last communication?" Sterling asked. His detective instincts had already switched on. He was thinking more like an investigator than a brother.

"Just after seven last night," Hanlon said. "He was traveling north on River Road and stopped to help a stranded truck."

"Has anyone found the truck?"

"Negative. Our men are out there right now, but there's no sign of the truck or the Professor's car."

Sterling had been on the other end of these phone calls all too often and knew that it was an unpleasant experience. But the fact that it was his only brother who was missing both scared and infuriated him.

"What time did Kay call in the missing person?"

"The first call came in to dispatch at twenty-one hundred hours. The second was logged in at twenty-three hundred, and the last at oh three hundred this morning." Hanlon's responses were short and automatic. No original thought, something that worried Sterling. Local police departments tended to be slow and lack creativity. Sterling knew exactly how they worked, having cleaned up many of their sloppy investigations. Now he dreaded the idea that his brother's life might rest in the hands of a small, untested department tucked away in a rural mountain town.

Sterling looked at his clock. "Have you entered him into NCIC yet?" The National Crime Information Computer centralizes criminal records and data on fugitives, stolen property, and missing persons. The FBI and authorized federal, state, local, and foreign law enforcement agencies can enter data into the elaborate system as well as extract information for the purposes of an active investigation. With just a few keystrokes, they can keep track of everything from the FBI's ten most wanted to stolen handguns. Sterling had used it many times to identify corpses.

Hanlon cleared his throat. He wasn't sure what Sterling Bledsoe did for a living, but it was obvious that he wasn't unfamiliar with police work. Bluffing would be a waste of time. "Mr. Bledsoe, typically we'd wait a little longer before entering someone into the computer. There's no reason to suspect any criminal activity or anything like that, at least not yet. We are, however, putting all available manpower on it. We realize that your brother isn't just anyone. He recently won that science award and a helluva lot of money."

"Big fucking deal about the award," Sterling shot back. "He also won the Nobel and nothing happened."

"That I know," Hanlon said. "But this is worth $2 million, double what the Nobel's worth."

Sterling knew damn well how much money his older brother had just won. He didn't need to hear it from some local cop who didn't even know which countries sponsored the awards. Sterling's gut was already churning and it was telling him that money wasn't the motive. Wilson was a frumpy academic, not some industrial titan. He and Kay had plenty of money, but they lived a pretty simple life. Not too many people would have a sense of how much they were actually worth.

"Have you called state yet?" Sterling asked.

"No, we're still treating this as a local matter between us and the department in Vermont," Hanlon said. "The investigation is just beginning. If the time comes when we need to bring them in, we will, of course, make the call."

"Where exactly did Kay say he was when she spoke to him last?" Sterling was in his apartment in New York City, but he was thinking like he was in Quantico.

"He was still in the car, just a few minutes from home."

"Did she get an exact location?"

"No, just that he was stopping somewhere on River Road, not far from the house."

"Is the area secured?" Sterling had already mapped out the scene in his mind.

"Like I said, Mr. Bledsoe, we're just beginning our investigation." Hanlon's voice wasn't friendly. "It's been less than ten hours since he was last heard from. It takes some time to gather all the facts and put everything together."

"Goddammit, Hanlon! If this is a missing person case, there's not a second to spare. Every tick of the clock can mean the difference between life or death. If River Road was his last identified location, don't you think it would make a world of sense to secure the area? Random car traffic or even roaming animals can destroy any evidence that's there."

There was a pause at the other end. "Anything else, sir?" Hanlon sighed.

"Yeah. Tell Kay I'm on the next goddamn plane!"

4

Sterling Bledsoe moved quickly and silently, packing enough clothes to last him a few days. He was more nervous than he wanted to let on, which is why he decided not to wake Veronica until he was heading out the door. Getting her upset wouldn't do either of them any good.

He walked into his small study and quietly closed the door behind him. He pulled out a small notebook that had been taped underneath his desk. He thumbed through the names of some of the most powerful people in Washington and stopped on Daniel J. Murphy, director of the FBI.

The phone rang once. "Murphy here." Even at five in the morning, the director growled like a man in charge.

"It's Bledsoe, Murph," Sterling said. "I've got some trouble up here."

"A student of yours has finally figured out what you really do for a living," Murphy cracked. One of the deals he had made with Sterling to keep him from leaving the Bureau was to allow him to teach an anatomy course at Hunter College one semester a year. Murphy never understood why it mattered so much to one of his top investigators to teach at some dinky city school.

"Wilson is missing," Sterling said.

Murphy's voice tightened. "How long?"

"About ten hours, from what I can gather. But who knows with the locals."

"Sorry to hear that, Sterling." He knew as well as Sterling that finding a missing person alive was always a race against the clock. The first twenty-four hours were critical. After that, the chance of a happy reunion dropped drastically with every passing minute. "Was he up at Dartmouth?"

"Yup. That's where I'm heading right now."

"Have they called us in yet?"

"No, but I'm sure they will soon."

"Anything suspicious?"

"A $2 million science award just hit the bottom of his bank account."

"Holy shit. You think it's a kidnapping?"

"I doubt it, which makes me feel even worse. Kidnappers would want him alive. Whatever the hell it is, I don't feel good about it. I need a favor, Murph."

"Shoot."

"If we get the call, I want to lead the case."

Murphy let out a sigh. "Sterling, you know I can't do that. Against policy."

"Fuck policy, Murph. This is my brother we're talking about. I want the case."

"Goddammit, Sterling," Murphy groaned. "You're putting me in a tough position. Sixteen Hundred will be down my throat if you fuck this up." Sixteen Hundred was their internal code name for the White House.

"So I'm in?"

"Every bone in my body tells me to keep you out."

"Murph, you know me. I can do it by the book with your blessing or I can do it on my own. It's your call."

"Doesn't sound like I have much of a goddamn choice."

"Thanks, Murph. I owe you."

"Be careful, Sterling. And for Chrissake keep a level head."

"Don't I always?" Sterling said before hanging up. He really didn't want to hear the director's answer.

S terling loaded his shield, his Beretta Tomcat because it was easiest to conceal, and several bullet magazines into his travel bag. Though most of his work centered on evidence collection and analysis, he always left home prepared. He returned to his bedroom to finish packing.

There were several things already bothering him about the call from Hanover. He didn't like it that Kay, who was always under control, was too distraught to speak. Then there was Hanlon, the local tight-ass, practically reading his answers from a police academy training manual. He had good reason to doubt the locals' ability to handle a case like this, especially if it really turned into something. Hanover was a quiet town centered on the college. Crime wasn't a part of their everyday lives; they weren't likely to have the kind of experience needed to crack a case like this.

Just as troubling to Sterling was his relationship with his only brother. Sterling didn't know Wilson—not like brothers should. In fact, he had spent most of his life hating Wilson, the chosen one in the Bledsoe household. Pops was constantly rambling about Wilson's success, and his mother openly worshipped him. Sterling's whole childhood was spent trying to figure out ways to escape his brother's shadow, but the comparisons were always there.

The fifteen years that separated the two brothers had something to do with their emotional distance, but Sterling's deep sense of inferiority played a much larger role. Nothing he did was ever good enough. If he proudly brought home a report card with all A's and one B+, his father glanced at it and reminded him that Wilson had had a *perfect* card all the way through high school. And when Sterling made the basketball team, his mother murmured that Wilson had been the champion of the chess team and won the state tournament two years in a row.

Sterling had acquired his love for science only through a desire to surpass Wilson. He decided, however, to distinguish himself in a different field. Sterling's choice was anatomy. In childhood, he had dissected the dead mice and birds his cat dragged home late at night. He loved probing the striated muscles and following the tiny network of blood vessels. It was his mastery of anatomy, both animal and human, that had put him on the fast track in the world of homicide. His college professor, a retired FBI agent himself, had discreetly suggested to Sterling after class that the Bureau could use a smart, ambitious young man like him.

For an entire year, Professor Martin Gilden, ex–field office director of the FBI, tutored his favorite student on the nonclassified inner workings of the Bureau. He delighted the impressionable Sterling with grand stories of horrible crimes solved by great detective work. The Bureau was a special place, he had assured Sterling Bledsoe, but it wasn't a place for those who dreamed of stardom. Many would benefit from his work, but most if not all of his efforts would be conducted in anonymity. The Bureau was full of unsung heroes, definitely not the place for those seeking celebrity. One afternoon, Gilden sketched a career outline that would shape young Sterling's behavior. He needed to keep up his grades, stay on the right side of the law, and always run in the opposite direction from trouble. If he could accomplish all three and was serious about a future in the Bureau, Gilden would make the necessary calls.

Sterling followed the outline to the letter, and Professor Gilden stayed true to his word. Sterling began just like the others, with a mandatory two-year training period, but in short order ambition and guts earned him a promotion and assignment to the most elite homicide unit. He led a team that was only called in on special cases—high-profile crimes or when the political stakes were so great that the director couldn't afford a botched investigation. Through the years, Sterling had earned a name for himself, twice receiving commendations from the director. Everyone in Justice, from the attorney general on down, regarded Agent Bledsoe as a comer.

Veronica opened her eyes as Sterling came back into the bedroom. She was gorgeous, like all his women. Wilson may have gotten their parents' attention, but it was Sterling who had always gotten the attention from women. He was tall and tightly muscled, and even as an adolescent, a flash of his smile would make married women fidget nervously.

"Where were you last night, baby?" Veronica purred in a morning voice that had made him late to class on more than one occasion. One of her long, toned legs was uncovered. Seeing it took some edge off his tension.

"I was over at the school finishing up a few things."

"But I waited up for you well past midnight."

"And I'm sorry for that. I should have called." He reached down and kissed her on the forehead, then he walked to the closet and pulled out a sweatsuit and running shoes. He was in no mood for being questioned.

"Where are you going?" she asked.

"Something's wrong up in Hanover," he said, stuffing more clothes into the suitcase. "They can't find Wilson."

"What happened?"

"He's been missing for ten hours."

"Where is he?" Veronica was the most beautiful girl that Sterling had ever dated, but she was certainly not the smartest, especially so early in the morning.

"They don't know, Ronnie," he answered teasingly. "That's why he's considered missing."

"It's too early for me to think," she said, slowly bending her exposed leg. She yawned but didn't bother to cover her mouth. Sometimes she had the manners of a guy, and when she did things like not cover her mouth it made her even sexier. Sterling fought the temptation to meet her back under the covers.

"I'll call you when I figure this out," Sterling said. He reached for a quick kiss, but she pulled him down farther and explored the inside of his mouth.

"That's so you won't forget about me," she said, finally releasing him. She fell back against the pillow.

"Little chance of that." He smiled. "Do me a favor and leave a note for the students on my office door. Cancel office hours for next Monday and Wednesday, but I'll be back for class next Friday." Sterling spoke with his usual confidence, but a bad feeling in his gut told him that his plan to be back in a week was overly optimistic.

5

Sterling grabbed his suitcase and caught the elevator down to his garage. Most New York City apartment buildings didn't have garages in the basement, and those that did weren't cheap. Though Sterling made decent money and lived well, he wasn't rich, but he had bought his apartment just after the stock market crash, when the once almighty dot-commers were forced to practically give their apartments away. It also didn't hurt that Pops Bledsoe had lived an excessively frugal life and saved a bundle. That, combined with the life insurance money, allowed the two sons to split a rather generous inheritance with their mother. Wilson saved his money, but Sterling used his to buy the apartment, and what was left over he poured into a life of fast cars and beautiful women.

He jumped into the shiny black Porsche 911 and turned on the ignition. The twin turbo engine roared awake, then settled on a loud hum. He pulled his cell phone from his jacket and dialed.

A woman answered. "Travel."

"SA 2378," Sterling said. "Reservation for one this morning."

"Agent Bledsoe? Is that you?"

"Ten-four," Sterling answered. "Monica?"

"Yes, sir," she said. "It's so good to hear your voice again."

"Yeah, it's been a while," Sterling said. "I've been on hiatus."

"I hope you enjoyed it. Where are you going now?"

"Hanover, New Hampshire, just outside of Lebanon."

"Lebanon, New Hampshire?" she repeated. "I don't think I've ever sent anyone there before."

"No good reason to," Sterling added. "It's a small, out-of-the-way kind of place in the mountains. Not much action up there. Most of the work in the area is handled by our field offices in Boston or Albany."

"When do you want to leave?"

"The next flight out of any New York City airport."

"Let me see what I have."

Sterling could hear Monica's rapid-fire typing. She had booked most of his travel since he joined the Bureau, and he liked it that way. Only the higher-ups were allowed to fly first class, but when Sterling playfully whispered to Monica, she always found a way to bend the rules. The irony was that after all these years he had never met her in person. The travel offices were somewhere in North Carolina. Several times he had promised that he'd stop by if a case brought him down there, but the closest he'd ever got was Atlanta for a grisly drug-trafficking case. Twenty-five bodies in all, including five cops. He was there for three weeks straight, but still couldn't string together enough free time to drive up and see her. To this day, he regretted the missed opportunity; a few agents from the Charlotte field office who had seen her happily reported to Sterling that he'd made a big mistake.

"There's a flight at seven o'clock out of La Guardia," she said. "Are you close to there?"

"Twenty minutes away this time of morning," Sterling said. "How long is the flight?"

"Only an hour and fifteen minutes. Nonstop. You arrive at eight fifteen. US Airways flight 5991."

"Good, that gives me a few minutes to grab something before we take off."

"It's a Beechcraft 1900," Monica added. She remembered that SA 2378 liked to know detailed information about the plane he'd be flying on. She thought it was odd the first time he asked, but then he explained about a college friend of his who was going home to West Virginia for Christmas break. He didn't like flying the small puddle jumpers into Morgantown, so his parents always picked him up at the Pittsburgh airport and drove the hour and a half home. No one was available to come get him this particular Christmas, so he'd agreed to fly the rest of the way from Pittsburgh. The plane went down on a heavily wooded mountainside, killing all nine passengers and the two-man crew. The pilot's body was the only one recovered whole. The rest had been shredded or burned—barely recognizable body parts hung from trees like snared kites.

"Capacity?" he asked.

"Nineteen max."

"Accidents?"

"First commercial flight was 1979. Fifteen accidents. The first on November 23, 1987. Many of them were out of the country. Two hundred eighty-two casualties total. Last accident September fourteenth of last year. Two occupants, no one died."

"Where was it?"

"St. John's, Newfoundland," she replied. "Agent Bledsoe, this plane has one of the best safety records in its class."

"Thanks, Monica. Grab a seat for me."

"Won't be a problem," she assured him. "Only three others on the flight."

"And, Monica, see if you can get me a rental car. I have a feeling I'm gonna need to get around up there."

"Something fast, preferably a convertible." Monica remembered everything. That's why the agents loved it when she answered the call.

"You're the best," Sterling said. "We'd be lost without you."

"Anytime, SA 2378. Don't be a stranger."

"When I'm down your way, I'll look you up."

"As always."

Sterling burned rubber out of his garage. It was almost six o'clock. He needed a tall glass of freshly squeezed orange juice and a warm bagel. He also wanted to get the early editions of the national papers to see if there was any mention of Wilson's disappearance. Unlikely, but worth a check anyway. He had to hurry, however. Security at the airports was ironclad even with his FBI credentials.

An image of Wilson flashed in his mind. They had grown a little closer during the last few years. They had most recently seen each other over New Year's, when Wilson and Kay spent the weekend in the city. They all went to a big party at the Rainbow Room overlooking the skating rink and Christmas tree in Rockefeller Plaza. That night, as he watched them holding hands and giggling, he found himself once again envious of his brother's marriage. Sterling wondered if maybe a wife would bring more calm in his own life. Wilson was so content as they looked out over the city, sixty-five floors in the sky. *It doesn't get much better than this.* His eyes had a gleam that night that Sterling had never seen before. The look of a man at peace with himself and the world around him.

Sadness, mixed with anger and guilt, misted Sterling's eyes as he raced the Porsche across 70th Street and turned onto a deserted Third Avenue. In less than an hour he'd be on his way to the tiny town of Hanover. He promised God that if he found his brother alive, he'd never ask for another blessing as long as he lived.

The small airplane weaved between the jagged white mountains of New Hampshire, its narrow body taking a beating from the turbulence. The copilot, who also served as the flight attendant, ducked his way down the tight aisle and informed the passengers that they'd be landing in fifteen minutes. He asked everyone to make sure their seat belts were fastened before disappearing into the cramped cockpit without checking that they had followed his directive. With only four passengers on board and an aircraft small enough to fit into the wing of one of the larger jets, there was no need to be a stickler for formalities.

The plane finally shook its way out of the sky and bumped onto the landing strip. Sterling looked out the window at the little airport. A short walk and they were inside a small building that resembled a town hall more than it did a terminal.

"Your reservation number?" the large woman behind the Hertz counter asked. The baseball cap she wore did little to disguise the fact that she hadn't combed her hair that morning. Sterling took quick notice of the dried coffee stains running down the front of her shirt.

"The name is Bledsoe," Sterling said. "Sterling Bledsoe."

The woman looked up slowly from the computer monitor with a pained expression. "Are you any relation to Professor Wilson Bledsoe?" she whispered.

"That's my brother," he said.

"I see," was all that she said before returning her attention to the computer. Sterling watched her fat hands pound the tiny keys. He sensed that she was avoiding eye contact.

"Is there something you want to tell me?" he pushed.

"No, sir," she said, eyes glued to the monitor.

Sterling looked into her meaty face and could tell there was plenty that she wanted to say. He had seen that same look thousands of times on the faces of reluctant witnesses who with gentle and not-so-gentle persuasion eventually came around and spilled everything they knew.

"I have you down here for our Mustang convertible," she said as the printer start spitting out paper. "The nicest car we have."

Monica had done it again. Sterling slid his credit card across the counter. She finally met his eyes and forced an awkward smile.

"Thanks for your help," he said, grabbing the papers, then turning to leave.

"Mr. Bledsoe?" she called before Sterling was too far. "These mountains have secrets. Good luck."

6

Route 10A. The only paved road that stretched from Lebanon to the center of Hanover. Sterling maneuvered the silver Mustang through what the locals considered a commercial district, a small strip of country stores and a used-car lot with big neon orange "sale" signs propped in the windshields. Less than a mile out of the Lebanon juncture, the road opened up in the heavily wooded area. Sterling mashed the pedal to the floor. The engine roared for a couple of seconds before the transmission kicked into a higher gear and the car lurched forward. The wind whipped as the car ate up the road, and Sterling temporarily forgot the dire situation that had prompted the journey.

For long stretches, Sterling saw nothing but a diamond blue sky and dense clusters of towering evergreens and maples. There were no cars or people, not even the occasional stray dog—just wilderness as far as he could see. This is what Wilson had said he loved most about living here.

Sterling pushed his way to the center of Hanover. Out of the expanse of tangled trees and tall, lazy grass emerged a small strip of low brick buildings straddling the two-lane Main Street. The road was barely long enough for two stoplights, one at the beginning of South Main, the other at the center of town, right before the massive Dartmouth Green.

Then he saw the sign: WELCOME TO HANOVER. Instantly his mind slipped back to a few years ago. They had found her body on the living room floor, and a neighbor had carefully explained to Sterling how she had been clutching that photograph so close to her chest. Sterling was hurt, but he wasn't surprised that his mother had taken her last breath holding that picture to her heart. She had always loved the image of that sign against the lush New Hampshire wilderness background and what it represented—

another Wilson accomplishment. Wilson had snapped the photograph on his first drive into Hanover and sent it home to their mother. And she had cherished it.

It hurt then and it hurt now, another painful reminder of Wilson's exalted place in the family hierarchy. Sterling had spent so many years angrily trying to break free from his shadow, only to be reminded at the end of his mother's life that he'd always occupy the distant second position. So here it was. Damn sign. Opening up old wounds that Sterling thought time and distance had finally healed.

He moved past the sign and the memories, then slowed the engine and eased into town as quietly as possible. He passed the Food Stop gas station on the southwest corner. ONLY SERVICE STATION FOR TWO MILES, it said outside in hand lettering. Sterling rolled up the quaint Main Street as students peddled by on mountain bikes and professors in rumpled tweed blazers engaged each other in the finer points of overly academic debates.

Sterling appreciated the fact that without Dartmouth, there wouldn't be a Hanover. Almost all the nine thousand residents had some connection to the school, whether as students, faculty members, employees, or landlords to the students. In most college towns Sterling knew, the locals developed a love-hate relationship with the school, but here the dynamics were completely different. In this land of granola and organic vegetable stands, Hanover townies took pride in their academic haven.

Sterling stopped at the red light in front of the Dartmouth Green. It was just warm enough for several students to toss a Frisbee to a golden retriever on the freshly cut lawn. He wondered if an open green would help relax his hardworking students back at Hunter, who spent their free time sitting on concrete steps and filling their lungs with the black exhaust from an endless stream of city buses passing through the middle of campus.

He pulled out a map, then took a left onto West Wheelock and rolled down the steep hill toward the slate-gray Connecticut River. As he crossed Ledyard Bridge, he noticed several teams of scullers out on the cool water, the strokes of their oars sweeping in perfect synchrony while the coxswain barked orders through a bullhorn. This is the Ivy League, he thought to himself. Mist was rising off the water as green and orange foliage hung over the water's edge in a perfect arch that stretched down the river. Picture perfect for the cover of a glossy school brochure.

To Sterling, the setting was almost disturbingly calm. How could anything too terrible have happened to Wilson here?

At the end of the bridge, Sterling took an immediate right on River Road. He was in Vermont now, distinguishable from New Hampshire only by its undecorated green license plates and its being home to the country's most sought-after maple syrup. Though the two states were not always political allies, they remained friendly neighbors in these sparsely inhabited mountains.

Sterling maneuvered his Mustang along River Road through a series of sharp bends. He was almost there. He tried mentally preparing himself for what he might find at the house. In a few minutes he'd be sitting with Kay, trying to piece together the mysteries of Wilson's disappearance.

His cell phone rang.

"Bledsoe," he answered.

"Agent Bledsoe, it's Lonnie Brusco from the Boston office. I don't know if you remember me, but we met on the Wharf cases a few years back."

"Don't be ridiculous, Lonnie. How could I ever forget you? You were the only one to pick up on those rug burns."

The Wharf murders had been the most gruesome collection of homicides in Boston since the Strangler. A janitor from one of the elementary schools in South Boston had kidnapped, raped, and murdered eleven teenage girls over the span of three months. All of their bodies had been found on the wharf along Boston Harbor, but it was Special Agent Lonnie Brusco who had noticed a similar pattern of rug burns on their legs. Then they got lucky. One of the victims still had her pants on when they found her. Underneath her left hem, they found a carpet fiber that the lab eventually traced to the janitor's apartment.

"We just got a call from the Hanover Police Department," Brusco said. "They're nervous. They want our help. Washington called and said you'd be leading."

"That's right. Are you on the team?"

"My flight leaves in an hour."

"Good, I could use another pair of experienced eyes."

"It's a horrible reason for us to see each other again, but it's good to be working with you."

"Likewise." Sterling closed the phone and negotiated a steep curve. He hit it too fast, sending the back of the car into a tailspin. This sure in hell isn't the Porsche, he thought. He cleared a thicket of trees, then slammed on the brakes. A police cruiser stood fifty feet ahead, painting the woods with its flashing red-and-white lights. Detective Hanlon had decided to take his advice after all. An officer with a wide-brimmed hat stood in front of the cruiser directing him to turn around. Sterling pulled the car up closer, then killed the engine.

"Gotta take it back around West Wheelock and up to I-91," the officer said. The strap underneath his chin was so tight he had to strain to open his jaw.

"Agent Sterling Bledsoe," Sterling said, flashing his creds.

"Oh," the officer said, pumping Sterling's hand. He was a big man, at least six foot five, maybe two fifty. All muscle. "I'm Officer McGran." A look of confusion etched his youthful face.

Sterling wasn't surprised. A black man in a sports car in this area wasn't exactly an everyday occurrence. "I'm also his brother," Sterling said. "I just arrived from the city."

"The city, sir?"

"New York City. I got the call early this morning." Sterling leaned his head slightly to see around McGran's massive shoulders. There were three other cruisers and an unmarked car. He counted at least five uniformed officers and three in civvies walking along the road and into the woods. They were wearing bright yellow jackets. "Have they found anything yet?" he asked McGran.

"Just getting started," McGran replied, swinging his arm wide so that Sterling could get a better view. He moved just like he sounded, stiff and mechanical. Everything about him was uneasy.

"Who's in charge?" Sterling asked.

"Captain Stangle," the officer replied.

"Which one is he?"

"The only one not wearing yellow."

"And Detective Hanlon?"

"Still at the house with Mrs. Bledsoe. She's taking all this kinda hard."

"Has she left the house yet?"

"From what I've been told, she drove down here last night herself, but she didn't see anything so she turned around and went back home."

"What time was that?" Sterling was in his element—a possible crime scene, local police, undiscovered clues, and a bad feeling in his stomach that was getting worse by the minute. He tried his best to forget that it was his brother he was looking for—the less attached the investigator, the better the investigation. *The heart has a strange way of blurring the mind.* One of the first lessons pounded into the trainees at the academy. Then again, who could ever be prepared to investigate a missing brother?

"I don't have all the details, Agent," McGran admitted. "Maybe you should speak to Cap." McGran turned on his heels and walked over to the captain, who was wearing a dark green windbreaker. The stub of a cigar hung from the right side of his mouth. Wisps of silver hair peeped out from underneath his black baseball cap, and the deep lines in his leathery forehead put his age near sixty. He looked in Sterling's direction, nodded once, and then headed over, the robocop trailing behind.

"Morning to ya," the captain said, extending a meaty hand. "I'm Captain Stangle from the Norwich Police Department here in Vermont."

"Agent Sterling Bledsoe," Sterling said. "Professor Bledsoe's brother." Sterling took Stangle's fleshy hand and immediately realized that it was too large for a firm grip. Wilson had told him that they grew them big here. Something to do with the water, he had joked.

"Sorry to have you up here on such an occasion," Stangle said, volleying the crumbling cigar from one corner of his mouth to the other. Not once did it look in danger of falling. He'd obviously had lots of practice. "It's the damnedest thing."

"What do you know so far?"

Stangle looked dismissively at McGran, who was hovering over his right shoulder. "Come with me," he said to Sterling. "Try to follow in my footsteps. We're still collecting evidence."

Sterling followed him to a small area just off the road. Stangle took out a notepad and flipped the tattered pages. "It just doesn't make much sense," he said, rubbing the creases in his forehead. The cigar was now on a continuous rotation. "Professor Bledsoe was being honored at President Mortimer's house last night for winning some big award."

"The Devonshire," Sterling interjected. "The richest science award there is."

"Two million big ones," Stangle added. He sang the amount like the jingle for a lottery commercial. "He leaves the party at approximately seven o'clock and calls his wife to tell her that he's coming home."

"Any sign of the car?"

"Nothing yet. But we're working with the phone company to get a log of his calls." Stangle flipped the page. "He calls Mrs. Bledsoe again about five to ten minutes later and says that he's gonna be late. There were a couple of guys having trouble with a truck down here on River Road, so he stopped to help."

"How far is President Mortimer's house from here?"

"Can't be more than ten minutes. It's over on Webster Avenue down the street from the fraternities." Stangle walked a couple of steps off the road and motioned for Sterling to follow. The river was just five feet from where they stood. Stangle pointed across the water. "When the leaves fall off in autumn, you can actually see the president's mansion through these trees. It's really not that far at all."

"But there's no way to get from there to here without crossing the bridge?"

"Not unless you got wings or you're strong enough to swim across the river. Gotta take the long way over Ledyard Bridge in order to access this road."

"Where did Wilson say he was helping these men?"

"Not exactly sure, but according to Mrs. Bledsoe, he was only a few minutes from their property. So we figure he was within a couple of hundred yards from this spot."

They had done some thinking on their own, which Sterling found surprising and encouraging. Often when he arrived on the scene only a small amount of real work had been done, and the authorities were more interested in quarreling over who was actually in charge of the case than in gathering evidence. A time line was always the centerpiece of any investigation, and they had started to construct a good one.

Sterling looked at the men. Some were crouched on the ground with magnifying glasses, others combed through the woods. They were working as a team, which was also important.

"How far did you block the road off?" Sterling asked.

"All the way to your brother's street—Deer Run Lane."

"How far is that from here?"

"About two miles or so."

Sterling looked down the narrow dirt road, which was smothered by large trees and heavy branches that blocked out most of the sunlight. There were no streetlights or road markings; it was as if someone had carved a road through the forest and forgot to finish it. He wondered how eerie it must've been going down this dark road with its unlit curves and narrow passages. What went through Wilson's mind as he traveled home last night?

"You say the president was throwing a party at his house in Wilson's honor?" Sterling asked.

"Yup, started at six." Stangle looked at his pad. "About two hundred and fifty people. The president and his wife like to throw big parties. They pack 'em in at least once a week."

"What about that truck? Did Wilson tell Kay what he thought was wrong with it?"

Stangle turned the page and skimmed the notes. The harder he thought, the faster his mouth rotated the cigar. "There we go. He told her that he wasn't sure if it was a dead battery or flat tire."

"What was the weather like last night?"

"Clear till about six or so, then a little drizzle. At about seven it started raining like the dickens. Damn winds were almost strong enough to blow my fat ass to the ground."

"That should be helpful for them," Sterling said, pointing at the men crawling on the ground.

"The wind?"

"No, the rain. That meant there was a lot of mud here last night—makes for deep tire tracks, especially when the next day is dry like today."

Stangle nodded. "Good point."

"Captain! Captain!" McGran was yelling from the cruiser. The trees swallowed his voice as if he were calling from inside a cave. He had the radio transmitter in his hand, but his fingers were so big, the only thing visible was the black cord dangling from his closed fist. Stangle and Sterling turned toward McGran. "They found the car!" he yelled.

"What?" Stangle grumbled. He and Sterling quickly walked back to McGran.

"Dispatch just called it in," McGran said. "The Hanover boys found the car about ten minutes ago."

"Where the hell is it?"

"Over behind Kellogg Auditorium in the medical school parking lot."

"Is Wilson in the car?" Sterling asked. He tightened his stomach for the blow.

"Negative. The car was locked and the windows rolled up. The keys are still in the ignition."

Sterling turned to Stangle. "Ready to go?"

Stangle looked at McGran. "Tell them we'll be there in five, six minutes tops," Stangle said. He took one last volley with the cigar then spit it to the ground with a determined grunt. "Follow me."

7

Sterling closely trailed Stangle's flashing cruiser through the narrow streets of Dartmouth's campus. They slowed down when they reached the expansive green in the middle of town, then took a series of turns before speeding past stately Baker Library. It was now eleven o'clock in the morning and the campus was waking up with a big yawn from the previous night's parties. The studious lugged heavy backpacks through the library's revolving doors, while others had squeezed into their spandex leggings and oversized sweatshirts to jog in small packs along the quiet roads.

Sterling took in the old buildings, their bricks recently washed, the wood boasting a fresh coat of white paint. As much as he preferred the jagged New York skyline and its imposing towers, he couldn't help but admire Hanover's rustic beauty and wholesome charm. While he had never visited the campus before, he had seen its picturesque vistas many times on the postcards that Wilson had sent home. Their mother had displayed them prominently. What Sterling found astonishing was that the campus was actually more pristine and majestic than the postcards had indicated.

Captain Stangle turned his sirens off, but kept the lights flashing as he made several turns down the sandy roads and approached a cluster of understated buildings. The modest sign on the lawn announced DARTMOUTH MEDICAL SCHOOL, 1786. Like most research buildings, these had been built for efficiency and practicality rather than for design—slabs of pale concrete piled carelessly on crumbling brick and large rusted beams.

They drove down a small incline to the back of the buildings and entered a deserted parking lot. A hundred yards or so into the lot, Sterling counted eight green-and-white cruisers. They were parked in front of an abandoned lime green parking structure that looked like it was begging for the wrecking ball.

Sterling stopped near the auditorium and surveyed the moss-ravaged brick and the two entrances, one on each side of the building. A walking bridge connected the auditorium to the bigger maze of ugly buildings.

He eased the Mustang toward the flashing lights and pocketed his small black-leather book before joining Stangle and the other officers. The cruisers belonged to both the Hanover Police Department and Dartmouth Security.

"Morning, Cap'n," one of the Hanover officers called out to Stangle as he approached the group. He was the shortest of the eight men, but had the cocky swagger of a man in charge.

"Well, Serge, it looks like the sun might be kind enough to keep us warmer today," Stangle said. Talking about the weather was the way most people began their conversations in these cold mountains, even when there was a serious matter at hand. "This is Agent Sterling Bledsoe. FBI. He'll be leading the investigation from their end. He's also the Professor's brother."

"Lieutenant Sergio Wiley from the Hanover Police Department," the short man said, offering a stiff right hand. He was even smaller up close, but his grip was firm. His face was serious, and unlike the other men, who wore big felt Stetson hats, he wore a dark blue Red Sox hat. The visor had been curled in the front the way the college students liked to sport their lids. A heavy black mustache hid his upper lip, and for a minute, Sterling thought it could've been fake. Wiley's compact body showed off a web of knotted muscles, straining the uniform across his chest. Sterling guessed he had been a wrestler in his younger days.

"Glad to meet you," Sterling replied. "Just wish it could've been under better circumstances."

"We all do," Wiley replied. "Your brother's a star on this campus, Agent Bledsoe. Never met him myself, but my neighbor's son took one of his courses a few years back and hasn't stopped talking about it since."

"Wilson's a good man," Sterling agreed. He suddenly felt an incredible urge to cry. "There must be some explanation for this."

Wiley got down to business. "One of the security officers spotted the car on his rounds earlier this morning. He didn't make much of it at first, because it's not uncommon for the medical students and faculty to leave their cars here over the weekend when they're carpooling out of town."

Sterling looked at the red Mercedes. He and Wilson hadn't spoken much over the years, but he vividly remembered their conversation about this car. Wilson had found it in the classifieds and purchased it from a doctor's widow in Windsor, Vermont, some thirty miles away. Poor eyesight had finally forced the old woman to give up her license, so she decided to sell the car. Before she signed the papers, she made Wilson promise that he would be mindful of the car's upkeep, something her husband had placed second only to the care of his patients. The car had only thirty-five thousand original miles on it, and the interior was in mint condition. Wilson would carry on about it for hours if you let him. Sterling glanced at the tires. The rims were shiny and except for a few splotches where mud had dried, the whitewalls looked like they had just been scrubbed. A smile flickered across Sterling's lips, then died. Keeping their cars spotless was one trait the Bledsoe men shared.

"When did the security officer first notice the car?" Sterling asked. He kept his eyes on the Mercedes.

"Oh three hundred this morning," Wiley returned. "There's not much activity back here, so they only make rounds every three hours. They do more patrols on the other parts of the campus where most people come and go."

"May I?" Sterling asked, nodding in the direction of the Mercedes.

"Sure, but don't touch it yet," Wiley said. "We're still waiting for state to come down and scrub for prints."

"Can't someone from your department lift the prints?"

"We could, but our guy is away this weekend," Wiley said. It seemed to embarrass him to admit there was only one man on the force who was proficient at dusting for prints. "State guys have more experience anyway."

"Understood," Sterling said. "There's a camera posted on the corner of one of the buildings back there," he said, kneeling down and examining the rear tires. "Does it work?"

Wiley and Stangle looked back at Kellogg Auditorium, then at each other. Wiley turned to one of the officers. "What's the surveillance back here?" he barked as if it was his idea.

"Not much beyond the patrols," one of the officers responded. He had a buzz cut that made his head look like it was covered in spikes and a stomach that hung so low he probably had to lift it to reach his belt buckle.

Sterling flipped on his back and examined underneath the car. "Anyone have a flashlight?" he asked. One of the officers placed a long metal light in his open hand. "Now can someone give me a definitive answer about that camera back there?"

Lieutenant Wiley shot a hard look at the buzz cut. "I'll have to check into that," the officer mumbled. He waddled to his patrol car and picked up the radio.

Sterling stood and slowly traced the car from the trunk to the hood. He took his time, knowing that most mistakes were made in the beginning of an investigation. He learned early in his career that being overly eager often resulted in missing the small details. Patience, at the right time in an investigation, could be an important ally.

"Can I get a pair of gloves?" Sterling asked.

Wiley motioned to one of the officers, who ran to his cruiser and returned with a pair.

They were a little tight, but Sterling eventually got them on. He walked to the front of the car and placed the back of his hands on the hood. He alternated them in methodical fashion until he had covered every inch.

"A cold engine and no forced entry." Sterling announced. Now he was squatting next to the door handle.

"But why would the Professor leave the keys in the ignition?" Stangle wondered aloud.

"Who said he did?" Sterling shot back. "There could be a million reasons why those keys are locked in this car, and him leaving them there is the least likely. Wilson loved this car." Sterling peered through the passenger-side window. "There's something on the floor," he said. "It's stuck between the seat and the door." He flashed the light through the window. The others gathered around. "I can't make out much of it from here, but it looks like the antenna of a cell phone."

Sterling looked at his watch and tightened his lips. It was a few minutes before noon. Wilson had been missing for almost seventeen hours and there hadn't been any calls from either him or anyone who might have seen something. Not good. "All done here," Sterling announced, handing the flashlight to Wiley. "Captain Stangle, how can I get to my brother's house without going down River Road?"

"There's a way higher up in the mountains that comes around the back of his property."

Sterling turned and faced Wiley. "Does President Mortimer know about my brother's disappearance?"

"He was informed at six this morning," Wiley answered. "It won't be easy, but we're trying to keep a lid on it for at least twenty-four hours. It'll give us time to get some answers before getting the campus all worked up."

"Makes sense," Sterling agreed. He started walking to his car, then turned back. "One more question, Lieutenant. If the security officer first spotted the car at three this morning and he makes a lap back here every three hours, then why didn't you guys hear about it till now?"

Wiley was prepared. "It wasn't until his third patrol at nine that the officer noticed the car didn't have a sticker. All cars that park in this lot must have a faculty sticker or they get ticketed. When the officer put the ticket on the window, he noticed the keys were still in the ignition, so he called the security office to have it towed. At approximately ten thirty, when the tow truck arrived, our dispatcher picked up the tow order over the radio. She knew that we were looking for Professor Bledsoe's car and the call fit the description. Our men were here within minutes."

Sterling looked around the parking lot, then something caught his eye. He walked back to the front of the Mercedes and knelt down. He was tracing something in the sand with his fingers. "Tire tracks," he said. "Wide enough for a truck. You might want to see if these match any over on River Road, Lieutenant. No way in hell Wilson voluntarily parked his car in the back of an empty lot with the keys still in the ignition."

Sterling walked to the Mustang with Stangle and Wiley following.

"Ready to go?" Captain Stangle asked.

"Yeah, but before I go to the house, I'd like to stop by Wilson's lab. I want to see inside his office." Sterling opened the door to his car and slid in.

"I'll take him," Wiley volunteered. "That was my next stop anyway."

Sterling knew that Wilson spent most of his time in his lab. He was confident that it would be the right place to start searching for the real evidence. The Mustang's rear wheels spun and kicked up a cloud of dust as he left the parking lot. He was convinced that someone in this small town must've seen or heard something, and as they often said in the Bureau, it would only be a matter of time before the clues started talking.

8

A Dartmouth Security officer dutifully guarded Wilson Bledsoe's locked laboratory. He stood with his thin arms folded across his chest, his chin slightly tucked back as if he were trying to suppress a cough. The solemn click of heels on newly waxed tile caught his attention.

"G'morning, Lieutenant Wiley," the officer said. He straightened his back as if he had spent some time in the military. Sterling was waiting for him to salute, but he didn't.

"Morning, Carlton," Wiley snapped. "This here is Agent Sterling Bledsoe. FBI. He's in from New York City." Wiley took his time pronouncing the last bit. It wasn't every day that they met someone from the big city, especially law enforcement.

"Couldn't've picked a better day to visit us here in the mountains," Carlton said, flashing a smile full of perfect teeth. "They say it's gonna climb into the seventies."

Lieutenant Wiley rocked back on his heels impatiently. "Carlton Gilly, Agent Bledsoe is Professor Bledsoe's brother. This is not a social call."

"I'm sorry, sir," Carlton stumbled. Sterling nodded his head in acceptance.

"Has anyone been in yet?" Wiley asked. He spoke in the deep, commanding voice of a man twice his size.

"Only a student came by," Carlton said. "It must've been six or seven in the morning. She told me that she worked here in the lab as a research assistant."

"Did you catch her name?" Sterling asked.

Carlton looked up at the ceiling and squinted his eyes till they were slits. Sterling noticed the length of his nose. It would've been a perfect diving board for a bead of sweat. "Not really," Carlton said. "But she was a good-looking girl, if you know what I mean. She showed me her ID, but the name just didn't stick with me. Helen or Heather—something like that."

Sterling scribbled in his black book. It wasn't terribly unusual for a research assistant to come in early on a Saturday morning. Experiments were often an around-the-clock proposition, and the low person on the totem pole typically was stuck with the graveyard shift, making sure everything was running smoothly. Sterling himself had spent many late nights and early mornings mixing reagents and running gels. For a graduate student, it was a rite of passage. "Did you let her in?" Sterling asked.

"No, sir," Carlton said, proud that he had at least gotten something right. "Chief Gaylor gave specific orders to keep the door locked."

"What time did you get here?" Sterling asked, still writing in his book. Every detail added to the time line.

"A little after five this morning," Carlton said. "The night commander sent me over as soon as I got to the station."

Sterling looked at Wiley for an explanation. "Since no one had heard from the Professor by the morning shift, we decided to take some extra precautions. Typically, we'd let more time go by before officially declaring a missing person, but these weren't typical circumstances, especially with that prize your brother just won. We thought it best not to take any chances, so we had the campus security send someone over here right away."

"Good thinking," Sterling said. A look of contentment softened Wiley's rigid face as he snapped his head for a quick nod. "Well, let's see what's up."

Carlton stepped aside to let Wiley and Sterling pass. As the door closed behind them, Sterling reached out and stopped Wiley from turning on the lights. He stood there quietly and slowly pivoted his head in the dark, trying to capture the essence of the spacious room. Unlike most researchers, who work away in anonymity, their work appreciated only by a select group of their peers, Wilson Bledsoe not only had made his mark in scientific circles but had crossed over into the broader public arena. Industry leaders recognized the importance of his research. On Wall Street, traders and analysts picked stocks according to a complicated algorithm Wilson had worked out that predicted how herds of animals will react to changes in environmental stimuli. The enormous size of Wilson's lab was only fitting.

Sterling and Wiley slowly walked along lab benches and tables piled high with slides and mounted specimens. An entire corner of the lab had been devoted to what looked to Sterling's urban eyes like otters.

At the back of the lab, Sterling spent a few more minutes in silence as he took in his brother's work space. Everything was so neat and shiny, all the way down to the microscopes perfectly aligned on the lab benches. He imagined Wilson striding down the aisles in his white lab coat, instructing his assistants, lending them a hand when they ran into problems.

"Clean enough to eat off the floors," Wiley said, admiring his reflection in one of the countertops. "Your brother runs a pretty tight ship."

"So I see," Sterling said, wishing his own lab were half as organized. He carefully reached into a box and grabbed a couple of pairs of latex gloves, one for himself, the other for Wiley. This wasn't the same Wilson whose bedroom was always a mess, papers and books all over the house, his clothes remaining for days wherever he happened to take them off. His mother would always tell him, *A great mind can't think clearly in a cluttered room.* After all these years he had finally listened.

"Doesn't look like the place has been touched," Wiley said.

"Looks that way, but too soon to say for sure, Lieutenant," Sterling warned. "We don't even know what we're after yet." Sterling walked over to a small metal desk in the corner. The computer screensaver had a family of owls sitting in a tree, their yellow eyes blinking. Every few seconds one would let out a screech, then dive to the ground and disappear off the end of the monitor. When the tree was empty, a whooshing sound could be heard, and the owls would fly back in a pack and reposition themselves on the branches.

"Technology is something else these days," Wiley said. "I barely know how to turn the damn things on. Tickles the hell outta my kids. But they can do the damnedest things with those electronics, especially the younger ones. The other night they were talking to some students in Europe through the computer."

"And that's only the beginning," Sterling said, tapping the keyboard to get rid of the screensaver. The screen cleared and revealed pages where someone had downloaded information from the FDA's drug reference section. Sterling scribbled the URL address in his black book.

"I know the Professor has an expertise with animals," Wiley said. "But what exactly does he do?"

"He's an animal behaviorist," Sterling explained. He scrolled down the FDA's home page to see if anything caught his eye. "Some people call them ethologists. He observes animals in their natural environment."

Sterling and Wiley continued to search the lab, carefully moving items for inspection, then putting them back in place. Finally they came to the door of Wilson's office and a sign that read CAUTION: WILD ETHOLOGIST ON THE LOOSE. This touch of humor wasn't the Wilson that Sterling remembered. Wilson had always been so serious, even when he wasn't working.

The door to Professor Bledsoe's office was unlocked, just as it had been for the last twenty years. He had always believed in an open-door policy, making himself available to his students and colleagues alike, whatever their problems, personal or scientific. Wilson wasn't like most laboratory directors, concerned strictly with the number of papers their assistants authored. Instead, Wilson stressed to his students that it was important to first get a handle on adult life; if they learned some science along the way, so much the better.

His office was even more meticulous than the laboratory. No loose pens or pencils on the desk, and the papers were neatly stacked to one side. Behind his desk hung a large black-and-white photo of the two brothers hugging after Wilson had received his graduate degree. Sterling was only ten, tall and lanky, flashing the same smile that kept him in trouble with women now. As reluctant as Sterling would have been to admit it to anyone, this had always been his favorite picture. He treasured it mostly because it was the only photo he could remember of the two of them together and happy. Since he had come to terms with his resentment of his older brother, his copy of the photo now sat on his nightstand back in his apartment. The day of Wilson's graduation was the only time that Sterling had seen the old man cry.

"This is some office," Wiley said. He was eyeing a picture of the Professor with some of his students. "You go to some of these professors' offices and it's a pigsty. Papers and books all over the place, moldy cups of coffee everywhere." He picked up the picture of the students and handed it to Sterling.

The photograph had been taken on the lawn in front of the lab or a similar building. Eight students surrounded Wilson. They looked so content and carefree. Sterling took his time and studied each of their faces. The student next to Wilson stood out from the others and not only because she was attractive. Her eyes, her posture, her smile—they all added up to an unmistakable air of confidence.

Sterling replaced the photograph on the desk and looked around. Floor-to-ceiling bookcases lined the wall, full of bulky textbooks and lab manuals. Three shelves had been dedicated entirely to fiction, something Sterling never imagined Wilson having an interest in or time to read. He had a lot of mysteries, Elmore Leonard and Walter Mosely and almost all of the Grishams. Sterling only remembered Wilson burying his head in the *New York Times* and *Scientific American*.

He walked to the other side of the large oak desk and pulled out the heavy, black-leather chair that slid on a square piece of Plexiglas. A small metal wastebasket in the shape of an elephant had been tucked against the right inside wall of the desk. Sterling emptied its contents onto the desk—three crumpled pieces of paper and a pen that had run out of ink. Sterling opened up one of the crumpled balls.

"Anything interesting?" Wiley asked.

"Not exactly sure," Sterling replied. "It seems to be a list of chemicals and their structures, but it's hard to make most of them out. They didn't print very well." He handed the first sheet to Wiley, then opened the second and third. More of the same.

"I can't even pronounce most of these names," Wiley surrendered. "That's why I never got along with science. So many damn words that take up too much space on a page. I always had better places to spin my wheels."

Sterling considered the names. He wasn't a chemist, but he had spent a couple of years studying organic chemistry. Changing just one number or a couple of letters, he knew, could mean two very different compounds.

"Does it say where that list came from?" Wiley asked.

Sterling couldn't find anything on the first couple of pages; most of the ink had been blurred or cut off at the bottom. He could, however, read some letters at the bottom of the third page: *http://www.fda*. The rest were illegible. "It's from the Internet," Sterling said.

Wiley stretched his neck, and brought the sheet of paper close enough to his face to practically smell the ink. Then he gave up on vanity and pulled out a pair of reading glasses from his breast pocket. "Part of getting older," he explained, sliding the thick glasses up his nose. "Was it normal for the Professor to be checking out something with the FDA?"

"It's possible. Researchers are always looking up scientific information on the Internet. The real question is whether the information on these pages had any special meaning." Sterling opened the closet door. More of the same—stacks of textbooks and boxes of paper, jumbled laboratory data, and copied journal articles. Various of Wilson's articles sat on one shelf, as did a shoe box full of Minicam videotapes. Sterling rummaged through quickly, before putting everything back in its original place. He pulled out his small black-leather book and scribbled some notes. He looked at his watch. It was one o'clock and he was starting to get hungry. He needed to sit and collect his thoughts.

It was time to go see Kay. The investigation was important, but he also had to be there for her. Wilson was all she had in the world, and everyone knew how close they were. For a brief moment, for no particular reason at all, the strangest thought entered Sterling's head. Was it possible that Wilson had run off with another woman? Unlikely, but every possibility had to be considered. One thing Sterling had learned after all these years with the Bureau was never to put anything past anyone.

Sterling neatly arranged the sheets of paper on the desk. "I think that'll do it for now," he said to Wiley.

"Once state has finished dusting the car for prints, I'll have them sent to the lab," Wiley said. "Shouldn't take more than a few hours."

"The sooner, the better," Sterling said. As they left, he took another look at the photo of Wilson and himself hanging on the wall. Though only for a brief moment, it warmed him to think that Wilson liked that picture as much as he did.

Carlton straightened up when he heard the door open. Sterling thought he might have been napping.

"How long is your shift, Carlton?" Sterling asked.

Carlton looked at his watch. "I came on at five this morning. I'll leave at three this afternoon, maybe stay later for some overtime."

"Any relief?"

"Someone will come by soon so I can take lunch."

"Make sure they don't let anybody in," Sterling said firmly. "That entire lab needs to be fingerprinted."

"Yes, sir," Carlton said. He seemed good at taking orders.

"And if anyone comes by saying they need to see the Professor or they work in the lab, make sure you take down their information—name, ID number, affiliation, and phone number where they can be reached."

Sterling and Lieutenant Wiley started down the hall. His lips moving silently, Carlton reviewed the instructions as the elevator doors opened.

"What about the cleaning man?" Carlton called after them.

Sterling struck his hands out to keep the elevator doors from closing. "What cleaning man?"

"He said he might need to come back later. He wasn't able to finish everything."

Sterling and Wiley stepped out of the elevator. "I thought you said the only person who asked to come in was one of the students," Sterling said. He was seeing red again.

"Well, I didn't think the cleaning people counted," Carlton said, shrugging his shoulders.

Sterling shook his head. Hanlon had made his blood simmer, and now Carlton had brought it to a boil. Only hours into the investigation, and he had already counted at least five mistakes that could seriously taint the evidence and hinder their ability to find Wilson. "Did you at least get his name?"

Carlton twisted his mouth. "I don't remember. He said he was running late and forgot his ID in his locker."

"How long was he in there for?"

"Not sure. He was coming out just as I arrived."

Sterling looked at Wiley. "We need the records of who was doing the cleaning this morning," he said firmly. "If this investigation is going to amount to anything, we've got to check on everything. Twice. This is the kind of shit that will blow the case before we even have a chance to get our hands around it."

Lieutenant Wiley nodded. He was accustomed to giving orders rather than taking them, but in this matter it was hard to disagree.

"No one enters that lab unless I say so," Wiley barked at Carlton. "No students, janitors, or police officers, not even President Mortimer himself."

"Ten-four," Carlton responded. This time, he did give a little salute.

Sterling looked down at Wiley. "If we come back, we're going to need one of Wilson's research assistants to take us through the lab. I just have a feeling that something in there isn't what it's supposed to be. Who knows what that janitor was cleaning."

9

A lone wooden stake leaning out of the ground marked the entrance to the Bledsoe property. The number 2 had been so inconspicuously hand painted that were one not looking for the address, it would completely escape detection. The modest entrance—a couple of tall trees interspersed with wild shrubbery—belied the expansiveness of the tract of land that Wilson called home. The Bledsoe house was one of only three on Deer Run Lane, and like the others, it hid in the dense woods, invisible from the small dirt road that joined the properties.

The beginning of the narrow gravel driveway was only large enough for one car, but after a couple of hundred yards, the trees and their bowing branches cleared into the open and the driveway circled in front of the massive house.

Sterling's reaction to his first glimpse of the imposing structure was shock. Wilson had described the house as comfortable; in fact, it was enormous. Like their father, Wilson lived a frugal and relatively simple life despite his hefty salary and lucrative awards. Sterling now realized that Wilson had saved all his money—and evidently a certain amount of flamboyance, too—and piled it into this colossal edifice. He had allowed the builders to clear only five acres surrounding the house, leaving the remaining acreage in its natural state. He was proud of it. *My own wildlife preserve. Full of enough animals for me to study for the rest of my life without setting a foot off my own property.*

Sterling passed three cruisers in the driveway, one each from the Norwich and Hanover police departments and an unmarked car with tinted windows and several antennae planted on the hood. State trooper. He settled the Mustang close to the front of the house.

The massive oak front door was unlocked. The first thing that hit Sterling was the smell of hot tea, fresh and minty. Sterling hated tea and everything about it. He hated to see people drink it, pursing their lips as if whistling, then gently pressing them against the rim of the cup. He couldn't smell or see or think about tea without a painful memory resurfacing. It was his ninth birthday and his parents had promised he could have a party at the house and invite all his friends over for cake and ice cream and games. He had never had a real party before, but this was going to be his first and he had planned every detail down to the table seating. He could barely fall asleep the night before, thinking about how much fun they'd all have and the gifts his friends would bring.

Then Wilson called and plans changed. Instantly. Wilson said he'd be coming home that afternoon but would only be passing through, as he planned on visiting friends in Philadelphia. He was in graduate school in Chicago and had just begun his midyear break.

Sterling's party was postponed and instead of a house full of balloons and rambunctious boys, hordes of his parents' friends from work and church descended on their small house. There were plenty of gifts that night, but they were all for Wilson. Books, sweaters, fancy pens and pencils—everyone came to pay homage to the golden boy. Sterling spent most of the night in his room crying, but the one time he left it to go to the bathroom, he took a quick glance down the stairs. That's when he saw them all, smoking their long cigarettes and sipping tea from his mother's china that she kept locked away for important occasions. Everyone had a cup in their hand, even Wilson. They laughed and puffed and sipped, acting just like the rich people he had seen on television. A bunch of phonies, he told himself. It was his birthday and Wilson was getting the attention. All these years later and he could still smell the sharp minty aroma. He could still see them crammed into the small living room and front hall, chatting importantly and tipping back those goddamn cups with the gold trim. It damn near killed him.

Sterling fought off the memory as he stepped farther into the foyer and heard voices from the back of the house. He dropped his bag and followed the voices, walking through the large family room, then into a den that was almost as big as his entire apartment. Kay was reclining on a beige leather chaise lounge. Her hair had been tied back in a bun, and she hadn't bothered with makeup. Not that she needed it. Even in her late forties, with age beginning to touch the corner of her eyes, she still possessed the attractiveness that had drawn Wilson to her. What a waste that her genes wouldn't be passed on to children.

The three officers made an odd picture, lined up on the couch across from her, all wearing different uniforms, hands folded in their laps. Something out of a seventies sitcom.

"Kay," Sterling said, walking into the open room. The ceilings were extraordinarily high, and his voice echoed for a while before the dark oak paneling swallowed it.

"Sterling!" she exclaimed, instantly rising to her feet. "Thank God you're here." Her eyes were swollen. Her black skirt fell just above her knees, showing off a pair of toned legs that would make most women envious. Her many years of dance still served her well.

Sterling wrapped his sister-in-law in a bear hug, and he could tell by the firmness of her clasp that she was as scared as he was.

He released her. "I'm Agent Sterling Bledsoe," he said to the cops, who had also gotten to their feet. He walked over and pumped their hands as they called out their names.

"I didn't know you were FBI," the tall one with a heap of red hair said. Sterling read the name Hanlon embossed on his shield.

"Most of the time," Sterling said, helping Kay to her chair, then claiming his own seat on an unoccupied sofa. It felt good to finally get off his feet. "Right now I'm teaching anatomy at Hunter College in the city."

"When did you get in?" Kay asked. Her voice was strained, desperate.

"A few hours ago," Sterling said. "Some of the officers have been showing me around."

"And?" Kay asked, her back straightening at the possibilities.

"They found the car over in the medical school parking lot."

"Yes, they called us here at the house." The disappointment dropped her back into the chair.

Sterling looked at the three men. "Who's actually leading this investigation from the local side?"

They all looked at each other before Hanlon took a stab. "We haven't entirely worked out jurisdiction yet, because we don't know exactly where he was last seen. We're thinking that it's probably Vermont."

Sterling was surprised no one had wrestled control yet. Local cops always fought for jurisdiction, sometimes harder than they did to find the perps.

The Norwich officer took his turn. "Professor Bledsoe lives here in Norwich, and Mrs. Bledsoe made her first call to us," he said. "We're assuming that he was last seen or heard from down on River Road. But Professor Bledsoe does spend a good part of his time over at the college in Hanover, so it only makes sense that we combine forces until we figure out what's happened." Diplomatic.

Sterling looked at the trooper. "They called us in for support," the trooper said. He was tall and had a fresh crew cut that perfectly matched the square shape of his face. He was broad across the chest and younger than the others. State troopers always seemed to be either monstrously big or Napoleonic. "We got a team out there dusting prints and collecting evidence."

Sterling directed his attention to Kay. "I know you're tired, but time is critical. Can you tell me a little about what happened last night?" He took out his black-leather book.

Kay looked up at the ceiling and closed her eyes. "Let me go back to yesterday morning," she began. "Wilson left for the lab a little earlier than usual. He wasn't himself. Wally and Serena were throwing a party for him last night in celebration of the Devonshire, and he couldn't stop worrying over how many people would be there. You know your brother hated crowds. And it didn't make things any better that I've been fighting this nasty virus that's been going around. So I decided not to go, which was fine with Wilson, since the plan was for me to stay here and fix his favorite dinner."

"Grilled salmon, mashed potatoes, and cucumbers," Sterling said.

Kay nodded. "Wilson has never been one for parties, so the only way I got him to go was to bribe him with dinner."

"What time did he arrive at the party?" Sterling asked.

"He called me from his office at about five thirty and said that he was heading over. The party was to start at six and I told him that he should get there a little early to greet the guests with the Mortimers. Even if he didn't want to be there, he still had responsibilities as the guest of honor."

"When did he leave the party?"

"It must've been around seven o'clock."

"Are you certain?" Sterling was back at work on the time line.

"I'm positive," Kay said. It was obvious that she had gone over the last night's events several times. The officers looked on quietly. "The news had just ended and I was turning to watch *Jeopardy*. That's the only game show that Wilson will watch." Kay cleared her throat and continued. "Alex was in the middle of announcing the contestants when Wilson called and said that he'd be home soon."

"Did he say if anything strange happened at the party?" Sterling asked.

Kay thought for a minute. "No, the party went well. Wait. He did mention that one of the students parking cars had asked for his autograph. But that was it."

"Was Wilson coming straight home?"

"For sure," Kay said. "He told me to have the food ready. Then he called back a few minutes later. There were a couple of guys having trouble with their truck." Kay stopped and closed her eyes. "If only he had never stopped," she cried softly.

"Would you like some water, ma'am?" Hanlon asked.

"No, I'll be fine," Kay said, waving him off. She took a deep breath. "I told him to be careful. It was dark and rainy and the wind was fierce." Kay took another breath. "He told me that he would be home soon and to make sure the food was warm." Tears leaked from the corners of her eyes.

"Was that it?" Sterling asked.

"That was the last I heard from him."

"And about what time was that call?"

"Couldn't've been more than seven fifteen, seven thirty."

"Did he say what type of truck it was—the color or make?"

"No, just that there were some guys who needed help, and he was going to lend a hand."

"When did you start thinking something was wrong?"

"After about an hour I got a little worried. I called his cell phone to make sure everything was all right, but there was no answer. I figured he was still out of the car helping the men."

Sterling nodded his head. His wheels spun. "When did you first place your call to the police?"

"At about nine, I think." Kay looked in the direction of the officers.

"Eleven minutes after to be exact," the Norwich officer confirmed. "Second call came in at twenty-three oh five."

"Yes, but between the calls I drove down River Road to see if I could find him."

"And?" Sterling asked.

"There was no sign of him or the two men he had mentioned. Nothing. It was pitch black, and the rain was coming down hard. I drove up and down the road three times, even went over to Hanover and traced the route that he would've taken from the Mortimers' house. Nothing."

"What did you do when you got back home?"

"I searched the house, hoping that by some miracle he had made it home and was waiting to surprise me." Her eyes started leaking again. "The house was empty, and I checked the answering machine to see if he had left a message." She shook her head. "Nothing. That's when I placed the second call to the police."

"And that's when we notified the guys in Hanover," the Norwich officer interjected. "It was still too early to get up in arms. It's not uncommon to get calls from spouses saying their loved one hasn't made it home yet. The weather up here can be nasty, and the roads can get tricky."

Sterling quickly reviewed his notes. Wilson was minutes away from home at approximately 7:15. He didn't answer his cell phone at about 8:15. Kay went looking for him at ten. So, between 7:15 and ten o'clock Wilson disappeared from River Road. Sterling stood up. He wanted to say something to the officers, but not in Kay's presence. "Kay looks beat, guys," he announced. "Maybe we should give her some time and pick up a little later."

The three men rose to their feet. "We'll be in touch," Hanlon said to Kay before they left the den. Sterling followed them out the front door and closed it behind him.

"I know they're working on the record of Wilson's phone calls and the one that Kay made to him," Sterling said. "But how long do you think that'll take?"

"All depends," Hanlon said. "This isn't something they do every day. It might take several hours."

"I'm getting beeped," the Norwich officer said, looking down at his pager. "I'll be right back."

Sterling took out his black book and asked some questions about procedure and the time line. He was also interested in the area's crime rate and any scandals that might have recently been exposed in the quiet college town. They were discussing the Mortimers' infamous parties at the president's mansion when the Norwich officer ran back to join them.

"They matched the tracks," he announced breathlessly.

"Which tracks?" Sterling asked.

"Both sets. Professor Bledsoe's car and a truck. Both were at the medical school and down on River Road."

"You guys have any dogs at the station?" Sterling asked.

"We don't have a canine unit," Hanlon said.

"Neither do we," the Norwich officer added before Sterling could ask.

"I think we sent some down," the trooper said.

"Good. We're gonna need all the help we can get," Sterling said.

A pain in Sterling's gut that had subsided to a dull ache now came roaring back. The more time that slipped away, the less chance they had of finding Wilson alive.

10

By two o'clock on Saturday afternoon, word of the mysterious disappearance of Professor Wilson Bledsoe had spread across the Dartmouth campus through frantic e-mails and whispered phone conversations. Everyone from the regulars in Lou's Diner on Main Street to the senior faculty had heard some part of the story. Like most other rumors, what news was passed on was largely the product of unrestrained imagination. Some stories had the Professor running off with another woman, while others had him skipping town because of gambling debts.

Sterling followed the campus map he had found in his car-rental packet and made a turn down Webster Avenue. Both sides of the street were lined with stately houses belonging to Dartmouth's famous sororities and fraternities. Most of the large brick buildings were badly in need of repair. The lopsided shutters barely clung to their hinges, and the beer cans strewn about the lawns offered evidence that the parties were hard and long. Toward the end of the street sat an enormous yellow mansion resting far back from the road, at least two hundred feet. A tall, black wrought-iron gate with an ornate pattern woven along the top protected the manicured lawn. A large circular driveway led visitors to the front of the house and then conveniently away when it was time to leave. This mansion was the largest, most elegant, and best-maintained house on the street, an appropriate distinction since it served as the official residence of President Wallace Mortimer.

While other schools tended to hide the opulence of their president's home, Mortimer lived like a king, and it was there in the open for everyone to see.

The gate to the driveway was open and two Volvos were parked quietly next to the house. The newer one was a black station wagon with the license plate WM III. The sedan, not more than a couple of years older, was dark green, with the license plate SM I. A Dartmouth Security cruiser was parked behind them. Sterling pulled in behind the cars.

It took a few moments for the door to open after Sterling rang the bell.

"Good afternoon," a short woman said. She was wearing a black, neatly pressed dress at least a couple of sizes too big and a white apron that wrapped her small frame like a cocoon. Her jet-black hair fell down her back, a perfect complement to her deeply tanned skin and sharp features. She was beautiful, but what immediately struck Sterling were her eyes. They were ocean blue and unforgiving. It was the first time he had seen a Native American—or anyone, for that matter—with eyes that color. For a moment they paralyzed his voice.

"Afternoon," he finally said, looking deep into her eyes. He could see the waves of the ocean. "Is President Mortimer home?"

"Who is it, Ahote?" a woman's voice reached out from somewhere deep in the house.

"Your name, sir?" the little princess asked. Her voice sounded like two pieces of silk blowing against each other in the wind.

"Sterling Bledsoe, from New York City."

The door opened wider and Sterling looked into another woman's face. Austere. Gray-tinged blond hair pulled back severely behind a black headband, eyes cold. Sterling found her plain and unremarkable, completely forgettable.

"How can I help you?" she asked. Her voice was strong and to the point. There was a hint of condescension. Ahote took a long look at Sterling and disappeared into the house.

"Agent Sterling Bledsoe," he said. "I was hoping to see President Mortimer."

The woman lifted her eyebrows, then wrinkled her forehead. "Please come in, Mr. Bledsoe," she said, stepping to the side to let Sterling pass. Her voice warmed, but it still wasn't friendly. "I'm Serena Mortimer, Wallace's wife. I just don't know what to say," she lamented, shaking her head several times.

"It's caught all of us by surprise," Sterling said. He stepped into the foyer and realized the house looked even bigger from inside. A grand staircase curved up to a mezzanine, then to the second floor. A massive chandelier sprinkled rainbows across the cream-colored walls. The pungent smell of cleaner immediately assaulted his nose.

"Awful," she said, leading him through a maze of large rooms, mostly decorated with dark, uncomfortable-looking furniture. Old paintings hung in gilded wooden frames. Heavily embroidered curtains shielded the windows from the sun. She spoke with the clipped New England accent of someone who had spent most of her childhood in country clubs. "Wallace is in the back."

The house was quiet and cold, sending a chill through Sterling that made him shiver. But the coolness didn't seem to bother Serena, who was wearing a short-sleeved shirt and plaid skirt. In the minds of those accustomed to winter temperatures well below zero, a cool spring day was just as warm as the middle of summer.

Serena walked Sterling through a long back hallway wallpapered in a green print. This finally opened up to a spacious sunroom overlooking the expansive backyard. Long glass panels trapped the sunlight in the room, keeping the air warmer and cozier than in the rest of the house. Two men sat across from each other speaking in low voices. They stopped when Sterling and Serena entered.

"Sterling Bledsoe," Serena announced. The two men got to their feet.

"I'm Wilson's brother," Sterling said.

"President Wallace Mortimer," the patrician man said. He shook Sterling's hand. His carefully combed black hair showed only traces of gray and a small amount of recession at the temples. He was quite a good-looking man, and in great shape for someone his age and in his position. He wore a forest green wool blazer with a white oxford shirt. His freshly ironed khaki pants had been meticulously tailored. His moccasins looked comfortable and expensive. Like most academics Sterling had met in the North, Mortimer didn't wear socks.

"This is Chief Nathaniel Gaylor," Mortimer said, pointing to the other man. "He's the head of Dartmouth's Security Department." Even the police officers have aristocratic names, Sterling thought. Gaylor extended a hand. He was a remarkably hairless man, with big ears and large bulbous eyes, exactly like an extraterrestrial in a cartoon. Sterling was fascinated by the perfect roundness of his bald dome.

"A pleasure to meet you both," Sterling said. "I apologize for just popping by like this."

"Apology completely unnecessary," President Mortimer said. There was that accent again, northern with a splash of haughtiness, perfect for an Ivy League president. "Please have a seat." The three men sat down. Serena lingered for a moment, then disappeared through the door.

"I was getting briefed on all that's happened so far," Mortimer said. He was just what Sterling had expected of the head of one of the most exclusive schools in the country. He spoke with a heavy and deliberate voice, going to great effort to articulate every vowel and consonant, comfortable in his superiority.

"I arrived this morning," Sterling said. "I've spent all my time so far trying to figure out how Wilson could suddenly slip away on a night that was so special."

"Yes, the party, of course," President Mortimer said. "It was quite a successful affair." He said that proudly. "The biggest scientists from all over the country showed up. Not an easy thing to pull off, I might add. Academics tend to be—well, shall we say, a little self-interested at times."

"I've been told that Wilson left the party at approximately seven o'clock," Sterling said.

"There were over two hundred people here, so I don't remember exactly when he left, but it was shortly after his address." Mortimer looked at the well-appointed garden and squinted from the sun. "I'd say he spoke sometime around a quarter to seven or so."

"Do you remember him behaving out of character at all? Maybe he said something strange, seemed anxious or nervous?"

"Not at all," Mortimer said. He shifted his long body in the chair until he found a more comfortable position. Sterling couldn't get over how young he looked for a man approaching his seventies. "Serena and I spoke to him earlier in the evening and again right before he left," Mortimer said. "He was anxious to get home to Kay. She had been sick, but was still preparing a special meal to commemorate the occasion."

"Have things been going well here for Wilson?" Sterling asked. Mortimer raised his eyebrows as if the question surprised him. "Sometimes things aren't exactly how they seem. Maybe some tension in his department?"

Mortimer's answer was emphatic. "Wilson is one of our most beloved professors," he said. "His scholarship has placed him among the giants, not only in our school's history but in the scientific community at large. No complaint or negative comment has ever come across my desk with Wilson's name on it. He was simply loved by all—faculty, student body, and support staff."

Sterling turned to the chief. "You may or may not know this, but I'm a special agent with the FBI." Gaylor nodded. "We've been called in to assist, and I'll be leading the investigation from our end." Sterling allowed his words to register before continuing. "I was hoping you could tell me what kind of video surveillance has been installed in the different campus buildings."

Chief Gaylor took a moment before responding. It was obvious that he wanted to say the right thing. "Some of our buildings have cameras, but most of them don't. We've been trying to upgrade our security detail over the last few years. To be honest, crime has not been a major concern here at Dartmouth. It's just not that kind of place."

"I noticed there was some type of camera in the entrance of Burke," Sterling said. "Where Wilson has his lab."

Chief Gaylor cocked his perfectly bald head and tightened his thin lips. He reminded Sterling of a hairless sphinx. "There's a library in Burke. That means it would've been one of the first in line for video surveillance installation. We decided to start with all the buildings that had libraries. They have the greatest need since they're open longer and students tend to come and go late into the night."

President Mortimer nodded approvingly, seemingly at the idea of his students putting the libraries to good use.

"Getting a copy of that tape might tell us something," Sterling said.

"What are you thinking?" President Mortimer wanted to know. He sat a little straighter in his chair.

"Just trying to cover all the possible places Wilson could've visited that night," Sterling said. "It probably won't turn up anything, but you never know."

Mortimer nodded. He did that a lot. "We've already gotten a few inquiries from some of the local press, and the *Boston Globe*," Mortimer said. "Someone in my office is working with Chief Gaylor's people to prepare a statement. I wanted the family to read it first before we release it."

"Thanks for the consideration," Sterling said. He knew the media would be sniffing around soon. There wasn't much in the way of crime in these small towns, so the disappearance of a popular professor was sure to stir some interest. After all of his years at the Bureau, Sterling had learned that the media could be your best friend or your worst enemy. The key was controlling them, before they controlled the investigation. When he moved to the special homicide division, he attended a two-week course on the media—how to speak with the press and how to use it to your advantage. While he was working on his first big case, one of the veterans had cautioned him that it was impossible to avoid ambitious reporters, and the minute it looked like that was what you were trying to do, the public relations game was lost. Go to the press before they come to you. As many crimes have been solved by well-placed leaks in the media as they have been by great detective work.

"One thing we've been discussing is a possible kidnapping," Mortimer said. "It was no secret that Wilson had just won the Devonshire. Two million dollars is a lot of money, even around here."

"And we've had a kidnapping in the past," Gaylor added. "About ten years ago, someone grabbed Pam Dolan. Big oil executive's daughter. No harm, just a couple of scratches. And we got her back within three days."

Sterling listened closely. He knew that a kidnapping was unlikely but was willing to hear them out. Everything had to be considered early in an investigation. Of course, there had been no ransom demands as of yet.

"This might be an uncomfortable question," Mortimer began. "But is it possible Wilson was having some type of personal trouble?"

"None that I know of," Sterling said. "But I guess it's something that has to be considered along with everything else."

"So many questions and no answers," Mortimer said. "It's damn frustrating." He was nodding his head again, and the habit was already bothering Sterling.

Ahote appeared at the entrance carrying a tray of glasses and a pitcher of water. When she stepped into the sunroom, the light penetrated the depths of her blue eyes. Sterling watched her movements—quick and efficient. He was captured by her beauty—simple but strong. He looked at his watch. It was almost three o'clock. Veronica was probably just pulling herself out of his bed—alone.

11

Solemn McKenzie Hall stood on the east side of the campus, directly opposite Memorial Field. Students didn't have much business there, since the facilities and operations personnel occupied most of its tiny offices. The dark building stood empty except for a couple of men sitting against the back wall of the lobby. They quickly stamped out their cigarettes as Sterling approached.

"We're closed today," the old one said. Smoking had turned his teeth a putrid yellow.

"I'm Sterling Bledsoe," Sterling said, ignoring the dismissive greeting. "I was hoping you could help me figure something out."

"Try the best I can. But no promises."

"Who's in charge of cleaning and maintaining the campus buildings?" Sterling asked.

" 'Pends on which ones ya talking about," the old man said. He started to reach for the pack of cigarettes in his pocket but changed his mind. "We're part of the custodial services, but then you have maintenance and the grounds teams."

"What are the functions of the custodial services?"

The two men looked at each other, then the old man stared hard at Sterling. "What exactly are you after, sir?" he said. His voice was starting to lose its friendliness.

"Just wondering who takes care of what."

The old man ran his eyes down Sterling's body. "Is this business or personal?"

"Both. I'm investigating my brother's disappearance."

The old man was clearly taken aback. "My sympathies. Professor Bledsoe was a helluva man. Lotta class. Treated us cleaning crews with the same respect he gave the other professors."

"Thanks," Sterling said simply.

"Those of us in custodial are in charge of opening and closing buildings, making sure the buildings are clean and safe," the old man said. "We keep track of lost and found and clear the bulletin boards when students post flyers without permission."

"We also handle all the recycling," the younger man said. It was the first time he had spoken, and Sterling quickly regretted that he had. His teeth were no better than the old man's and looked even worse, with oversized gums that were closer to black than to pink.

"How can I find out who cleans which buildings?" Sterling asked.

"Gotta check with the office," the old man said. "They keep all the assignments and time cards."

"Is anyone in there now?"

"Nope, nobody's in on the weekends. Gotta wait till Monday or call the troubleshooter."

"Troubleshooter handles all emergencies on the weekends," the younger man added.

"How do I reach him?"

"Go over to that white phone and dial 2344," the old man said. "Somebody will pick up."

"Thanks for all your help, gentlemen," Sterling said. He watched the men walk out the front door and jam fresh cigarettes in the corner of their mouths. They were already pulling long drags by the time the door closed behind them.

Sterling dialed the number and waited. "Power plant," a muffled voice answered. A loud radio cranking out the oldies made it difficult to hear him.

"I'm looking for someone from Facilities," Sterling said.

"You have an emergency, sir?" the man asked.

"You could say that," Sterling said.

"Either you do or you don't," the man snapped.

"Something suspicious has happened in my lab, and I need to talk to someone in charge."

There was a pause on the other end. The music suddenly cut off. "What do you mean by suspicious?"

"Exactly that. Suspicious. Not right. Something wrong. Do I need to call Safety and Security?"

"If ya just give me a minute, sir, I'm trying to help." His tone had changed. "What exactly do you need to know?"

"Who cleaned Burke on Friday night?"

"You're talking about Burke labs just down the hill from the observatory?"

"Exactly."

There was another pause. "Where are you?"

"In the lobby of McKenzie."

"Is this really important?"

"Important enough for me to call Security if you can't help."

"I'm at the steam plant. Wait for me and I'll be over in five minutes. What's your name?"

"Sterling Bledsoe."

The rattle of the front door roused Sterling from deep thought. A short man with square metal-framed eyeglasses lumbered across the lobby. He wore dark brown uniform pants and a grease-stained beige shirt with the sleeves rolled up. His right sleeve secured a box of cigarettes. Probably Marlboros. Sterling stood and intercepted him.

"I'm Sterling Bledsoe," he said, extending his hand.

"Otto Winter," the man said, offering a firm handshake. Winter had to be well into his sixties, but his grip was strong and the muscles still bulged in his forearm.

"Thanks for doing this for me," Sterling said. He didn't want to alarm the man, so he kept things unofficial. At least for now. "I normally wouldn't bother, but I'm concerned about some very expensive equipment that's been moved."

Otto grunted and shook his gray frizzy top, badly in need of a haircut. "I doubt one of our people would take anything, sir, especially equipment like that. We ain't got no use for those high-tech gizmos."

"Hopefully they haven't taken it, but maybe they can tell me if it was moved," Sterling said.

"Maybe." Otto reached down to his side and pulled up a wad of keys on a circular ring that looked big enough to fit over his head. He fumbled with a couple of keys before finding the one he wanted. He opened the door to an office off the lobby and flicked on the light. "I used to know the schedule by heart," he said, walking Sterling behind a counter and stopping at a tall metal cabinet along the back wall. "I made the schedule for twenty years before retiring. Now I just fill in on the weekends to get away from the wife." He let out a strange laugh that sounded like he was choking. Then he pulled open the third drawer.

Otto knew exactly where to go and which folder to pull. He took it over to one of the desks and carefully pulled out the papers. "Here it is," he said, showing it to Sterling. "The Friday-night Burke crew was Bretta Winslow and Norma Jean Donnelly."

Sterling looked at the names and scribbled them in his book. "What time do they clean Burke?"

"Right after the library closes," Otto said. "Precisely at midnight."

"And how long does it take?"

Otto bit his bottom lip and tightened his eyes. "I haven't been over there in years, but I suspect three hours tops. That's one of the cleaner buildings, mostly offices and labs. Not a lot of students making a mess. Their biggest cleanup is in the library, where they have to vacuum the rugs and clean the bathrooms. For some reason, those goddamn kids make a helluva mess in the bathrooms. Used to bug the shit outta me when I was cleanin' them."

Sterling continued to scribble as Otto waited patiently for the next question.

"What are you writing, a book or something?" Otto smirked.

"Just my way of keeping things clear," Sterling said. "Is it possible that one of them could've called in sick that night?"

"I doubt it. Bretta maybe, but Norma Jean, never. That woman is a workhorse, bless her soul. She hasn't missed a day of work in fifteen years." Otto shook his head. "They don't make 'em like her anymore."

Otto walked back to the cabinet and shuffled through another set of papers before finding a thick folder—simply labeled "Time Cards." He pulled

out two long manila cards and brought them to Sterling. "They were working all right," he said, handing the cards to Sterling.

Each card had a name on top, and underneath that a formatted weekly
schedule. Bretta had punched in that day at seven, Norma at six forty-five.
They punched out together, Bretta at 3:30:05 and Norma Jean at 3:30:15.
Sterling recorded the times and handed the cards back to Otto.

"Is it possible that someone else would've come after they left to help
clean up?" Sterling asked.

Otto raised his eyebrows. "I can't imagine why. When we finish cleaning a building, we're finished. No reason for anyone else to come and clean
up a cleanup, if you get my drift."

"Who would have access to the labs and offices at Burke?"

"That's a tough one," Otto said. He brought his hand to his chin, and
exposed a tattoo of a naked mermaid on the underside of his forearm. "The
individual custodians that clean Burke would have a key. The custodial
office has a master, so does campus security. We have one at the troubleshooter's office in case of an emergency. Beyond that, I can't think of
anyone else who would need one."

"What door would they use to enter and exit the building?" Sterling
asked.

"The back," Otto said. "Always. The cleaning supply room is just inside
the back door. No real reason to go through the front."

Sterling nodded. "One more thing, Otto," he said. "I notice that you're
not wearing an ID. Does everyone carry one?"

Otto pulled out a wallet thicker than a balled fist. Papers and receipts
fell to the ground, but eventually he produced a photo ID. "Everyone car-
ries ID on their person. Nonnegotiable. A few years back we got hit by a
big theft ring. A bunch of men and women come up from Boston pretend-
ing to be college employees and students. Stole us outta house and home.
Cleaning supplies, computer equipment, textbooks—anything they could
get their hands on, they were taking. Since then, everyone, regardless how
long they've worked here, has to carry their identification. Don't do it and
you're outta here."

Sterling gritted his teeth. They had missed a major opportunity when
Carlton didn't ask the man leaving the lab for his identification. Didn't he
have enough damn sense to be suspicious of someone leaving Wilson's

office only hours after he was reported missing? Then the good-looking girl who had come by claiming to be one of his students. Why had she really come to the lab that morning? If she was checking on an experiment, she hadn't put up much of a fight when Carlton denied her access. Wouldn't she at least have asked him to chaperone her inside if what she was doing was that important?

"You've been a big help," Sterling said, replacing the book inside his breast pocket. "I'll be sure to call the office on Monday if I have any other questions."

"Ask for Darius Brown," Otto said. "He's the big boss."

Sterling left the office and walked into the dark lobby. Whoever went into Wilson's lab between three thirty and five on a dark Saturday morning wasn't making a social call. The clues weren't talking yet, but they were at least starting to hum.

12

The sturdy old bell high above Baker Library had just finished its fourth strike of the afternoon when one of the officers discovered the half-naked body of Professor Wilson Bledsoe. One of the German shepherds from the Vermont State Police canine unit had sniffed his way to the decrepit barn at the edge of Potter's farm. The dog dragged Officer Beck until he spotted the light-gray fabric partly buried underneath a cluster of bushes. First the black wingtipped shoes, then the shirtless upper torso, facedown. Beck touched the inside of the left leg with his shoe and gave a hard nudge. No response. The dog smelled death and started barking furiously as it skipped in restless circles. Beck pulled the leash back, then radioed to the rest of the search crew.

Sterling was finishing up a bowl of cereal when his cell phone rang.

"Bledsoe," he answered.

"Wiley here. Where are you?"

"At the house," Sterling said. He pushed back from the table. "What is it?"

"There's no way to put this easy, Agent Bledsoe. But we found him."

"Wilson? Dead or alive?"

"He's been murdered."

Sterling heard the words, but they didn't register. "Is he alive, Lieutenant?"

"I'm sorry. He's dead." There was a long silence before Wiley spoke again. "Are you there, Agent?"

"Where is he?" Sterling said.

"In a wooded area off River Road."

"I'm on my way."

A s Sterling raced down River Road he heard the buzz of a chopper overhead, but he couldn't see it through the heavy trees. He ignored a sharp curve, skimming hedges and branches that crawled onto the road. He slammed on the brakes when he reached the flurry of activity. The cordoned-off area was much different from when he had left it a couple of hours ago. Hordes of uniformed men wearing different colored jackets scrambled around like rats in a maze. Anxious dogs barked and strained at their leashes, and at least twenty marked and unmarked cars were haphazardly strewn along the road. The army of bright lights swirling atop the cruisers only added to the chaos, giving it a carnival-like atmosphere. Sterling took a few moments to observe the pandemonium. Some officers screamed into walkie-talkies while others yelled at each other, not in anger but in confusion.

Sterling approached the yellow tape. Two state troopers stood guard with their bulky arms folded across their chests. Twin sentries. "Sir, this is a sealed-off crime scene," one of them said. "Please vacate the premises and move your car."

The words "crime scene" ripped through Sterling's gut like a shotgun blast. He flipped his wallet open and flashed his tin, not bothering to waste words on them. He spotted Lieutenant Wiley in the middle of the chaos, barking orders to anyone who would listen. The two sentries moved aside and let Sterling pass.

"How far away is he, Lieutenant?" Sterling asked when he was close enough for Wiley to hear him above the noise. He leaned onto a nearby cruiser to steady himself and inhaled deeply, hoping he could clear his head. Everything seemed to be moving in slow motion.

"About three hundred yards from here," Wiley said. "He was just outside an old barn up on the Potter property."

"When was he found?"

"About twenty minutes ago. I called you as soon as I got the word. They're taking photographs and prints now."

"Which direction?" Sterling bit his lip hard to fight back the tears. He refused to believe that his only brother was dead until he saw the body himself.

"I don't know if you want to go up there, Agent Bledsoe," Wiley cautioned. "I'm not sure how bad it is." Sterling's chin fell to his chest and he closed his eyes. Wiley stepped forward and placed a hand on his slumping shoulders. "Maybe you should let our men handle it from here."

"I'm going to see my brother, Lieutenant." Sterling's voice was strong and full of anger. "Then I'm gonna figure out who the hell did this."

"Everyone's on board," Wiley informed him. "State, the local departments from both towns, and some of your men from Boston are already up there."

"Did he struggle?" Sterling had to know.

"I think so," Wiley said, shaking his head. "His clothes were dirty and tattered. Blunt trauma to the side of his head."

Sterling looked along the side of the road through a slight clearing in the thick trees. He could see the calm rolling waters of the Connecticut River. A family of ducks floated down the current, the sun illuminating their brilliant green, black, and blue feathers. How could something so horrible happen here, a place of such natural serenity—no hustle and bustle like in the big city. His mind raced through scenes of his youth, when Wilson would come home from college and their mother would prepare his favorite meal. Wilson's wide smile had always brought her such pleasure. It was the smile that Sterling had learned to hate.

Sterling allowed himself to get lost in the memories. They had always been a hardworking family. The academic success of the children had become the old man's pride, and he would boast about it to anyone willing to listen. Sterling remembered the warm glow that would light up his mother's face when the ladies at church asked how Wilson was doing in Chicago. They asked every Sunday morning, as if things might've changed one week to the next. In their small manufacturing town in western Pennsylvania, most of the children finished high school and then went to work in the factories and textile mills. It was a big deal to have a son off in college, then graduate school, and an even bigger deal that he was a scientist.

Wilson's Nobel came at a time when their parents' health was declining but good enough for them to make the trip to Sweden. That same glow returned to his mother's cheeks as Wilson accepted his award from King Carl XVI Gustaf. They'd died before he won the Devonshire, but they'd known that their small-town boys had turned out to be successful men of the world.

"Agent Bledsoe." Lieutenant Wiley tapped Sterling on the shoulder. "Maybe you should let us clean things up a bit and identify him at the morgue."

"No," Sterling insisted. "I want to see him now."

Wiley walked over to one of the cruisers and pulled out a fresh box of latex gloves. He led Sterling through the dense trees, stepping over fallen branches and walking around areas where the ground was wet and soft from the previous night's rain. They crossed a small ravine, then climbed their way up to the pond. A few minutes later they had reached the clearing that led to the back of the Potter property. Both men were breathing heavily by the time the barn came into view.

The chopper continued to make passes in the sky. A group of officers, too many for Sterling to count, huddled just outside the barn, their heads bent toward the ground like kids playing marbles. A flash from the photographer's camera popped every couple of seconds. Sterling took a series of deep breaths, hoping to untie the knot in his stomach. This was going to be the most difficult thing he had ever done.

The solemn voices grew quiet as he and Wiley approached.

"Gentlemen, this is Agent Sterling Bledsoe," Wiley announced. "Brother of Professor Bledsoe."

The men turned and nodded, but didn't say anything. Their faces were long and dark. Death had that kind of effect, even on grown men. They all moved back to give Sterling some private time. He was pleased that they stood behind him, making it impossible for them to see the tears in his eyes.

The dog that had found the body had finally settled down, though it occasionally let out a distressed yelp. Sterling took one last breath, then moved closer. The body hadn't been moved. Both shoes were untied, their soles packed with mud that still hadn't dried. Wilson's gray pants were covered with dirt marks and the right leg had a large tear in it.

The upper torso was naked, but there weren't any abrasions or fresh wounds on the back. Sterling looked at Wilson's waist and noticed the extra pounds he had put on in the last few months. His face was planted in the ground, but strangely the arms were extended above his head. His fingers had stiffened in a slightly curled position.

"Are you done with location and position photos?" he asked the photographer.

"I think we've got enough," the photographer answered. He patted his vest pocket bulging with rolls of film.

A short, burly man approached. "I'm sorry, Sterling," he said. His voice sounded like sandpaper dragged across a piece of rotted wood. His heavy black mustache drooped past the corners of his mouth and curled back in perfect loops. Sterling recognized Special Agent Lonnie Brusco right away. "I got in about an hour ago." They pumped hands firmly. "You sure you don't wanna wait till we take him to the morgue? This won't be easy."

"Nothing about this damn business is easy," Sterling said. "I need to see what they did to my brother."

Brusco sighed in acknowledgment. He understood the pain, and he also knew what it meant to be a homicide agent. There was something buried deep inside all of them that compelled them to see and learn every grisly detail of the killing. Even if it was family. He gave Sterling his space.

Sterling snapped on the latex gloves. He had done this hundreds of times, in the lab and in the field, but never had he imagined it would be over the dead body of his brother. He closed his eyes, bowed his head, and mouthed a small prayer. When he finished, he knelt beside Wilson, then turned him over with considerable effort. Nothing could have prepared him for what he found. He had to reach out to stop from falling.

The word NIGGER had been inscribed across Wilson's chest. The cuts were so deep that Sterling could see large tangled chunks of bone, muscle, and fat. Sterling couldn't get out more than a painful grunt. He scrambled to his feet and looked away.

One of the other officers started heaving. He grabbed his stomach before doubling over to vomit.

"Get him the hell out of here," Wiley barked. Two other men escorted the sickened officer away from the scene. Even with the buzz of the chopper overhead, they could still hear him retching on the side of the barn.

"What the hell?" one of the other men said. He spoke for everyone staring at Wilson's mutilated body.

Brusco walked behind Sterling and placed his hand on his shoulder. "Let us take it from here," he said. "You've seen enough."

Sterling dried his eyes with his hands, then stepped back. He watched quietly as the other men went to work. They began dusting the body for prints, then took samples—tissue, skin, hair, fingernails, and some of the blood that had clotted on his chest. The team worked quickly and expertly, gathering the evidence and sealing it in large plastic bags, then labeling them with black markers. As Sterling watched, he mentally checked off the steps that should be taken during the early collection of evidence. Reflex. This was his area of expertise, and despite the pain in his heart and the fog clouding his mind, the FBI agent in him monitored their movements carefully.

Sterling stepped closer to the body. The more he looked at the word "nigger" carved into Wilson's chest, the angrier he became. Didn't the evils of racism have any boundaries, play by any rules? Sterling was painfully reminded of what Pops had always told them growing up. *No matter how high you climb, don't ever forget the color of your skin because they won't. The amount of money you have in the bank or the number of degrees hanging on your wall won't mean a damn thing. To some of them you'll always be a nigger.* And that's what Wilson was to them, even after all that he had accomplished. Sterling cursed his father because his words rang so true. He cursed Wilson's killers for senselessly wasting a good and productive life.

Sterling felt a wave of hate surge in his body. He wanted to kill them—all of them—racists, bigots, hate mongers, and anyone else who had spewed the venomous ideology of racism. If they could kill someone like Wilson who rarely, if ever, even whispered a harsh word about anybody else, then no one was safe.

His jaws tightened as he examined the carved letters. If this was the work of a hand knife, it must have taken the killer a long time to complete the disfigurement. The letters were well formed and in a strange sort of way they were neat. Most troubling, however, was the depth of penetration. Spicules of bone were fixed in the dried, matted blood as if they had been stuck in glue. Sterling prayed that Wilson had been dead long before they mutilated him. The skin along the incised areas remained puckered, the edges uneven and actually frayed in some parts. Sterling knew this had to be the work of a jagged blade. The cuts seemed too deep to be carved by hand. He had cut through bone for years during autopsies, and he knew the effort it would take to accomplish it with a knife.

The men pulled the body so that Wilson's face emerged from underneath the bushes. He wore an expression of terror. His eyes were wide and glassy, his mouth was open. It looked like he had been killed while in the middle of saying something. Sterling peered over the shoulders of the men kneeling beside Wilson's body. There weren't any marks on his face, nor was there blood in his mouth. But that expression. Sterling knew it would haunt him forever.

Sterling found Lieutenant Wiley standing a few feet away deep in thought, his hands clasped behind his back. "Whose property is this?" Sterling asked.

"Potter's farm," Wiley said.

"Who owns it?"

"It belonged to one of the richest men in the Upper Valley—Ezra Potter."

"Belonged?"

"The old man died years ago. Actually, he was killed somewhere on this property in a hunting accident." Wiley slightly stressed the word "accident."

Sterling heard the skepticism. "You didn't buy it?"

"I was only a teenager at the time, but I remember it well. Just too damned strange. He heads out here one afternoon with a couple of buddies and returns in a body bag."

"But hunting accidents do happen."

"Not when you're shooting up in the air at fowl and all four men have been hunting since they were kids."

"So who lives here now?" Wiley took Sterling by the arm and led him a few yards away from the chaos. He pointed at the distant trees. The mountain peaks reached into the sky, piercing the bed of clouds suspended above them.

"The main house is about half a mile on the other side of the property," Wiley said. "His wife is still knocking around up there. She must be damn near ninety, but she's as sharp as a tack. She's lived by herself all these years since Ezra's death, but someone told me she finally got some live-in help."

"Has anyone gone up there yet?"

"Not that I know of."

"Then we need to pay Mrs. Potter a visit."

13

The Potter farmhouse was a great, rambling, faded-red structure that stood alone in the middle of an open field. The weathered wood and drab color were clear indications that the house had seen much happier times. An antique maroon Porsche with a black soft top sat in front of the garage. The polished chrome shone in the sunlight like a mirror. Sterling made a mental note of the car before approaching the front door of the old farmhouse. The massive structure of ancient wood slats screamed out for a fresh coat of paint. Forget a modern contraption like a doorknob. A heavy rusted knocker hung in the middle of the door, looking like it was too tired to announce any more visitors. Wiley cleared away the cobwebs and reached up to give it several firm taps. A few seconds later the door creaked open.

A young woman stood in the doorway. She was wearing jeans and a pink blouse buttoned to her neck, and her blond hair was pulled back in a long ponytail. Sterling got the strange feeling that he had seen her before. He never forgot a pretty face.

"Officer Wiley, ma'am, and this here is Agent Sterling Bledsoe. We were hoping to get a word with you and Mrs. Potter."

A look of concern spread across her face. "Is there a problem, Officer?" Her accent was hard, maybe German, Sterling thought. She couldn't have been more than twenty-four.

Wiley looked at Sterling before answering. "I'm afraid there is," he said. "We've found a body on the edge of the property."

The fair-skinned girl lost what little color she had, covering her mouth with her free hand. "A body? Here?"

"Yes, ma'am, we found it about an hour ago." The girl shook her head until it settled into a tremble. Her eyes were fixed in disbelief. "May we come in?" Wiley asked.

"Oh yes, please do," she said. "Mrs. Potter is in the living room. Wait here for a moment." She disappeared before Wiley could ask her name.

Inside, the house looked much better than one might have expected from the poorly maintained surrounding property. Large oil canvases hung on dark walls, mixed with black-and-white still photographs, the oval kind where the faces had started to turn sepia from age. The backgrounds had completely faded to an ash gray. Two doorways flanked the room, one on the left, the other farther back along the right wall. Identical deer heads had been mounted above the entrances. In the far corner sat a dusty gun cabinet filled with an assortment of shotguns and rifles. A vast collection of plaid, wool, fur, and bright-orange hunting caps burdened a crooked hat pole. A serious hunter had once lived here.

The young woman returned. She looked much calmer now. "Mrs. Potter will see you."

Sterling and Lieutenant Wiley followed her through a series of cluttered rooms and a sitting room big enough to seat a family of twenty. They walked down a short hallway and through a door that opened to a spacious living room. The floor-to-ceiling windows gave the otherwise dark room a jolt of life. An old woman sat propped in a chair, leaning over a small table. She was just finishing a sip of something hot. Her skin sagged in some places but was stretched tight in others. Her eyes were strong. Chestnut brown. The diamonds in her ears were big enough to comfortably send someone into retirement.

"Good afternoon, gentlemen," she said, placing the cup back on the tray. "What in God's name is going on?"

"I'm Lieutenant Wiley from the Hanover Police Department," Wiley said, removing his cap. It was the first time that Sterling had seen him with it off. His dark hair was surprisingly wavy and youthful-looking. "This here is Agent Sterling Bledsoe."

"Have a seat, gentlemen," she said, waving her wrinkled fingers at an empty sofa. "You too, Heidi, for God's sake." The young blonde followed the command. "This weather is a real treat, especially after the rain last night," she said. Sterling had expected this would start the conversation.

"It's a fine one, Mrs. Potter," Wiley said. "Probably still hovering somewhere in the sixties." There was a brief pause, and then it was time for business. "Mrs. Potter, we found a body on the edge of your property about an hour ago."

Mrs. Potter sat back from the table and rested her head against the chair. "I thought Heidi had been mistaken. What's a body doing on my property?" Her voice was still strong for a woman climbing into her nineties. Wiley's statement didn't scare her. Instead, it made her more indignant.

"That's what we're trying to figure out," Wiley said. "One of our men found him by the old barn not far from the pond."

"I haven't been down there since Ezra died." She looked out the window and mumbled something. The sun on her face illuminated the web of tiny blue veins beneath her paper-thin skin. "Do you know who it is?"

"My brother, ma'am," Sterling said, speaking for the first time. "Professor Wilson Bledsoe."

Nel Potter let out a shriek, her face twisted in horror. She looked at Heidi, then at Sterling. "My God!" she exclaimed. "Did you say Professor Wilson Bledsoe? The one who lives just over on Deer Run Lane?"

"Yes, ma'am. That's my brother."

"There must be some mistake," she said, shaking her head as if someone had just slapped her. "I just saw him a couple of days ago."

"You knew my brother, ma'am?"

"Did I? I saw him at least once a week. There must be some mistake." She couldn't stop shaking her head. "No one would want to hurt that lovely man." The room fell silent as Mrs. Potter struggled with the news. She turned to Heidi. "Child, get these men something cool to drink." Wiley and Sterling waved away the offer, but it was of no use. Heidi was already through the door. Sterling caught her wiping her eyes. "Wilson was a prince of a man," Mrs. Potter said. She stopped suddenly and closed her eyes. Her chin dropped to her chest. "I've already referred to him in the past tense."

"It's tough for all of us," Sterling said. "This has come as quite a shock. Now we're beginning a murder investigation."

"It feels so strange even hearing the word murder," she said. "That just doesn't happen around here. Why in God's name would someone murder Wilson?"

"We don't know who or why," Sterling said, "but I'm not stopping till I have the answers."

"And to think that he was killed on my property," Mrs. Potter sighed.

Heidi returned to the living room carrying a tray of tall glasses and a large pitcher of lemonade. In just the short time since she had left, her eyes had already swollen and reddened. She had been crying hard. She poured drinks for everyone but herself, then took a seat. Sterling still couldn't place her face and it bothered him.

He looked at Mrs. Potter. "How did you come to know my brother?" he asked after a long pull on the sugary liquid. The sweetness followed by the sharp bitter aftertaste made his lips pucker.

"I met the Professor a few years ago, after he and his beautiful wife moved over to the Karlson property on Deer Run. That piece of land had been in the Karlson family for four generations, but the mother was the last one alive and didn't have anyone to leave it to. Poor woman. The Professor and his wife bought it, and there couldn't have been a more perfect couple for that property. They were young and Wilson was crazy about nature."

Sterling noticed Heidi nodding in agreement. "Heidi, what's your last name?" Sterling asked.

Heidi turned to Mrs. Potter almost as if asking for permission to speak. "Vorscht," she said. "I'm a graduate student at Thayer, the engineering school."

"Do you live here?" Sterling asked.

"Yes, sir."

"She's from Germany," Mrs. Potter took over. "Just outside of Stuttgart. Every few years I get a new live-in student to help me around the house. I've been quite lucky with the German girls. They're hardworking and good around the house." Mrs. Potter paused. "And they always do well in school."

"Did either of you hear anything unusual last night?" Sterling asked.

Heidi and Mrs. Potter looked at each other. Mrs. Potter went first. "I had dinner at seven in the kitchen, as always. I watch *Jeopardy* every night. I get most of the answers right when these young people with all their fancy degrees can't even answer the easy ones. Just goes to show you the old way of schooling wasn't that bad after all. After the final *Jeopardy* question, Heidi sets me up in the family room for my dessert. That's where I watch *Wheel of Fortune*. That Vanna White is just the loveliest." Sterling indulged the old woman's rambling. "When that's over, it's a little shot of whiskey for the heart, and then I'm off to bed."

"Did you hear anything strange during that time?" Sterling asked.

"Nothing at all," she said. "But that's not surprising, since I sleep like a log."

"What time did you get up this morning?"

"I get up the same time every morning, five thirty."

"What about you, Heidi?" Sterling asked.

"After I put Mrs. Potter to bed, I went downstairs in the den to study," she said. Her English was perfect, but still weighed down by her heavy German accent. Sterling looked at her carefully. She was even prettier than he first thought—the way her eyes turned up at the corners, high cheekbones and long, slender nose. Her turtleneck sweater clung across her ample chest. She was in excellent shape. "I like the den, because at night the house gets cold and the fireplace in there works the best."

"What time did you go to sleep last night?"

"About one o'clock this morning."

"And when did you get up?"

"About eight."

Sterling looked intently at Heidi's delicate hands. They were trembling. He couldn't help but think how ironic it was that Wilson's body was found on the property of friendly neighbors who would have done anything they could to help him. He motioned to Wiley, then stood up. Lieutenant Wiley grabbed his hat off the sofa and stood beside him.

"Thanks for all of your help, Mrs. Potter. You too, Heidi," Sterling said. "Sorry we had to meet like this."

"The Professor was a wonderful human being," Mrs. Potter said. "I can't imagine why anyone with a sane mind would want to take his life." She stood with great effort, ignoring Heidi's outstretched hand. She reached for an old wooden cane leaning against her chair and started walking slowly, but after a few warm-up strides she picked up her pace.

"We might come back for a few more questions, if that's all right," Wiley informed the two women.

"I'm always here," Mrs. Potter said. "I don't get out much. Come and have a cool drink anytime you'd like."

Heidi opened the door for them to leave. "By the way, Mr. Bledsoe, what will ever come of his blackbirds?"

"Blackbirds?" Sterling asked.

"They were his passion," she said. "That's how we first came to meet. I'd see him taking what he called his night scouts. He'd be out walking on the property before the sun was even awake, gathering information about all kinds of animals, didn't matter how small or how big. And he was such a . . . such a . . ." She struggled for the word. "Such a crusader for those blackbirds."

He made a note in his black book. Why the hell was Wilson studying blackbirds so early in the morning, and where had Sterling seen this beautiful girl before?

Kay stood at the counter putting away dishes when Sterling entered the kitchen. He watched her for a few moments, then looked over at the table. Wilson's plate of salmon was still there, covered in Saran Wrap. Seeing it only worsened the pain gnawing at his stomach. Sterling had never been a religious man, and the last twelve hours had done very little to put the Bible at the top of his reading list. At this moment he had a lot more questions than he did faith. He walked farther into the kitchen and hung his coat on the back of a chair. "Kay," he finally said.

She turned and faced him. The stress of uncertainty had not been kind to her. Her mental fragility had unmasked age's creeping effects around her eyes. He looked at her desperately, then nodded and turned away.

Her woeful scream filled the air, a scream of bottomless anguish. She sagged to the ground and lay there in a fetal position, her sobs causing her to heave uncontrollably. She kept repeating Wilson's name and asking God for his mercy.

Sterling knelt beside her, pulling her to his chest and spilling his own tears into the flood pouring out of her eyes. "It's gonna be okay," was all that he could say, trying to console himself as much as her. "Even if it takes me to my death, I'll find whoever has done this."

"Where is he?" Kay sobbed.

"Over on the Potter farm. They found his body near an old barn."

"Is he really dead?" she cried.

Sterling hugged her tighter. "They've taken him away."

Kay hung her head and fell back into Sterling's chest. They remained in that position for a long time, begging for hope where there was only despair.

$\mathcal{S}$terling spent most of the night sitting in the darkness of Wilson's study, a tumbler of Jack Daniels within arm's reach on the desk. The whiskey slipped down his throat easily, warming his insides deep into the night. He looked out the window into the darkness. It all just seemed to be crashing down on him at once. He and Wilson had grown closer the last several years, but there was still work to be done. He needed to bury the demons forever and continue to open his mind. That was the conclusion he had come to during his last session with Dr. Lieteau. Therapy had been a painful process, and many times he had wanted to bolt out of the room and never go back. But she had kept him searching inward. He had planned a long weekend for just himself and Wilson, trying to repair some of the damage. Then this. Sterling couldn't help but feel the sting of guilt, remembering how he had refused to visit Wilson and Kay in Hanover, repeatedly pushing aside the olive branch that his brother extended.

He closed his eyes, then leaned his head back. But he stopped. Tapping. Was there someone at the door? "Hello?" he called out. No answer. More tapping, but it was faint. He rested the drink on the desk and opened the door slowly. The hallway was dark, except for the moonlight cutting through the windows. He eased down the hall, looking into the dark, empty rooms. The sound of metal on metal, but it was coming from outside. He grabbed his gun from the closet and snapped in a magazine. First he checked Kay's room upstairs, opening the door quietly. She was asleep. He took the back stairs down. One loud tap, then it stopped.

Sterling slipped through the sliding glass doors of the kitchen. He looked out back first, then walked around until he reached the garage. Everything seemed normal, but then he saw the door—slightly open, swinging softly in the wind. He took a deep breath, kicked the door open, and crouched with his gun drawn, ready to fire. No one there. He searched around, first looking under Kay's car, then opening the doors and checking inside. Confident that he was alone, he clicked on the safety lock and slid the gun inside his waistband. He turned on the light, then examined the door lock to the garage. The lock had been jammed. Deep grooves cut the steel where it had been forced open. Someone had definitely been there, but why?

Sterling walked back to the house and checked on Kay once more, then headed off to his room at the other end of the hall. He kept his door open when he got in bed and placed his gun on the nightstand beside him. If they were willing to come once, they were willing to come again. It took hours before he finally dozed off. It had been a long time since he felt so much fear for his own safety.

14

Sterling ran hard along the Connecticut River, the sound of waves lapping against the banks following him in the darkness. He preferred to run just before dawn. Three days a week, four if something was bothering him. Hitting the road, however, was not something that had always come easy to him. As a trainee in Quantico he could barely sleep through the night knowing that he had to wake up at the crack of dawn to run miles in the woods and then survive an obstacle course. Several times he had almost quit before his career had even started. He was much better suited for the laboratory, where he could put his mind instead of his muscles to work. Unexpectedly, the exercise slowly became a drug, and by the time he finished basic training, he had fallen in love with the very drills that had caused him so much pain. Long, quiet runs had become the perfect balm for his cluttered mind and tangled nerves. While others required a daily jolt of caffeine in the morning, Sterling only needed to feel his feet pounding the pavement.

The run along the Connecticut River, deep in the cool mountains, was a welcome change. It reminded him of how beautiful nature could be when it was protected from ambitious developers and their gigantic machines of mass destruction. Hearing hundreds of strange, anonymous cries and the unbridled songs of animal joy made it easy to understand why Wilson started so many of his mornings with a nature scout.

Sterling turned onto Deer Run Lane and picked up his speed for the last half mile. He had gone to bed exhausted, but whatever had happened in the garage had made it difficult to sleep. When he was finally able to shut his eyes, the photographer's bright bulb flashed in his dreams, waking him up to darkness. Then the images would start again like a movie reel stuck in a loop—Wilson's body lying under the bushes and the deep letters carved into his chest. Sterling had woken this morning, searching for reasons someone would want to kill a man who had loved life so much. When the answers didn't come, he took to the road to find some peace.

Sterling reached the gravel driveway of the property and ran toward the large house, which looked much more imposing in the low light. He always finished his run where he had started; it gave him a sense of closure. He looked at his watch. Thirty-six minutes. Just over seven minutes a mile. He was pleased, especially for his first run at a higher altitude and on challenging terrain. He walked over to one of the wide birch trees and leaned against it to stretch his muscles before they tightened.

As he stretched, he heard the crunching sound of tires on gravel. A white cruiser pulled slowly along the driveway and came to a rest just in front of the house. Lieutenant Wiley jumped out of the car and walked over toward Sterling. His hard, compact body seemed in danger of exploding.

"G'morning, Agent," Wiley said, touching his cap slightly.

"Morning, Lieutenant," Sterling said, pulling his outstretched leg from the tree and meeting Wiley in the middle of the yard. They pumped hands earnestly.

"Supposed to be another warm one," Wiley said, looking up at the gray sky. "Clouds are gonna move out and give the sun a shot." He let the thought sink in. "I see you've already taken advantage of the good weather."

"Great place to jog," Sterling said. "No one to bother you or cars forcing you off the road. I could run all day on these country roads."

"One of our hidden secrets," Wiley said proudly. A rare smile cracked the corner of his mouth. "Yesterday you asked Chief Gaylor about video surveillance on campus."

"That's right," Sterling said.

"Well, we got something yesterday, but I'm not sure if it's going to be of any help."

Sterling stopped in the middle of a bend and straightened up.

"It looks like that camera you spotted by the medical school hasn't been working for years. It got disconnected during a storm, and no one ever bothered to hook it back up."

"I didn't have my hopes up too high about that video," Sterling said. "But it was worth a shot."

"You got a great eye, Agent Bledsoe," Wiley said. "And you did hit the nail on the head about there being a camera over at Burke. We just got the tape in a couple of hours ago."

"Anything on it?"

"We haven't looked at it yet. I figured I'd come get you first."

"Thanks for waiting, Lieutenant." There was a sense of hope in Sterling's voice. Maybe their first big break. Getting that first one was always difficult, but when it came, more often than not the others were soon to follow. "Let me run up and change, and I'll be back in a few."

"No problem. I'll be waiting in the car. By the way, how's Mrs. Bledsoe?"

"Not well at all," Sterling said. "The news broke her right down. Then hearing that it was likely a race crime just tore her to nothing."

Wiley winced slightly. "This isn't the spirit of the Upper Valley," he said in a tone of apology. "Whoever did this is not one of us."

Sterling accepted Wiley's words without protest. He was more determined than ever to catch the person who had done this to his brother. With his other cases he'd been motivated by the chance to bring the killer to justice; this time he was driven strictly by revenge.

The Hanover Police Department was in an inconspicuous single-story building squatting next to the eighth hole of the Dartmouth Country Club golf course. It had a simple entrance just off Lyme Road, mostly hidden by the tall evergreen trees that kept it in perpetual shade. Except for the name across the front of the building, the few cruisers parked in the rear were the only indication that matters inside revolved around police work. As Wiley pulled his car to the back, Sterling parked the Mustang in a spot marked for visitors.

"We'll be using this as headquarters for the investigation," Wiley said, taking Sterling down a couple of narrow hallways. "We've all agreed that the Norwich department is just too small for all of us to fit."

Wiley opened a black unmarked door that led to a large room with several small cubicles along the perimeter. A long conference table in the middle of the pit was filled with phones and fax machines. A large map of the Upper Valley had been taped in the center of the far wall. Sterling recognized most of the faces from the previous day. Agent Brusco talked quietly to a group of officers. He stopped when Sterling and Wiley approached.

"Just in time, Agent," he said; the scratch in his voice sounded like it hurt him to talk.

"So, this could be our first break," Sterling said. He raised his eyebrows with uncertainty.

Brusco nodded. "Just waiting for you to play it," he said. He pointed to a woman seated across the room in front of the video player. A screen had been hung on the largest wall. Next to the screen, the beginnings of a time line had been posted. It was mostly blank except for Wilson leaving the Mortimer mansion, his phone calls to Kay, and the discovery of his body.

The woman pushed a couple of buttons and fidgeted with the remote control before the tape finally played. Most of the video was grainy and out of focus. The faces were barely distinguishable. No audio, just the constant flow of bodies, mostly students, passing in and out of the front door. Occasionally someone would walk outside and smoke a cigarette. The best part about the tape was the time code running along the bottom of the frames.

"Let's fast-forward to early yesterday morning," Sterling instructed the woman running the controls.

"Tell me when," she said.

The video images raced across the screen. Sterling pulled out the black book from his vest and reviewed his notes. According to Carlton, the officer standing guard at Wilson's laboratory, the cleaning man was just leaving as he began his watch a little after five o'clock.

"Stop it there," Sterling said. The time code showed 4:00:30.

The room sat in silence for twenty-five minutes, watching a still front door with no movement other than the jumping shadows of tree limbs blowing in the wind. At 4:25:10, action outside. A figure approached the front door, looked around, and quickly entered. They couldn't tell if it was a man or a woman, so Sterling had her rewind the tape and play it in slow motion.

The face could barely be seen, but in one frame, just as the door opened, an image could almost be made out. A dark baseball cap hid the eyes, the nose and mouth only slightly visible. "Can you zoom in on that?" Sterling asked the woman.

"Not with this machine," she answered.

"Can you print from it?" Sterling asked.

"Unfortunately not."

"Okay, let the tape play," he said, resigned.

When she released the Pause button, the person quickly disappeared. Then another thirty-five minutes of no activity, until another figure came into view and opened the door. The security uniform was obvious, as was the shield that shone under the lobby light. The time code showed 5:02:03.

"That's Carlton," Sterling announced to the room, checking his notes.

"Who's Carlton?" Brusco asked

"Carlton Gilly," Sterling answered. "One of the Dartmouth Security officers. He was assigned his post outside of Wilson's lab when he reported in that morning."

"He was in the middle of his shift when we stopped by yesterday," Wiley added.

"Let the tape play," Sterling said.

Another five minutes of the empty lobby before a shadow appeared and the back of a figure temporarily blocked the camera. The person quickly opened the door with his right hand and left the building. In less than a second he had disappeared. Time code: 5:07:24.

"Go back," Sterling instructed. "Right before that figure appears."

The woman rewound the tape, then pushed play. "Stop!" Sterling shouted.

Everyone stared at the screen, and then at each other. They weren't seeing what Sterling had seen.

"What is it?" Wiley finally asked.

"The door," Sterling said, walking over to the screen. He pulled out a pen. "There's a reflection of the face in the door. It's faint, but it's there."

Everyone gathered around Sterling and took turns looking at the image. They all agreed there was something, but it was too faint to make out.

"It's the cleaning man Carlton mentioned," Sterling said. He looked down at his notes. "Carlton said as he was taking his post a man was leaving the laboratory. Carlton didn't question him too hard because he looked like he had really been cleaning."

"I wouldn't've questioned him either," one of the officers said. "They probably clean those labs early in the morning when less people are around."

"They do," Sterling said, turning the pages in his book. "But according to Facilities and Operations, the Burke labs are cleaned between midnight and three."

"Maybe the janitor got a late start?" someone offered.

"Not on Saturday morning," Sterling corrected. "Bretta Winslow and Norma Jean Donnelly clean the Burke labs every Friday night. They punched off the clock at three thirty Saturday morning."

"It's possible they forgot something," someone else suggested.

"Winslow and Donnelly always enter and exit from the back of Burke," Sterling said. "I talked to the weekend troubleshooter, Otto Winter. He said all the cleaning supplies are stored in the back. There's no real reason to enter the front."

Agent Brusco looked at Sterling. "Makes a lot of sense," he said. "But if that's not a janitor, then someone has some explaining to do."

Sterling kept his eyes on the still door on the screen. "Let's send this down to Harry's lab in Quantico. The tech guys can work miracles with this footage." Sterling smelled his first scent of blood.

15

Sterling drove around the Dartmouth Green and parked in front of the newest-looking building in Hanover, the Hopkins Center, or the Hop, as it was better known. Large arcaded windows stood in stark contrast to the antiquated colonial structures that composed most of the campus. People filed in and out of the glass doors, some lugging large instruments, others dressed for the symphony. Small children ran ahead of their parents, disobeying commands to stop.

An old woman sat hunched at the information desk. "I'm looking for the Student Employment Office," Sterling said. "Is it open today?"

"It's open every day, sir, but you're in the wrong building," she said, shuffling over to a table covered with glossy brochures. She pulled one out and opened it. "You want to go over to the Thayer Dining Hall, just behind the Collis Center. It's a big brick building, just west of the green."

As he turned to leave, Sterling noticed a small pile of newspapers stacked carelessly in a metal bin. It was the college paper, *The Dartmouth*. He spotted Wilson's name in one of the headlines. "How much for one of those papers?" he asked.

"Oh, those aren't for sale," she said. "They're waiting to go to the recycling center. They're over a month old."

"Can I take one?"

"If old news interests you, be my guest," she said, straining to bend down and grab the paper.

"Just trying to catch up," Sterling said, unfolding the thin newspaper. He noted a small article on the front page entitled "A Walk on the Wild Side with Professor Wilson Bledsoe." In the article, Wilson had described some of his remarkable observations about the behaviors of different species of animals that he had encountered on his long night scouts, everything from the mating behaviors of the red fox to the territorial aggression of the wild snapping turtle. The article ended with Wilson's promise to bring more attention to his recent findings about the blackbird population in the Upper Valley and a mention of the new course he planned on adding to the curriculum next semester.

Sterling carefully tore off the front page, folded the article, and tucked it in his vest pocket. He handed the rest of the paper back to the old woman. "Here's to the recycling efforts."

Sterling decided to walk the short distance to Thayer. It gave him more time to think. Despite the accumulating evidence, he still wasn't buying the random hate crime theory. It just didn't make sense. On a campus so intent on proving its openness and tolerance of difference, a star faculty member and its most accomplished African-American professor is killed by racists.

He crossed the green, now full of students lying out in the sun, reading books, and tossing Frisbees. He walked through a cluster of large brick buildings, then asked a group of noisy students for directions to Thayer Dining Hall. They pointed him to a long narrow building in the shadow of its towering neighbors.

Thayer looked like any other college building, with sales notices and student organization bulletins plastered just inside the lobby. The smell of pizza and french fries floated from the cafeteria as students dumped their knapsacks and coats in a makeshift coatroom before heading in for lunch. Sterling descended the narrow staircase and followed SEO signs posted along the dark hall. The small office bristled with eager students reading job offerings on the small index cards tacked to the wall. Others sat at computer terminals, checking e-mail or searching the job database.

"May I help you?" a student called from behind a cluttered desk. Sterling could hardly see him over the stack of papers.

"I was hoping you might help me find someone," Sterling said. The student got up and came over to him. "Do you keep files on which students get assigned to the various jobs?"

"Absolutely," the student said. He was tall and thin—a great body for long-distance running, Sterling thought. "We need to keep track of the job matches to make sure the right person gets paid. Also, if someone doesn't show up, we need to know where to send a replacement worker."

"Then maybe you can help me figure out who was parking cars at the president's house this past Friday night."

The boy's expression suddenly changed. "I'd like to help you, sir, but I can't just give out information like that to anyone."

"I'm Agent Sterling Bledsoe." Sterling flashed his shield. "Brother of Professor Wilson Bledsoe."

"I'm sorry, sir, I didn't know," he said. "I'll be right back." The lanky student hurried to the desk and rummaged through a drawer full of loose papers. He returned after a few minutes with a narrow look on his face.

"All the parties at the president's house are serviced by our seniors," he explained. "Those jobs are always in high demand, because the president pays a little more for student services and his guests usually leave bigger tips. That night there were nine students—two behind the bar, three serving hors d'oeuvres, two checking coats, and two parking cars."

"I'd like to speak to one of the valets."

The student traced his finger across the page. "Carlos Sandoza and Michele Leone," he said.

"I'm looking for Carlos. How can I get ahold of him?"

"Let me call his room."

Sterling observed the busy office, watching the students scribble down names and phone numbers of potential employers. His undergraduate years were different. Extra money was hard to come by unless you shot a good game of pool or could play a mean hand of poker. Things seemed much easier now.

The student came back in a minute or two. "I talked to one of his roommates. You're in luck. Carlos left the dorm about five minutes ago. He's heading over here to pick up his paycheck."

"How far away is his dorm?"

"Just on the other side of the green. It won't take him long to get here." Students continued to file in and out of the office.

"I'll wait for him," Sterling said, stepping back into the empty hallway and taking a seat on the small bench outside the office. He pulled out his black book and slowly turned the pages. Carlos Sandoza was probably one of the last friendly faces his brother saw.

Carlos Sandoza was a strongly built kid with dark, wavy hair that had been combed back and gelled into a perfect helmet. His Sean John headband, baggy denims, and black Timberland boots were the clothes of his neighborhood—the South Bronx—and he walked with the swagger of someone familiar with the life of the streets. Sterling had a feeling that he hadn't grown up with the same advantages as the other students, and he wasn't going to make any excuses for it. In an Ivy League town full of privileged prep schoolers, Carlos Sandoza wore his hardened Bronx upbringing defiantly.

"You looking for me?" he asked.

"Carlos Sandoza?"

"Yeah, that's me. Who wants to know?" A long toothpick dangled from the corner of his mouth.

"I'm Sterling Bledsoe, brother of Professor Wilson Bledsoe."

Carlos sized up Sterling. "Your brother was the shit," he said. The toothpick seemed like it was about to fall out, but it didn't.

"What part of the Bronx?" Sterling asked.

"You know the city?"

"I can find what I need," Sterling answered.

"Hundred and Thirty-ninth and Beekman. South Bronx."

"Mott Haven," Sterling said. "Number 6 train to Brook Avenue."

Carlos nodded his head in approval. "You know the 'hood. Most people don't."

"Not many reasons to go to that part of the city."

"That's right, not unless you got business."

"I want to ask you some questions about the night you were parking cars."

"I don't know anything," Carlos said. "He came out, got in his car, and left. Someone called me this morning and said he was dead."

"Not just dead," Sterling said. "Murdered. And it was someone with a grudge against him. Messed him up real bad."

"That's fucked up!" Carlos said. The toothpick finally escaped his mouth and landed somewhere on the ground between them. "Who would kill the Professor?"

Sterling grabbed Carlos's arm and walked him away from the employment office and into an unlit hallway. "That's why I'm here," Sterling said. "I think you might be one of the last people he saw."

Carlos put his large hands on his hips and shook his head. Disappointment and shock wrinkled his forehead, making his hard countenance appear even tougher.

"What can you tell me about that night?" Sterling asked.

Carlos paused. "Everybody wanted to work that party because a lot of big names were coming from across the country. It was a nice set. Bigger than usual. I only went inside a couple of times, because I was parking cars. Most cats have too much pride to park cars, but not me. Parking gets you the biggest tips. By the time people leave President Mortimer's parties drinking all that fancy shit, they ass is tore up. When I bring their cars around, they're so drunk they give me whatever's green in their pocket—fives, tens. I even got a twenty that night. I remember Professor Bledsoe was one of the first to leave." Carlos stopped and shook his head. "I can't believe he's dead."

"Try to think back, Carlos. Did Wilson appear to be drunk? Was he acting unusual?"

"Not at all," Carlos replied. "I've served him at parties before, and he never drank more than one glass of wine. I think he liked red. I was surprised to see him leave so early, you know, because it was his party and all."

"He never was much of a partier," Sterling said. "He'd rather be in the classroom or working in the lab."

"When I saw him getting his coat, I ran and got his car so that it would be waiting when he walked over to the driveway. I have much respect for your brother. A lot of us looked up to him. He might've been the quiet type, but he kicked some serious academic ass at this lily-white school."

"Did he say anything that was out of the ordinary?"

Carlos squinted hard. "Not really. I asked him to autograph one of his textbooks for me, but he laughed and wouldn't sign it. He said that autographs were for famous people and that he was just a small scientist daring to dream big. He was keeping it real. I'm telling you, your brother was the shit."

Sterling nodded his head slowly. "Did he say where he was going?"

"Not really. Not that I remember."

"After he left, did you hear anything funny that night?"

Carlos thought hard. "It was a rainy night. Up here in the boonies you hear all sorts of strange sounds. When the rain started coming down harder, I went in the house to get an umbrella. As soon as I walked back outside, I heard a pop. It sounded familiar. Reminded me of gunshots back home."

"You think it was a gun?"

"It definitely sounded like one, but it was off in the distance. I heard the same thing a few minutes later. I thought maybe one of the frat houses was setting off firecrackers or something—sounded like an M80."

"Which direction did the sounds come from?"

"From the back of the house," Carlos answered. "That's another reason why I didn't hear it too well."

"Do you remember about what time it was?"

"I remember exactly. Between seven thirty and a quarter to eight."

"How can you be so sure?"

"Right after I heard them, one of my boys hit me on my cell to see if I was going out that night. The Kappas were having a party at Collis, and everyone was leaving Shabazz House together at eight, getting some chow at the Hop, then heading over to the party. He told me the crew would be leaving in about fifteen minutes."

"Did you go out with them?"

"I couldn't. I didn't finish getting cars till nine thirty, then I had to go over to Baker to study for midterms."

Sterling closed his book. "You've been a big help, Carlos. Just do me a favor and don't talk about this to anyone. We're still trying to figure out what the hell is going on."

Carlos pounded his chest three times—a street sign for secrecy. He turned back before leaving. "What part of the city do you live in?"

"Upper East Side in the Sixties," Sterling said.

"High society." Carlos laughed. "You fuckin' sellout." He plucked a fresh toothpick out of his pocket and slipped it in his mouth. He slid his hands in the pockets of his jeans and strutted down the hall to collect his paycheck. Attitude back in effect.

16

The investigative team decided to conduct Professor Wilson Bledsoe's autopsy at the morgue of the Dartmouth-Hitchcock Medical Center, known to the locals as the Hitch. The hospital had been gracefully assembled on more than two hundred acres of rolling hills and green meadows, a colossal structure of white stone and glass two miles outside of Hanover in the town of Lebanon. The Hitch looked more like a hotel than a hospital. Its modern design and well-appointed decor were a refreshing break from the traditional dull brick and steel beams, and it had garnered numerous awards. Even the *New York Times Magazine* had run a small feature, calling it "the inevitable future of hospital construction."

Most autopsies performed at the Hitch fell under the auspices of the chief pathologist and his lab assistants. In the majority of cases, the doctors already had a good idea of the cause of death but performed the inspection to either comply with insurance regulations or bring closure for a disbelieving family. The autopsy of Professor Wilson Bledsoe, however, was like none other ever performed at the Hitch. There were few murders in the region, and the racial nature of the crime and the profile of the victim mandated that the state's chief medical examiner and his team travel up from Concord to conduct the highly publicized autopsy.

Sterling was waiting outside the examining suite when Dr. Gerald Withcott entered with two young assistants trailing. Dr. Withcott walked fast, with his head slightly down and his hands planted deep inside his lab coat pockets. He was a wisp of a man, standing only five feet two, even when he straightened his curved spine. He looked to weigh all of a hundred and ten pounds after his biggest meal. Before moving on to the CME's office five years ago, he had been the longtime chief pathologist at Dartmouth's medical center.

The owner of the biggest and most successful organic farm in the Upper Valley, Withcott was something of a celebrity in the community. His fruits and vegetables were shipped throughout the region, and twice the White House had specially ordered crates of his plump, sweet melons to serve at state dinners. But while his neighbors most admired him for his prolific farm, his work as a pathologist had brought him national recognition. In the relatively short time since he had left the Hitch and taken his position with the state, he had made a name for himself handling some of the toughest cases. Withcott was a stickler for detail, and efficiency fell second only to accuracy on his list of priorities. Wasting time in his lab was a cardinal sin.

"Good morning, all," Withcott said, not bothering to look up at those gathered. He remained focused on the body bag.

"Dr. Withcott, this is Agent Sterling Bledsoe," Lieutenant Wiley said. Even Wiley spoke in a tone of deference. "He's also the brother of the deceased."

Dr. Withcott lifted his head and nudged the large round glasses up the bridge of his narrow nose. "My condolences, sir, and my apologies," he said. He spoke in a cadence that seemed like it was rehearsed, but this was how he always spoke. "I typically don't like the family of the deceased to be present while I work. But I have little choice since I've been told you're leading the FBI team. I've also heard that you share this line of work."

Sterling nodded slowly.

"Well, as you know, no two autopsies are the same, nor are the techniques. I've been doing this for more than twenty years, but even I make mistakes and miss things." He pointed his thumb at the two assistants. They had taken up positions on either side of the body. "That's why I always bring my help. Stephanie Elam and Patrick Riley. Both of them trained here at Dartmouth."

The two offered friendly nods, but neither smiled.

"I've heard only good things about you, Dr. Withcott," Sterling said. "In fact, I studied some of your cases when I was in basic training. Your case résumé is quite impressive."

"Well, now that you've raised the stakes, let's hope that I don't disappoint," he said. "Feel free to comment as we go along. Collaboration is always a good thing."

Dr. Withcott motioned to his assistants. They unzipped the bag and removed the body. Patrick, tall and gangly, snapped open the autopsy kit while Stephanie, prettier than any lab assistant Sterling had ever seen work a cold body, wrapped the headlight around Withcott's tiny dome. He snapped on two pairs of gloves, then opened his hand for the measuring tape.

Dr. Withcott worked mostly in silence, and Sterling appreciated his well-orchestrated movements—nothing short of art. His assistants anticipated his needs, slapping the instruments into his palm without his looking up. Their sequence of inspection was standard, starting with the external examination, taking measurements of the body's length and using the specially designed table scale that calculated its weight.

Withcott turned on his headlight, and with a magnifying glass bigger than half his narrow face, he began to inspect the skin. His assistants worked on their own, clipping finger- and toenail samples, cutting small patches of hair from Wilson's head, from under his arm, and from his groin. Sterling watched quietly, admiring the fluidity of the autopsy and how well the three worked together, always seeming to know one another's next move.

Withcott remained emotionless, his expression never changing. Until he reached Wilson's chest. He paused for a moment and shook his head. His jaw tightened as he inspected the carved letters and pulled out jagged pieces of bone matted with clotted blood and hair. "Awful," he groaned, carefully examining edges of the skin, relaying the wound measurements to his assistants, who dutifully recorded them. Then he stopped.

"Forceps and another light," he instructed. It was the loudest he had spoken all evening. At the second G, something deep inside the chest cavity had caught his attention. Steadying the forceps in one hand and a hooked probe in the other, he worked his way in until he grasped something. He slowly pulled out a twisted metal object covered in blood. Everyone else in the room moved closer for a look.

"Exactly what I thought," Dr. Withcott said to no one in particular, his magnifying glass covering the object. "The instrument used was some type of saw, maybe a portable jigsaw."

Stephanie produced a small vial of clear liquid and handed it to Dr. Withcott. He dipped the twisted blade until it was free of the clotted blood. He picked it back up and looked at it. "Bingo," he said. "Half of the blade is gone, but they left us the important part. The serial number is stamped across the bottom. AE4390-289."

"Is there a make on it?" Sterling asked.

"Doesn't appear to be," Withcott answered, still examining the blade. "But it still might be possible to make the match." Withcott dropped the evidence in a bag, leaving Stephanie to seal and mark it. He continued with his external inspection, humming a tune that Sterling eventually recognized was from *Carmen*.

Withcott reached the neck and stopped. "More light here," he commanded. "And get me a block." Stephanie adjusted the overhead light while Patrick brought over a wooden block with a semicircle carved into one side. Patrick lifted Wilson's head and carefully slid the block underneath, exposing more of Wilson's neck.

Withcott peeled off one pair of gloves, leaving the inner layer intact. He reached into his coat pocket and pulled out a small camera no bigger than his hand. He snapped five pictures of the neck from different positions, then returned the camera to his pocket.

He looked at Sterling. "What do you think, Agent Bledsoe?"

Sterling moved closer and immediately noticed what had drawn Withcott's attention. Small disk-shaped bruises no more than a couple of centimeters around covered the middle of the neck. The area along the jaws had longer, irregular marks of the same discoloration. Sterling pointed to similar bruises along the sides of the neck and just above the clavicle. At first, the two men had a difficult time discerning the bruises on Professor Bledsoe's dark skin, but the overhead light made them more visible.

"Strangulation," Sterling said. "Classic findings, especially the small circular bruises."

"And it looks like he put up one hell of a fight," Withcott said.

"No doubt," Sterling agreed. "Look at the number of bruises and how they run up and down the neck. Long marks. The attackers must've lost their grip as he tried to fight them off." Pops would have been proud of the way Wilson fought for his life. Sterling was proud of him too.

For the next two hours, Dr. Withcott and his assistants continued their meticulous inspection, extracting, weighing, and examining Wilson's internal organs, stopping to take photographs when something caught their attention. Sterling occasionally stepped out of the room when he found it too much to bear, returning only after he had regained control.

Another hour elapsed before Withcott called out. "There's something here. More light and the camera."

Withcott had Wilson propped on his side, supported by two large sandbags. Withcott lowered his magnifying shield and swabbed a small area of skin just above the left hip. "It's an eagle," he announced. "It's branded into his skin. The impression is clean and deep."

Sterling stepped closer to the body. One of the assistants handed him a magnifying glass. He easily made out the eagle with its ruffled wings spread wide. The head had been drawn in profile with a perfect triangular eye.

"This is no coincidence," Sterling said. "It's a signature. Someone knew we'd find this."

"WLA," Wiley announced from the back. He stepped closer to the body and everyone turned to face him. "White Liberation Army. A group of rednecks down in Claremont. Nothing but a bunch of beer-swigging rabble-rousers."

"Where's Claremont?" Sterling asked.

"About twenty-five minutes or so down Route 120. Used to be a small farming town, but now they have commerce and transportation."

"What does the WLA do?" Sterling asked.

"Not much of anything. But they talk a big game, how they hate everyone who's not white and born in America. I've read some of their flyers. Pure venom. But nobody really pays 'em much mind."

Sterling thought about Wiley's words. It just seemed too damn convenient for Wilson's death to come at the hands of white supremacists. Content to drink and brawl, most of those groups never acted on their words. Why would they suddenly elevate their rhetoric to murder? And why would they decide to hit the highest-profile member of the Dartmouth faculty?

"How many are in this group?" Sterling asked.

"Not many," Wiley said. "I don't have the exact number, but I'd be surprised if there were even a dozen."

"Do you know them?"

"Not really, but the boys down in Claremont do. I'm sure they can help us round 'em up and bring 'em in for questioning."

"If they can still be found."

"Oh, don't worry. If they're still in Claremont, we'll find 'em. Not many places to hide down there."

Withcott continued his methodical autopsy, saying very little, rarely lifting his head from the body. He had settled into what pathologists, like athletes, call "the zone," something familiar to Sterling from his own hours of examining lifeless bodies in cold, sterile rooms, the smell of alcohol and preservatives keeping his mind alert. Dissecting a cadaver requires detailed knowledge of the tissues and organs and their relation to one another, but it also requires immense concentration, especially when one is looking for subtle abnormalities. There's a point when the dissector has reached a state of ultimate detachment—the cadaver no longer has a name or face or history. Even for Sterling, the body on the table, once a vibrant person—once his brother—had become nothing more than an elegant network of failed organ systems holding tiny clues to the cause of death.

"Down here," Patrick called. He held Professor Bledsoe's stiff right ankle above the table. "There's something written here."

The others quickly gathered around and Dr. Withcott flashed his light on the block letters:

CHOGAN

It could have easily been mistaken for a tattoo. They took turns pronouncing the strange word that no one recognized. Then Sterling took a closer look at the letters—neat, but definitely rushed. He had never seen the word before, but he recognized the writing style. He thought hard, searching his memory. It had been in his childhood, somewhere around the house. Then it hit him. Wilson had written the word in his own hand. It was exactly the style he used for all of those letters and postcards he sent home to their mother. Sterling thought about the postcards stacked on the television set. Wilson only wrote that way for her, because her eyesight had gone bad after years of poorly controlled diabetes. Her vision had faltered so much in her later years that even her glasses failed to help her make out most of what she read. So when Wilson wrote home, he'd write it just like this—neat block letters—so perfect you'd think they had been written by machine. These letters weren't as neat, understandable given the situation, but that was his G with the unmistakable tail hanging down. His trademark. Sterling started to share this with the others, but quickly decided against it. He figured Wilson must've written it this way for a reason. Wilson was clever. Maybe he counted on Sterling seeing this and only wanted him to know that it was his hand. Wilson's last message before he died— maybe the key to finding his killers.

Withcott took the final measurements and consulted briefly with his assistants. Then he turned to the others and announced his preliminary conclusion. Professor Wilson Bledsoe died from manual strangulation after a blunt trauma to the side of his skull. The word "nigger" had been carved into his chest by some type of electric saw, but only after he had already expired.

17

Sterling drove out of town with no particular destination in mind. He opened up the engine and challenged the car's engineering, making it prove why it should be called a sports car. He took in the beauty of the land, as the winding roads brought him to the peaks of mountains, his tires spinning only feet from the edges of cliffs. The strong sun and racing wind felt good as he sang along with Bob Marley's "I Shot the Sheriff." For the next hour, he allowed nature's freedom to take him away from all that had troubled him the last couple of days.

He climbed another mountain and pulled over to the side of the road in an area that, according to the sign, offered the best scenic viewing. The Mustang's engine kicked a few extra revs, then sighed to rest. Sterling walked to the front of the car, pleased by the smell of burned rubber and hot oil. He thought about his Porsche back home. It was good for a sports car to get a thorough cleansing every once in a while, especially when it spent most of its time leisurely traveling the streets of a small country town.

Sterling stretched his eyes across the valley. He was only a few hundred miles from New York City, but still in another world. He thought about how invigorating a trip to the great outdoors would be for so many of his fellow New Yorkers who fought the inevitable hassles of the fast life, cramming onto packed subway cars, holding on for dear life as the trains screeched and careened down the dark tracks, or else waiting endlessly in the back of boiling cabs stuck on gridlocked streets.

Wilson's death had been an immeasurable blow, but the surrounding irony gave it the sting. When Wilson had told his family and friends that he wanted to settle down in a small mountain town, they laughed. Had it not been for Dartmouth, Hanover wouldn't have even registered on the map, and it certainly didn't figure in the consciousness of black America. His friends had teased Wilson that he better not get caught out late at night because people in the mountains would mistake him for a predator and shoot him dead. As a going-away gift, they had given him a bright orange vest emblazoned with the words DON'T SHOOT, I'M HUMAN.

Now those playful taunts took on an ominous resonance. Wilson had been murdered in the very place that he'd equated with his freedom. A place where front doors were left unlocked and gas stations didn't ask customers to pay before pumping. Students had their professors' home numbers, calling at any hour they needed help.

A cooing sound disturbed the silence. Sterling looked up as a crow appeared overhead, floating effortlessly on the invisible gusts of wind. It flew lazy circles in the sky, flapping its wings only when necessary, slowly descending out of sight into the valley below. If Wilson had been alive, he would have loved to be sitting right here where Sterling was—alone and observing the open space only wildlife claimed as home. For the first time since his brother's body had been discovered, Sterling Bledsoe didn't just tear up, he cried. Big sloppy tears. He hated himself for hating his brother and hated whoever had taken Wilson away before he had the chance to apologize.

18

Four days after the discovery of Professor Wilson Bledsoe's body, an army of state trooper sedans and police cruisers raced down Route 120 and descended on the small town of Claremont, New Hampshire. Billy "Tex" Norkin, one of two founding leaders of the WLA, was their first stop. They found him in the back of his two-room trailer parked in an abandoned lot behind De Franco's Used Cars. It was almost noon, but he was still sleeping off a hard night of boozing. His body was too long for everything, especially the small mattress wedged into the corner. When they finally roused him to his feet, he had to duck to walk down the narrow corridor. His face was thin with a three-day stubble spiking underneath his chin and across the top of his lip. His long black hair had been tied back into a ponytail with a rubber band. A real hard-ass.

The troopers apprehended Tex quickly and without incident, but when they searched his trailer, they found a stash of weapons and ammunition that could outfit an entire battalion. "I got licenses," Tex snarled as he watched them carry out the guns by the armful. "All my papers is in proper order."

Anyone who knew the history of the Norkin clan knew that the privileged Norkin bloodline made Tex the unlikeliest of insurrectionists. He descended from a long line of prominent Norkins who at one time owned practically the entire village of Claremont. The Norkins made most of their money on livestock and dairy farming, at one point producing almost the entire supply of milk for the state of New Hampshire and most of southern Vermont. Norkin Farms and its vast commercial interests were as close to a monopoly as the state had ever seen.

One Friday some years back, the entire clan of aunts and uncles,

Ian Smith

cousins and in-laws had assembled inside the basement of the enormous farmhouse for their weekly all-night poker game. Old Grandpa Jedsell Norkin still officiated at the family gatherings. While the Norkins built most of their fortune peddling milk, they found their greatest pleasure emptying liquor bottles. Alcohol, cards, money, and loaded shotguns were, for the Norkins, a time-honored family tradition.

After a couple of hours of intense competition and steady drinking, an argument erupted when Priscilla Norkin, Jedsell's oldest daughter, accused her only brother, Weymouth, of cheating in a game of seven-card stud. The argument stretched beyond the game to inheritance and who rightfully deserved the bulk of the Norkin fortune. Anger and greed quickly drew the battle line between the offspring of Priscilla and Weymouth. By the time the last bullet had been fired, Lynn Norkin was the only bloodline left standing. Her son was born a few months later in a small hotel room in Texas, thus his name, William "Tex" Norkin.

Brusco joined the team that drove Tex up to Hanover. They had decided to separate Tex from his partner, Gordie "Buzz" Gatlin. So while Tex would be questioned at the Hanover Police Department, Buzz would be taken to Norwich. It was the old ploy of separating co-conspirators for interrogation.

As they took Tex in, another group of officers broke into the apartment of Sheila McCray, Buzz Gatlin's on-again, off-again girlfriend. Sheila and Buzz bunked in a small two-room apartment perched over the garage of Mr. Haskins's gas station. Buzz and Sheila were inside the tiny bathroom enjoying each other when the door suddenly flew open. "Goddammit! At least let me finish my business," Buzz growled at the officers and the phalanx of drawn guns. "Just settle on back and I'll be right with you."

The troopers wrapped Sheila in a sheet and gave Buzz enough time to throw on jeans and work boots. They were surprised at his calm when he placed his own hands behind his back, as if he had been expecting them. "Don't worry, honey," Buzz said to a crying Sheila. "Let me have a conversation with these boys, and ole Buzz will be back to finish what he started."

Sterling and Wiley watched from one of the cruisers as they packed Buzz into the car. He was a big man with a heavy beard, but he looked entirely peaceful.

"That's one mean bastard," Wiley said to Sterling.

"Why do they call him Buzz?" Sterling asked.

"One night he caught some guy hitting on his girlfriend and nasty words spilled into a brawl. Buzz was in a drunken stupor, and the other fella let him have it. But about two weeks later, they found the poor guy underneath one of the bridges. His body had been cut up into small pieces with a chain saw and stuffed into a crate."

"Why is Buzz still a free man?"

"Never could pin it on him. Everyone knew he did it, but after years of trying to connect him to the murder, they came up with nothing. They've called him Buzz ever since."

"How long ago was that?"

"Must've been about ten years ago. It was right before I was promoted to lieutenant."

"Do you think he killed Wilson?"

Wiley shrugged. "Tough call," he said. "Ever since that murder, Buzz has been kinda quiet. He talks the liberation bullshit, but that's about it. The question that has to be answered is why after all these years of just preaching hate, he would decide to commit murder and get caught so easily. Buzz Gatlin might be a country boy, but he ain't nobody's fool."

The Hanover Police Department had squeezed in a makeshift interrogation room on the other side of the pit. Tex Norkin slumped back in his chair, pulling nonchalant drags on a cigarette, his long legs handcuffed to the table. A nervous-eyed officer stood in the corner of the room, his hand impatiently resting on his revolver. On the other side of the one-way mirror, it seemed like the entire investigation team had crammed inside the tiny observation room. Even Chief Gaylor graced them with an appearance, his first since the investigation started. Sterling eyed him carefully as he stood off in the corner, avoiding contact with the others. Though little light seeped into the room, his polished dome still shone like a fresh wax job. Unlike the other officers, he was dressed in street clothes. Sterling studied his face and wondered if he always wore that expression of apathy or if he was simply uninterested in the proceedings because they were interrupting his daily round of golf.

Brusco entered the interrogation room and took a seat across from Tex. The two men sized up each other before Brusco began.

"Tex, we want to ask you a few questions."

"What's your name?" Tex said. His voice had the scratchy hoarseness of a chain-smoker whose larynx had finally been destroyed.

"Agent Brusco."

"You don't have a first name?"

"Lonnie. Special Agent Lonnie Brusco."

"Good, now we're getting somewhere. Are you arresting me, Lonnie?"

"No," Brusco said. "We've just brought you in for questioning."

"Then why am I strapped down like some goddamn criminal who raped your mother?" Tex pulled so hard on his cigarette, the insides of his hollow cheeks almost touched.

Brusco nodded to the officer, who unfastened the cuffs on Tex's legs. The officer's right hand remained near his holster.

"I have to tell you that this is completely voluntary," Brusco said.

"So that means I can get up and walk out of here anytime I want?"

"Technically."

Tex flashed a smile of rotten teeth. "Let me hear what you have to say first, then I'll make a decision."

"Have you been in Hanover the last couple of weeks?"

"Nope. Not much up here I'm interested in. Well, 'cept those little college sweeties. You ever had 'em real young, Lonnie? They taste a lot better right after mommy and daddy drop 'em off at school. You look about old enough to have a daughter just the perfect age."

Brusco kept his gaze fixed on Tex. He had handled a lot tougher. This lowlife was nothing more than a rookie. "Have any of your friends been up here? Anybody from the WLA?"

"Does she wear those tight little sweaters? Your daughter, that is. You know, the ones you almost have to rip when you take 'em off." Brusco wasn't biting. "Looking at you," Tex said, "I bet she's got a good head on her shoulders. Did you know the smart ones are the best? They almost always got some inferiority complex about their looks 'cause every boy in the school is running the other way after Susie the cheerleader. All you gotta do is whisper a few nice things to 'em, and they just melt in your hands."

"Have any of your boys from the WLA been up here lately?" Brusco persisted.

Tex sucked on the cigarette, looked at the officer standing in the corner, then blew across the table into Brusco's face. "You're gonna have to ask them, Lonnie," he said. "I ain't my brother's keeper."

"Okay, then what have you been doing lately?"

"What I'm always doing—enlightenin' the masses to the importance of white liberation. This is our land, ya know. We have to protect our rights against foreigners and niggers and them damn Jews. Every time you turn around, another one has taken something of ours."

"How many members do you have?"

"Why? You wanna join?" Tex said, snickering. He tapped a long column of ashes on the table.

Sterling mentally recorded everything, including the way Tex held the cigarette with his thumb and index finger. He was a lanky, almost gaunt man, the kind whose pants were always too big and sleeves too short. But what most caught Sterling's attention were his fingernails—remarkably manicured, sparkling under a fresh coat of clear polish. Most women would be jealous. Most men would find it odd.

"Have you ever heard of a man named Professor Wilson Bledsoe?" Brusco asked.

Tex shook his head. "Don't ring a bell."

"Jog your memory again," Brusco said.

"I heard of a Wilson Bledsoe," Tex said. "No nigger need to be walking around with the title Professor."

"How do you know Professor Bledsoe?"

"I might not have some fancy degree and high-paying job, Lonnie. But even us mountain folk read the paper, ya know. Let me guess where you're from. Somewhere from the boring Midwest. That's right, the heartland of America, maybe Missouri or Kansas. But now you're all grown up, living near Boston. I can hear that cheap-sounding accent you adopted. All those 'ahs' where you can't pronounce 'r' anymore. And you don't live in the city, do ya? Still too fast for a prairie boy. Maybe a little ways out, somewhere like Revere or Waltham."

Brusco never broke his stare. "Professor Bledsoe was murdered five days ago."

"And whoever did it should be congratulated." Tex smiled. "Them highfalutin niggers can be the worst, demanding equal rights and memberships in things they ain't even got no interest in. They just wanna join to ruin our purity. Slave mentality."

Sterling stood quietly behind the mirror, watching Tex but also continuing to observe Gaylor. The security chief still hadn't said a word to any of the other men. He remained aloof, almost as if his mind were somewhere else. He looked uncomfortable with his arms folded tightly across his chest.

Brusco reached inside a large manila envelope and slid a photograph across the table. An autopsy picture of the branded eagle. "Does this look familiar?"

Tex smiled. "Ain't the symbol of liberty just a thing of beauty?"

"Found on the dead body of Professor Bledsoe."

Tex looked at the picture again, as if taking a new interest. "Ain't our work then," he said.

"It's your signature. Your eagle has the diamond eye."

Tex pulled up his sleeve and showed Brusco his spindly right bicep. "Oh, it's definitely our eagle," Tex said. "But I can tell you that none of my men killed that nigger. Unfortunately."

"Then how did this get there?"

Tex shook his head. "You're the goddamn po-lice. Not me. You figure it out. As much as I'd like to lay claim to it, we ain't responsible for this. No way, no how."

"Maybe one of your members did it and you don't know about it. You just said you weren't your brother's keeper."

Tex moved in his chair. For the first time he seemed uncomfortable. He dragged twice on his cigarette before answering. "Let's not start twisting my words here. I know none of my men didn't do this 'cause I ain't commissioned it."

"Commissioned?"

"That's right. Do you make moves without your superiors giving the goddamn okay? I know they're all sitting on the other side of that mirror watching you. Watching us. My men can't make a hit like this without me knowing."

"What about Buzz Gatlin? Does he need your approval before making a hit?"

Tex thought hard. "Buzz and I are both generals," he said. "Technically, one general ain't gotta consult the other, but out of respect, we always work as a team. Keeps our activities coordinated."

"Are you sure Buzz is gonna protect you like you're protecting him?"

"Now the old divide-and-conquer routine, huh, Lonnie?" Tex choked a laugh. "Buzz and I go back a long way. We started this movement with just the two of us and built it up to what it is today. I know damn well that Buzz would never sell me out to a bunch of sorry-ass cowards hiding behind uniforms."

Brusco pulled back the photograph and slipped it into the envelope. There was a tap on the door, and the officer leaned his head out to talk to someone. He returned and whispered into Brusco's ear.

"I think I'll be taking advantage of that voluntary clause and get the hell outta here," Tex said. "It's obvious you boys ain't got nothing but a dead nigger."

"I'm afraid that option to leave is no longer valid," Brusco said. Now he was the one smiling. "Seems like the computer found some of your outstanding summonses. You stood up Madame Justice a couple of times and now she wants an explanation."

"Bullshit!" Tex yelled, flicking the cigarette to the ground and jumping to his feet. His first display of physical aggression. The door flew open and a gang of police officers swarmed Tex; every one of them was needed to restrain his flailing limbs.

Brusco turned back before leaving. "And as for your partner, Buzz Gatlin. In my experience, the prospect of serving life in the joint can make a man think real hard about what it means to be loyal."

19

Buzz Gatlin sat solemnly at the small rectangular table, cracking his knuckles loud enough to be heard in the observation room on the other side of the one-way mirror. He was an enormous man, mostly fat, but his shoulders were broad and strong. His stump of a neck gingerly balanced his massive cranium. A woolly beard blanketed the lower half of his face, reducing his lips to nothing more than slits of dried flesh. His insulated plaid lumberjack shirt barely stretched across his chest and belly. What could be seen of his brass belt buckle looked like the shape of Texas. He was a big man no doubt, but he was surprisingly kempt. His rectangular wire-rimmed glasses softened his countenance, and Sterling could easily see him teaching a high-school chemistry class.

Unlike Tex, who had asked for a cigarette the minute he sat down, Buzz requested three things: that day's edition of the *New York Times* crossword puzzle, a pen (because, according to him, he rarely if ever made mistakes), and a large black coffee with four packets of sugar. His only complaint was that the cuffs linking his legs to the chair were digging into his skin, something that couldn't be fixed since they had already used the biggest pair in the station.

The locals had already convicted the two men of murder in their minds, but Sterling remained skeptical, even doubtful. Maybe it was because most of his cases had been complicated and the investigations long, but he had never been involved in a murder case with so few clues and suddenly the suspects got picked up so easily. The branded eagle was the only real evidence linking them to Wilson's murder, but even that was too convenient. They might as well have just walked themselves into the station and confessed.

The observation room wasn't as packed as it had been in Hanover. There were either fewer officers attending the spectacle or the room was a little larger—Sterling couldn't tell which. But what remained the same was Chief Gaylor standing back from the rest, his arms folded across his chest, a look of disinterest turning down the corners of his mouth. He had no official role in the investigation, but Sterling had already surmised that he was the eyes and ears of the college. Mortimer might have been keeping a comfortable distance from the central investigation, but Sterling was certain he was being apprised of the developments. Solving the murder quickly meant the school could leave the whole horrible mess behind and get on with the business of education.

Buzz sat quietly, sipping his coffee and working the crossword puzzle. He grunted occasionally when a question stumped him. Then he smiled when he finally figured out the answer.

"Don't be fooled," Wiley whispered to Sterling. "Looks like the perfect gentleman, but that sonuvabitch would carve your heart out with a dull pocket knife and not think twice about it."

"What does he do?"

"According to the Claremont boys, he works part-time fixing televisions and other electronics. Supposed to be damn good at it, too. The rest of the time he's organizing the WLA, holding meetings and stuff. Informationals, they call 'em. He's the real brains behind the operation. Tex is more a front man."

"Any relatives?"

"Not sure. They think a cousin or two somewhere out West, but they don't keep in touch much. At least according to the phone records. He was an only child and his parents died in a boating accident when he was a teenager. He spent some time with an aunt, but he nearly ate her out of house and home. A neighbor took him in till he was old enough to go out on his own."

"Have they found the neighbor?"

"Moved somewhere up in northern Vermont. They're trying to track her down as we speak."

"Anything in the way of education? Not many people can do the *Times* puzzle with a pen."

"Not much, believe it or not. He taught himself most of what he knows.

They say he's been reading books since he was little. Memorized the entire Constitution in grade school. He'd stand in front of the supermarket and recite it for anyone willing to part with some change. The man's got a decent head on his shoulders."

"Not your run-of-the-mill murderer."

"No, but he's more than capable. Just as sure as I'm standing here, he killed that man down in Claremont and chopped him up. He's got a mean streak running through him that don't wanna end."

Brusco entered the room, and Buzz looked up from his paper quizzically, then nodded in greeting.

"I'm Special Agent Lonnie Brusco," Brusco said as he took his seat. He dispensed with the bit about this being a voluntary appearance. Gatlin's background check already showed that he had missed two court dates for a speeding ticket on I-91 earlier in the year. The outstanding warrants were enough to keep him in for a few days, or as long as they could bungle the paperwork.

"How can I help you, Mr. Brusco?" Buzz said. He creased the newspaper and straightened in his chair.

"We've had some serious trouble up here, and I was hoping you could answer a few questions for us." Buzz said nothing. "Let's start by talking about your organization, the WLA. What exactly do you do?"

"Are you forgetting something, Mr. Brusco?"

Brusco shrugged his shoulders.

"Don't you want to ask me if I want legal representation before answering your questions?"

"You haven't been charged with anything. Yet. I'm just trying to get your help with some questions."

Buzz thought for a moment, flipping the pen in his hands. "Our organization is one of the purest patriotic groups in the country. We are constitutionalists, the protectors of the rights granted to us by our Founding Fathers."

"Would that include the right to commit murder?"

"Consult the Second Amendment, Mr. Brusco. 'A well-regulated militia being necessary to the security of a free State, the right of the people to keep and bear arms shall not be infringed.' "

"But in your opinion, does that mean you have the right to commit murder?"

"Depends on whether the government is protecting our rights."

"And which rights might those be?"

"The inalienable rights of life, liberty, and the pursuit of happiness." Buzz paused for a pull of his coffee. "It's right in the second paragraph of the Declaration of Independence. 'That to secure these rights, Governments are instituted among Men, deriving their just powers from the consent of the governed,—That whenever any Form of Government becomes destructive of these ends, it is the Right of the People to alter or to abolish it, and to institute new Government, laying its foundation on such principles and organizing its powers in such form, as to them shall seem most likely to effect their Safety and Happiness.' We have a right to be safe and happy."

Brusco nodded his head slowly. Buzz Gatlin would be much tougher to crack than Tex Norkin. He was not a dumb man.

"Have you or any of your men had any activities up here?"

"This is a dead zone," Buzz said.

"What does that mean?"

"There aren't enough potential comrades to support the movement up here. We tried a few years back, but most of these kids are brainwashed with far-out liberal ideas. College towns aren't a great breeding ground for our mandate."

"So that means you haven't been here in the last couple of weeks?"

"I haven't been here since Nixon swung through back in seventy-one. Talk about the fall of a great man. The party hasn't been right ever since."

"How many members do you have in the WLA?"

"Fourteen."

"Care to share their names?"

"We're not a secret organization, Mr. Brusco. We're proud of what we stand for. Do you want to write them down or shall I?"

Brusco motioned to the officer, who produced a small pad and placed it on the table. Buzz calmly wrote down the names and slid the pad to Brusco. Sterling didn't have a clear view of the pad, but Buzz's writing seemed to be neat and tight.

"What kinds of activities is your army involved in?" Brusco asked.

"Mostly community service," Buzz said. "We do a lot with the veterans. After putting their lives on the line for this great country, they got a raw deal in the end. We try to help them out as much as we can. Everything from getting health benefits to work around the house if things need fixing."

"Noble," Brusco sighed.

"That's the idea behind the group. We do a lot of good, but most people just don't understand it."

"You know of a Professor Wilson Bledsoe?"

"Who doesn't? His name has been all over the radio and papers. Even our little *Claremont Bee* has run stories on him. Who would kill a man doing such good?"

"Cut the shit, Buzz. Your men killed Bledsoe and you couldn't give a damn."

Buzz took more coffee. "Killing isn't something I believe in. It's usually best to work things out peacefully, like civil-minded people."

Back in the observation room, Wiley rolled his eyes at Sterling.

Brusco opened the envelope and slid the photograph across the table. "Is this your idea of peaceful?"

Buzz surveyed the photo of Bledsoe's disfigured body. He swallowed hard, but his expression never changed. Then Brusco handed him a second photo. Buzz turned it several times until he got the correct orientation. He nodded slowly. "That's our eagle," he said. "But we didn't put it there."

"Who did?"

"No idea. Maybe someone trying to implicate us."

"Possibly commissioned by Tex Norkin?"

"Not at all. I would've known beforehand."

"Not according to Tex. He said that as a general he could commission a hit without your approval." Buzz flipped the pen in his hands. He didn't appear as calm as he had just minutes ago. "He also said that you could do the same," Brusco said.

"He told you all that, huh?"

"Just an hour ago." The two men stared at each other. "Anything you'd like to say about that?" Brusco asked.

"Sure. Now I'd like to speak to my attorney."

There was a collective sigh in the observation room. Wiley nudged Sterling. A few of the men slapped hands.

"They didn't do it," Wiley whispered to Sterling. "I can't put my finger on it, but something's not right about this."

Gaylor walked toward the observation room door and opened his mouth for the first time. "Don't make it harder than it has to be, Agent Bledsoe," he said. "These two lowlifes murdered your brother." Then Gaylor unfolded his twill blazer and slipped it on. Time now for that round of golf.

20

After Kay had gone to bed that night, Sterling locked himself in Wilson's study and booted the computer. He waited patiently, then logged on to the Internet and called up Google. He typed in "chogan" and within seconds the search engine had produced more than three thousand hits. He scrolled through the first page and found an esoteric website index created by Chad Hogan. The garbled text spelled out a list of instructions that created a header and footer for Internet HTML pages. By the looks of Hogan's e-mail address, he was part of the astronomy department at the University of California, Irvine. Sterling jotted down the address, which began with chogan—an obvious combination of his first and last names.

The next entry was more interesting. It was devoted to the game of polo, also known as chogan. The Circle of Ancient Iranian Studies, part of the School of Oriental and African Studies at the University of London, provided a detailed history, suggesting that the Chinese learned the game from Iranian nobility who sought refuge in Chinese courts after the invasion of the Iranian Empire by the Arabs. The history explored another possibility—that Indians were also taught by the Iranians. According to the website, polo claimed an exalted place in Chinese culture, especially under the rule of Ming Huang, the Radiant Emperor, an enthusiastic patron of equestrian activities. He was so fond of the sport that he mandated that chogan sticks appear on the Chinese royal coat of arms. But the game's acceptance quickly deteriorated under Emperor T'ai Tsu, who ordered all the other players beheaded after one of his favorite players was killed in a match.

Sterling finished reading the history, but still couldn't find anything that might be in any way connected to Wilson or his research. He printed out the text and continued searching the other entries.

Next he found the Chogan Ugama, part of the Royal Regalia of the Sultan of Brunei. The gallery photo showed an ancient silver religious mace. Nice but seemingly irrelevant. The next website was that of the Chogan Bed and Breakfast in Coventry, England. Wilson and Kay had visited the United Kingdom several times over the last few years, both for pleasure and as part of Wilson's lecture schedule. Maybe this was where they had stayed on one of their trips. Was Wilson directing him there? Sterling wrote down the address and phone number. He would ask Kay about it or call the bed-and-breakfast himself.

Then he found it. Sitting in the middle of the third page of results. Damian Cherry's myth simply titled "The Story of Two Blackbirds." Sterling clicked on the entry, and the brightness of the page lit up the room. Images of white cumulus clouds floating in a pale blue sky filled the background. The text was simple.

THE STORY OF TWO BLACKBIRDS
BY DAMIAN CHERRY

Long ago there was a tribe called the Ojibwa. They were a large tribe of about 6,000 known for being great warriors and creative artists. They lived between the Nemadji River and Lake Superior in Minnesota, before being chased into eastern Wisconsin by the French explorers and traders. There was a little boy named Chogan who loved everyone and everything and was loved by all in return. Chogan had been given his name by the Ojibwa chieftain, because his jet-black hair and free spirit were similar to the friendly blackbird who traveled openly across the empty wilderness. Chogan had a warmth to his presence that could heat cold rooms on a winter day and make those who were sad feel good again. But what he was most known for was his singing. As he walked among the fields of crops or the banks of the river, he sang songs that he heard the animals sing. His voice was so beautiful that people would come from miles around to hear the singing Chogan. Even the French traders would ask for him, to hear his lovely voice.

One summer day, Chogan was playing along the river, singing his songs and collecting rocks. Ganzera, the goddess of the mountain birds, heard his courageous voice and flew down in the form of a bald eagle to listen closely to the boy. Ganzera was known for her magical powers. She approached Chogan and told him that his love for the wild and his free spirit were qualities that others should always admire. As a reward for his gentle heart and beautiful voice, she would grant him any wish he desired. Chogan thought long and hard and even considered making himself the chief of the tribe or a rich French trader. Then he saw a pair of blackbirds flying together across the water, singing along as they played together, letting the world know how happy they felt. Chogan decided he would forever become not just one bird but two birds, to represent those he now watched flying loops in the sky. The first bird would be all black, except for the red feathers on his shoulders to represent the fire of passion to love all that is good. The second bird would be smaller and have black and white and brown feathers to represent the truth that the white traders and the different Indians could live together as one if they all agreed to be happy and kind.

Ganzera granted Chogan his wish and in seconds he had been split into the two birds. At first he was sad, because he would miss his family and friends. No longer could he collect the rocks on the river or swim deep in its cold water. But Ganzera told him not to be sad. Now he could spread his wings and fly all over the world, spreading warmth and joy not only to his tribe but to the Sioux and Cheyenne to the east and the Menominee and Potawatomi to the west. From then on, Chogan soared across the land, following his people on their summer hunts across the great plains before going north to eat sunflowers and insects on the open farms. Today, the red-winged blackbird is the only blackbird who can sing a song that still makes others stop and listen.

What surprised Sterling even more than the content of the story was the author. A fifth grader from Pembroke Elementary School, whose location wasn't disclosed on the website. According to a brief caption, the story had been created as part of a school project. The students had been assigned to research the various inhabitants of the Northeast Woodlands, then create a myth to share with their classmates during story time. A small photo showed the students gathered around a makeshift campfire in the middle of their classroom, eating, playing games, and exchanging tall tales. Damian Cherry had told the story of Chogan.

Sterling read the story a second time, now convinced that Wilson had sent him a message about blackbirds. Hadn't Mrs. Potter's Heidi called them his passion? But what was Wilson trying to say?

21

Kay Bledsoe requested that the memorial service be simple. Reverend Roderick, the university's portly chaplain, happily obliged with modest arrangements at the school's stately Rollins Chapel. The program would be short: a few comments from Wilson's closest friends and two choir selections. All of the television trucks and intrusive reporters only made Kay more steadfast in her decision to honor her husband's life quietly, exactly as he had lived it.

The waiting, hoping, and praying—and finally the discovery—had been a long nightmare, and it would continue until they found out who killed Wilson and why. The answers wouldn't bring him back, but they would at least give her some sense of closure. It had happened so fast. One night, preparing her husband's favorite meal; the next night, a widow at forty-eight. It helped somewhat to have Sterling in the house and looking after things, but it was still awkward mourning with a brother-in-law who was little more than a stranger.

At first, she had been relieved by all of the familiar faces gathered in the chapel, but then came the painful realization that once they went their separate ways, she'd be spending another night alone, relying on those little blue pills to help her sleep.

President Mortimer delivered his address first, giving a moving history of Wilson's work inside and outside the classroom. He recounted the first time they had met at a faculty dinner and how Wilson had more questions about the family of deer that grazed on the president's property than about Mortimer's academic plans for the college. Mortimer closed with a poem by Wendell Berry:

When despair for the world grows in me
and I wake in the night at the least sound
 in fear of what my life and my children's lives may be,
 I go and lie down where the wood drake
 rests in his beauty on the water, and the great heron feeds.
 I come into the peace of wild things
 who do not tax their lives with forethought
 or grief. I come into the presence of still water.
 And I feel above me the day-blind stars
 waiting with their light. For a time
 I rest in the grace of the world, and am free.

President Mortimer's deep voice reverberated in the chapel and by the time he had recited the last line, his words had already been smothered by a chorus of plaintive sobs.

A young dark-skinned woman, wearing a simple blue dress without much in the way of adornment, stepped to the podium and bent the microphone down. The airy chapel made her soft voice sound angelic. "My name is Donica Holmes, and I'm a senior," she announced. "I'd like to begin my comments with something Emily Dickinson once wrote: 'Unable are the Loved to die / For Love is Immortality, / Nay, it is Deity.' Professor Wilson Bledsoe saved my life," she said. "He taught me much more than science and the principles of animal behavior. He showed me what it meant to be a good and loving citizen. But more important, he taught me to always dream big. While his scholarship was acclaimed and his lectures entertaining, I will best remember him as someone who loved life and all of the opportunities that it had to offer. There were many times when I was ready to give up and leave Dartmouth, but his gentle encouragement and willingness to lend an ear kept me here and on the path to graduation. Mrs. Bledsoe, thank you for allowing us to share your amazing husband." She looked up to the ceiling, then closed her eyes. "God, thank you for sending us one of your angels."

Nel Potter spoke last. Heidi helped her stand and walk to the podium. The old woman looked even more ancient under the bright lights, her thin gray hair pulled back from her chalk-white face. She didn't have any notes, but instead spoke slowly and freely into the microphone.

"Even at my advanced age, I don't understand death," she said, looking around at the packed room. "One day I will come to know it—maybe even sooner than I think. What I do understand, however, is the goodness of man and how undeniable it can be even in the face of evil." Mrs. Potter's voice cracked and she paused briefly to collect herself. "I have lived in the Upper Valley for all of my adult life. I can say with certainty and unfaltering conviction that Professor Wilson Bledsoe was a giant amongst men and a gentle spirit to all forms of life he encountered. When you've been around as long as I have, you come to appreciate the smaller things in life that to others might seem unimportant. Wilson Bledsoe and I shared those appreciations. He was an extraordinary scientist and an even greater man."

Mourners in the packed chapel rose to their feet and filled the cavernous room with applause.

The organist slowly woke up the organ and the choir stood to sing Wilson's favorite hymn, *One Day at a Time, Sweet Jesus*. The poignant lyrics brought more sobs, and as Sterling looked around he noticed Carlos Sandoza, sitting near the back, dabbing his eyes with the back of his hand. After the choir finished their last verse, President Mortimer once again stood behind the microphone and welcomed everyone to the mansion for light refreshments and fellowship. The choir belted out another hymn, and as the doors to the chapel opened, white-gloved ushers released five doves into the air, each representing a decade of Wilson's abbreviated life.

Sterling stood at the back of the church next to Kay, accepting handshakes and condolences, making small talk. He watched Kay and admired her strength as she smiled through her exhaustion and grief.

An old man with unruly white hair stood at the end of the recession line. Sterling watched as he hobbled on a black cane, tightly gripping the brass elephant-head handle. His badly wrinkled dark suit begged for an earnest wash and pressing. His black rectangular eyeglasses sat slightly askew on the bridge of his bulbous nose.

"My condolences, Mr. Bledsoe," he said, gripping Sterling's hand with what little energy his emaciated body could muster.

"Thank you for coming this afternoon," Sterling said.

"I'm Professor Mandryka," the old man said. He shifted his weight on the cane. "I've heard a lot about you, Special Agent."

Sterling was surprised the old man knew his occupation. "How did you know?"

"Your brother was proud of you. He told me everything about your accomplishments. He derived as much pleasure from your career success as he did from his own."

This brought a reluctant smile to Sterling's face. He never imagined Wilson taking an interest in his career, let alone talking to others about it.

The old man continued. "Your brother and I go back a long way. I was one of his professors when he was doing graduate work at the University of Chicago. He was the best damn student I ever had, and let me tell you, I've had many in my day."

"What a coincidence that the two of you ended up teaching here at Dartmouth," Sterling said.

"Oh, it wasn't a coincidence at all." The old man hacked a dry cough. "Before Willie arrived, there was only one other faculty member here of any true scholarship who was interested in the study of animal behavior. I called Willie and alerted him that this faculty member was going to retire within the next couple of years and the path would be wide open for him to come here and make a name for himself."

"So he followed your advice."

"And became one of the giants in his field."

The old man paused and looked up at the chapel's stained-glass windows. Sterling could tell that he had something to say, but didn't want to rush him.

"Willie was more than a scientist and teacher," the old man finally said. "He was a humanitarian with an insatiable appetite for giving to others."

"That's what I've learned," Sterling said. He now found himself fighting back tears.

The old man looked around and waited for others to pass before stepping closer. He stretched his neck and whispered into Sterling's ear. "I'd like you to come by my laboratory tomorrow morning at seven, before my research assistants arrive. There's something I want to show you." The old man's voice had taken on an ominous tone.

"Where's your lab?"

"Third floor of the Gilman Life Sciences Laboratory. Over on College Street. It's just in front of the medical school. You can't miss it."

"What's your room number?"

"There is none. The entire third floor is mine. Oh, and Sterling, make sure you come alone."

Sterling started a new page in his book and scribbled down the address. "What do you want to show me, Professor?"

Mandryka rested his arthritic hand on Sterling's shoulder and looked deep into his eyes. "Blackbirds."

A crowd had once again filled the Mortimer house, but this was far from the kind of cheerful gathering that had become customary at the rambling mansion. The music had been silenced and the alcohol had been replaced with coffee, tea, and soda. Kay didn't want to attend, as the ceremony at Rollins Chapel had already exhausted her, but she remained strong, graciously accepting countless condolences and words of encouragement.

Sterling stood by her side most of the afternoon, listening to various anecdotes that attested either to Wilson's goodwill or to his scientific brilliance. But after an hour the stories and the faces of those telling them blurred into each other, and Sterling decided to duck outside for a breath of fresh air. He disappeared through a side door and made his way to the backyard.

The sun had begun its descent toward the horizon, but it still showered wide beams of warmth. Sterling walked across the lawn and stopped at a small, meticulously maintained garden just on the edge of the property. A few flower buds poked through the recently turned topsoil. As the warm wind jostled the tree branches, Sterling thought about New York. He longed to be back in the concrete jungle, picking up his orange juice and bagel at the corner deli and taking his students through the art of dissection and human physiology. He had reached down to pick up an odd-shaped leaf when he heard his name. He turned and recognized Ahote, the petite Native American who worked for the Mortimers.

"Good afternoon, Mr. Bledsoe," she said as she approached. The sun made her black hair look like hot oil. Her skin, too, was on fire, an exciting mix of pink and brown with daring splashes of red. Seeing her in the sunlight only enhanced the sense Sterling had had of her beauty.

"Ahote," he said, flashing his wide smile. "How are you?"

"Fine, thank you," she said. "I wanted to share my sorrow with you."

"That's very kind. Everyone has been so nice to me these last few days."

Ahote looked back in the direction of the house. When she turned, Sterling noticed a small purple flower resting in her hair. He wondered how it stayed there without anything holding it.

She stepped so close that they almost touched. The sun made her deep blue eyes even more intense. It was difficult not getting lost in them.

"Everyone is not so nice," Ahote said.

Her terse words startled Sterling.

"What do you mean?" he asked.

"My people have lived in these mountains for a long time," Ahote said. She spoke in a kind of singsong. "We know the land and the way that nature prefers things to be. Everything is not as it should be or as it appears."

"Does this have anything to do with my brother's death?"

Ahote looked down for a moment, then back into Sterling's eyes. "Askuwheteau was a man of love and peace. His death is not only your loss but a loss to my people and the wonderful animals that roam these great mountains."

"Why did you call him that?" Sterling asked.

"In the Algonquin tongue, Askuwheteau means 'Always Keeping Watch.' "

"What did he watch?"

"Everything. He had the eye of a great warrior and the mind of a wise man."

"Ahote, how did you come to know my brother?"

"All of my people knew him. His heart was with us. He respected nature's freedom as we do. He understood our way of life."

Sterling wondered if Wilson had also found her attractiveness irresistible. "Did you spend time with him alone?"

"He spent time with all of us, Mr. Bledsoe. Like many of us, he believed that the world was best served by allowing all living things to enjoy nature's beauty."

Sterling looked deeper into Ahote's eyes. He saw jagged specks of green floating in the deep blue waves. Her strength was well hidden, but it was there, buried within her beauty. He reached out and touched her shoulder. "Ahote, I'm going to ask you a question, and I need you to be completely honest with me."

"I am an honest being, by nature," Ahote said. "Ask your question."

Sterling lowered his head and spoke firmly. "Do you know who killed my brother?"

Ahote never flinched. She'd expected the question and responded immediately. "I do not," she said. "But my people and I share your determination to catch the killers and punish them." Ahote reached underneath her shawl and produced a folded sheet of paper. She handed it to Sterling. "This is the name of the person you should speak with."

Sterling unfolded the paper. The word "Kanti" had been written in small black letters. "Who is this?" Sterling asked.

"Kanti knows all," Ahote said. "He is our great leader."

"How can I find him?"

"Don't worry, Mr. Bledsoe. You don't find Kanti. He finds you."

"Agent Bledsoe," a man's voice echoed from across the lawn. Sterling turned and saw Lieutenant Wiley waving his hands. He folded the paper and placed it inside his black book. By the time he turned to thank Ahote, she was already floating across the lawn in the other direction.

Sterling walked over to Wiley. "What's going on, Lieutenant?"

"I just got a call from the station," he said. He was short of breath, as if he had been running. "They got those pictures back."

"Which pictures?"

"The stills you wanted from the video over at Burke. Someone just delivered them fifteen minutes ago."

"What's on them?"

"No one wanted to open them till we got back to the pit."

"Let's not keep them waiting."

"One more thing, Agent. We definitely have the wrong men."

"What makes you so sure?"

"I talked to Jack Spriggins, the sheriff down in Claremont. An old friend. He did some digging around. Nothing."

"What if he's wrong?"

"Jack Spriggins is a bit of a loose cannon, but when it comes to these matters, he's never wrong. He rules that town with an iron fist. He said Tex and Buzz have air-tight alibis. The night of your brother's murder, Tex was down at the Chicken Shack, eating wings and throwing back Buds. One of my nephews tends bar there and said Tex came in around six and his girl carried him out sometime after midnight."

"And Buzz?"

"Locked tight. He and Sheila ate dinner that night at the Mountain Roadhouse. Had dinner from seven to eight thirty, then went over to the Elks lodge for bingo. They didn't get out till after the jackpot round, a little after one."

Sterling nodded. He wasn't surprised. "If they didn't do it, someone in their crew might've been involved or could know something."

"Negative. He's checked them all out."

"But we should do some work on our own to make sure."

"I'm skeptical, but I agree. That's why our men are out there looking for them. And for now we're keeping Tex and Buzz in custody. Spriggins says he hasn't gotten this much sleep in years."

"We better get to the pit. Those pictures are all we have going for us right now."

"I'll work the phones on the way over."

22

The large black envelope sat by itself in the middle of the conference table like a bomb waiting to detonate. An index card with Sterling's name on it had been stapled and taped to the outside flap. The room was uncharacteristically busy—some officers shouted into phones while others dusted off the last of a large pepperoni pizza. With the autopsy over, the phone records collected, and the time line almost completely filled in, they were confident that Professor Wilson Bledsoe died between his last phone call, at a quarter after seven, and eleven o'clock that evening. The scratch marks on his stomach were evidence that he had been dragged for several feet, then deposited underneath the bush where he had been found.

Almost everyone, except for Sterling and Wiley, believed that they had caught the real killers. They weren't buying the alibis. At first brash and cocky, Tex Norkin had become less cooperative and more combative. A true sign of his guilt, the local officers claimed. Only a guilty person with something to hide would have shifted attitude like that. Teams of investigators had searched his trailer several times but still hadn't found anything that directly linked him to Wilson's murder. Beyond not having any hard evidence, time had also become a concern. It would be impossible to keep him locked up while they waited out his confession. He had been scheduled for his court appearance in a couple of days, and unless they produced credible evidence linking him to the murder, the judge would have no choice but to levy a fine for the outstanding warrants and release him. Tex remained stubborn. Despite their intimidation, he still refused counsel, claiming innocent people didn't need to bother with small men showing off their fancy vocabulary. But they continued their interrogation and even hinted at offering a deal if he gave up the goods on Buzz Gatlin. His eyes widened at the offer and they were already collecting bets that he'd soon be asking for representation.

Buzz Gatlin. Ice. His only communication—a daily request for the *New York Times* crossword puzzle, a pen, and a large black coffee with four packets of sugar. Elmer Gallows, a local litigator with a storefront office in Claremont, had taken the case. Gallows wasn't a member of the WLA nor did he believe in their cause. But he was one of those liberal lawyers who firmly believed that protecting freedom of speech was important above all else, even if it meant allowing a group of hateful racists to spew their vitriol.

Buzz and Gallows had known each other since high school. Buzz was smart and stubborn even back then, but Gallows had always thought he was a decent kid who'd had some tough breaks. The idealist in Gallows hoped that by taking the case, he'd have a chance to talk some sense into his old classmate. So for the time being, Gallows had advised Buzz not to talk. He needed to get a better handle on what the other general, Tex, might be saying and if he was trying to work out a deal. With both men potentially facing a first-degree murder rap, Tex could be as much an enemy as he could be a friend.

Looking down at the dull black envelope, Sterling knew their real suspect was only a video image away. The others watched intently as he slit open the flap and pulled out three glossy black-and-white photographs with a handwritten note scribbled on FBI stationery.

> Sterle,
>
> I know this is a tough time for you and your family. I want you to know that all of us down here have been sick over this and wish you all the best. This is the first crop of photographs, but as usual Artie is working around the clock for better enhancement. As the images become clearer, we'll send them to you via e-mail. We miss you down here, where you really belong. But if anyone can crack this case, you can. We're rooting for you.
>
> Warmest,
> Harry
>
> P.S. We got a new batch of recruits. The women in the group are anxious to meet the legendary Agent Bledsoe. I'm doing my best to keep your reputation intact.

Sterling smiled to himself, slid the note into his pocket, then took a look at the first photograph—a wide shot of the reflection in the door. The resolution still needed work, but they had cleaned up a lot of the tape's graininess. Sterling nodded when he flipped to the second photograph. The face, now clearer, obviously belonging to a man—there was the beginning of stubble sprouting under his chin.

"This is our man," Sterling said as the others gathered closer. "This is our man."

Sterling walked over to the large time line on the wall and pointed to the section marked Burke. "Look at the times here. This man first appears at 4:25. Carlton comes in at 5:02." Sterling moved his finger along the line. "The man leaves at 5:07. He stayed for a total of forty-two minutes, then decided to call it quits." Sterling turned and faced the rest of the group. "It's possible that someone who legitimately worked there stopped by the lab at 4:25 in the morning, but it's pretty damn unlikely and suspiciously coincidental that they show up after Wilson was murdered."

Sterling looked at the last photograph, the best of the three. "Can someone get me a magnifying glass and a few sheets of colored paper?" He placed the photograph on the table and turned it in several directions. Someone handed him three sheets of blue paper, and he used them to cover the entire photograph except for a small area of the face. He picked up the magnifying glass and examined that portion of the image. "If I'm not mistaken, there's some type of mark on this man's face. Maybe even the beginning of a scar." He stood up and passed the magnifying glass to Wiley.

Lieutenant Wiley, already close to the ground, didn't need to do much bending to examine the picture. "I don't see it, Agent," he said, his eyes still glued to the photograph. "It's hard to tell if that's just artifact from the video or something real."

Wiley passed the magnifying glass to the others, and they took turns poring over the small mark. None of them, including Brusco, was willing to confirm what Sterling had seen.

"There's something there," Sterling said, sensing the overwhelming doubt in the room. "I'm telling you, this is the real suspect. This photo might not be enough right now, but believe me—it will lead us to our answers."

Sterling next went to the board covered with gruesome photos of the crime scene. Wiley joined him. The most disturbing shot had been taken right after they had flipped over the body. Wilson had such a look of terror on his face, as if he were trying to say something before the air had been choked out of him. Sterling took the three photographs from the FBI lab and tacked them up next to the crime scene shots. Something was bothering him. There were clues hidden somewhere, connections that he hadn't been able to figure out.

Detective Hanlon approached Sterling and Wiley and placed a hand on each of their shoulders. "Let it go, gentlemen," he said. "We've already got the killers. Now it's just a matter of connecting the evidence."

"And that's exactly the problem," Wiley said. "The evidence we have doesn't point to them at all." Wiley looked at Sterling and then the others. The two of them were alone on this. He could read the doubt in their eyes. To hell with them. Even if he hadn't had confirmation from Spriggins, he knew the WLA hadn't done this. This was their man in these pictures. He hadn't gone to Burke in the wee hours of a Saturday morning to diddle around with the test tubes of an experiment or mop the floors.

Sterling looked up at the board as if reading Wiley's mind. "This man went there looking for something," he said. "The question is whether he got it."

23

Only late afternoon, but the day had been long and hard. Sterling decided to head back to the house to eat and take a quick nap. A million thoughts jammed his head at once. Most pressing, Professor Mandryka wanted to meet him the next morning to show him blackbirds—the very things Wilson seemed to refer to in code on his ankle before he died. Wilson had been clever to the end, leaving the message for Sterling underneath his sock so that his murderers wouldn't find it, and writing in a way that only Sterling would recognize. Genius, even near death. A pang of jealousy shot through Sterling.

Then the strange encounter with Ahote and her ominous words. Who was this mysterious Kanti that she mentioned, and how could he help them find the real killers? Tex and Buzz were nothing more than pathetic racists and well-chosen decoys. Someone wanted them to take the fall. The real suspect was in that photograph. Sterling was certain. As soon as Harry worked his magic with the tape, they would have their answers.

As Sterling turned from the center of town and headed toward the bridge, his cell phone rang. Chief Gaylor's voice surprised him.

"The president and I were wondering if you had time to come by for a chat," Gaylor said. It was less a question and more a demand. And it was in that damn haughty voice.

"Has something happened?"

"No, it's just been a while since the three of us have caught up on the case together. President Mortimer would like to know how the investigation is going."

Sterling found the request odd. Gaylor had every right to attend their daily briefing sessions in the pit, yet he had never come by once since the official murder investigation started almost a week ago. He made one grand appearance—at the interrogations—and even then he refused to speak to the other men, except to proclaim Tex and Buzz guilty. Now he was requesting a sit-down. Sterling knew that Gaylor was nothing more than Mortimer's messenger, and he also knew that Mortimer's primary concern was damage control—keeping Dartmouth's reputation from being tarnished by the grisly murder of a popular professor. Image was everything, even in the insular world of academia.

"When would he like to meet?" Sterling asked.

"Can you do it in an hour at his office in Parkhurst?"

"I'll be there."

Gaylor didn't bother saying thank you or good-bye. The phone just went dead. So damn superior, Sterling thought to himself. A security chief in charge of a small school in the middle of nowhere and you'd think he was the goddamn U.S. attorney general.

Sterling checked in with Wiley.

"We've located most of the WLA, except for Skeeter Wilkins. He's in Canada on a fishing trip. They've all been put through the mill. Spriggins was dead-on. Their alibis check out solid. A group is heading up to find Wilkins as we speak."

Sterling replayed Gaylor's parting words as he'd left the interrogation. How were he and the others so sure? Sterling had seen that false confidence many times, when everyone smelled blood and their desire for the kill distorted their judgment. It benefited all of them to have this case wrapped up quickly and cleanly. The longer the case went unsolved, the greater the town's fear grew. Convicting two outsiders like Tex and Buzz would return a sense of security to the close-knit community.

Sterling walked across the green toward Parkhurst Hall. He stood for a few minutes and watched some students playing soccer, using their backpacks as goal posts. There was such innocence in their play and laughter. Everything so perfect. Too perfect. It was just impossible for him to believe that no one had seen or heard anything that night.

President Mortimer's office took up the entire top floor of the expansive brick building. A couple of deans had their offices on the floors below, but those were surely no comparison to the suite of rooms reserved for Mortimer and his staff of fifteen. A pair of heavy glass doors, prominently embossed with the college shield, and a portrait of Mortimer wearing a navy blazer and green-and-white-striped tie dominated the entrance. He had that imperious look of a man accustomed to getting his way.

Sterling gave his name to the effusive receptionist, who ushered him into the inner sanctum. The office was as extravagant as it was massive. Thick beige carpeting blanketed the floor, and dark green leather furniture gave the room an appearance of a country club. A large glass chandelier hung from the middle of the ceiling and tall portraits of stoic, ancient white men looked down on the room as if demanding that anyone who entered the president's office first meet with their approval.

Mortimer and Gaylor were seated on a couple of wingback chairs when Sterling entered.

"Sorry to bother you on such a tough and emotional day," Mortimer said, rising to shake Sterling's hand. Gaylor stood and did the same. "I know you've been quite busy lately with those men from Claremont. As you can imagine, there's been a lot of pressure on my office, from parents to trustees. I just wanted to see where everything stands at the moment."

Sterling sat in a less comfortable chair close to the wide mahogany desk. He imagined this was what it felt like to sit in the Oval Office, only here the U.S. flag flanked one side of the desk and the Dartmouth flag was positioned on the other. The overbearing desk had been meticulously arranged with a matching leather-bound date book, writing pad, and calendar. Two pictures were prominently displayed at the front edge. One was of Mortimer standing with several books in his hand, lazily leaning against a tree and looking away from the camera—he couldn't have been more than twenty. The other photograph was an equally young Serena Mortimer with darker hair and longer eyelashes. She was wearing a tight black-and-orange Princeton cheerleading uniform. Not exactly a knockout, but worth a second look. She had signed the picture *To Clipper with love, Serena.* The handwriting surprised Sterling. He would have expected it to be slanted and severe, the way intellectuals tend to write. Instead, it was extremely girly—loops and fat letters—and there was even a small heart with an arrow drawn through it underneath her name.

"The killers are still out there," Sterling said. "We have these two men in custody, but that won't last very long."

"Why do you say that?" Mortimer asked.

"There is absolutely no credible evidence of any kind that links them to the murder. No prints, witnesses, plans. Nothing. And they've got alibis that have checked out. We're only holding them on a thread. A couple of outstanding warrants in traffic court." Sterling noted Mortimer's natty, camel-brown tweed blazer and green polka-dot bow tie. This was their third meeting, and each time he had worn something with school colors. Sterling wondered if he had green pajamas.

Mortimer digested Sterling's words, lifted his eyebrows, and looked at Gaylor. He started nodding his head. Habit. "It's come to my attention that these men are part of a hate group," Mortimer finally said.

"They call themselves the WLA," Sterling said. "The White Liberation Army. Their ideas aren't much more creative than their name."

"But they are the prime suspects?"

"The only suspects. And for me that's a problem. Their motivation isn't strong enough."

"But whoever killed Wilson did have a racial motive. It certainly wasn't anything as simple as robbery."

"The racial angle is superficial. That's what the killer wants us to believe."

"You're not convinced." Mortimer sounded disappointed.

"Not at all. This race angle is a distraction. Nothing more. We've questioned these men and their cohorts for the better part of two days now, and they've given us nothing but their radical ideas of white liberation and protecting the Constitution. No real reason to believe they killed my brother."

"But it's no secret Gatlin is a murderer," Gaylor interjected. "If he's killed once, what makes you so sure he wouldn't kill again?"

"I didn't say that he wouldn't," Sterling said. "But if I were a betting man, that's not where I'd stack my chips. Preaching hate is much different than committing cold-blooded murder. The killer knew the exact time Wilson would be heading home that night."

"Is that what the evidence shows?" Mortimer asked.

"It's not about the evidence," Sterling said. "Pattern. Most murders aren't random acts of violence. There's almost always an established link between the murderer and his victims."

"That's exactly what you have with this hate group," Mortimer pressed.

Sterling shook his head, reminding himself to be patient. "There are a lot of questions that have to be answered before I believe those men killed Wilson."

Mortimer raised his furry eyebrows till they met in the middle of his forehead.

"To start, why would they decide to commit a murder after all these years of harmless barn rallies and misspelled flyers?" Sterling said. "And why Wilson, a prominent and beloved professor living thirty miles away?"

"He just won that award," Mortimer offered. "Lots of money. All the papers carried the story."

"But they didn't want the money. They didn't steal anything. They could've taken his car, his wallet, anything. Besides, if they were kidnapping him to get the money, why kill him?"

Mortimer exchanged blank stares with Gaylor.

"To believe the WLA could kill my brother you'd have to believe they knew specific details. They had to know exactly when Wilson left your party and the route he'd be taking to get home. Those men who ambushed Wilson on River Road either killed him or knew who did."

"That would seem like a pretty easy thing to do," Mortimer offered. "They found Wilson's address in the white pages. After that, it's not hard to figure out the fastest way to his home from the campus is across Ledyard Bridge and up River Road. The only other route into Norwich would mean driving an extra fifteen minutes. So they guess he takes the shortest route. It's not rocket science." Mortimer either thought quickly on the fly or had already given these possibilities some serious consideration before he called the meeting. Sterling was inclined to believe the latter.

"Agreed," Sterling said. "But beyond that, whoever killed Wilson knew his exact movements. The timing had to be perfect."

"What makes you say that?" Gaylor asked.

"Not many cars travel River Road at that time of night, but there would be enough for at least one person to notice the truck on the side of the road. And the rain was coming down pretty hard. Certainly someone would've stopped to offer these men some help."

"I'd agree with that," Mortimer said. "People here in the Upper Valley are quite willing to help their neighbors."

"And that's exactly why no one has called us about seeing the truck that night."

"I don't understand," Gaylor said, wrinkling his face into a scowl.

"If someone had seen that truck or offered help, certainly they would've called in a tip by now. But no one has called. Not a single person. No prank callers or even mistaken identities. Highly unusual for such a prominent murder. I don't believe anyone saw the truck except for Wilson, because it wasn't there when other cars passed. Those men put that truck in position only at the precise time they knew Wilson would be heading over the bridge. Wilson's murder was almost perfect—excellent timing, no prints left at the scene, and no witnesses. Whoever did this knew a lot about crime. Sorry, but a ragtag group of beer guzzlers and hatemongers like the WLA doesn't fit."

"What about the branded eagle?" Mortimer asked.

"Interesting, but inconclusive. Anyone could've done that. It led us to Norkin and Gatlin, but it doesn't make a case."

The three men sat in silence for a moment before Mortimer cleared his throat. "How much longer do you think all of this will take?" he asked.

"This isn't a term paper, President Mortimer. Murder investigations don't operate on deadlines. They operate on evidence and facts."

"I've been getting a lot of calls from our trustees," Mortimer said. "There's a growing concern about how people are perceiving the school. Most parents and their children are drawn to the college because of our excellent faculty. But we also know that the area's safety and comfort factor in heavily when they make their decisions. It's why some of them choose us over the urban Ivies like Yale and Columbia." Mortimer had a way of making "urban" sound like a bad word.

Sterling stood and glared down at Mortimer. "With all due respect, Wally, I don't give a goddamn about this school's reputation and your trust-fund prodigies. Tell your trustees there's a murder investigation going on, and I'm not leaving till I've got the killers. The WLA is about as guilty of murdering my brother as your little bubbly receptionist sitting up front. The real killers knew Wilson's plan that night, and they knew it down to the second. And I'm starting to believe that whoever did this didn't do it alone. They had help on the inside."

24

Sterling was too dizzy with anger to return to the pit. He needed some quiet time before he did something he might regret. Dr. Lieteau would be proud of his decision. Anger management, she called it. Then he heard the director's warning. *Be careful, Sterling. And for Chrissake keep a level head.*

He walked back across the green and reclaimed the Mustang from in front of the Hop. He thought about grabbing a deli sandwich but instead steered the car toward Ledyard Bridge. He could fix something back at the house or maybe order a pizza—if they even had delivery service so far from civilization.

He drove down the long driveway, slowly so that he could appreciate the splendor of Wilson's creation. He remembered what Kay had whispered to him his first night there. *Wilson always took his time coming up the driveway. It gave him more time to appreciate the house as he approached. I would never let him take all the credit, but he really designed it himself, all the way down to the door handles in the bathroom.*

And it really was a thing of beauty, the way the narrow row of trees lining the driveway slowly opened up to the full expanse of the house. The length of the driveway and the positioning of the house had been measured perfectly, making the house grow bigger every twenty feet, each spire and window coming into view the closer you approached. Maximal effect. The house was enormous by any standards, but revealing it gradually like this made it an architectural wonder. Damn him, Sterling thought. Was there anything Wilson couldn't do?

A white station wagon taxi was sitting out front, its driver leaning out the window smoking. Sterling parked next to the garage and went inside. Three floral-print suitcases sat inside the foyer. He found Kay in the back of the house.

"I can't stay here any longer," Kay said as he walked into the spacious family room. She was alone, sipping her coffee. The rest she had gotten these last couple of days agreed with her. Traces of pain were still there, but they were no longer etched so deeply in her face. "I see him in too many places," she said. "He loved this house, Sterling."

"Where are you going?"

"I'm flying to Chicago in a couple of hours. My parents still live there. I'll stay with them the next few months. They're getting old and could probably use some help around the house. It'll give me a chance to make up my mind about what I'll do next. I can't think here. Not right now. Too many emotions. Too much anger. Someone has ruined our lives and is still walking around free."

"Everyone thinks those rednecks from Claremont did it," Sterling said.

"But you don't. I can hear it in your voice."

"Doesn't make a lot of sense to me. First of all, they're too damn convenient. Second, I don't buy the motive."

"Did they know Wilson?"

"I don't think so. They'd heard about him from his awards and articles in the paper, but they didn't really know him."

"After all these years we lived here," Kay said. "Wilson dedicated his entire life to this school and the community. He loved it so much. And this is how he's taken away from us. Killed in the woods like some animal." She shook her head hard and looked away.

"Was everything all right with Wilson?" Sterling asked.

"What do you mean?"

"Was his health all right?"

Kay shrugged. "Just out of shape. Wilson exercised with a fork more than anything else." A soft smile escaped her face. It was the first since Wilson had been declared missing. "He did have a touch of high blood pressure. Wilson loved his salt."

"How about arguments, conflicts?"

"None. Your brother avoided tense situations at all costs. He hated confrontation. He would tell me that the time people spent arguing and getting upset over silly things was time that was lost forever. He spent his time on good things."

"Like what?"

"Other than teaching and working in the lab, Wilson loved to walk in the wilderness and videotape the animals. He'd have such a look of contentment when he came home."

"I met with President Mortimer and Chief Gaylor. I get the feeling that Mortimer wants this to be over as soon as possible."

"I'm not surprised," Kay said. "Wally has always had one thing on his mind—Dartmouth. He'll do anything to protect the school's name."

"But after twenty years of friendship, you'd expect more from him than worrying about satisfying a bunch of trustees. He's just lost the biggest name on his faculty and someone who supposedly meant a lot to him personally."

"He's a complicated man," Kay said. "It took many years for me to be comfortable around him. He's one of those people you feel like you never really know. He and Serena are made for each other. They're both very cold people, interested in their own things."

"Did Wilson confide in him?"

Kay took a long swallow of coffee. "I'd be surprised if he did. Wilson was closest to Yuri Mandryka. He's been a mentor to Wilson since his grad days at Chicago."

"Kay, I know you've gone over that night a hundred times, but I need you to focus on the party. I can't get a clear picture of that hour and a half that Wilson was there."

"I don't really know much," Kay said. "He left his lab about five thirty or so. Since he was the guest of honor, I thought he should be there early to greet people as they came in. The next I heard from him he was in the car and on his way home."

"Did he say anything about the party that struck you as odd?"

"We only talked for a couple of minutes. He was surprised at the turnout. A friend of his had flown in from Stanford. Even Wilcox had come up from Harvard."

"Wilcox?"

"Laurence Wilcox, the chairman of biology at Harvard. He's never forgiven Wilson for not accepting a position in the department. But Wilson loved it here. He didn't want to go down there and deal with all the politics." Kay shook her head. "And that's all I know about the party."

"Well, I was hoping he might've mentioned that something unusual happened. But maybe not."

"Nothing that I remember."

"That's what I figured," Sterling said. "This hasn't been easy for me, Kay. There's so much that I needed to tell Wilson. So many things that happened between us that I wanted to explain."

Kay put up her hand. "No matter what you guys had between you, Wilson loved you, Sterling. You need to know that." Kay smiled gently, knowing nothing would bring back the only man she ever loved.

Standing barely an inch over five feet, Elmer Gallows was exactly what one would expect of a small-town mountain lawyer. No tie or even a blazer, instead a wrinkled button-down oxford and a pair of khakis whose hem needed to be let out at least two inches. His curly dark hair had been combed in every imaginable direction in a losing battle to hide his baldness. Everything about him was miniature, especially his small hands that always seemed to be moving. He walked into Wiley's cramped office and took a seat without being asked.

"What's on your mind, Lieutenant?" he asked.

Wiley stood and closed the door. Neither extended his hand.

"Off the record," Wiley said, falling back into his chair.

Gallows nodded his head.

"I don't think your boy did it," Wiley said.

"Good, that makes three of us. Now how do we convince everyone else?"

"Tensions are pretty high around here. Everyone down the hall is anxious to pin this on someone."

"Even if it's the wrong person?"

Wiley half nodded. The answer was yes, but Wiley didn't want to admit to something like this even if it was off the record. The man sitting in front of him was still a lawyer.

"I've talked to Spriggins," Wiley said. "He says they're clean."

"How do you know Spriggins?"

"That's irrelevant. Let's just say we know of each other." Wiley had met the legendary Jack Spriggins on several hunting trips the two had been part of many years ago. Spriggins not only looked tough at six foot four, but he walked and talked tough. And he had the best eye-hand coordination Wiley had ever seen in a hunter. "What's important is that Spriggins has made inquiries separate from ours and has turned up nothing."

Gallows nodded his head, his tiny hands working hard on his collar. "Why are you telling me this, Lieutenant?"

"Because I want you to ask your client who he thinks might be out to get him. Maybe someone's setting him up, trying to settle an old score."

"Why don't you ask him yourself? You sure as hell have had enough time."

"Because you and I both know clients have a different version of the truth when it comes to talking to their lawyers."

Gallows weighed Wiley's words, rolling his fingers in a small circular motion the entire time. "And if my client is able to help you, what will he get out of it?"

Wiley stood and opened the door, signaling the meeting was over. "A one-way ticket back to the hell he came from."

Gallows started to say something, but instead shook his head in frustration before storming out of the office. His hands were still hard at work.

Sterling spent several hours flipping through his black book, trying to tie the loose ends together. For most of the investigation, he had attempted to figure out who would want Wilson dead. But now he was beginning to wonder if his scope had been too narrow. Had he spent too much time trying to find the guilt in others and not enough time exploring Wilson's actions that might have precipitated his murder? Anything at this point was possible—debts that had gone unpaid, a kidnapping attempt that had taken a deadly turn, even a vindictive student who had finally gotten revenge.

Then there was still the whole business with the WLA. Tex and Buzz were definitely innocent, but someone had gone to great lengths to implicate them. They had carved "nigger" into Wilson's chest and branded the diamond-eye eagle into his side. They knew that these clues would lead to the WLA.

What had happened at the party at the mansion that night—or better yet, was there someone there who wanted Wilson dead? The closer Sterling thought he was to figuring things out, the more questions surfaced that didn't have answers. He went into Wilson's study and read the copy of the will that Kay had left him. Kay had been named the primary beneficiary, receiving the bulk of the estate, including the house, cars, and other hard assets. Sterling was next in line, receiving the surprising sum of $3 million and Wilson's entire book collection, which included many signed first editions of best-selling novelists. Sterling felt guilty about Wilson's generosity.

Wilson left his Nobel and Devonshire medals and diplomas to the school with the stipulation that "they be displayed not prominently but honorably." There were three other names on the list, none of which Sterling recognized. They would receive $25,000 apiece and small tokens such as minor pieces of art and the various electronic devices he had collected over the years.

Sterling found the entire affair of death and wills dizzying, so he climbed into bed early that night, a stranger in a big empty house full of a brother's spirit he had run from most of his life. He was tired, angry, and lonely, and he hoped a sound sleep would reenergize him. Before he turned off the lights, he looked across the room at a framed picture of Wilson and Kay on the dresser. They were standing on a bridge with a long, winding river and old buildings in the background. It had a European look, maybe London or Rome. How could two people be so much in love? Now, one cold night of evil had changed it all. Forever.

For the next hour he lay in darkness, staring out the window at nothing. The wind gently knocked against the window. Shadows of tangled tree limbs squirmed across the naked walls, looking like menacing monsters of untold horrors. Sterling fell asleep wondering about the agony Wilson must have felt knowing he was going to die only minutes from the safety of his home.

At first he thought it was part of his dream, but the second time he heard it, he opened his eyes and waited. Footsteps on the hardwood floor. They were steady. Cautious. Somewhere on the first floor.

Sterling sat up in bed quickly and pulled his gun off the nightstand. He slipped into his sneakers, then eased the door open and moved quickly toward the staircase. There was definitely someone there. Something heavy like a box or a stack of books crashed to the floor. Then silence. Sterling snaked down the stairs. The noise had come from Wilson's study.

Just as he hit the last step, a gunshot exploded. He couldn't see who had fired it. He struggled to get his orientation, but before he could figure out what was happening, another shot boomed through the dark house. This one missed also, but he dropped to the ground and crawled to the other side of the stairwell. It had been a long time since someone had taken a shot at him—actually several years. He was working a case in Alabama and a gang member who had committed the murder circled back while they were walking through the crime scene and sprayed a round. One agent took a shot to the shoulder, while a lab tech took one to the spine. It didn't kill him, but severed three of his nerve roots and left him paralyzed below the waist.

"Who the hell is it?" Sterling yelled, aiming his gun at the invisible intruder. "What do you want here?"

No answer. A few moments of silence, then the thud of heavy footsteps heading down the hall in the opposite direction. Sterling stood and fired a couple of shots into the darkness, but the footsteps continued with the sound of crashing glass and overturned furniture. He cautiously ran after the fading footsteps, then heard a door swing open. The intruder was already out through the kitchen. By the time Sterling reached the door, he could hear an engine turn over, then the sound of rubber spitting rocks in the air. He ran down the steps. All that he could see was a dark figure speeding away on a motorcycle. The bike was too far away for Sterling to read the license plate.

He ran down the driveway and fired a couple more shots, but it was useless. The driver had escaped and the only thing left was the fading sound of a motorcycle engine roaring down River Road. Sterling stopped near the entrance of the property and bent over to catch his breath. He returned to the house and turned on every light before searching the study. It was immediately obvious the intruder had come for something specific. Wilson's desk drawers had all been opened, with papers and files spilling onto the floor. The top of the desk was a mess—pencils and pens strewn across the blotter, papers everywhere. An entire wall of books had been emptied on the hardwood floor.

Sterling opened the closet door. There wasn't much in it except for an old computer monitor, a filing cabinet that was largely empty, and a couple of overcoats hanging on hooks. It didn't look like it had been disturbed. Sterling wondered if the intruder had run away before he had a chance to go through it. He reached up to the top shelf and blindly ran his hand along the paneling. He found an old baseball, a catcher's mitt, and an ancient pair of boxing gloves. Why did Wilson have these? Nothing else caught his attention.

Sterling locked all of the doors and windows, then went into the front living room and found a comfortable spot on the sofa—half sitting, half reclining. He rested his gun on a small end table within arm's reach, before quietly looking out the window into the empty shadows of night. Wilson's secret must not have been lost with his death. Whoever killed him still hadn't gotten what they were looking for.

25

Sterling rubbed off the film of sweat misting his watch crystal. His run completed, he stood in front of the house waiting for his breathing to return to normal again. He had shaved a full minute off his morning jog, a sign that his lungs were adjusting to the altitude and his legs were growing more comfortable with the hilly terrain. He raced into the house, took a quick shower, and changed before returning outside to rev up the Mustang. He wanted to grab a bagel and the New York Times before heading over to Professor Mandryka's lab.

The Bagel Basement was Hanover's most popular morning joint, inconspicuously situated in the basement of a two-story building on Allen Street, a small one-way path in the center of town. Grumpy Oscar Nederhoff lit the old cast-iron ovens at five every morning, and for the next twelve hours—long after Nederhoff had gone home for the day—the smell of freshly baked dough pulled in customers from miles around.

Sterling settled the Mustang in an empty parking lot behind the building and bounded down the stairs. A young woman in her late teens stood behind the counter filling the baskets with warm bagels. She had pink-and-green fluorescent hair with a big silver loop dangling from her nose. Her oversized clothes hung wrinkled and loose.

Sterling looked around at the early arrivals. An older man in a long trench coat sat at a corner table, reading the thin Valley News. He dipped his bagel in hot coffee, then nibbled it as he moved from one news item to the next. The woman sitting next to the window pored over what looked like a term paper, vigorously marking it with red ink. She had barely touched her poppy seed bagel, but the tall cup of coffee was almost finished.

Sterling took his toasted cinnamon-raisin bagel and orange juice and sat down at one of the small back tables. It was only six thirty; he wasn't expected at Professor Mandryka's for another half hour. He flipped open the *Times* and began skimming the front page. Nothing. He then scanned the nation section. There was the headline DARTMOUTH PROFESSOR MUR-DERED IN VERMONT.

It was a short article, starting at the bottom of the page and continuing in the science section. Most of the space was devoted to Wilson's scientific accomplishments. A biologist whose name Sterling didn't recognize was quoted as calling Professor Bledsoe one of the most important ethologists in the history of the discipline, in the same class as the Austrian Konrad Lorenz.

Sterling thought it odd that only the last paragraph dealt with Wilson's murder. The details were sketchy at best. He had been killed after a party in his honor, and the authorities had no suspects or motive for the killing. There was no mention of the racial disfigurement or that he had been found in a heavily wooded area. The quote from President Mortimer was brief but it expressed the sadness felt not only by the community but by Mortimer himself, who had been a colleague and friend for almost twenty years. That at least was heartening.

Sterling pulled out a dollar and left it in the empty tip jar on the front counter. The fluorescent-headed girl gave him a lazy nod of appreciation. Professor Mandryka was waiting.

Professor Yuri Mandryka spent most of his time in a dark, musty laboratory that took up the entire third floor of the Gilman Life Sciences Laboratory building. His lab was housed in three rooms, all of them with views overlooking downtown Hanover and the greenery of the surrounding area. Sterling found him lighting a Bunsen burner underneath a column of foamy blue liquid.

"Good morning, Professor Mandryka," Sterling said.

"Morning to you," Mandryka replied. "But call me Yuri. No need for titles and formalities. Those things don't matter so much when you get to be my age." Mandryka poured more of the blue liquid into the glass column, then turned his attention to Sterling. "Did you bring any company?"

"No, just me, as you asked."

"Good. Privacy could be important."

Mandryka continued to fiddle with the bubbling solution while measuring a charcoal-gray liquid in two other graduated cylinders. He whistled a tune as he fidgeted with the experiment, hobbling from one side of the lab bench to the next. Though he moved slowly and deliberately, his decades of experience still allowed him to deftly handle the solutions and instruments.

"Just a second," Mandryka said, still rearranging the glass beakers and eyeing the levels of the fluids. "I want to get these reagents going so we can talk without being interrupted. I'm trying to degrade some proteins."

"I thought you did animal research," Sterling said, looking around the room. It was full of smoky glassware, microscopes, and test tubes. "This could be a chem lab."

"It is," Mandryka said, wiping his hands on a lab coat that looked like it had survived a chemical war. He folded his wire-framed glasses and tucked them in his breast pocket. "I'm from the old school. When I was coming up in science, there was a lot of crossover in the disciplines. Chemists were biologists and biologists were chemists. These days, everyone is super-specialized, just working on a small part of the problem. I like to work a problem from beginning to end. My lab has been trying to develop new ways to analyze the mitochondrial DNA in monkeys. We're almost there."

Mandryka rinsed out a couple of glass beakers in the sink and brought them to an empty lab bench. He poured equal amounts of clear white solution into each beaker, then put them on a rotating mixer. He opened one of the drawers and pulled out a timer, turning the small knob with great effort and setting it on the counter.

"Follow me," Mandryka said.

Mandryka opened a door to an expansive office. Windows filled one entire wall, overlooking a vast wooded area that dropped into a valley—a spectacular view of unblemished wilderness.

"Quite a view you have here, Yuri," Sterling said, walking over stacks of books and papers to get to the windows. Mandryka hobbled to his chair without using his cane and took a seat behind the cluttered desk.

"That's one of the few perks that comes with all these gray hairs,"

Mandryka said. "Or at least what's left of them. Choice lab space goes to the most senior in the department."

They looked out over the endless mountains, quietly taking in the soaring peaks and deep valleys. It was still early in the morning, but the haze had lifted and visibility extended for miles. Sterling knew that back in the city rush hour was just beginning, with cars jamming the narrow streets and buses careening down the wide avenues. But outside Mandryka's lab, Sterling counted only three cars on the road below and no signs that it would get much busier anytime soon. He turned and found an empty chair across from the old scientist. It was time to talk.

"How much did Willie say to you about what he'd been doing lately?" Mandryka asked.

Sterling shrugged. "Not much. We only spoke to each other once every couple of months, and when we did, we didn't talk much about our work. We spent more time catching up on our lives. Personal things."

"I see." Mandryka removed a stack of papers and cleared off a small oak humidor on the corner of his desk. He opened the lid and pulled out a fresh cigar. "Care for one?"

"I don't smoke, but thanks anyway."

"One of my students is from London," Mandryka explained. "When he goes home for vacation, he always brings me back a box of Cubans." Sterling watched as Mandryka clipped one end, lit the cigar, then took a long drag. "Of course, I pay him," he said, blowing a cloud of bluish-gray circles toward the ceiling. Sterling looked at the no-smoking sign tacked to the bulletin board and smiled.

"I've already told you that your brother and I go back a long way," Mandryka said, allowing the cigar to rest in the corner of his narrow mouth. "Willie knew that I spent a good portion of my time studying animal anatomy. I took an interest many years ago after I hit a deer one morning on the way to work. When I went to move the poor thing to the side of the road, I noticed that it had been severed in half, just as if someone had taken a saw and buzzed it right down the middle. Its innards were spread all over the hood of my car and the ground. The heart muscles were still in spasm."

Mandryka took another drag on the cigar and leaned back in the chair, making his small frame look like that of a child who had climbed into his father's recliner.

"I lost my old car in that accident, but I found a new interest in anatomy. For years I had studied animals, their behavior, and their relationship to environment, but now I was going to find out not only how they behaved but why they behaved as they did."

"Anatomy is my area of expertise," Sterling said.

"Yes, Willie told me, which is why I thought you might appreciate that story. A few months ago, Willie called me at home very early in the morning and asked if he could bring something by the lab. I, of course, said yes, and he came that morning with a brown bag that had been wrapped in a larger plastic bag. I thought he was bringing me breakfast." Mandryka took another drag and let out a soft cackle. "Wilson had brought me breakfast all right. It was a dead blackbird."

"Where did he get it from?" Sterling asked.

"The back of his property. You see, what made Willie such a good scientist was that he lived his craft. He didn't just sit in front of the classroom or laboratory and teach these kids. He went out in the field and collected data, developing his theories and putting them to the test."

Sterling thought of the story he had read on the Internet about Chogan and of how Wilson had spent his last minutes alive writing the word on his ankle. Sterling was unsure how much Mandryka knew, but to call a clandestine meeting like this, he knew something.

"Birds and other animals die all the time," Sterling said. "I'm sure Wilson could have found plenty of dead animals in those woods if he had looked long enough."

"Yes and yes," Mandryka said. He leaned forward to stand, grabbing on to the edge of his desk. "Come and let me show you something."

Yuri Mandryka waddled around his desk, barely able to lift his legs high enough to clear the stacks of science journals and papers littering his floor. He ignored the cane resting next to the door and instead reached out to different pieces of furniture to maintain his balance. Before he left the office, he snuffed out the cigar and slid it into one of his coat pockets. Sterling followed, noticing the nasty curve that twisted the old man's spine and bent his head downward. He had probably been half a foot taller in his younger years, but the curse of osteoporosis and its insidious thinning of the bones had robbed him not only of his height but of the ability to straighten his neck for long periods of time.

Professor Mandryka led Sterling to the other end of the long hallway, where they caught the elevator to the basement. He didn't say anything during the ride, instead keeping his eyes straight ahead, weighing something serious. The doors opened onto a dimly lit, bare hallway that looked like a storage room for custodial supplies.

Mandryka continued to waddle down the hall, reaching out to the wall with every step to balance himself. They walked through one heavy steel door, then another, which Sterling helped the old man open. Mandryka fumbled with his key ring for a few minutes, then inserted a long key in the lock of the third door. It took all of his effort to push the door open, and once he did, Sterling was immediately hit with the room's teeth-chattering chill and the heavy smell of formaldehyde. Mandryka turned on the light, but Sterling was not prepared for what he saw.

"Jesus Christ!" Sterling exclaimed. "What the hell is this?"

Blackbird carcasses were everywhere. In cages, on top of cabinets, lined up on metal tables, wrapped in bags on the floor. There must have been hundreds of dead blackbirds in that tiny room. Mandryka stood there quietly and allowed Sterling's mind to catch up with his eyes.

"You see, Sterling," Mandryka finally said. "Willie did walk farther into the woods, and as you surmised, he did find lots of dead animals. The only problem was that they were all blackbirds—not one or two, but hundreds."

"I've never seen anything like this before," Sterling gasped.

"And neither had Willie, which is why he brought them to me." Mandryka let out a violent cough.

"What did he expect you to do with them?" Sterling asked.

"He needed to find someone who could help explain all this death, but he didn't want to raise too many eyebrows. He knew my chemistry background, so he thought I could help."

Sterling walked around the room, looking inside the cages and picking up the bags on the floor. There were so many birds, it was hard to believe that they were real. Some had black bodies, others were a streaky brown.

"There are two different species here," Sterling said.

"Not true," Mandryka said, shuffling to a stainless steel table covered with an opaque plastic bag. He reached underneath the table for a box of gloves and snapped on a pair. "Not to worry—your mistake is common. This is one species." He removed the plastic table cover.

Five birds had been lined up in different stages of dissection. The first three had been dissected down to the skeleton with all of their organs exposed and tagged. The last two were completely intact. Mandryka offered Sterling a pair of gloves, then picked up the last two birds. "These are the red-winged blackbirds," he said, holding them up in the light. "They're arguably the most abundant type of blackbird in North America." Mandryka handed one of the birds to Sterling.

"But they look so different," Sterling said as he turned the bird in his hand.

"Only on the outside," Mandryka said. "What you're holding is the male red-winged."

Sterling grabbed a tuft of small scarlet feathers that sprouted from the rest of its shiny black feathers. "And this is how it got its name."

"Precisely," Mandryka said, taking the bird from Sterling's hand and spreading its wings. "This area is called the *epaulet*, from the French word meaning shoulder. As you can see, the males are glossy black everywhere except on the shoulder of their wings." Mandryka brushed the scarlet feathers, which were bordered with a yellow stripe. The bill was also black, thin and pointed.

Sterling picked up the other bird. "And this is the female."

"Exactly. And to the untrained eye it looks like a different bird altogether. The females are blackish-brown on top, streaked with buff and chestnut. The head is streaked and the cheeks are brown. You can see how the throat is pale with a pink tinge and the breast and belly are whitish with heavy dark lines. They share some of the male's red coloring in the wings, but not much."

"What killed them?" Sterling asked.

"That's why Willie brought them to me over the last couple of months. I've been dissecting them every day, comparing the size of their organs and looking for an abnormality that might be common to all of them." Mandryka went to a large refrigerator and opened the top door. A puff of cold mist dusted his face. Hundreds of tiny vials had been separated in long metal baskets. They were full of a dark-crimson viscous liquid.

"Serological studies," Sterling said.

"That's right. I've been running blood tests since Willie brought me the first bird." Mandryka closed the cooler and hobbled over to the back wall, where he pulled a notebook from a rusted metal drawer. He placed the book on the corner of a table so Sterling could read over his shoulder. The word "Chogan" had been carefully written across the top.

"Willie and I made some interesting discoveries," Mandryka said, flipping the wrinkled pages. "All of the blood samples we tested were positive for a compound called bufalin."

"Lethal?"

"Take enough of the stuff and it can kill you in seconds," Mandryka said. "Its common name is toad venom. Several pharmaceutical companies used to synthesize a derivative, because it had cardioactive properties similar to the digitalis plant, which is used in the heart medication digoxin."

"Why did they stop making it?"

"Two Japanese women back in the eighties. Lovers, ostracized by their families and community. They committed suicide by taking high doses of the Chinese medicine Kyushin, which contains a bufalin derivative. They died in a matter of minutes. Autopsies showed their hearts had doubled in size. The pathways that conduct electricity throughout the heart had been so badly destroyed that the medical examiner suspected the muscle lost its rhythm and began beating erratically like a bag of worms. Horrible way to die."

"So the FDA wouldn't let the companies develop the drug here?"

"As you might expect. We have the most conservative drug approval policy in the world. If a drug makes you sneeze one extra time, patient advocates are down the FDA's throat not to approve it."

"That explains what I found on Wilson's computer. The last website he had visited was the FDA. I found some of the printed pages in one of the trash cans. They didn't say much, but he had been looking at the safety alert pages."

"That's right. We found a posting in the archives that warned consumers and scientists about the dangers of this toxin and the products that were being made from it."

"But how do you know that bufalin killed all these birds?"

"Take a look at this," Mandryka said, hobbling over to another cooler.

He opened the door and pulled out a covered tray. He carried it back to an empty lab bench and rested it on the counter, then removed the cover.

"What are those?"

"You've probably never seen these before. They're bird hearts."

Fifty beefy-red hearts, smaller than olives, covered the tray. They had been divided so the larger hearts were on the right and the smaller ones on the left.

"The hearts on the right side belong to the birds with the highest levels of bufalin in their blood," Mandryka explained. "Those on the left either had trace amounts or none at all."

"So the poison is causing the hearts to enlarge to the point that it kills them," Sterling deduced. "How fast do they die?"

"All depends on how much they consume and how concentrated it is. If I had to guess, I'd say a matter of hours to a couple of days. When I opened the hearts and dissected the muscles and septum, I found that all of their electrical systems were ruined."

"So these birds are coming in contact with the toads that carry this poison?"

"Impossible. First of all, the poison is located in the toad's skin glands, so they'd have to eat the toad or its skin to be poisoned. Blackbirds don't feast on toads. Secondly, bufalin is found almost exclusively in the *Bufo bufo gargarizans* species, toads which predominantly live in China. The European toads—*Bufo bufo vulgaris*—contain a similar compound, but it's not as lethal as the Chinese bufalin. But there's something else." Mandryka turned the pages of the register. "I've taken blood from at least a couple of hundred of these birds and I've found that not all of them contain the poison."

"So the birds that don't have the poison are dying from something else?"

"No, I still think they're dying from the poison. They have the enlarged hearts and the ruined electrical systems. It's just that there's no detectable poison in their blood."

"Degradation," Sterling said. "By the time you run tests on the blood, the poison has degraded beyond recognition."

"Exactly. And when I did an external examination of the birds, I found that the longer the birds had been dead, the less likely they were to have traces of the poison."

Mandryka pointed to a series of columns for Sterling to analyze.

Everything he had just said made sense. The birds had been listed from those most recently killed to those that had died a long time ago. The new deaths had the highest concentrations of poison while the older deaths simply had "undetectable" scribbled beside them.

"In some of the specimens, the poison is completely intact, but in others, I can only find traces of the bufalin. It's a perfect poison. It does its dirty work over a matter of hours, then quietly degrades and disappears."

"Amazing," Sterling said. "Hundreds of blackbirds are dying in the woods of the Upper Valley from some type of mysterious poison and no one knows about it."

"Willie only found hundreds, which means there are probably thousands," Mandryka said. "Something strange is happening out there. Willie and I were hot on the trail."

"Who else knows about your discoveries?"

"We haven't told anyone," Mandryka said. "At least I haven't. That's why I've kept everything stored down here in this basement. No one has the key to this room but me."

"None of your research assistants helped you in this?"

"Not a bit," Mandryka insisted, clearly understanding Sterling's line of questioning.

"What about Wilson's lab? Would any of his research students know about this?"

"I don't think so," Mandryka said. "We agreed to keep a tight lid on things until we had a better idea of what was going on and who was involved. Willie was writing a paper or case study for *Science*. I don't know if he finished, but he was close to it. He'd been working very hard the last couple of weeks. He wanted to have it done before the party, but I'm not sure if he made it. He left that night before I had a chance to ask."

"Some of these pieces are starting to fit," Sterling said, flipping through the pages of his little book. "Nel Potter's live-in, Heidi, mentioned that Wilson's night scouts would often take him onto the Potter farm. She said that he would come over early in the morning to observe the blackbirds."

"She wouldn't have known about this," Mandryka said. "Willie didn't even tell Kay. He was too worried about who might be behind these killings. This toxin isn't just some simple compound anyone can mix up in a lab. This is powerful stuff. Someone knew what they were doing."

Sterling flipped another page in his book. "A month or so ago there was an article about Wilson in *The Dartmouth*. I picked up a copy when I was over at the Hop. In the article, Wilson mentioned that at a future date he'd be delivering some information about his recent discoveries on blackbirds."

Professor Mandryka walked over to another table full of dead blackbirds and began inspecting them. "He gave that interview after we were certain something was going on. He was about to reveal everything he had learned, but then I found something that gave both of us pause." Mandryka lifted two blackbirds from the heap, one male and one female.

Sterling examined them. Mandryka pulled on the tiny white metal bands strapped to their legs. "What's that?" Sterling asked.

"Bird ringing. Look at the tiny numbers stamped here."

Sterling picked up one of the birds and peered at the ring. "Where did this come from?"

"Your guess is as good as mine. That's where we left off. Bird ringing can be something that bird-watchers do as a hobby, but usually it's done by professionals. This is how ornithologists mark birds and track their movements. It's been an effective way of studying life histories, population dynamics, and bird migratory patterns. Started in Denmark in the late 1800s. A researcher there fitted starlings with metal rings engraved with successive numbers and a return address. Then he released them into the wild. Bird ringing is now practiced in every corner of the world."

"And you have no idea who might've been ringing these birds?"

"Not in the least. But one thing's for sure, someone else out there knows that these birds are dying and isn't saying. Willie placed a call to the Animal and Plant Health Inspection Service in Washington. Sometimes they get involved with migratory studies. He thought they might be behind the ringing."

"Their answer?"

"They couldn't deny or confirm, but agreed to look into it."

Sterling closed his book and slid it in his pocket. "Something's going on here, Yuri, and it sounds like Wilson was getting close to it." Sterling hesitated, unsure whether to take Mandryka into his confidence. "Someone was fishing around in Wilson's office the night that he was killed," he finally said. "I haven't been able to figure out who it was or what they wanted, but I'm certain they came specifically to find something."

"Check his research records," Mandryka said as he opened the door and turned off the light. The two men stood facing each other in the dark hallway as the sound of water dripping on concrete echoed in the distance. "One thing about your brother, he was meticulous at documenting everything. I taught him that when he was my student in Chicago."

"Yuri, are you sure no one else knows you have these blackbirds?"

"I'm the only one with keys to this room. The maintenance people can't even get in."

"I'm not sure why Wilson was murdered, but if it has anything to do with these blackbirds, then you could be in danger too."

"I'm an old man," Mandryka said. "I'm not much use to anybody."

"But the information you have could be. Be careful, Yuri."

Mandryka didn't have to answer. The concerned look on his face said it all.

The two climbed into the cranky elevator and left the dank basement. As Sterling had predicted, the evidence was starting to talk.

26

The Mustang left a cloud of smoke and dust in its wake as it raced up the dark driveway, eating up patches of dead grass and snapping twigs like broken pencils. Vermin and other four-legged animals scrambled into the woods as their imminent death bore down on them like a runaway freight train without brakes. Sterling couldn't wait to get back to the house. With the information that Mandryka had just told him, he was convinced that he knew what the intruder was after. He went directly to the study, then systematically searched the room. First, he removed all the books from the shelves, opening each one to make sure there wasn't an envelope or a message hidden between the pages. Then he opened the closet. He had looked at everything the previous night, but what he hadn't done was check the top shelf carefully. He stood on his toes and tried reaching back, but the shelf was too deep. He pulled over a chair to stand on. He was ready to step down, when he felt it. A small keyhole all the way in the back wall, which he would surely have missed had he not run his finger along the paneling. He cleared the other items, then knocked on the area around the lock. A secret compartment. It had a much hollower sound than the rest of the wall. He searched the entire study for the key, making more of a mess than had already been made. Frustrated, he considered his options for opening it without the key and thought about hammering his way through. But that would risk destroying whatever was inside.

Sterling sat in Wilson's tall leather reclining chair and closed his eyes. Where would he hide something as small as a key? Sterling lifted the blotter. Nothing. He slid out the middle desk drawer and completely emptied its contents on the floor. He placed the drawer on top of a pile of books, but seconds later it tipped and fell to the floor before Sterling could catch it.

That's when he saw it. Affixed to the underside of the drawer was a small black metal box. Sterling opened it and pulled out a tiny key.

He stood on the chair and stretched to the back wall. After a couple of tries, the lock clicked. The small compartment door swung open. Sterling didn't know what to expect, but it certainly wasn't what was sitting there. A compact Sony mini-DV camera. He pulled it out and ran his hand along the empty space. Nothing else. He sat behind the desk and opened the pop-out LCD monitor. It was a nice camera, state of the art, loaded with buttons and connection ports and a high-powered mega-pixel zoom lens. But why had Wilson locked it away in a secret compartment? Surely there were more expensive items sitting openly in the study.

Sterling pushed the Eject button and found a tape in the cassette holder. He rewound the tape, then pushed Play. The picture was out of focus at first, then he recognized trees and rocks and a tiny ravine. The camera jostled as whoever was holding it stepped over branches and lost his footing on the rough terrain. Sterling could hear labored breathing. The video went on like this for several minutes, then Wilson's voice. "This is where it starts and runs for about two hundred yards into the northeast corner of the Potter property. They're here by the hundreds." The camera now focused on a blackbird lying on its back, its beady eyes staring blankly into the sky.

Sterling watched the next thirty minutes of tape, blackbird carcasses by the hundreds, scattered under rocks, floating in the water, caught between dead branches, covering dirt paths. Most of the tape had been shot with natural sound, the crunching of leaves under Wilson's steps, animals calling from a distance. Every few minutes, Wilson could be heard as he identified his location with precise compass directions, pinpointing the specific degrees along the horizon, as well as the lines of latitude and longitude. He distinguished male from female birds, and when he came across a heavily concentrated area, he zoomed in on the bodies, turning them over with sticks to make sure he had captured everything. Before the tape ran out, Wilson turned the camera on himself, his face barely visible. Once he had framed himself as best as possible, he spoke decisively. "You have just witnessed the physical evidence of immense wildlife death. This is no mere accident. These birds are being poisoned. But by whom and why?"

27

Sterling returned the camera and tape to the secret compartment and slid the key in his wallet. He jumped into the Mustang and started toward the hospital. He wanted to speak with the chief pathologist to find out if there had been any reported cases of human bufalin toxicity. It was a reach, but he figured if this many birds were dying in the wild from a rare poison, it might have found its way into humans as well. A quick check of the hospital toxicology reports and cause-of-death statements might provide some insight.

His cell phone rang. "Bledsoe," he answered.

"Agent Bledsoe, Lieutenant Wiley here."

"Good morning, Lieutenant. What's cooking?"

"How soon can you get to the pit?"

"Ten minutes if I obey the traffic signals, five if you grant me immunity."

"Then make it seven." Wiley sounded anxious, which was unusual.

"I'm on my way." Sterling hung up and immediately screeched into a U-turn.

He entered the police station through the side door and walked down a couple of hallways before reaching the pit. He opened the door to sheer pandemonium. Everyone screaming, phones ringing, fax machines squealing. Wiley and Brusco stood at the head of the table. "Bledsoe," Brusco yelled over the noise.

"What's all the commotion?" Sterling asked.

"Another body," Brusco said.

"Who is it?"

"No idea," Wiley said. "Unable to make a positive ID."

Brusco looked grim. "This one was bad."

"How bad?"

"They found her stuffed in a freight box in a dumpster behind the Grand Union grocery store. Completely naked. Bruises and scratches all over her body."

"Sexual?"

"Hard to tell right now," Brusco said.

"Facial injuries?"

Brusco shook his head slowly. "It's headless."

Sterling took a hard swallow and then scribbled in his pad. "Who found the body?"

"Garbage man emptying the dumpster this morning," Wiley said. "It fell out of the crate in the back of the truck. He noticed a human leg sticking out."

"Where's the body now?"

"At the morgue," Wiley said.

"Autopsy?"

"Dr. Withcott is already on his way up from Concord. He should be here in less than an hour."

One of the officers walked over to them. "We just received an e-mail from Quantico."

Three large computers had been set up in the middle of the pit, all connected to their own color printers. Sterling followed the officer to the middle computer and clicked on the mail icon.

> Sterle,
>
> These are the latest. We did some fidgeting and the quality is much better. We just got some new software that allows us to digitally manipulate the image, so we're trying more reconfigurations. I'll be sending updates as soon as I get something that works. I hope this helps. Let us know if there's anything else we can do.
>
> Warmest,
>
> Harry

The first picture showed the man's reflection almost as if the glass door were a mirror. His eyes were still hidden, but his lower lip was more visible. He seemed to have a smirk on his face, but there wasn't enough exposure to make any real determinations. It wasn't even clear if he was black or white or somewhere in between. Sterling passed the photo to Wiley and Brusco.

The next photo was a wider shot, focusing on the lower part of the reflection. Harry had zoomed in on the reflection of the man's left hand. A perfectly clear image. He carried three videotapes. Sony stickers marked the outer cases.

"Videotapes?" Sterling thought aloud.

"You were right all along, Bledsoe," Brusco said. "The sonuvabitch wasn't there because he couldn't fall asleep. There's something on those tapes that he wanted."

"Wilson had a shoe box full of those tapes," Sterling said. "When I first went to his office, I saw them but didn't pay them any mind. They were sitting on one of the shelves in his closet." Sterling zoomed in on the gloved hand holding the tapes. The three men reexamined the photo. "He's a fairly tall man," Sterling said.

"How can you tell?" Wiley asked, looking at the computer screen.

"Look at how long his fingers are. And check out his arms, the way they reach far down his body."

Wiley and Brusco followed Sterling over to the dry-erase board and picked up the marker.

"We know it's a male," Sterling said, writing the word "male" on the board. Then he wrote "left-handed."

"How do you know he's left-handed?" Wiley asked.

Sterling took out his cell phone and tossed it to Wiley. "Go out the door, and then come back in."

Wiley looked confused but went along with the drill while the others watched. He left the room and returned a few seconds later. "Now what?" he asked.

"What hand is holding the phone?" Sterling asked.

"The right."

"What hand did you open the door with?"

"The left."

"Exactly. When people are carrying something they care about or don't want to drop, they put it in their dominant hand. Then they use the free hand for something that doesn't require fine motor skills, like opening a door."

"Not bad," Wiley conceded.

"There are tiny pieces of evidence all around us, Lieutenant," Sterling said. "The key is to look everywhere, especially in places you least expect to find them." He went back to the board and reviewed the photos of Wilson's body, then tacked on the new-photos of their number-one suspect. "Wilson's skull was cracked on the right side of his head," Sterling said. He fingered the blown-up photo that showed dried blood caked in the Professor's curly hair. "Exactly how a lefty would strike."

The officers stood around Sterling. "Let's get over to the hospital," he said. "I want to see how this woman was decapitated."

Withcott stood on a footstool, leaning over the table with his headlight focused on the remnants of the neck. He hummed as he worked, not bothering to look up when they entered. "Good afternoon, gentlemen," he said. "This was a vicious murder. Any idea who she might be?"

"None," Wiley said. "Nothing yet we can even remotely identify. No sign of clothes, purse, or anything personal. And nobody's filed a missing persons."

"There was quite a struggle," Withcott said, lifting up the badly bruised and scratched arms. Withcott turned her hands over. "Look at the cuts on the palmar aspects of her hands." Withcott pointed to the first web space of her right hand, the area between the thumb and index finger. A large, gaping wound that reached through the superficial and deep-tissue layers down to bone. Similar wounds stretched across the finger joints. "This injury pattern is classic for defensive knife wounds. She must've grabbed the blade several times in self-defense."

"Any idea what type of blade?" Sterling asked.

"That's what I was trying to figure out as you came in," Withcott said. "Come and take a look."

They moved to the neck. Wiley had never seen a decapitation before. He felt his stomach lurch and took deep, quiet breaths through his nostrils to keep from being sick.

Sterling put on a pair of gloves and moved closer to the body. "Look at the skin edges," he said. "They're jagged, not smooth like they would be if cut by a sharp knife."

"That's right," Withcott said. "The edges are not only torn, but there's a rather consistent pattern to how the skin is puckering."

"As if it were done by a machine," Sterling observed.

"You're reading my mind," Withcott said. His female assistant returned to the table with a folder and opened it. Withcott riffled through the photos and papers until he found what he wanted. "Look at this," he said, showing the photo to Sterling. It was of the wounds on Wilson's forearms.

"The cut pattern along the skin edges is similar," Sterling noted. "Maybe the same instrument."

"Very possible," Withcott said. "If you look here, the neck has been severed quite evenly."

Wiley took this opportunity to look the other way.

"Much different than what you'd expect if someone had been hacked at the neck," Sterling thought aloud. "An ax or heavy machine could cut quickly and decisively. But they wouldn't leave the skin edges jagged like this."

"And they would've shattered the cervical vertebrae," Withcott said, pulling back layers of red tissue and yellow-brown lobules of fat to expose the bones of the spinal column. One of the vertebrae looked as if it had been cut in half with even strokes. "An ax wouldn't be able to make such a clean cut."

"What's going on with the saw blade we found in Professor Bledsoe's body?" Wiley asked.

"It was sent to the state office to see if they could figure out the company that manufactured it and where the blades were sold," Withcott said. "We don't have an answer yet."

"That blade could be the critical link between the murders," Sterling said. "There's not much else to go on right now."

"There's something under the nails," Patrick, the lab assistant, said. He held the right hand of the corpse carefully, using a magnifying glass to examine the fingers.

Withcott took a closer look. He grabbed a pair of forceps and a small, hooked probe and carefully scraped underneath the fingernail of the woman's right index finger. He pulled back the forceps and carefully deposited the tiny debris on a sheet of white tissue paper. "Looks like skin," he said, carefully moving around the mangled debris. "Send it to the lab for DNA."

A thought suddenly came to Sterling's mind. He took off his gloves and walked to the door. "Let me know if anything else shows up," he said to Withcott. "You can reach me on my cell."

Sterling left without waiting for Wiley. He needed to take another look in his brother's lab, but this time with some help.

28

Sterling drove back to the campus and up Main Street. He took a quick detour to the Food Stop and picked up a cheesesteak with everything—except peppers. He continued to the center of campus, keeping a casual eye on the townspeople and students as they went about their business. This bucolic New England town hardly seemed like the setting for one brutal murder, much less two.

Sterling put his cheesesteak on the passenger seat, took out his cell phone, and dialed Sean Kelton's number. He'd gotten the home number of Wilson's lead post-doctoral student from Kay.

Sean had been expecting the call. All laboratory operations had been suspended pending the outcome of the investigation. Many of the researchers hadn't even been allowed back in to collect their personal items.

"I was hoping you'd go with me to the lab," Sterling said. "I want to take another look around, but I need someone who's more familiar with the layout."

"No problem, Mr. Bledsoe. When do you wanna go?"

"How soon can you get over there?"

"I live a few minutes past the golf course. I can be there in fifteen."

"I'll meet you outside," Sterling said. "What will you be wearing?"

"A bright red shirt with Big Red on it."

"I'll be waiting."

Sterling turned off Main Street and into the parking lot of the Grand Union. The area around the dumpster had been marked off with yellow police tape and orange pylons, and a crowd of curious onlookers had gathered. Several uniformed and plainclothes officers were still working the scene. Sterling recognized one of the officers who worked in the pit.

"How's it going?" Sterling asked.

"Trying to make sense of all this, Agent Bledsoe," the man answered. "Two murders like this so close together. The damnedest coincidence."

Sterling nodded slowly. "Hasn't been a murder in this area in over fifty years. Suddenly two murders within a week. I'm not buying coincidence. Have the store employees been questioned?"

"We've talked to everyone who was on duty when the body was found," the officer said. "Last night's crew doesn't come on till three o'clock, so we'll have to wait a couple more hours for them to get here. But so far, no one saw or heard anything strange when they arrived to work this morning."

"I'm not surprised. She probably wasn't murdered here. The body was brought here and dumped." Sterling left the officer and walked farther along the side of the building until he stood in the small area directly behind the store. He looked along the building and up at the lights attached just underneath the gutter. He walked back to the officer. "Is the manager here?"

"Over there, in the brown shirt," the officer said, pointing to a nervous-looking man raking his hands through what remained of his thinning hair. He was of average height and probably somewhere in his late forties. He had the disgruntled look of a chronic underachiever.

Sterling approached. "Agent Sterling Bledsoe," he said, extending his hand. "FBI."

"Miles Borwind," the manager said, his eyes darting back and forth.

"I was hoping to ask you a few questions," Sterling said.

"I've already told everything to the police. I don't know much."

Sterling looked away from the manager's darting eyes before they made him dizzy.

"Yes, I understand," Sterling said. He had plenty of practice dealing with nervous and uncooperative interviewees. Confrontation rarely worked. The trick was to make them feel at ease. "I'm sure you told them everything, but sometimes when you answer the same question a second time, it helps to jog your memory."

Borwind shrugged in resignation. Sterling noticed that he had a nervous tic that made him jerk his head slightly toward his right shoulder. "What time does the store close at night?"

"Eleven o'clock Monday through Friday and nine o'clock on the weekends," Borwind squeaked.

"Who's the last to leave?"

"I'm the weekday manager. I typically leave at five, then one of the assistant managers works till eleven and closes up."

"Who's that?"

"Kathy Geddes, but she didn't work last night. She called in sick, so I came back to close up."

"Did you leave out of the front or back door?"

"Back. I locked the front door from the inside, turned off the lights, and then left out the back." Borwind's tic settled down. Sterling's questions were easier than he had feared.

"When does the garbage truck come to empty the dumpster?"

"Three times a week. Monday, Wednesday, and Friday mornings. They collect the garbage before I open up in the morning at nine."

Sterling continued to enter the details in his book. He was about to put it away, then asked one more question. "Did you see any other vehicles in the back of the building when you went to your car?"

Borwind thought hard. The officers hadn't asked him that earlier. "Not really," he said, still thinking. "There was an old truck parked at the far end of the building, but no one was in it. It probably belonged to someone in one of the houses next door. Sometimes they park in the back of our lot even though we have signs all over telling people it's customer parking only."

"What did the truck look like?" Sterling asked.

"I didn't pay it much attention. One of those old pickups. It was a rusted red or brown. Nothing fancy. It had tall wood railings in the back to keep cargo from falling out." Borwind massaged his temples. "That's about it."

"Thanks a lot for your time, Mr. Borwind," Sterling said. He didn't make the mistake of extending his hand again. "I'm sure things will get back to normal soon."

Borwind sighed and shook his head. He glanced at the growing commotion around the dumpster before lowering his head and hurrying back into the safety of the store.

Sterling quickly surveyed the scene, then found the crime scene photographer and pulled him to the side. "Follow me," he instructed. The two disappeared behind the store.

"What are we looking for?" the photographer asked. He was a short, bald man with a rim of wispy black hair that seemed to be hanging on just for the heck of it. He carried two cameras around his neck and a portable flash big enough to light an entire studio.

"Tire tracks," Sterling said. "A truck was parked back here last night. There's a strong possibility it's linked to all this."

The two searched the lot, an empty asphalt surface with a heap of used boxes and crates haphazardly piled next to the door. The area was small, not more than thirty feet wide and a hundred feet long. A row of hedges and small trees separated the Grand Union's property from the adjacent houses. But there was enough of a gap between the trees to entice neighbors to ignore the "no parking" signs.

Sterling and the photographer walked shoulder to shoulder, their eyes fixed on the sandy, uneven surface. Then Sterling spotted something off in the corner where weeds and crabgrass sprouted through the cracked asphalt.

"Hold it," Sterling said, bending down over a faint impression. He traced tread marks, their grooves barely holding, vulnerable to even a strong wind. "Shoot this."

The photographer immediately went to work, snapping photos with the small camera first, then alternating with the bigger one whose long lens made it look like a menacing creature. As he snapped away, Sterling walked back in a semicircle and stopped. "This is another one," he said, pointing to the ground. The photographer reloaded the cameras, then sent off a flurry of flashes. By the time he finished, he had four rolls ready to be developed.

"How soon can we get these?" Sterling asked.

"A few hours. I'm using a developing outfit over in Norwich."

"As soon as they're ready, call me on my cell."

"Do you want me to bring them back to the pit?"

"No, just hold on to them."

"What are you looking for?"

"I want to see if these tracks match those we found on River Road and at the medical school. I have a strong suspicion they will."

29

Sterling noticed the bright red shirt from the other side of the lawn. Sean was patiently leaning against the building near the entrance.

"Sean Kelton?" Sterling asked as he approached.

"Mr. Bledsoe," Sean said, straightening up quickly. "I got here as fast as I could."

"I had to make a little stop before coming over."

"My condolences, sir. I apologize for not making the memorial service, but I was out of town visiting my in-laws in California. We only see them once a year, and that was this week."

"Not a problem, Sean," Sterling said. "And thanks."

"This is so unbelievable," Sean said, hanging his head, a mop of burnt-orange hair piled recklessly with nowhere to go. A series of freckles started high on his cheeks and marched across his face until they met on the bridge of his nose. "Everyone liked Professor Bledsoe," he said. "I can't imagine why anyone would kill him."

"Neither can I," Sterling said. "But when I first arrived here, a woman told me something that really started me thinking. She said, 'These mountains have secrets.' She wasn't lying."

Sterling and Sean rode the elevator in silence to the fifth floor. A uniformed security officer stood outside Wilson's lab, his hands clasped behind his back. All business.

"Agent Sterling Bledsoe," Sterling said. It was the first time he had seen this officer. Carlton must have already finished his shift.

"No one can enter the lab without special permission," the officer said stiffly. His face was full of pockmarks. Too much pimple popping when he was a teen. He had the rehearsed scowl of someone who had played a lot of cops-and-robbers as a kid.

Sterling pulled out his wallet and flashed his tin. He couldn't be mad at the man for following orders.

Awe stole over the man's sober expression. A real FBI badge. And it was shiny like those he had seen in the movies. "Sorry," he stammered. "Go ahead in."

Sterling and Sean entered the lab and closed the door firmly behind them. When they were out of earshot of the officer, Sean turned to Sterling. "That was cool," he said. "The Professor never told us that his brother worked for the FBI."

Sterling tossed Sean a pair of gloves. "I want you to walk me through every inch of this lab and tell me if you notice anything that seems to be out of place."

"Yes, sir," Sean said. "Where should we start?"

"Let's start at that end of the lab and work our way to Wilson's office."

Sean led Sterling to the far corner and began his investigation. He opened cabinets, pulled out drawers, and thumbed the books stacked underneath the windows. He even went to the storage cabinet and sifted through the shelves of test tubes, beakers, and graduated cylinders. The inspection took over an hour before they reached the door to Wilson's private office.

"Everything looks exactly like we left it," Sean said. "Professor always insisted on a clean and organized lab. He said the mind couldn't focus in a cluttered environment."

"Did you ever go into his office?"

"Sure," Sean said. "We usually went in to discuss our latest experiments or review the papers we were writing. Professor did most of his writing and correspondence in there."

Wilson's office was stuffier than Sterling remembered. He and Sean stood for a minute and looked around.

"I really can't tell you much about the office," Sean said. "We pretty much just sat on the couch and talked our problems out."

Sterling went directly to the closet and grabbed the box of tapes. He set it down on the desk and removed the lid. Like everything else in the laboratory, the tapes were neatly organized and clearly labeled. He emptied the tapes in numerical order. He stopped at tape forty-three. Tapes forty-four to forty-seven were missing. The numbers continued from forty-eight to fifty-one. The photo had shown the man carrying only three tapes. One tape was missing. It must've been the tape Sterling had found in the video camera locked away in Wilson's study.

Sterling remembered what Mandryka had said about Wilson almost completing the case report on the blackbirds. "Was there a special place you all kept the draft copies of the papers that were sent in for publication?" he asked.

"Professor had a very strict rule," Sean said. "Whoever the lead researcher was for that experiment was always entitled to first authorship on the paper. But that also meant they were responsible for putting together the first draft. And Professor was very specific about how he wanted us to deliver our drafts. When we were done, we would copy a version onto a diskette and leave that on his desk along with a printed version. We'd also e-mail him a copy. Then as a final precaution, we'd go to the post office and mail him a copy."

Sterling's eyes widened. "I understand being cautious, but that seems a little extreme."

"Yeah, but he had his reasons. He told us that a few years ago, one of his research assistants had written a twenty-page review article, references and all. She had written it on her laptop, but never backed it up. Her hard drive crashed when she was writing the last paragraph. They lost everything and had to start from scratch."

"I guess that's happened to all of us at some time or another," Sterling lamented. He had done the same thing as a grad student. It had cost the lab a $50,000 grant, something the director never let him forget. Sterling turned on the computer on Wilson's desk. A few seconds passed, a melody played, and the screen sprang to life. When the computer had finished booting, he moved the mouse and clicked on the icon for the computer's hard drive. The folder opened, but it was empty. "That's strange," Sterling said. "How could there be nothing on his hard drive?"

"That's impossible," Sean said. "Professor downloaded all the manuscripts on this computer. He liked to edit them here because his monitor is so large."

Sterling clicked on the recycle bin. "There's nothing in the trash, either," Sterling said.

"Let me take a look," Sean said. He clicked on the various icons, searching through different directories, even restarting the computer in hopes that it would bring everything back. Nothing. No documents. No application programs. Sean shook his head. "This doesn't make sense at all. Professor saved everything on his computer, and now there's nothing."

"What about backup?" Sterling asked. "Is there another computer in the lab that would have a backup of his files?"

"Never," Sean said. "The way the computers were configured, he had access to the hard drives on our computers but not the other way around. This is really strange."

"Did he ever use a laptop?"

"Professor hated laptops. He always complained that the keyboard was too small for his fingers. He liked his desktop because it had the expanded keyboard and oversized monitor."

Sterling paced around the office. Everything would be lost if Wilson hadn't backed up his files. Sterling searched the office again. The computer diskette holder was empty. He checked all the papers that had been printed out. Still nothing.

Then he saw that picture again—the one he and Wiley had noticed on their first inspection. Wilson and his students gathered on a lawn in front of one of the white academic buildings. Their faces were happy and free from worry. He spotted Kelton, but next to him, he saw another familiar face—Heidi Vorscht, Mrs. Potter's live-in help. Why was she in this picture? When he had told her that Wilson had been murdered on their property, she didn't even mention that they had been more familiar than just neighbors. She stood closest to Wilson in the picture, her hand lightly resting on his shoulder. There was a connection between them that didn't exist with the other students. Sterling's gut was at work again. He was certain Heidi hadn't told him everything. He slipped the picture inside his jacket.

Sterling turned his attention to the computer monitor, then knelt on the ground and searched the hard drive tower. He found what he was looking for and pulled out his black book. He wrote down the number that had been stamped on the back: DC 1617. "This is a college-issue computer," he said.

"How can you tell?"

"There's an inventory number stamped on the hard drive. Now the question is whether these computers are networked."

Sean thought for a minute. "I don't know, but the computer administrators would. They're over in a building called Kiewit."

"Where's that?"

"On the other side of the green. Can't be more than a ten-minute walk."

Sterling picked up the phone and dialed the operator. She connected him to the Kiewit administration office.

After five rings, a student's voice answered. "Kiewit Computing."

"What time do you close?" Sterling asked.

"The building's open twenty-four hours, seven days a week, except Christmas and New Year's."

"What about the administrators?"

There was a slight pause on the other end. "I'm not sure if anyone's still here. They usually leave around four."

"But that's ten minutes from now."

"Well, four, ten of four, same thing."

"If you see anyone from administration, please ask them to wait five minutes. I'm on my way over."

"Who should I say is coming?"

"Agent Sterling Bledsoe, FBI."

Sterling and Sean quickly closed the lab and raced down the hall. They took the stairs rather than wait for the elevators.

"I'm going to do this alone," Sterling said as they walked through the front door.

"I'm willing to help," Sean offered.

"You already have. I'll call you if anything else comes up." Sterling could see the disappointment on Sean's face, but at this point in the investigation, information containment was critical. He was also hoping to find the blackbird paper Wilson had been writing, and there was a good chance he might uncover it while at Kiewit. It was best to keep it all under wraps until he had a better handle on it.

As Sterling drove to Kiewit, his cell phone rang. It was Wiley.

"Where are you right now?" he asked.

"Just following up on some leads."

"Well, we've got some results from the lab today that might be of interest to you. Can you talk?"

"For a few. I'm all ears."

"Remember when you asked us to sweep the lab for fingerprints?"

"That's right, and compare them to everyone known to have entered the lab in the last month or so."

"Well, we did that. We got a list of everyone who might've entered the lab the last couple of months and fingerprinted them. Our guys entered the prints in the computer and ran a program that matched them against those collected in the lab."

"How many matches did you get?" Sterling raced to Kiewit, ignoring the red lights, stop signs, and one-way arrows.

"We were given a roster of eleven people that had entered the lab recently. But we found thirteen different sets of prints in the lab and his office."

"Two people unaccounted for."

"That's what's troubling us."

"Let me guess where you found one of those prints," Sterling said. "The computer keyboard in Wilson's office."

Sterling could hear Wiley shuffling papers. "How the hell did you guess that, Agent?"

"Let's just call it a hunch. Did you run prints on the custodial staff?"

"We've printed over a hundred people, everyone who cleans even a sidewalk on this campus. Nothing's turned up."

"Maybe they belong to people who visited the lab a while ago and no one remembers them. Are all the prints in the computer?"

"Yup, the matched and the two unmatched."

"Tell Brusco to transmit them down to the lab in Quantico and have them enter the unmatched prints into the federal computers. Our database will match them against prints of felons from every police station and law enforcement authority in the country."

"Do you really think that will tell us something?" Wiley asked.

Sterling slammed the Mustang to a stop in front of Kiewit. "It's a long shot, but it's worth a try. I've been surprised before. No reason why it can't happen again."

"I'll get on it right away."

"One more thing, Lieutenant. Any word yet on that saw blade?"

"I think they found the manufacturer. Now they're trying to find the shipping information to see if they can figure out which batch it was in and where it was sold."

"Thanks, Lieutenant."

Sterling jumped out of the car and raced into Kiewit. He followed the administration signs and ran down the narrow hall. The door was still open when he arrived at five minutes to four.

30

A woman with reading glasses perched on the tip of her nose sat behind a big metal desk that dwarfed her tiny frame. She looked up at Sterling, then impatiently at the clock. "May I help you, sir?"

"I'm Agent Sterling Bledsoe," Sterling said. Her expression suddenly grew cooperative. "I need to speak with someone who understands the networking of the campus computers."

"I think everyone might've left for the day," she said, stretching her neck to look down the back hallway. "Let me see if I can find someone." She looked at Sterling again, almost as if she were about to offer an apology, but instead stood up and walked through an open door in the back of the room.

Sterling looked around the office for any big computers or some indication that this was the campus computing hub. If the computers were networked, there had to be a large space where they kept the system hardware. Back at Hunter College, the network administrators occupied an entire floor of the IT building. Several students and managers sat in a dark room around the clock, budgeting their time between solving computer problems and playing video games when the phone lines fell silent.

The woman returned a few minutes later accompanied by a tall man with a thin build and white-blond hair that looked like it had been bleached in his kitchen sink. He had two-day-old beard stubble that seemed more calculated than accidental. His right earlobe had multiple piercings and was pulled down by a strip of alternating silver hoops and heavy studs. His black shirt bore an image of a rock band that Sterling didn't recognize.

"How can I help you, sir?" the man asked. He couldn't have been more than thirty. A hint of California slowed his delivery.

"I'm Agent Sterling Bledsoe."

"You're the one who called a few minutes ago?"

"That's right. I'm investigating Wilson Bledsoe's murder. I have some questions about his computer and the information that was stored on it. What's your name?"

"Jeff Cullins. I'm one of the system administrators."

"Just the person I need. Are the academic computers networked?"

"It all depends." The diminutive woman lost interest and disappeared through the back door. "We don't network all the computers, only those issued by the college and wired into the system."

"How do you know if the computer is on the network?"

"That's easy. Each computer has an inventory stamp on the hard drive beginning with DC. Stands for Dartmouth College. We keep a list of all the computers and where they're located."

"Does your office have a way of backing up the information stored on those computer hard drives?"

"Absolutely. That's a major reason why we networked everyone. Too many professors were forgetting to save their data and losing information. Then we had problems with viruses. People were downloading infected programs and crashing their hard drives."

"Can you retrieve the backed-up files from here?"

"Yes, but it takes some time to go through all the files. We have hundreds of computers on the network." Cullins looked down at his watch. "And we're just on our way out the door."

The woman returned wearing her coat and a straw hat with a fake butterfly attached to the side. "Good night, Jeffrey," she said as she left. "Good night, Mr. Bledsoe. My sincerest condolences. Professor Bledsoe was a beloved member of our community." Sterling acknowledged her sympathy with a nod, then she hung the closed sign and pulled the front door shut behind her. The echo of her clicking heels faded down the long, empty hallway.

"Let me be blunt, Mr. Cullins. I'm not here to learn how to change fonts and margins." Sterling flashed his tin for emphasis. "This is an official investigation, dammit, and I'm looking for a killer, some heartless bastard who carved my brother up like he was turkey on a dinner table. Now the sooner you cooperate and answer my questions, the sooner both of us can be on our way. Am I clear?"

Cullins looked back at the wall clock, then shrugged. He picked up the nearest phone and informed someone that he was going to be late. "Follow me," he said to Sterling. They walked through a maze of small rooms stuffed with large monitors and cables, then descended a long staircase. They passed through two unmarked doors and entered a large oval room crammed with computer equipment—everything from large flat-screen monitors to stacks of hard drives and switchers connected with an array of multicolored cables and tangled cords.

The terminals had been set up adjacent to one another around the perimeter. A row of printers sat on a long table in the middle of the room as did several trays of food that had been picked over. Six people were glued to the monitors—most of them young—but a couple of older men who looked like they were in charge sat behind a glass partition in what seemed to be a master control center. Soft-rock music buzzed over the din of noisy printers and fingers tapping on keyboards. Most of those working didn't acknowledge Sterling's presence, and those that did barely gave him a nod of welcome.

"We call this the wire hub," Cullins said. There was a hint of pride in his voice. "We're able to handle the entire campus network out of this one room." He took Sterling to an unoccupied terminal. "I'll begin a program to search for Professor Bledsoe's computer."

"I actually have the inventory number, if that'll make it faster," Sterling said, pulling out his book. "DC 1617."

"That's the easy part," Cullins said. "The key will be finding where his information is stored on our backup drives."

Cullins punched the keys with a flurry of movements. He bobbed his head to the music as hundreds of files and directories scrolled across the screen.

"How long do you save the backed-up files?" Sterling asked.

"Two months. There's a limit to how much we can store before we reach capacity. We figure sixty days is enough for someone to report missing data."

"Does the computer user have to do anything special to get their files backed up on your hard drives?"

"Nothing at all. Backups are automatic. We've configured the system so that every hour all files stored on each computer get saved here. We've also been testing a program that allows us to save not only the hard drive but every version of a document, for the entire two-month period."

Cullins worked in silence for the next twenty minutes, bringing up a series of screens with jumbled text messages that would only make sense to a techie. While Cullins continued his search, Sterling took a few minutes to reflect on the investigation. Tex Norkin and Buzz Gatlin had finally been released and were now back to barn rallies and preaching hate in Clare-mont. Many of the local officers had argued that they were making a big mistake letting them go, but Sterling held his position. He was sure that Wilson was murdered because of what he knew or had on those tapes. Why else would someone break into the lab hours after his death? And why were all of his files deleted from his computer?

Then the second murder. A young woman, decapitated and dumped in a trash bin. Norkin and Gatlin were in custody when it happened. It could be the random work of a serial killer, but more likely than not, the two murders were connected. Sterling's theory had the truck that Miles Bor-wind had seen behind the Grand Union as the same truck that Wilson had stopped to help the night he was murdered. All of this was somehow con-nected to the killing of hundreds of blackbirds. Dots of information, but still nothing certain enough to connect them.

"Shazam!" Cullins shouted. His face almost touched the computer screen. "She was hidden in the wrong directory. I don't know how that hap-pened, but here it is."

"How much is there?"

"Let me see." Cullins searched through four screens of document titles. "There must be a good two hundred documents."

"Does that include his e-mails?"

"No, those are in another directory. What we have here are just the documents that he worked on the last couple of months."

Sterling leaned closer to the screen. He wasn't surprised to see that Wil-son had been working on so many things over the last couple of months. Unlike many other intellectuals, Wilson actually produced results. With two textbooks and over two hundred articles to his name, he had accom-plished in a short time what most scientists couldn't dream of accomplish-ing in two careers.

"Is there any way to check which documents he worked on last?" Sterling asked.

"We don't have a program pre-designed to do that, but let me try something." Cullins's fingers danced across the keyboard. He twisted his face into a grimace as the computer sent back an error message. A few minutes later, a smile of confidence. "Voilà," he said, pushing back from the terminal so that Sterling could get a better view of the monitor.

"What did we do before we had technology?" Sterling said. He began reading the titles of the last one hundred documents, looking for anything that might have alluded to the blackbirds. Nothing caught his attention. "Are you sure these are all the documents?"

"One hundred percent. Anything your brother worked on over the last two months would be here in this directory."

"What if he erased a document? Would that also show up?"

"Yup. That's the beauty of this software. Even if he deleted a file, our system still keeps a backup here. Many professors have accidentally deleted manuscripts, grading reports, even their address books, and we've been able to restore them from our computers."

Sterling shook his head, still reading the titles but having no luck finding a document that sounded like it might have anything to do with the blackbirds. "How can I get a copy of these files?"

"Which ones?"

"All of them."

Cullins looked at his watch. "I could print them, but that could take at least half an hour. Could we do this first thing tomorrow morning?"

"Hell, no!" Sterling said. "There's already been two murders. I'm trying to prevent a third."

Cullins opened his eyes wide. "Another murder?"

Sterling continued to work him. "That's right. A young woman was found in the dumpster of the Grand Union this morning." Sterling spared him the details.

"This is fucking radical, man. Two murders here at Dartmouth? It's like something out of a bad movie."

"It's anything but a movie. A killer is on the loose, and we need everyone's cooperation to catch him before he strikes again."

Cullins didn't need any more prompting. He turned back to the monitor.

"I'm gonna print them over there," he said, pointing to the long row of printers. "I'm also gonna condense all the files and save them on some zip disks so you have an electronic backup."

Sterling watched as Cullins furiously tapped the keys and made the printers in the middle of the room jump to life. "What about his e-mails?" Sterling asked. "How difficult would it be to get those?"

"A piece of cake," Cullins replied. "The blitzmail files are much easier to access."

"What's blitzmail?"

"Our e-mail system. It was one of the first college-wide e-mail systems in the country. A couple of students were trying to figure out a way to send messages to each other and ended up inventing our e-mail program. You can access it from any computer on the network."

Cullins tapped the keys with a renewed sense of purpose. His eyes remained glued to the screen. "I can give you all the blitzmail files from his very first one," he said. "We store them on a different server. Printing them is gonna be a bear." He pressed several keys. "Professor Bledsoe has over eighty thousand e-mails."

"Then save them to a zip disk and just print the last two hundred."

"On its way to the printer," Cullins said.

After an hour and a half of papers flying out of the printer with Cullins inserting and ejecting disks, the task was complete. Sterling had a box full of documents and e-mails and a box of disks.

"I hope you find what you're looking for," Cullins said.

"There's not a doubt in my mind that I will."

Cullins walked Sterling upstairs and led him to the front door. "One question, Agent Bledsoe. If there's a killer on the loose, how safe are the rest of us?"

Sterling looked hard into his eyes. "We don't know when or even if this killer will strike again. If your front door has a lock, use it."

Sterling slipped out the front door of Kiewit and loaded the box and disks into the trunk of the Mustang. He hadn't had this much reading ahead of him since studying for his doctorate.

31

Forty-eight hours after the headless body had been discovered in the Grand Union dumpster, the police still hadn't identified it. Then the call arrived from Mrs. Nel Potter. Her live-in student, Heidi Vorscht, was missing. Mrs. Potter had last seen her two mornings ago as she left for class. It wasn't uncommon for Heidi to spend the night at a friend's apartment, especially if she had been studying late in the library. But two days of no contact was worrisome. "She never would have stayed away that long without having someone come by and check on me," Mrs. Potter said.

Sterling walked into the pit as the dispatcher finished the call.

"Nel Potter's girl is missing," Wiley said.

"The student we spoke to?" Sterling asked.

"Heidi Vorscht. Mrs. Potter hasn't seen her for a couple of days."

"Does the body fit her description?"

"Hard to say. Probably the same height. Young enough to match."

"Has she heard anything from the girl?"

"Not a word."

"Let's go."

Sterling and Wiley rushed over to the Potter farm, followed by a couple of cruisers. The door to the rambling farmhouse was slightly ajar when they arrived. Sterling knocked loudly, called out Mrs. Potter's name, and then pushed the door open. They found Mrs. Potter in the kitchen, standing over a sink full of dishes. Her hair was disheveled and her clothes unkempt. The stress of Heidi's disappearance made her look even older than her advanced years.

"Mrs. Potter," Sterling said, startling her. She turned off the running water and faced the group of officers who had rushed into her kitchen.

"This awful weather is a sign from God," she said, pointing out the window at the furiously gray sky. "It was just like this the day they killed Ezra on the back of the property. Shooting accident my foot."

"Come and have a seat, Mrs. Potter," Sterling said, helping the feeble woman to a chair at the small table. "Tell me what's happened."

Mrs. Potter rested her trembling hands on the table. A look of desperation turned down the corners of her mouth. "It's a most confusing affair. A few days ago Heidi was heading off to class like she does every morning. She fixed my breakfast and served it to me in my bedroom. Then she left."

"Did she say what her plans were that day?" Sterling asked.

Mrs. Potter looked out the window. "We didn't have much of a conversation. I don't like to talk much in the morning, especially before I've finished my breakfast. She simply said that she'd see me around dinnertime. She has exams coming, so she was spending a lot of time studying in the library."

"Do you know which library she studied in?"

Mrs. Potter shook her head. "I'm sure she's told me before, but I can't recall the name right now. I think it began with a K."

"Have you noticed anything different in Heidi's behavior the last couple of weeks?"

"Not really. She was studying a lot more, but like I said, she had exams coming." Mrs. Potter looked back out the window and sighed. "She still kept up with her chores around the house. She is good for that, you know."

"Did she have a boyfriend?"

"She never brought a boy home," Mrs. Potter said. "But kids are kids. She is an attractive girl, so I'd expect someone took a liking to her."

"Do you remember her talking on the phone to anyone who might've been special?"

"I don't know. I couldn't have heard most of what she said anyway, with my bad hearing."

"Try to think back, Mrs. Potter," Sterling insisted. "Can you remember anyone that might've called her?"

Mrs. Potter squinted hard. "Well, there was that one time we answered the phone at the same moment, and I heard her talking to a man. He had never called her before. At least not from what I remembered. She called him Clipper."

"What did they talk about?"

"I don't know. She took the phone upstairs and closed her door. She did that often. These kids like to have their privacy."

"Are you sure that was his name?"

"Positive. I laughed when I heard it. My grandfather's nickname was Clipper."

"Mrs. Potter, we found a body a couple of days ago," Wiley said. "It had been squeezed in a freight box and tossed in a dumpster."

The old woman leaned forward with an expression of anguish. The veins swelled under her thin pale skin. "Was it Heidi?"

"We don't know," Sterling said. "It was a woman, but she had been decapitated, and we haven't located her head."

Mrs. Potter fell back in her chair and buried her chin in her chest. Her shoulders twitched as she began to sob. She moaned words, but they were indecipherable.

Sterling waited before speaking. "Some of the officers are going upstairs to Heidi's room to take a look at things," he finally said. "We need some pictures and some strands of her hair to run genetic tests."

"What do you mean, genetic?" Mrs. Potter asked between sobs.

"Samples of her hair or from her toothbrush will give us cells to analyze in the laboratory. We can run special tests to see if they match the corpse. It's new technology. Pretty standard procedure nowadays."

"Which room is hers?" Wiley asked gently.

"The big one at the end of the second-floor hallway. Take the front steps and turn right." The sky had turned an angry black and rain thrashed against the old house. "Dear God, I hope it's not Heidi," she cried to the backs of the officers.

Everyone else in the room already knew that it was.

As word spread that the headless body found in the Grand Union dumpster belonged to graduate student Heidi Vorscht, fear paralyzed the small town of Hanover. The customary safety and innocence of the quiet mountains had quickly become a mere memory. A stream of concerned parents arrived in expensive foreign cars and marched to the front door of President Mortimer's mansion. They demanded proof that the campus was a safe place for their children.

Meddlesome reporters and aggressive cameramen from around the country descended on Hanover, renting every available room in the closest three towns. The journalists were relentless in their interrogations of the unassuming townspeople. Small children, the elderly, it didn't matter. Everyone was a potential source and equally liable to have a mike thrust in their face. Photographers snapped endless rolls of film for their scandal-hungry editors. Two gruesome murders in such an unlikely setting were sure to sell papers.

The Dartmouth Security office issued new guidelines that closed the sprawling campus to anyone without a direct affiliation with the school. The entrances to most of the academic buildings were guarded by security personnel who manned sensor machines and checked the identification of each person entering and leaving. State troopers had taken up posts around town, their presence comforting to some, a disturbing reminder of the recent tragedies to others.

The students had in a way created their own curfew, restricting their travel after dark. Even the menacing-looking football players moved in pairs after the sun faded. Hanover evenings, typically energized by students crisscrossing campus to the library or the Hop or Murphy's Bar and Grill on Main Street, were unnervingly quiet. Overnight, the Upper Valley had been transformed into a ghost town.

Fear hung in the air. Sterling heard it in the hushed tones and saw it in the eyes of the local police officers. The entire town was on edge, and so far there was no good reason to believe that things would get better anytime soon.

32

One trick to surviving long, exhaustive investigations is to find a reliable strategy to relieve the tension. For some, it's big dinners and plenty of liquid refreshment; for others, rented late-night movies. But for Sterling it was running. And this he did relentlessly—up at six, on the road for a five-mile run, then over to the Bagel Basement for his morning fare of juice, bagel, and the *New York Times*. The small shop was crowded this morning, so he decided to walk to the green where he could sit outside and catch up on matters around the world. Wilson had a satellite dish that captured all of the television stations and even some international programming, but that wasn't enough to make Sterling feel in touch. Like any New Yorker, he needed his copy of the *Times*.

As Sterling sat down, he looked around and noticed how quiet the campus had fallen since the discovery of Heidi Vorscht's body. He opened the paper to the sports section, always his first stop. He enjoyed a lengthy article on Barry Bonds of the San Francisco Giants, then read through the box scores of the baseball games, before he turned to national news. He glanced at the headlines. Then at the top of the second page he saw an article: "Yankee Clipper Sets Sail." Sterling closed his eyes and put down the paper. It wasn't the ship that had caught his attention but the name—Clipper. He remembered where he had heard it before. Mrs. Potter had said that a man with that name had called Heidi days before her death. But he had also seen the name somewhere else. He thought back over the last several days. It had been written on something he had seen in passing. He checked his notes. He could find only the reference from Mrs. Potter. Then it came to him—President Mortimer's office. At least, that's what he thought.

He dialed Mortimer's office and got the world's happiest receptionist.

"It's Agent Bledsoe," Sterling said.

"Good morning, Mr. Bledsoe. It's Vivian Sinclair. How can I help you?"

"I think I might've dropped something in President Mortimer's office the other day."

"Are you sure? No one turned in anything to me."

"It was a special silver pen that a friend gave me. It's very small. Someone could've easily overlooked it. Is President Mortimer there?"

"No, he and the rest of the staff will be gone all day. They're over at the business school for a big fund-raiser. Lots of VIP alums are up for some events. Gotta keep the money coming in."

Perfect, Sterling thought to himself. "I'll stop by and take a look myself if you don't mind. It's so small, someone could've stepped on it or kicked it without even knowing."

"Are you sure you want to come all the way over here? I can go check and call you if I find it."

"I know you're busy there by yourself, so I don't want to bother you. It's just as easy for me to come over. I'm only a few minutes away."

Vivian agreed and Sterling wasted no time getting to Parkhurst. She greeted him with her permanent smile as he entered the office. How could anyone be so damn cheery all the time? She showed him back to the office and got on her hands and knees with him as he pretended to search for the pen.

"I was sitting here," he said, walking closer to the desk. "Maybe it rolled under." As he leaned back toward the floor, he found exactly what he had come for. There it was—the picture of Serena Mortimer in her cheerleading uniform and the inscription *To Clipper with love. Serena.* What were the chances that this was the same Clipper whom Mrs. Potter overheard speaking with Heidi?

"I guess it's not here," Sterling finally said. "Maybe I dropped it in the car."

"I'm sorry, Mr. Bledsoe. Do you think you can get another one?"

"Probably not," Sterling said. "I've had that pen for fifteen years."

As Vivian walked Sterling to the heavy glass doors, an idea popped in his head and he took a gamble. "I'm sure you really miss Heidi around here," he said.

"Words can't describe," Vivian sighed. "She was such a beautiful girl in every way."

"What did she do?"

Vivian thought for a moment. "A little bit of everything, I guess. She really didn't have an official position."

"Did she work directly with you?"

"Not really. She spent most of her time with the president."

"Sort of his personal assistant?"

"I guess you could say that. She was one smart cookie. I know he thought the world of her. She was so ambitious. Most of the students that are lucky enough to get a job here must go through the whole application process. But Heidi just walked in one day and asked to meet the president. Didn't even have an appointment. I normally would've turned her away, just showing up like that, but she said she'd wait all day if necessary. He agreed to meet with her for a few minutes, and she's been around ever since."

This surprised Sterling. Why hadn't anyone from Mortimer's office called when the body had finally been identified as Heidi Vorscht? If she had been so beloved, then why had everyone, including Vivian, remained quiet about their connection to her?

"Do you know if she spent a lot of time at the Mortimers' home?" Sterling asked.

Only the two of them stood in the room, but Vivian still looked around nervously. She grabbed Sterling by the arm and led him into an empty office. She didn't speak again until the door was closed.

"I don't mean to talk out of school," she whispered. "But Mrs. Mortimer was not one of Heidi's fans. I never could really figure it out, but those two were like oil and water."

"How did you know something was wrong?"

Vivian shook her head. The smile was gone. "You had to be deaf, dumb, and blind not to notice. This is an awful thing to say, and I don't want you to get the wrong impression. I really don't make a habit of listening to other people's conversations, but I happened to be walking by one day and the president's door was open just a little. He was talking so loud I couldn't help but hear. He wasn't saying very nice things to Mrs. Mortimer, and I kept hearing him mention Heidi's name."

"Was Heidi in the office with him?"

"No, she had just stormed out crying minutes before. I asked her what was wrong, but she said she was too upset to talk about it. The president and Mrs. Mortimer must've argued for another twenty minutes."

"Did anyone else hear it?"

"No, everyone had left for the day but me. It was an awful afternoon. Of course, I've heard him yell before, but that day it was something altogether different."

"If Heidi and Mrs. Mortimer had such bad blood, why would he keep Heidi around?"

"Heidi was a special girl," Vivian said. She was still whispering and holding on to Sterling's arm. "Heidi had an irresistible charm. The president tried his best to soothe things over between her and Mrs. Mortimer. Nothing worked."

"An unfortunate situation," Sterling said, opening the door. They walked back to the reception area. "Give me a call if anyone knows about that pen," he said.

"I'm sorry we couldn't find it."

Sterling shrugged. "Don't worry. It always shows up when I least expect it." He walked out the door certain he had found something much more valuable than a silver pen.

Sterling walked back to the green and found a quiet bench. He scribbled some notes into his book, then dialed Sean Kelton's number. Sean was standing next to Heidi in the picture on Wilson's desk. His wife answered the phone, and Sterling could barely hear her over the screaming baby in the background. Exactly why Sterling wasn't ready to walk down the aisle. She told him that Sean had left an hour ago to run some errands in town. She gave him his cell phone number.

"What can you tell me about Heidi Vorscht?" Sterling asked when he reached Sean.

"Not much. I didn't spend much time with her."

"Was she one of Wilson's lab assistants?"

"I'm not so sure I'd call her that. Supposedly she had an interest in our research, but the craziest thing is that she was getting her master's in engineering at the Thayer School."

"Then why was she working in the lab?"

"We never could make the connection. And I wouldn't exactly call what she did work. She was just around. Then all of a sudden she stopped coming in."

"When was that?"

"A few months ago."

"Did she have an argument with someone?"

"Not that I know of. We just noticed that she wasn't stopping by and chatting up Professor like she used to."

"What did she and Wilson talk about?"

"Not sure. They always closed the door when she went into the office. Supposedly her dad had committed suicide right after she arrived at Dartmouth. We just figured she was having a difficult time adjusting."

"This is an important question, Sean, so I want you to think hard before you answer it. Do you ever remember Heidi talking about a boyfriend?"

There was a pause. "Never," he said. "And I always found that strange. She was a very pretty girl, but she never talked to any of us about a boyfriend. To be honest, the other girls thought she was kind of strange. They said that whenever the conversation got too personal, she'd just clam up or change the topic."

"Do you know the names of any of her friends?"

"No. She was a loner. I never saw her with anyone, even when she was walking on campus. Guys thought she was cute, but she gave off the vibes that she just wanted to be alone."

"Thanks, Sean. You've been a big help."

"Are you guys any closer to figuring this out?"

"A hell of a lot closer than when we started."

33

$\mathcal{S}$pring comes much slower in the mountains than it does in the lower-lying areas. Winter slides into hibernation grudgingly, unleashing punishing freezes well into April. Sterling welcomed the morning chill. With two miles left in the run, he inhaled the crisp morning air deeply. Running in the quiet of the wilderness the last couple of weeks had spoiled him. There were no honking yellow cabs or heavy black exhaust fumes blowing out the back of city buses. Instead, he was treated to the cries of the wild and the relaxing sound of the powerful river awakening for its southern journey. This was Sterling's favorite part of the day, when he was left alone to sift his thoughts.

The last part of the run was mostly downhill, giving Sterling a jump-start to his final kick. His strides were long now and his breathing rhythmic. He galloped down River Road, then up Deer Run Lane, turning into the driveway and finishing the last thirty yards in a dead sprint. When he reached the front of the house, he quickly looked at his watch and slowed to a jog around the circular drive. As always, he finished at the large birch tree in the front yard.

He hadn't noticed the small red car parked on the side of the house.

"Mr. Bledsoe," a man's voice called.

Sterling jumped out of his stretch. An enormous tanned-skin man with jet-black hair stared down at him. Menacing. His features were wide and heavy, his countenance could only be described as serious. Very serious. Everything about him was big, including the clothes that draped his mountainous mass. He wore a dark leather headband that matched the turquoise-studded vest just visible under his colorful shawl.

Sterling had already planned two escape routes by the time he spoke.

"Who are you?" Sterling asked.

"They call me Bigfoot," the man grunted. He hadn't walked fifteen yards and he was already short of breath. "I've come to take you to Kanti."

"Who the hell is Kanti?"

"Our leader. Ahote gave you the message?"

Sterling remembered the paper she had slipped him the day of the memorial service. "Yes, she said that someone would come looking for me. What the hell took so long?" Sterling's attempt at comic relief was dead on arrival. The gigantic man's face never cracked.

"Kanti does things according to his schedule," Bigfoot said. "Now he's ready to meet with you."

"I'll go in for a quick shower and change. Want to come in for some coffee?"

"No thanks," Bigfoot said, shaking his massive head. "Your kind of coffee has become a drug in this society. I will wait out here."

Sterling rushed into the house. He had almost forgotten about the conversation he had had with Ahote and her insistence that he would be contacted when the time was right. Sterling finished his shower, threw on some fresh clothes, and grabbed his gun and black book. He plucked a banana off the counter, then went outside to follow the large messenger.

Bigfoot shifted his wide girth into the small red car and immediately flattened the two tires on that side. Sterling laughed to himself, remembering something his mother had said to him when he was a little boy. *For some reason, big men love small cars. I've never understood why.*

He followed Bigfoot down River Road, but instead of turning left to cross Ledyard Bridge into the center of Hanover, Bigfoot took a right and climbed into the layered hills of Vermont. Sterling had never been in this part of the Upper Valley, but it was even more remote than what he had already seen. Except for an occasional sign that warned motorists of deer crossings, there was little if any indication that human life was welcome in this great wilderness. They spent most of their journey negotiating winding roads that climbed for short stretches and then fell in others. Every few hundred yards a mailbox showed up near the edge of the road, tucked under bushes and large branches. The houses, however, couldn't be seen behind the impenetrable wall of wide trees and wild vegetation.

The red car made a sudden turn into the woods, then scraped along a dirt road that curved its way up the mountain. Bigfoot's car kicked up rocks into the grill of the Mustang, and they hit the metal like pellets fired from a BB gun. Sterling was relieved that the Mustang was only a rental. Had it been his Porsche, he wouldn't have had kind words for Bigfoot, however many tons the man had on him.

When they reached the top of the mountain, Bigfoot stopped his car in a small clearing. Sterling didn't see any signs or houses, just trees and wild hedges. The red car rose nearly a foot and sighed as Bigfoot made his exit. He lumbered over to Sterling. "Park it here," he instructed. "We must walk the rest of the way." Bigfoot detected doubt in Sterling's face. "Kanti doesn't allow motor vehicles of any kind on his property. The noise and fumes are not one with nature.".

Sterling reluctantly turned off the Mustang and took a quick look at the tiny nicks in the grill. They were small enough to escape the detection of the car rental agency, but another five minutes behind the red car and he would have had a lot of explaining to do. He followed Bigfoot along a zigzagging path of trampled weeds and grass. Every few yards they ducked underneath branches or stepped over fallen limbs. Sterling heard Bigfoot's labored breathing as the rough terrain pushed him to his limits.

Sterling wondered if his meeting with Kanti would shed any light on the intruder who had almost blown his head off. He kept his Beretta tucked inside his waistband for the unexpected.

A few more minutes and suddenly they emerged from a thicket and entered a large clearing. An imposing log cabin stood in the middle of a perfectly groomed oval lawn, flanked by what in summer would surely be a riot of blooms. The sun at that moment shone directly on the house and the lawn, so that it felt much warmer than it had in the woods. It was peaceful. The house and its landscaping looked as if God had woken one morning and decided to drop a swath of paradise on top of the mountain.

Bigfoot and Sterling were about to walk up the front steps of the house when a shrill cry filled the sky. Sterling had never heard anything like it before, halfway between a scream and a demonic laugh. "Kanti is in the back," Bigfoot said. "Follow me." They walked around to the back of the house and the most breathtaking vista Sterling had ever seen. The lawn extended for about a hundred yards, then the trees suddenly disappeared and all of the mountains and valleys that one could ever dream of seeing at once slipped into view. Sterling felt like he was in heaven looking down on earth. Another deafening cry cracked the air, but this time it was followed by short bursts of a whistle.

Bigfoot continued toward the edge of the lawn, where they finally spotted the source of the cries. A small man stood with his back to them, looking up into the sky, slowly surveying the air as if he were expecting something to fall. His shiny black hair had been tied into a ponytail and rolled up around a thin red stick that stuck to the back of his head. He wore a long leather dress that draped from his shoulders to his ankles. His small feet were buried in fur-lined moccasins.

Bigfoot walked to within ten feet behind the small man, then refused to take another step. He put his finger to his mouth to keep Sterling silent.

The little man, still not acknowledging their presence, let out another cry. He put his hands to his mouth as if he were going to shout, cupped them, then quickly opened and closed his fingers as the strange sound escaped his throat. It was the most unusual sound Sterling had ever heard. When the cry was over, the man once again rotated his head, looking into the sky. Suddenly, a flock of blackbirds appeared overhead, flying a few hapless circles before making their descent some fifty yards away. They had been drawn to a specific area in the lawn that seemed familiar to them as they landed and immediately shoved their beaks into the ground.

Over the next few moments the small man watched the birds ravenously forage on the land. When he was content that they were well fed, he turned to welcome his visitors.

The small man faced Bigfoot. "Kwe-kwe," he said in friendly tones. Bigfoot closed his eyes and slightly bowed his head. "Good morning, Mr. Bledsoe," the man said, extending his right hand to Sterling. He was certainly old, but it was difficult to tell his age. There were deep wrinkles at the corners of his eyes and a couple across his forehead, but in some places his skin still had the appearance of youth. His features were more regal than they were handsome, and he looked as if life had been kind to him over the years. "My name is Kanti. Welcome to our land."

"It's a pleasure to meet you, Kanti," Sterling said. "That's some skill, the way you called those birds from the sky."

Kanti turned and looked at the birds digging into the ground. A smile had softened his face when he turned back to Sterling. "Those birds are like family to me. They are the red-winged blackbirds, the most noble of their kind. Look at how they work for their food." The three men stood in silence and watched the birds walk around each other, planting their bills in the ground, spreading the earth.

"What exactly are they doing?" Sterling asked.

"In your language, it's called gaping. You see, one of the remarkable things about the blackbird is their unusual way of feeding. The secret to their success is that they can find prey that's unavailable to other birds. This allows them to be great hunters. They can feast on several types of food and in many different habitats. Let's walk a little closer."

Sterling and Bigfoot followed Kanti as he softly walked in a zigzag fashion toward the birds. They were no more than fifteen feet away when he stopped. "Look closely at their bills."

Sterling focused on the faces and their short, pointed bills. They were continuously at work, spreading the earth and plunging into the ground. Some were chomping on black-and-white seeds, while others pulled up wet, succulent earthworms from the ground. If nothing else, they were persistent, repeatedly striking the ground, struggling to open their bills in the hard earth. If one direction didn't work, they changed positions, rearranged their bills, and dug back in.

"There aren't many other birds that have mastered this skill," Kanti said. "Only the starlings, crows, jays, and magpies search for their food this way. If you were to watch them long enough, you'd even see them flipping over tiny stones and small branches on the ground, exposing the insects attached to the undersurfaces."

Kanti turned back to the birds. Sterling could see that whatever the reason was he had been brought here, it would be up to Kanti to decide when he wished to explain it. He couldn't be rushed into conversation. Sterling looked at the birds, then at the distant mountains and valleys in their muted colors. Patience in this encounter would be essential.

"Follow me," Kanti said. He moved quickly and deliberately through the woods, ducking under branches and stepping over water-soaked ground. They walked for a few minutes until they came to a marsh the size of a football field. Kanti guided them to the other side, then stopped when they approached a small patch of ground whose fresh soil looked as if it had been recently turned. He grabbed a nearby stick and moved the soil with smooth raking motions. After a couple of minutes he stopped. "Look at that."

Sterling looked into the small hole and saw a pile of bird carcasses. He could tell they were red-winged blackbirds, like those he had seen in Professor Mandryka's lab, by the red tuft of feathers surrounding the shoulder of each wing. Epaulet was the word that Mandryka had used to describe the area.

"There are hundreds of these birds buried here," Kanti said. "I've put them in the ground with my own hands."

"What are they dying from?" Sterling asked. He wondered if Mandryka and Kanti knew of each other's work.

"The white man's poison for sure," Kanti said, kicking the soil back over the birds until they were no longer visible. He walked a few feet from the burial ground and looked over the marsh. "I've been playing with these birds since I was a little boy. My grandfather taught me their customs and cries, and I watched as he fed the hungry and mended the sick. They have been an important part of my life, and we've had thousands of them on our property over the years. They like this area back here."

"What's so special about this land?" Sterling asked. Bigfoot stood silently and listened.

"The red-winged blackbird may be the most abundant bird in North America, but it hasn't always been this way," Kanti explained. "One of the major reasons their numbers have grown is the increasing amount of lakes and marshes like this. Great feeding grounds. Blackbirds live and breed where food is most available."

"How do you know it isn't the food that's killing them?"

"I don't know for sure," Kanti said. "And that's why I sought your brother's counsel. I had been told that he knew the land and animals as if he were one of us."

"You knew Wilson?"

"We all knew and loved Askuwheteau. That was his Algonquin name—Always Keeping Watch. He had great eyes and curiosity. Nothing got past him. He was sent to us by God. His work was that of honor. He used his knowledge for the advancement of all living things, doing good in a world where there's much evil."

Sterling decided to take a chance and push the conversation. "What did Wilson say about these blackbirds?"

"It's funny how things happen sometimes," Kanti said. As he walked along the edge of the marsh, Sterling stayed beside him. Bigfoot dutifully followed. "About a year ago I started to notice dead birds back here on the property. At first I thought they were killed by other birds or ground animals, but the numbers were too great and I couldn't find any fighting wounds on their bodies."

Kanti stepped closer to the water's edge and pointed along its perimeter. "This is why they like it back here. This land is full of insects. Grasshoppers, butterflies, spiders, snails, and worms. In other parts of the country like the West and Midwest, they live off the flower seeds and corn. Your brother, Mr. Bledsoe, was on to something. Too many birds have died out here the past year for this to be an accident. Askuwheteau was brought to me, because he was finding dead red-wingeds on his property and the adjacent lands."

"How did he know you were also finding dead birds?"

"He didn't at first. One of our friends overheard him discussing blackbirds with a woman who lives near the river. He spent many hours walking along her property. First, he only noticed a couple of dead birds. Then the farther out he went, the more he found. They were stacked in groups of ten and twenty."

"Was this woman Nel Potter?"

"You know her?"

"We've met."

"I've never met the woman, but Askuwheteau was very fond of her. He told me she was quite generous with her land and allowed him access whenever he wanted."

"Did he tell Mrs. Potter about the dead birds?"

"He didn't want to tell her something like that on account of her age. He was concerned that involving her in something like this would only worry her unnecessarily. That was his way, always thinking about others."

Sterling thought a minute before speaking. "Who was this friend who brought Wilson to you?"

Kanti took a couple of more steps with his head down, then stopped. "A beautiful young woman whose passion for nature was as great as my people's. She was one of us born in their skin. We called her Wogan—someone who loves nature. They called her Heidi."

"Heidi Vorscht!" Sterling exclaimed. His words hung in the open air until the wilderness swallowed them. "Dammit! Of course. That's the connection I couldn't make."

"What connection?" It was now Kanti's turn to inquire.

"Heidi Vorscht's body was found a few days ago in a dumpster outside of the Grand Union in Hanover. Her killer had beheaded her."

Kanti looked away, pained. "Yes, I was informed that her life had been taken with such indignity." He shook his head. There were tears in his eyes. His voice was softer now, like that of a grieving father. "The evil forces that menace this great world are often beyond even my ability to comprehend."

"I knew that her murder must've had something to do with Wilson's, but for the life of me I couldn't draw the connection," Sterling said. "I only met her once, but she had asked me what would come of his blackbirds. She called him a crusader. She must've known something was going on."

"Wogan knew everything," Kanti said. "Like I said before, she brought Askuwheteau to us. Her dedication was like no other."

"They brought some of the birds?"

"They brought a couple of them, but the pictures are really what got my attention."

"Pictures?"

"He used a video camera to record the dead birds. There were hundreds of birds on the ground. It was the worst sight I'd ever seen. I was sick for days after watching that video." Kanti turned to Bigfoot, who nodded in agreement.

"When did he last show you this video?"

"The same day he was killed. He came out the day of his celebration party. I remember him complaining about having to attend a party at the president's mansion. He was happy to win that prize, but he didn't want to make a big fuss over it. Forever modest."

It hit Sterling then that the last tape Wilson had shown Kanti was the tape he had found in the camera, the tape the intruder had come back looking for. Sterling could barely keep up with the thoughts racing through his mind. He was sure now that he had his motive. Wilson and Heidi had been murdered because they knew about the blackbirds. But something didn't fit. Professor Yuri Mandryka and Kanti also knew about the blackbirds, but they hadn't been harmed. Either the murderer hadn't struck yet or he simply didn't know that the other two also knew about the birds. They desperately needed to find the man in that surveillance video before someone else died.

"Who do you live with?" Sterling asked.

"I live among my friends," Kanti said, sweeping his arm in a wide gesture. "All of the animals you see and don't see are part of my life."

Sterling turned to Bigfoot. "There have been two murders already, and we don't have any idea who's behind the killings. You need to protect Kanti." Bigfoot nodded his head solemnly. "Around the clock. This killer can strike anytime."

"Do you have any idea who might be behind all of this?" Kanti asked.

"Not right now. But I believe whoever's killing these birds has killed my brother and Heidi Vorscht."

The three men began walking back toward the house. A light gust of wind rustled the trees and stretched the necks of the tall cattails. The land looked serene.

"Do you remember the last thing you discussed with Wilson?" Sterling asked.

Kanti closed his eyes in thought. "Askuwheteau said he had a good idea what was killing the birds and who was responsible. He was waiting for a response from an agency in Washington."

The three approached the house. Kanti pointed to the bare feeding ground. "They've taken food back to feed their little nestlings. In the next few months, those nestlings will make their first trip here to my property, and I'll train them like I've trained thousands before them."

"I'll be in touch," Sterling said. Bigfoot turned to accompany him, but Sterling shook his head. "No, you stay here. I can find my way back to town."

"May Glooskap guide your most noble mission," Kanti said. "Glooskap is our spirit of good. He formed the sun and the moon, animals, fish, and the human race. His brother Malsum is the evil spirit, the one who made mountains, valleys, serpents, and every manner of things which he thought would provide an inconvenience to the race of men."

"What does your name mean?" Sterling asked.

"Kanti is an Algonquin name. My grandfather gave it to me when I was a little boy. The first few years of my life, I didn't speak language like other children. Instead, I imitated the sounds that I had heard in the wild. Kanti means 'sings.' My grandfather always said that I sang with the animals. That's how I learned the call of the blackbird."

"If you eat off the land, be careful," Sterling said. "Whatever's poisoning those birds could also be affecting the rest of the wildlife."

Kanti nodded his head sternly and took Sterling's hand. He held it firmly for a few seconds and with his free hand made a small gesture, mouthing what seemed to be a prayer. "Go in peace and wisdom," he said.

Sterling looked into the eyes of the small man, then up at Bigfoot, before quickly turning and disappearing down the narrow path that had delivered him.

34

The sharp ring of Sterling's cell phone snapped him awake. "Yeah," he answered, too tired to say much of anything else.

"Wiley here. Did I wake you?"

Sterling looked at the clock on the nightstand. "That sounds about right."

Wiley was unapologetic. "Well, I wouldn't have called if it wasn't important. We just got another e-mail from your friends in Virginia."

This made Sterling sit up. He wiped his eyes and took another look at the clock. "It's eleven o'clock."

"Yup. The overnight desk commander called me at home."

"There must be something in there Harry wants me to see right away." Sterling slipped into his pants. "Otherwise he could've waited till morning."

"That's my guess. Somebody there is burning the midnight oil."

"Don't open it. Call Brusco and get him over there. I'll be there in fifteen."

Sterling sped along River Road, wondering if Wilson was up in heaven sending down help to catch the killer. He crossed Ledyard Bridge, eerie-looking as thick layers of menacing fog hunched quietly over the dark water. By the time Sterling had reached Lyme Road, he didn't even notice the car was pinned over 100 miles per hour. He pulled into the police station before the sleep had cleared from his eyes. There were only two cruisers parked underneath the massive evergreens that towered over the squat building. That's strange, he thought to himself. There were usually ten or more lined up. Maybe they were getting serviced overnight. Sterling made his way through the side door and down the short hallway that led to the pit. The room was empty. The quietest it had ever been. It looked different without all the frenzied activity, more like a classroom than the nerve center of a major investigation. Wiley stood alone facing the big board. He wore a uniform even at this late hour. He didn't turn when Sterling came in.

"You know, Agent Bledsoe, I'm sitting here looking at this board trying to put these two murders together," Wiley said. "But it's just not making a lot of sense. Where's the damn motive? The night of a big bash celebrating his award, the Professor is mysteriously murdered and no one sees or hears anything? Bullshit! It's not like he had death threats against him or some property feud with a neighbor."

Sterling considered revealing the dead blackbirds in Mandryka's lab and the gunshots Carlos Sandoza heard after Wilson had left the party. He could also explain the meaning of Chogan. But his instincts kicked in. In cases like this, when it was unclear who knew what and what their potential connection was to the murder, it was always best to work a lead alone until there were concrete answers. It wasn't that he didn't like Wiley. The lieutenant was tough, determined, and proud as hell to be a police officer. In fact, he was one of the best local cops Sterling had come across in a long time. Lessons, however, often came hard, and Sterling had learned early in his career that solo work was especially needed in cases as sensitive as this one.

"The killer has struck twice, which doesn't necessarily make him a serial killer," said Sterling, "but it does get me thinking. For the sake of argument, let's say we are dealing with a serial killer. The most important thing to nail down is the thread—the connection between the choice of victims. It can be easy at times, but it can also be the most difficult part of the investigation. I've found in previous cases that once you firm up that connection, the rest of the answers you've been searching like hell to find just jump out at you."

"Maybe we're making too much of a possible connection," Wiley said. "It could be a coincidence that the two murders happened so close together."

Sterling looked up at the board. "Think about it, Lieutenant. Do you really believe it's a coincidence that a peaceful community like this that hasn't seen a murder in more than fifty years suddenly has two of them in the span of a week? And we're not talking about simple murders, a barroom brawl that turns deadly or a wife's jealous rage. These killings were gruesome. Evil. The killers weren't leaving any doubts that the victims were dead. And they did a helluva job covering their tracks."

"What about the saw blade?"

"The only mistake we've seen and one they couldn't erase. I don't have to tell you, Lieutenant, that committing the perfect murder is a lot more difficult than most people think. A lot of nerves and adrenaline are involved."

"I agree. It just doesn't make sense," Wiley said, rubbing his temples in slow circular motions. "Something's missing."

"Where's Brusco?"

"He called in while you were on your way. Said to go ahead without him. He'll catch up when he gets here."

Sterling shrugged. It was unlike Brusco to be late, especially for something important like this. He went over to the computer. "For them to send this so late, Harry must've really wanted us to see something." Sterling opened the e-mail and read Harry's message.

> Sterle,
>
> We worked with the colors and contrast. We also took the liberty of playing with the face a little. We've got a new kid down here from California who's a wiz at this stuff. It's not perfect, but it'll give you a little something to work with. I'll be out of town the next few days, but if you need me, I'll be up at the house in the Adirondacks. I hear the fish are biting like hell, and I could use the break. The number is the same.
>
> Warmest,
>
> Harry

A smile grew across Sterling's face. No one loved fishing more than Harry Frumpton. Sterling had gone on a weekend trip with him once a few years ago. A lover of cities and all their modern trappings, Sterling had been slow to adjust to the rural village of Tupper Lake. But by the second day of relaxing in the hypnotizing quiet of the wilderness, away from gridlock and honking horns, Sterling understood why Harry was always counting the days until his next outing.

Sterling clicked the download icon. Only one picture this time. Unlike the other images, this one began revealing from the bottom of the screen. It was immediately obvious that the clarity and resolution were much better than on the previous photos. What the video camera hadn't captured, the computer had generated and filled in with color. First his neck, long and caramel colored. His chin came to a handsome point with stubble sprouting sporadically, heavier on the sides of the face.

Then his lips, full and symmetric, a soft pink tinged with brown. The image pixels slowly revealed smooth skin with a faint hint of beard shadow. The nose was narrow, the bridge slender and straight.

"I'll be right back," Wiley said abruptly.

Sterling waved his hand and kept his eyes glued to the screen. Not exactly the hard face of a murderer, he thought to himself. The image continued to crystallize, and Sterling got the strange feeling that he had seen the face before. It was a black man, light-skinned.

The complete image finally uploaded.

"What the hell is this?" Sterling shouted. He looked in amazement at the computer screen.

The image he saw was himself.

He stood there for a few seconds, his mind struggling with what his eyes clearly saw. A burning wave of pain exploded upward from the base of his skull. Confused, he turned to get Wiley. But Wiley was already there—pointing a service revolver inches from Sterling's face.

"We need to talk, Agent Bledsoe. You've got a lot of explaining to do."

"What the hell are you doing, Lieutenant? Have you lost your goddamn mind? Get that gun out of my face!"

"Not until we reach an understanding," Wiley returned. "Now don't do anything we'll both regret. Slowly open your coat and let it drop to the ground."

Sterling complied, keeping his eyes on Wiley's finger hooked around the trigger. Just a slip and he was a dead man.

"Okay," Wiley said. "Now take your gun out slowly. Put it on the floor and kick it over to me."

Sterling followed Wiley's command. Once the gun had come to a stop across the linoleum, he raised his hands. "Do you really think I killed my own brother?" he asked.

"I'm not sure what to think," Wiley said. "All I know is there are a lot of unanswered questions and your face is staring at me from that computer screen."

Both men looked back at the computer. Sterling felt dizzy.

"That picture is bullshit," Sterling said, "and you know it. There has to be an explanation for it."

"I'm listening."

"For God's sake, I was in New York at 5:00 AM! You people called me there," Sterling said incredulously. "How the hell could I be in two places at once?"

"According to the time line, you didn't have to be. Withcott put your brother's time of death at eleven o'clock. New York City is just a little more than a four-hour drive, and a lot less at that time of night for someone in a year-old Porsche with a twin turbo engine. Plenty of time for you to get back home and get that call." Wiley looked hard into Sterling's eyes. "So maybe you might want to start by telling me where you were between the hours of eleven and five."

Sterling felt trapped, especially since he knew his alibi couldn't be corroborated.

"I'm waiting for an answer, Agent Bledsoe," Wiley said.

"Not that you'll believe it, but I was looking at student papers," Sterling said. "And before you ask, no one was with me to confirm that."

Wiley nodded slowly, his hand gripping the gun even tighter.

"Oh c'mon, Lieutenant. Someone is playing a sick joke on all of us. My image was electronically transported into that e-mail." Sterling read the doubt on Wiley's face. "It's not the most difficult thing to do. With the right software any decent hack could've done it."

"But why, Agent? Why would someone want to put your image in an incriminating e-mail directly implicating you in your brother's murder? Seems like a big effort to play a joke, never mind the risk of being caught interfering with the federal investigation of a murder. Just doesn't play for me."

Sterling's head started aching as he raced through all the possibilities. It was a legitimate point and he didn't have an answer, at least not without having some real time to think everything through. He shook his head slowly. "I don't know why the hell someone is doing this. But look at what it's done, divided us once again on who the real suspects should be. It's another distraction, just like the WLA. Can't you see they're trying to turn us against each other?"

Wiley nodded but he kept the gun aimed at Sterling's chest. "I need something stronger than that, Agent. There are a lot of questions I still have that don't have answers. I need you to start filling in some of the blanks. In a hurry."

"Like what?"

"Let's take it from the very beginning. You hated your brother. You have for years. Why would you want to lead this investigation? We didn't even have a chance to call the feds in before you were already up here running the show. You volunteered your services, and quite adamantly from what I've been told. And according to Bureau procedure, it's completely against policy to be involved in an investigation dealing with a family member. Even more of a violation to be the lead."

Sterling was caught even more off guard. How did Wiley know about their troubled relationship? Sterling could count on one hand the number of people who had been aware of his strained history with Wilson. Two of them, his parents, were already dead.

Wiley was on a roll. "That's right, Agent, I know all about it. You might not expect much from a mountain cop, but I've been doing my homework too. I had a long conversation with Mrs. Bledsoe a few days after the Professor's murder and just before she left. Both times she raised some interesting points that I never would've known had I not spoken with her privately."

"Like?"

"She distinctly remembers your relationship with your brother heating up right after he won the Nobel and all the money that came with it."

Sterling alternated between dizziness and anger. Had Kay really said these things? Why hadn't she told him that she spoke with Wiley? He didn't know what to think, but he knew if he didn't start coming up with some answers, he'd be in the shitter for sure.

"Put the gun down, Lieutenant," Sterling said. "My relationship with my brother is none of your goddamn business. We had our differences like most brothers do. But you can't believe that our not being close has anything to do with all of this. For Chrissake, sibling rivalry is not a motive for murder."

"But there was a lot of money at stake, Agent. Close to $3 million. You had more than ample time to tell us you stood to inherit that much money."

Sterling thought about explaining the word "Chogan" and telling Wiley about the mysterious deaths of the blackbirds that Wilson and Mandryka had been investigating. But Sterling knew he hadn't tied enough loose ends together to make a valid case. At this point, Wiley would discard it as conjecture, an elaborate theory Sterling had concocted to shift the blame away from himself.

"So why the insistence on investigating your own brother's murder?" Wiley pressed. "We both know it's not normal procedure for a family member to be involved in that kind of investigation. Conflict of interest."

"I didn't know it was murder at the outset," Sterling said. "All I was told was that he was missing. I knew right away that something wasn't right. Wilson wouldn't be away from Kay for an hour without telling her where he was going. Call it an investigator's intuition or whatever you want, but something deep down told me things were much worse than what I was hearing."

"That's fair, but it doesn't explain everything else. Why the hell is your picture sitting in that e-mail?"

"Goddammit! Listen to yourself. If I were the murderer, do you think I'd send the video from the lab down to Quantico to have it analyzed, knowing that it would come back with my face on it? That would be pretty stupid."

As they spoke, Sterling kept watching the door for Brusco to enter. It had been almost half an hour and he hadn't even called. That wasn't like him. Maybe he too believed that Sterling had been behind the murders and decided to sit on the sidelines while they apprehended him. Sterling knew there were few options left. With his picture in that e-mail, there was little he'd be able to do right now to prove his innocence, alibi or not. And he couldn't afford to lose time while they checked that out. He needed more time to work through everything. He looked down at his watch, and stayed in that position.

"What are you doing?" Wiley asked.

Sterling counted to three under his breath, and when he looked up, he took a quick step forward and swung an open hand at the gun. A shot rang out, and for a moment, both men froze. Then Sterling jumped on the smaller man and grabbed the hand holding the gun in one motion. Wiley was strong and wiry, but was outmatched by Sterling's power. A second bullet was fired, striking one of the pit windows and sending glass crashing to the floor. They struggled for a few moments until Sterling had control. Wiley released the gun and Sterling turned him on his stomach, jammed his forearm into the back of his neck, and crushed him with his weight.

"I hate to do this, Lieutenant, but you've left me no choice." Sterling unclasped Wiley's handcuffs and snapped them around his wrists. "Time will prove my innocence but not fast enough."

"You're going to get caught, Agent," Wiley said. "You can kill me, but they will eventually find you."

"Don't be stupid, Lieutenant. I'm not going to kill you, just like I didn't kill Wilson or that Vorscht girl. I just need some time to get this case together so you and everyone else realize that the real killer is walking around free somewhere laughing at how much he's making fools of us."

Sterling pulled Wiley up and led him out of the pit and down a flight of stairs to a small, dark room of holding cells. Sterling found a paper cup and straw in one of the cabinets. He filled the cup with water from a nearby fountain and set it up on the small desk in the cell.

"I don't want to do this, Lieutenant, but I'm sure you understand." Sterling slammed the bars shut, then ran for the stairs, stopping to retrieve his gun before racing out the door. For the first time in his life, he was a fugitive.

35

The murderer had proven to be a more formidable opponent than Sterling had expected, killing two people in the span of a week, setting up the WLA, and now trying to frame him. Someone was certain to find Wiley soon. Sterling knew he needed to get out of town in a hurry. He drove across Ledyard Bridge and rocketed up River Road, struggling to keep the Mustang from wiping out on the blind curves. He needed to get his bag from the house, but more important, he needed that videotape that was locked in the wall safe. It was a critical piece of evidence that could possibly lead to the capture of the real killer.

Sterling skidded up Dead Man's Curve, then floored the accelerator once he reached an open stretch. He couldn't get beyond the computer image of his face. Had Harry really sent that, or had someone doctored the image and sent it under Harry's name? Either way, an insider was targeting Sterling, and others were sure to believe he had some type of involvement.

Less than a minute from the house, Sterling slammed on the brakes. Strobe red-and-white lights painted the darkness. Sterling looked through the trees toward Deer Run Lane and spotted the source of the light show, a gang of police cruisers huddled at the entrance of Wilson's driveway. Sterling thought back to his arrival at the station. That explained why there were only two cruisers parked outside. It all must have been part of the plan—lure him to the deserted station where Wiley was alone while they searched the house for any evidence linking him to the murders.

Sterling turned the car around on two wheels and flew back down River Road. The tape would be safe for now, as it was unlikely that anyone would find the secret compartment. At least he still had the box of disks and the printed documents from Wilson's computer stashed in the trunk. When he was no longer in danger, he could finally sit down and go through everything, seeing if he could find that important thread weaving through the blackbird deaths and the two murders.

He picked up his cell and let his home number ring precisely three times before hanging up and dialing again. Veronica would recognize the code.

"Hi, baby," she answered with her bed voice. "Why are you calling so late?"

"Ronnie, I need you to listen to me and not ask any questions."

Veronica could hear the urgency in his voice and immediately sat up. "I'm listening."

"Go to my office and look under my desk. You'll find a small black book taped underneath the middle drawer. Got that?"

"Yup."

"Look on the second-to-last page. There will be a series of numbers. That's the combination to the wall safe."

"Baby, you never told me you had a wall safe." She sounded more disappointed than surprised.

"Please, Ronnie, not now. Just listen. The safe is in the kitchen behind the microwave. Open the safe with those numbers and take out all of the money and the gun. There should be $50,000 in small bills."

"Fifty thousand? What are you doing with so much cash?"

Sterling ignored her. "Take the gun, the cash, and the black book, pack yourself enough clothes to get through the week, and get out of my apartment."

"Then what?"

"Stop by the store and grab some food that won't spoil. You won't be eating gourmet, but you'll be able to survive for a couple of days. There's a small hotel in the East Village. Not a nice one, but they rent rooms by the hour, mostly for local prostitutes. It's called the Hotel DeWitt. Tell them you want to pay for two days. Give them the cash. If they ask for identification, tell them you don't have any. They won't press the issue once they see the cash."

"Sterling, why do you know about a hotel like this?"

"Goddammit, Ronnie! It's a long story and I don't have time to get into it right now. I need you to do exactly as I've said. Don't leave the hotel and don't use the phone. Wait until I call you. Do you understand?"

"I'm scared, Sterling."

And so was he, but admitting it to her would only make things worse. "There's nothing to worry about, sweetie, as long as you follow my instructions."

"Are you all right?"

"I'm fine. Now go and get the hell out of my apartment as fast as you can."

"I'm already in your office."

"And one last thing. Don't go directly to the hotel. Someone might be following you. Make sure you take a cross-town subway to the West Side, then take the shuttle back. Take a cab downtown once you get back to the East Side, but make sure he drops you off a few blocks away from the hotel. The DeWitt is on the corner of Avenue B and Tenth Street, upstairs over a florist. There won't be a sign. It has a faded blue door."

"Be careful, Sterling."

He could hear the tremble in her voice. "Just do as I've said, and everything will be all right."

Sterling finally weaved his way to I-89 and opened the car's engine. He knew it wouldn't be long before they put out an APB, if they hadn't done so already. He drove west for thirty minutes, then took an exit marked with a gas station and lodging sign. He pulled into the brightly lit station and bought a bottle of water, a packet of Tylenol for the explosions ricocheting through his head, and a Rand McNally street map of upstate New York. The young attendant behind the counter asked where he was going so late at night, and Sterling, realizing the kid could be a potential witness, explained that he was going to Canada to visit his dying mother.

Sterling drove down a few more exits before turning off at a rest stop and mapping out the fastest route to Harry Frumpton's cottage in the Adirondacks. Sterling couldn't recall the exact address, but he remembered the name of the street—Moody Road. The houses were few and far between, and most of them had been built around Tupper Lake. Harry's cottage was the last house at the southernmost point. It had been in his family for three generations. As a rambunctious child, he had hated the house's remoteness, but in his adult years it had become a great source of relaxation and spiritual fulfillment, allowing him to escape the intense pressures of his Bureau work and vacation anonymously in the wilderness.

Sterling pushed through the two-hour journey, trying to make sense of this sudden turn in the case. He kept repeating to himself that there had to be a connection between Wilson's and Heidi's murders. There had been a lot more to this innocent-looking foreign graduate student than he had first thought. At the very least she hadn't been up front with him that afternoon in Mrs. Potter's house. At the very worst she had been deceitful. She knew a lot more about Wilson than that he walked the property and watched birds. She was the one, according to Kanti, who had brought Wilson to him when both had independently noticed dead blackbirds in the mountains. Heidi Vorscht had her hands in everything from Wilson's lab to President Mortimer's office. But no one could really define what she did in either place or the kinds of friends she had kept. Kelton had actually called her a loner, which seemed to contradict everything else Sterling had learned about her. Now she, too, was dead, murdered in such a way as not to leave a single clue why someone would kill her so savagely. They must have wanted more time. The decapitation was a perfect way to obscure her identity and give them a chance to plan their next strike or to get away.

As the exits flew by, Sterling shifted thoughts to the last e-mail. He and Harry had been friends since Sterling joined the Bureau. Harry had been an instructor for one of the evidence collection trainee classes. He and Sterling started chatting one afternoon and once they discovered each other's interest in anatomy, they'd spend hours after class discussing forensic pathology and the exciting new world of DNA that was making it easier to identify and capture criminals as well as prove the innocence of the wrongly convicted. Harry Frumpton was the classic middle-aged bachelor with little interest in activities that involved large numbers of people. Fishing was perfect for him.

Sterling's heart wouldn't let him believe that after all these years Harry would try to implicate him in a murder. He thought about the message, then picked away at a small inconsistency he had previously ignored.

If Harry was trying to set him up, why had he included such a friendly message about fishing and suggested that Sterling call him?

He pressed on through the darkness, scaling the steep mountain roads before descending into their lifeless valleys. The roads were narrow and bumpy, at times almost sending the Mustang skidding off the embankments. He thought about Veronica. It had been almost an hour, more than enough time for her to be checked in.

He dialed her cell phone.

"Hey, sweetie," she answered. She must've seen his number on her caller ID.

"Everything all right?"

"This place smells like an armpit," she whined. "And there's all this knocking into the walls and strange noises."

"I never said it was the Plaza, Ronnie, but the most important thing right now is that you're safe."

"I don't feel safe."

"Did anyone follow you?"

She exhaled loudly, out of frustration and exhaustion. "Impossible. I took ten trains and two cabs."

"That's my girl. What name did you use to check in?"

"My high-school English teacher, Maureen Bierbower."

"Nice touch. What room did they give you?"

"Five seventeen. At least I have a view of the park across the street."

"Are you near the window right now?"

"The room's so small, everything's near the window."

"Well, pull down the shades and get as far away from the window as possible." Sterling could hear the creaking of the shade's cylinder as she pulled. "Now sit tight. I'll be there tomorrow."

"What time?"

"I don't know. Just wait for me to call."

"Are you in trouble, Sterling?"

"I don't know right now. Something strange is happening and I'm trying to make sense of it all."

"I'm getting scared."

"Don't panic, Veronica. Sit tight and don't leave your room or answer the door. And don't use your cell phone. Understand?"

"Yeah. Hurry up, sweetie. Being away from you is making me sick."

"Don't worry. I'll be there."

Sterling hung up the phone and looked down at the map. If the route had been marked properly, he'd be at Harry's in less than twenty minutes. His mind drifted back to the e-mail. Maybe Harry had been coerced into sending that picture. What had he really been trying to say in that message? He made a point of telling Sterling that he'd be fishing in the Adirondacks for a few days. He also said that the number hadn't changed. Why hadn't he included it with the message just to be sure Sterling had it? Maybe he knew that someone else would be looking at the e-mail before he sent it and didn't want them to see the number. Was he reaching out to Sterling for a face-to-face meeting? It made a lot of sense. Harry knew the phones in his office would be tapped, but not the cottage. He had been around long enough and had witnessed firsthand the Bureau's internal surveillance of its own agents, so he had his line in the cottage configured so the number couldn't be traced. And if the line did get tapped, the number automatically rolled over to a scrambled line that changed on an hourly basis.

Sterling had all of Harry's numbers programmed into his cell. He started dialing the cottage, but hung up before it rang. It had been almost two hours since he left Hanover. Certainly they had found Wiley and were out looking for him. If they hadn't already, soon they'd be tracing his cell phone calls. He pulled off the highway and found a small shopping center not far from the exit. He pulled up to a pay phone in front of a pharmacy. He dialed Harry's number and waited. The answering machine kicked on after five rings, so he hung up and tried again. No answer. It was two o'clock in the morning. Sterling couldn't remember if Harry had a phone in his bedroom. Maybe he just couldn't hear the ringer.

Sterling got back into the Mustang and found his way onto the main road. There were almost no streetlights and the farther he traveled into the wilderness, the fewer street signs he passed. People in this small lake community had lived here long enough to know their way not by street names but by landmarks like the old synagogue in the center of town that had been founded more than a hundred years ago by Yiddish-speaking peddlers from Eastern Europe. There was also the no-frills Rotary Track and Athletic Field behind the L. P. Quinn School, which had been paid for partially by the 140,000 pennies collected in one week by the elementary-school students.

Sterling had visited the cottage only once, but the quaint charm of the village had left a deep impression. The streets slowly started coming back to him, especially the long road with a hundred-yard stretch of perfectly manicured tall hedges. Harry had told him that the adjoining property had been owned by a German industrialist by the name of Volgezang. The family had been a pillar of the small community until the father had an affair with a maid half his age. She eventually had his child, and when he told her that she would have to leave, she poisoned his wife. Harry had played with the children, but once the scandal hit and the maid had been convicted, the father packed up their bags, moved the family back to Germany, and sold off the estate in smaller parcels.

Sterling turned at the end of the Volgezang hedges and found the small dirt road that weaved around the lake. Harry's cottage was hidden beneath an arcade of evergreens and tall birches. He slowed the car once he approached the driveway and could see the house. All the lights were off. He drove closer, parking the Mustang fifty yards from the house. Harry had left his old station wagon with the chipped wood paneling in front, something he did only when he was home. Sterling scaled the front steps and looked into the living room windows. Darkness. The porch wrapped around the entire house, so Sterling quietly slipped to the back, lifted a window, and let himself in. Once inside, he pulled his gun from his waistband and tiptoed into the kitchen.

"Harry," he called out. "Are you here?"

No answer. The floorboards creaked under his steps. "Harry Frumpton," Sterling called again. He stood inside the doorway between the kitchen and small living room. Silence.

Sterling didn't like it. He readied himself with the gun, then looked into the living room. The two bedrooms were tucked away upstairs in the back of the house. Sterling made his way to the front hallway, then suddenly stopped.

"Oh shit!" he whispered. A man's body was stretched out in the front hallway. Sterling knew right away that it was Harry. He could tell by the beard and the gray ponytail. Sterling knelt beside him and felt the carotids in his neck for a pulse. Nothing. His skin was cold. He had been dead for at least several hours.

Sterling walked quietly into the other two rooms on the side of the house, then took the back steps to make sure no one was upstairs. He checked both bedrooms and a small TV room, but nothing looked like it had been touched. He replaced the gun in his belt slide holster and returned to Harry's body. Harry was dressed in oversized striped cotton pajamas and slippers. Sterling grabbed a pen from his coat and moved Harry's head to the side. There was the bullet wound, no bigger than a pencil eraser. A small stream of blood had dried on its course down his face before collecting in his ear. Sterling figured it was probably a .22, small but powerful. There was no exit wound. He searched the rest of Harry's body but found nothing else.

Sterling opened the front door with his sleeve pulled down over his hand. He checked the lock first, then the frame, looking for splintered wood or scraped metal. No signs of forced entry. Sterling figured Harry had known the shooter. There must have been a knock on the door late at night. Harry gets out of bed, comes down to greet the visitor, and opens the door. The shooter pulls out a gun and fires at point-blank range, hitting Harry with one bullet to the head. Harry falls a few feet from the door and dies instantly.

Sterling searched first the porch, then the yard and driveway for footprints. Close to a row of bushes, he picked up what looked like motorcycle tracks. They were too narrow to be a car, but too deep to be a bike. They ran several feet alongside the house, but disappeared where the driveway ended. It was difficult to make out much in the dark, but Sterling guessed by the depth of the grooves and how intact their borders remained that the tracks were fresh.

He returned to his car, now assured that his suspicions about Harry had been correct all along. Harry must have known something, maybe the identity of the killer. Sterling was convinced of a leak on the inside. Was it someone working for Harry? Was it someone in Hanover who was part of the investigative team? Sterling started the car and was halfway down the street when a thought came to mind. What if Harry knew all along that someone was trying to frame Sterling? So he sent the message figuring

Sterling would pick up the subtle hint that they meet at the cottage. That would also explain why Harry was taken by surprise and the shooter gained easy access. He had let the shooter in, expecting Sterling. Harry had something to show Sterling, otherwise he wouldn't have gone to the trouble of driving all the way up from Virginia.

But someone had definitely altered the message. Harry had said the fish were "biting like hell," but how could that be when the serious fishing, according to their past conversations, was still another month away? Harry never would have said that, but someone who had tampered with the message and knew little about the fishing season could easily have made that mistake.

Sterling pulled back up to the house and went in again, this time through the front door. He checked the ground floor first, pulling out drawers and opening cabinets. Nothing. He climbed the steps and entered the master bedroom. He wasn't sure what he was looking for, but he kept searching. He checked Harry's desk, then opened his closet. His suitcase had been tucked in the back corner. Sterling pulled it out and sat it on the bed. The key was still in the lock. Sterling unzipped it only to find that it was empty. All the same, he rummaged through the pockets and sleeves along the inner lining. He ran his hand across the vinyl floor of the suitcase, and suddenly he felt it. A flat oversized envelope.

He opened the hidden pocket and immediately recognized the gray confidential FBI envelope typically used for evidence transport. He ripped open the flap, and pulled out the contents. Two pictures. One of a man entering a building, presumably the "janitor" who came to clean Wilson's office. The resolution was almost perfect, showing his entire face, including the long scar that wrapped down from his hairline to his left ear. The second picture was even more surprising. It was a black-and-white of Heidi Vorscht and Kanti. They were sitting in the grass speaking with each other. Like everything else so far in this investigation, the new evidence only confused matters. How the hell had Harry gotten his hands on that photo and what exactly did it mean?

36

The body count had already risen to three and Sterling was convinced that whoever was behind the murders wouldn't stop until everyone who knew the truth had been silenced. But what was the truth? He needed to go back to the basics and sit down and map everything out. Luckily, he had copied the time line they had constructed in the pit inside his black book. Every road led to Heidi Vorscht, then turned into a dead end. She was front and center in the picture on Wilson's desk, on friendly terms with President Mortimer, living on Potter's farm where most of the dead blackbirds had been found, trusted by the Algonquin Indians, and now in a picture in Harry's suitcase.

Sterling needed to get back to New York, where he could move around by getting lost in the crowd. Harry's death was a clear signal that not only was someone out there watching but they were one step ahead. Sterling pulled off to another rest area and parked next to a pay phone. He dialed information and had them connect him to the Hotel DeWitt.

"Room 517," he said to the receptionist.

"Name of the guest?"

"Maureen Bierbower."

Veronica sounded uncertain when she picked up. Sterling could tell that she hadn't been asleep. A feeling of deep guilt engulfed him and he regretted that she had been dragged into this mess. Veronica had been nothing but good to him, and now she was running from a pack of professional killers who wouldn't think twice about hurting her to get to him.

"It's me, Ronnie. How's it going?"

"As best as can be expected, I guess. I'm sitting here in this filthy room, afraid to touch anything. Every time I start falling asleep another couple starts in the room next to me and the sound of a vacuum cleaner begins in the room above me. Like they're on a timer. Everything begins and ends exactly on the hour."

Sterling knew her nerves were frazzled. "I'm sorry, baby, but this is the best place I could think of right now. It's under the radar and the front desk is trained not to ask questions. It's only temporary till I can get my bearings."

"Are you going to tell me what's going on?"

Sterling thought about it. He owed her some type of explanation, but there were many things that still concerned him. If he told her everything and they found her, they'd have little problem coercing the information out of her. He also didn't want to scare her, which was pretty easy to do. She might try to do something that was helpful and only get herself or him hurt. Limited knowledge would have to satisfy her for now. It would be best for both of them.

"There've been three murders so far, Wilson included. I don't know the reason or reasons, but someone is now after me. Maybe I was getting too close to cracking the case. I don't know. But until I figure all this out, you need to stay out of sight. One way they could get to me would be through you, which is why I want to make sure you're secure. These guys are playing for keeps, Ronnie. There will be no mercy."

"I could go down to my parents in D.C.," Veronica offered.

"No, that's the last thing you should do. We're dealing with professionals, Ronnie. They already know everything about your family and close friends and where they live. That's the first place they'll check if they haven't already. That's why I don't want you to call anyone. No family, no friends. Understand?"

"This is getting scary, Sterling."

"I know it is, but everything will be fine in a couple of days. I just need more time to put all the pieces together. Where's your cell phone?"

"In my purse."

"Good, leave it there. Don't answer it or make any calls. Actually, turn it off so it doesn't even ring. Where's the gun?"

"In the bag with the money."

"Take it out and keep it next to you. Don't answer your door for anyone. No housecleaning or management. Nothing. If someone forces their way in, aim and shoot."

"I don't know how to shoot a gun." She was crying softly now, something she rarely did, and the sound pained him.

"Pull down the safety lock, aim at their chest, then squeeze the trigger. You might not hit, but at least you'll scare the shit out of them."

"When will you be here, Sterling?"

"Sometime tomorrow. Just hold on. Everything will be all right."

Veronica blew kisses into the phone, then the line went dead.

Sterling's next call was to Professor Mandryka. The phone rang eight times before it was answered.

"Hello," Mandryka said.

"Yuri, it's Sterling Bledsoe. Thank God you're all right."

"Why wouldn't I be?"

"Because three people are dead right now and at least two of them knew about the blackbirds."

"Who else other than Wilson knew about the birds?"

"Heidi Vorscht."

"Was this Heidi Vorscht the girl they found in the Grand Union dumpster?"

"That's right. She lived with Mrs. Potter. But she also knew Wilson. Her name has surfaced on every lead I've found so far."

"And who was the third killing?"

"One of our agents helping me with the investigation. I don't know how, but he found out something about Heidi Vorscht and her involvement in this mess. I'm not sure exactly what he knew, but it was enough to get him killed. Knowledge of those blackbirds is proving deadly."

Mandryka grunted. "Have you learned anything else about the birds and who might be killing them?"

"I'm making some headway, but not enough to draw any real conclusions. My working theory is that whoever's killing them will spare no expense or life in keeping it secret. That means your life's at serious risk just like the rest of them."

"I'm an old man, Sterling, long past my prime. I'm not much use to anyone. Don't worry about me."

Sterling had to stop himself from slamming the phone against the wall. "Dammit, Yuri, stop it with that fatalistic bullshit. Someone could put a bullet in your head the minute we get off the phone. If for no other reason, I need you alive to help me put this thing together and catch Wilson's killer. I'm counting on you, Yuri, and so is Wilson."

There was a brief pause at the other end. "What do you want me to do?"

"First, stay away from the lab, at least until I get things sorted out. Call one of your assistants tomorrow morning and tell them that you're sick and taking the rest of the week off. Do you have another house nearby or relatives?"

"No relatives, but I have a small place up near Killington Peak in Vermont. I haven't been there in a few years."

"Does anyone else know you have it?"

"Only Wilson knew. We went up there for a few days of eagle spotting. Wilson always loved the eagles."

"Good. Pack as much as you can as fast as you can and get up there. Is there a working phone in the cabin?"

"Are you kidding? I probably don't even have running water."

"Then take down my number." Sterling gave him his cell number. "If you think of something else about the blackbirds or Heidi or anything else we might've missed, call me. Otherwise, check in with me in twenty-four hours. Agreed?"

Mandryka read back the number. "I got it. Are you all right, Sterling?"

"I'll feel a lot better when this is behind us. Be careful, Yuri. And most important, don't trust anyone."

S terling filled up the Mustang at an all-night gas station, then raced out of the Adirondacks and toward the city. He couldn't get his mind off Heidi Vorscht and the central role she played in this. He took out his black book and read the notes he had made during his conversation with Vivian Sinclair, the receptionist in Mortimer's office. According to Vivian, Heidi had walked into the president's office looking for a job without even so much as an appointment. Vivian was surprised that President Mortimer had agreed to see her right away. Students typically went through layers of bureaucracy before getting a chance to see him. Why was he so agreeable about bending the rules for this foreign student?

Vivian also recalled the nasty argument she overheard between Mortimer and his wife. The divisive issue—Heidi Vorscht. Vivian had said that Heidi and Mrs. Mortimer were "like oil and water." But why was Mortimer such a big fan, and why was he so hell-bent on patching things up between his wife and this student? It just didn't fit. Mortimer was an aloof, guarded bureaucrat who hid behind his presidential position and spent the greater part of his time worrying about his legacy at Dartmouth. Why take such an interest in a student who meant nothing to him or his school?

Then the pictures.

Sean insisted that Heidi didn't work in the lab, but she was in that group photo they had taken on the lawn. And she wasn't just in the picture, but had been prominently positioned next to Wilson. Even in an informal picture, one would have expected to see the most senior post-doc fellow standing next to the lab director. Hierarchy was always preserved in academia.

Sterling had been bothered by something else in the picture, the way Heidi rested her hand on Wilson's shoulder. Too familiar. Now Harry had another picture of Heidi, but this time with Kanti. Sterling turned on the car light and looked at the photo again. They seemed so peaceful sitting there, both with their legs crossed, the tall grass blowing in the wind. Kanti was explaining something with his hands and she watched with laser intensity. Who had taken the photograph and how had it ended up with Harry?

By the time Sterling worked through all the possibilities, he had reached the outskirts of the city, passing the Yonkers Raceway. His first order of business would be to get some sleep, but he didn't want to go to the hotel just yet. Veronica probably wouldn't let him sleep anyway with all of the questions she had in store for him.

He raced through the Bronx and past Yankee Stadium, then crossed the Willis Avenue Bridge, merged onto FDR Drive, and headed down the East Side of Manhattan. He looked across the East River and saw a glint of light breaking on the distant horizon. It had been a long night. First the confrontation and struggle with Wiley, then finding Harry murdered in his cottage. Now he had the picture of who he believed to be the real killer and a mysterious photo of Heidi and Kanti sitting in tall grass. Veronica was penned up in an hourly, and Yuri was hopefully on his way into seclusion on Killington Peak. Now he needed to focus on his own safety and well-being.

Sterling followed the signs to the Manhattan Bridge that would lead him to Brooklyn. It would be easier to find a secluded spot somewhere in that vicinity. He could easily hide the Mustang and at least get a couple of hours of sleep. Just as he was turning off the FDR, his cell rang. He looked down at the caller ID. Unknown. He held the phone in his hand and debated a moment before flipping the lid open.

"Yeah," he said.

"What the hell are you doing, Bledsoe?" It was the unforgiving voice of Director Daniel J. Murphy.

Sterling couldn't suppress his sarcasm. "I was wondering what was taking you so long, Murph. Isn't this kind of late in the game?"

"Cut the goddamn bullshit, Bledsoe! I want a full rundown of what has transpired over the last twenty-four hours and why one of my best agents is on the run."

Sterling was too tired for the harangue. "The honest answer is that I myself don't even know what's going on. But right now there are three people dead and some assholes have the bright idea that I'm behind it. Go figure."

"I only know what I've been told so far, and it ain't good. For any of us. What are you doing right now?"

"Knitting a scarf for the local Girl Scouts. What the hell do you think I'm doing? Trying to find the real killer and save my ass."

Murphy groaned loudly and Sterling took some delight in picturing the director ensconced in his Potomac, Maryland, mansion, wearing silk pajamas and fur-lined slippers, massaging his temples to fend off the impending headache. Murphy was a deeply political man, and this growing embarrassment could hurt his not-so-secret ambitions to run for the Senate.

"Stop playing cowboy, Bledsoe," Murphy barked. "This case is blown wide open and every law enforcement agency in the states of Vermont and New Hampshire is looking for you."

Sterling mashed the car's accelerator. "You're not getting the message,

Murph. I don't give a damn, because I didn't do it. Not only is someone trying to set me up, but I'm starting to feel like they have some inside help."

"Why in the hell are you running? People don't run unless they have something to hide."

"Fuck you, Murph. You know damn well if I sat and talked, the chances of me walking away from this is next to nothing."

"Then who's the murderer?"

Sterling looked down at the picture on the seat next to him. "I might be able to figure it out if you called the hounds off of me. All I'm asking for is a few more days to put everything together."

"You know damn well I can't do that. I'm already getting questions from Sixteen Hundred. Come in on your own and we'll get through this, save us both a lot of trouble. There's still time to make it work without any more repercussions. What you did to that lieutenant up there makes you nothing better than a goddamn ciminal."

Sterling looked out over the Brooklyn Bridge. He was leaving the Manhattan skyline behind and heading toward the squat buildings of a sleeping Brooklyn. In the city now, he was on his own turf, which meant the odds had turned slightly in his favor that he could avoid capture and still have a fighting chance of figuring out who the killer was.

"We've known each other for ten years, Murph," Sterling said. "I haven't always followed procedure, but I've always delivered for you. I'm asking you, no I'm begging you, hang with me on this and buy me a little time. There's something big at work here. A lot bigger than my brother and the girl."

"How do you explain Frumpton?"

"Collateral damage. Harry must've found out something they didn't want him to know. He wasn't a primary."

Murphy's groan rumbled through the phone like the slow roll of a drum. "There are just too many bodies without enough answers," he said. "I can't let you stay out there and freewheel it. Bring it in and I'll personally see to it that you're given a fair deal."

Empty words from a politician-in-waiting, and Sterling knew it. "Can't do it, Senator. It's not business anymore. It's personal."

"I'm sorry you feel that way," Murph said. "You leave me no choice but to consider you armed and dangerous. From here on out, Bledsoe, all bets are off."

"Your support is overwhelming." Sterling hung up as he came off the Brooklyn Bridge and steered the car along the water's edge. The phone rang again. Murph having second thoughts? Sterling ignored the phone this time, as he should have the first. He weaved in and out of a maze of one-way streets and back alleys until he found what he was looking for—a small, cobblestone, dead-end road hidden underneath the long shadows of a row of boarded-up warehouses and burned-out buildings. He pulled up alongside a chain-link fence, feet away from the heavy steel columns of the Manhattan Bridge. He fell asleep with his hand on his gun and the twinkling lights of Manhattan blinking in the distance.

37

The constant tapping was part of his dream. He had locked himself in an office and a team of agents were hunting for him. They were going door to door, busting into offices that had been locked for the night. He reached by his hip for his gun, but realized he had left it in the car. A sense of doom squeezed his heart. He covered his ears, but the knock was still there. Slow. Constant. He wanted to scream. Why didn't they just break down the door already? He turned left, then right, but it was still there. Then the knocks grew more forceful.

Sterling opened his eyes slowly and shielded his face from the blazing sun. He looked left. A police officer was standing at the window, one hand on his stick, the other on his gun. He was a short, barrel-chested white man with biceps straining his sleeves. He sported one of those hard-ass buzz cuts, close on the sides, sticking straight up on top. There was a tap on the right window. His partner. A tall black man with a shiny bald head. He gave Sterling the roll-your-window-down motion. Sterling squeezed his right hand. The gun wasn't there. It must've fallen between the seats, which right now was a good thing.

"How's it going, Officer?" Sterling said, as he rolled down his window. "I guess I lost track of the time." The easy approach.

"License and registration," the cop drilled away, skipping the whole pleasantry exchange. "And proof of insurance." Another robotic local. No personality, all attitude.

"Is there a problem?" Sterling asked. He almost reached for his FBI shield, but thought better of it. He was on the run.

"There's no standing after eight," the officer maintained in flat tones. His left hand was free, but he still used the stick to point at the parking sign. Thinly veiled intimidation. "Not only are you parked, but you're sleeping. What are you doing down here?"

"Waiting for a buddy," Sterling said. "We're supposed to meet here and carpool over to the city. That lame two-person commuter requirement to get in over the bridge." Sterling handed his license through the window.

"You have New Hampshire tags," the officer said. "You live around here?"

Sterling chuckled, giving himself more time and trying to defuse the mounting tension. "The tags. Not mine. My car's in the shop. Busted transmission. This here is a rental. Wish it were mine, though. I'd have a lot less problems than with my piece of shit."

The officer looked at Sterling's license, turning it over in his hands a couple of times. "You live here or in Virginia?"

"Just moved up from Virginia, about thirty miles out of D.C. I've been here for a month, staying with a friend over in Fort Greene."

"Can I see the rental papers?"

Sterling reached into the glove compartment, pulling out the sleeve of papers. He shuffled through them as if he were trying to get them organized, but he was quickly checking to make sure there were no references to the FBI. He put the origination paper in the back, hoping the officer wouldn't notice the car had been rented in New Hampshire.

"Everything's here," Sterling said, handing the papers to the officer.

The officer looked at the rental agreement, then matched the name to Sterling's license. Satisfied, he glanced across the car at his partner who hiked his shoulders, signaling he believed the story. Sterling considered what to do if they still went back to run his info through the computer. A simple check and they'd be ready to call in the National Guard for backup.

"When's your partner coming?" the buzz cut asked.

Sterling looked at his watch. "Typical. He's already ten minutes late. Punctuality isn't his strong point, but luckily, he's the boss."

"Open the trunk, please," the black officer said.

Sterling popped the trunk and waited while they inspected. There wasn't anything back there except for the box of documents and diskettes. Nothing suspicious. They returned to the windows, taking their respective sides.

"What kind of work do you do?" It was the short officer again. Now he was leaning his outstretched arm against the window frame. The bottom portion of a tattoo appeared just underneath his sleeve. It looked like the rear wheel of a Harley. Sterling read his nameplate—Bronchetti. It should've read "Tough Guy."

He continued to play along. "I'm a computer programmer, Officer Bronchetti. Small company in the Flatiron District."

Bronchetti looked at the license again. "This is a no-standing zone, Mr. Bledsoe, even if you're waiting for someone. And if you've moved to the city, you should be carrying a New York license. The next time you get stopped, the officer might not be so lenient and issue you a summons." He handed the license back to Sterling.

"Thanks, Officers," Sterling said. "I'll get that done right away."

They gave him one last look-over. "And maybe you need to get some more sleep at home," the tall officer said before turning to leave. "You look horrible, buddy."

Sterling thought of a few choice words, but resisted answering. He watched as the officers returned to their car then slowly pulled off. He let out a deep sigh, waited a few minutes, then started the Mustang. The sweat running down his back made his shirt stick to the seat like glue. The car had definitely become a liability and it was time to dump it, but not before he made a drop-off.

He drove over the Manhattan Bridge into the city. At Houston Street, which separates SoHo from Greenwich Village, he turned west, then raced to the Avenue of the Americas and headed north. He passed the famous West Fourth Street basketball courts, and even at this hour some of the hoopsters were dazzling the morning work crowd, acrobatically flying through the air and dunking the ball in positions that he had only seen in the circus. Continuing north, then west, he reached Eighth Avenue. Rush hour was in full swing, but he raced the Mustang in and out of traffic, finally bringing it to rest in front of the enormous federal post office across from Madison Square Garden. He pulled the car into an illegal spot, the only one he could find, then removed the box of papers and diskettes from the trunk. A cab almost wiped him out as he dodged the traffic to cross the street.

Pennsylvania Station, New York's greatest interstate railroad hub, occupied the entire basement of the Garden. Millions of travelers crisscrossed the durable linoleum, making their way to trains and subways or upstairs to join the long line of suits waiting for yellow cabs. Sterling knew that he had to move quickly and quietly. Since 9/11 and the Iraq war, the Office of Homeland Security had tightened controls around large public venues like Penn Station and Grand Central Terminal. Several National Guardsmen walked through the fast-moving crowds, green berets sloping across their heads, their hands cautiously massaging machine guns. Small packs of NYPD officers also patrolled, moving the homeless along and chasing panhandlers.

Sterling walked past the big Amtrak board and entered the eastern hall, which housed the New Jersey Railroad and the city subway lines. He walked past Zabar's and Starbucks, then turned the corner and stopped. The threat of terrorist bombs and anthrax had led to the removal of most of the lockers, and this was the last cluster that remained. There were sixteen lockers in all, but as Sterling surveyed the door locks he noticed all of the keys were missing. They were already being used.

He leaned against the wall and considered his options. Going to his apartment was out of the question. With Murph's go-ahead, teams were surely already posted up and down his street and his phone lines would be tapped. But he could drop the box off at the hotel until he found a more permanent location. As he turned to leave, he almost plowed into an old woman who had stopped at the bottom row of lockers. She rummaged through her pocketbook for a few moments before finally taking out a key. Opening a locker, she removed a small suitcase and shopping bag, whispered something to herself, then joined the hordes of commuters scuffling to the trains.

Sterling waited for the woman to disappear, then turned his back to a group of National Guardsmen walking toward Zabar's. Once they had passed, he slid around the corner and squeezed the box into the locker. He dropped a handful of quarters into the door slot and grabbed the key before quickly turning to exit. Safely outside, Sterling swiped the parking ticket off the Mustang, started the engine, and headed west on 34th Street. He stopped by a small grocery store on Ninth Avenue and purchased a can of charcoal lighter fuel and two of the morning papers. He moved the Mustang into the long line of cars heading through the Lincoln Tunnel to New Jersey. As he sat in traffic, he asked himself if perhaps he had missed something. This time he focused on the blackbirds. First, who knew about their deaths? Heidi, Mandryka, Kanti, and Bigfoot all were aware of the birds, but no one knew about all of the others except Heidi, which struck Sterling as more than peculiar. Wilson hadn't even told Kay about the birds, so why had he confided in Heidi? Did he tell her of his own volition or did she find out about his discoveries and confront him?

Kanti had said that Heidi had brought Wilson to him. Wilson and Heidi had shown him a video of the blackbird carcasses that Wilson had taped on one of his nature scouts. That led Sterling back to the initial question— why was someone intentionally killing the birds? He had gotten no closer to answering that question than when Mandryka first showed him the dead birds in the basement lab.

Sterling finally made it out of the tunnel and turned onto the New Jersey Turnpike. He headed south and exited at the town of Elizabeth. He had only been there once before and that was after making a wrong turn when he tried to find the discount Swedish furniture store IKEA. He had gotten off one exit too soon and found himself lost in a rundown neighborhood of small streets and dilapidated homes. Though it was the middle of the day, there were few people out and those who were walked quickly with their heads down and their hands jammed in their pockets. He remembered thinking at the time about the countless murders that had been committed on those desolate streets and never even reported. It wasn't like New York's ghettos, with their tall brick complexes and glass-strewn courtyards scarred by graffiti. But it still had the electric feel of imminent danger. Most people lived in one- and two-family dwellings plastered with brightly colored aluminum siding. The small one-window bars and gated-window corner delis served as a warning to unlikely visitors that this was not the most friendly of places to stop for a can of soda and bag of chips. Few police cars patrolled the area and that wasn't by mistake.

Sterling took a series of turns, working his way to the pier. He passed a group of teenagers throwing gang signs at each other, then puffing their chests as he drove by. He found a road that ran along the pier, passing a series of junkyards, tow yards, and shipping docks. Then he found the street he had been looking for. A row of abandoned houses was on one side and a string of deserted lots on the other. Several cars had been left to rust away on cinder blocks, their bodies stripped down to the frame, their windows either smashed or missing. Sterling pulled into the back of the lot and killed the engine. He took out the can of lighter fuel and doused the car's interior first, then the exterior. When he had emptied most of the can, he threw it on the backseat, then lit a ball of newspaper. Standing as far back as he could, he tossed the newspaper at the car and ran for cover as the car erupted into flames.

As a small burst of explosions sounded, Sterling ran across the street and waited on the other side, only willing to leave once the car had been incinerated beyond recognition. The license plates turned black first, then melted under the intense heat. The windows popped out sequentially and the flames shot hungrily into the sky. Sterling looked up and down the street to make sure no one else had been watching. When the seats had been torched down to the floor and the nauseating smell of burning rubber reached him a hundred yards away, he flipped off the safety lock on his gun and headed into the edgy town, searching for the nearest train that would take him to the city.

38

Sterling walked out of Jerry's Den on 125th Street in Harlem feeling like a new man. He had shaved off all his hair and his bald dome glistened in the hot afternoon sun. He stopped at a Korean sporting goods shop and purchased a black skullcap that he rolled down to his eyebrows. At a Salvation Army thrift store he picked up a lightweight-canvas green military coat that made him look ready for the fiercest of battles. He kept his jeans, but completed the hip new look with a pair of trendy black Timberland boots that he had seen many of his students wear.

Sterling headed east on 125th Street and, forgetting the jam he now found himself in, took his time to absorb the rhythmic sounds and bright colors unique to the Harlem streets. It had been several years since he last visited this neighborhood, and he felt pangs of guilt that he rarely took the easy ten-minute drive north to enjoy the spirit of his people and the zest of their rich culture. Africans hovering at the corner of Adam Clayton Powell Boulevard wore their traditional multicolored garb, hawking dashikis, masks, and colorful lamps. The Jamaicans owned the corner at Malcolm X Boulevard, sitting behind small tables of burning incense and bootleg reggae CDs, their roping dreadlocks falling to the middle of their backs.

Young mothers pushed crying babies and old men exchanged war stories as they leaned against the buildings sharing laughs. Sterling bought a bean pie from one of the young Muslim men dressed in a freshly ironed black suit and wide bow tie, then caught the downtown express train on the east end of 125th Street. A couple of high-school girls in his subway car giggled and flirted with him, the confirmation he needed that his new youthful disguise might actually work. He crossed over to a local train at 86th Street, then exited when it reached 68th Street—Hunter College. He needed to find out as much as possible about blackbirds and if they held any type of significance that would cause someone to intentionally poison them by the hundreds. If anyone would have the answers, it would be Xao Zhang, an ornithologist from Guangdong Province in China and one of his oldest friends at the school.

Sterling blended into the crowd of students, listening to a few of them argue about the hottest rap song as he kept an eye out for uniforms or agents from the Bureau. He waited for the Lexington car traffic to stop before crossing. That's when he spotted the first car. It was parked on the northeast corner of 68th and Lexington, facing east. He could see the wires hanging from their earpieces and snaking behind their collars. They were wearing identical blue blazers. Sterling crossed to the south side of the street and joined a group of students rushing to a class in the Hunter East building. He caught a side profile of the agent seated in the passenger seat and his jaw tightened. Skip Dumars. He and Sterling had hated each other ever since a tense confrontation many years earlier.

Skip had just been assigned to the New York City field office and had landed the East River murders, his first high-profile case and a chance to make a name for himself. He had spent weeks on the tedious investigation, questioning witnesses and sorting through the evidence. Then a decision had come down from high up the Bureau's food chain, and Sterling had taken over the case. Skip reluctantly handed over the files to Sterling, but not without a major fight that had left them enemies for life.

Sterling thought about the venom in Skip's eyes the last time they had seen each other. He knew that Skip must have tasted blood when he took this assignment.

Sterling remained camouflaged by the group of students as they made their way along 68th Street. Twenty yards more and he'd be clear to duck into the Hunter East building where he could backtrack his way to the zoology department. Sirens rang out in the background, cabbies honked at a stalled car, and city buses lumbered down the crowded street. Keeping his eyes focused ahead, Sterling spotted the second car. They were parked farther east on 68th Street, facing west toward Sterling. A male and a female agent, both sporting dark glasses that wrapped around their faces.

"Bledsoe," a man's voice called from behind. Sterling didn't turn, but he recognized the raspy bark of Skip Dumars. "Stop right there, Bledsoe."

The group of students suddenly stopped and turned toward the commotion. Sterling busted out into a full sprint. The agents at the other end of the street jumped out of their car, guns drawn. Sterling slipped into the lobby of Hunter East, running past the security guard, knocking over a couple of students as they waited in line to present their IDs.

Sterling ran up the back escalators to the third floor and heard Skip's barking before he entered Wexler Library. He quickly moved down the carpeted aisles, trying not to draw any unnecessary attention. Minutes later, he exited the library and ran to the glass walkway bridge that connected Hunter East with Hunter West. Several students sat against the far wall typing away at the bank of computer terminals, while another group waited in line at the portable ATM. Sterling slowed to a walk on the bridge and looked down at the street beneath him. An army of police cars had strangled traffic north of 68th Street and angry drivers were getting out of their cars looking for the source of the holdup. Several government sedans had lunged up on the sidewalks, their lights flashing. Sterling ran across another bridge and entered the Hunter North building. He turned back and was relieved not to see any signs of Skip or the other agents.

Sterling raced to a back stairwell and hurtled down four flights, then crossed through the basement bookstore into a service elevator. A tunnel, which few people other than the janitors knew about, connected Hunter North to a small townhouse on 69th Street that was used for a bunch of administrative offices, including the zoology department. Sterling plowed through the swinging doors, then sprinted through the dark tunnel. Once he reached the other end, he removed his cap, wiped the sweat pouring from his shaved head, and took a moment to catch his breath.

He walked down a maze of narrow hallways to the corridors of the zoology department. Large posters of zebras and fish and felines adorned the walls, leading to a back stairwell that most ignored for the more convenient bank of elevators. Sterling hopped the three flights of stairs and walked the length of the fourth floor to Zhang's lab, nestled in the corner of the building. The door was open when Sterling approached.

"Zhang, you here?" Sterling called out, stepping into the dimly lit lab. Large skeletal remains hung from the ceiling and stuffed animals had been mounted on the wall. A wide, scaly snakeskin had been cut open, stretched, and pinned across the back wall. Footsteps echoed on the linoleum.

"Bledsoe," Zhang said. He was in his usual attire, a long, white coat stuffed with pencils and markers and utensils only a professional ornithologist would carry. He wiped the corner of his mouth as if he had just finished lunch. "What brings you to my small corner of the world?"

"I need your help, Zhang."

"You sound so serious. Why the military fatigues? They shipping you off to a war I don't know about?" Zhang let out a small chuckle, his plump cheeks rising high enough to cover his eyes. He stopped when Sterling didn't join in.

"I'm in a bit of a tight situation," Sterling said, leaning against one of the workbenches. "I need to pick your brain about something."

"Not much to pick, but you can work with what's there." Zhang's self-deprecation was more out of habit than necessity.

"I need to know about blackbirds."

Zhang's face tightened. "Blackbirds? Which ones? There are at least six species in North America alone."

"The red-wingeds."

"Ahh, my favorite, and in my opinion the most interesting. What do you want to know about the red-wingeds?"

"Why might someone want to kill them?"

Zhang repeated the question to himself, something he often did. "To my knowledge, the red-winged is not a bird that hunters care about."

"I'm not talking about hunting, Zhang. I mean kill. Poison. Can you think of any reason why anyone would want to poison blackbirds?"

"Depends on what part of the country you live in and your occupation."

"What does that mean?"

Zhang waved Sterling to a lab table and pulled out a tall stool. When they both had settled into their seats, he explained. "The red-winged blackbirds are arguably the most abundant blackbird in North America. Great for ornithologists like me, because that makes them easy to study and their movements well documented. But if you're a farmer in the northern Midwest, then that doesn't make you happy at all."

"The same for the Northeast?" Sterling asked, trying to focus on the blackbirds in Vermont.

"Different situation," Zhang said. "See, at least 70 percent of the country's sunflower crop is cultivated in western Minnesota, North Dakota, and South Dakota. This sunflower crop provides most of the country's sunflower oil and birdseed. So it follows that many farmers' livelihoods are based directly on the success of their sunflower crop. The blackbirds, however, have only made it difficult for them. The red-wingeds in particular love the succulent sunflower seed and sweep down on those fields, ravaging millions of dollars' worth of crops."

"How big of a deal is it?" Sterling asked. He was already scribbling notes.

"Some estimates of the yearly damage can reach as high as $10 million when you include the cost of trying to keep the birds away from the crops. What you have to understand is that in just the upper Midwest alone, sunflowers can be a $300 million-plus business. We're not talking about chump change. To many of these farmers, it's a matter of financial life and death. This is why the National Sunflower Association in Bismarck, North Dakota, has made such a big deal of this down in Washington. They've spent a tremendous amount of time and money lobbying the Washington bigwigs to fund a program that would kill many of the blackbirds and save their crops."

Sterling digested the new information. Wilson had discovered hundreds of dead blackbirds, but there were probably thousands more hidden back up in the mountains. Everything would fit together nicely if he could somehow link the regions.

"What's the likelihood that farmers in Vermont and New Hampshire are also growing sunflowers?"

Zhang shook his head. "Agriculture isn't my thing, but I think it's highly unlikely to find sunflower crops in those areas. Topography and weather are critical for certain crops, but any more information about the sunflower crop is pressing beyond my knowledge."

"Did Congress ever decide to fund that killing program?" Sterling asked.

"Yes and no," Zhang said. "The last time I read something on it, controversy, dirty politics, and in-fighting had bogged everything down. The alliances keep changing. Early on, farmers picked up a lot of sympathy in

Washington. Then the animal rights advocates heard about the planned killing and cried foul. No pun intended." Zhang laughed at his own joke. "The animal rights people have their Washington support, too."

"How were they suggesting the blackbirds be killed?"

"Poison. I think they've used DRC-1339 in the past, but I'm not sure if they were going to stick with that. Hold on for a minute." Zhang went back to another office, where Sterling could hear him opening and closing desk doors and rummaging through papers. He returned a few minutes later carrying a folded sheet of paper. "This is an old friend of mine," Zhang said, handing Sterling the paper. "His family sponsored me when I immigrated here from China. He was an important man in the Audubon Society. Call him and tell him that I referred you. He's a little grumpy, but stick with him. He knows more about the politics of wildlife than anyone in the country."

Sterling took the paper and slid it inside his coat. He closed his book and extended his hand to Zhang. "You've been a big help, Zhang."

"I like the new look," Zhang replied, pointing to Sterling's head. "Makes you look fifteen years younger."

The two men shared a brief smile. "I need one more favor," Sterling said. "The conversation we just had never happened. You haven't seen me in weeks."

Zhang's eyes narrowed as he frowned. "Is everything all right, Bledsoe?"

"I don't know right now. But until I figure things out, it would really help if you kept this little talk between you and me."

Zhang nodded. "When you find Mack, tell him you want to know about the project."

"Does the project have a name?"

"You bet it does. The Blackbird Project. He'll know all about it."

39

The avuncular Windsor McGovern lived in a one-bedroom apartment overlooking Gramercy Park. When Sterling had first called and inquired about the Blackbird Project, he hung up the phone, saying he was tired of meddlesome reporters and their nasty habit of distorting his words to fit their stories. When Sterling called back and said Xao Zhang had referred him, McGovern invited him over and asked him his favorite tea flavor. Sterling said plain water would be fine.

Sterling rode the creaky elevator to the eleventh floor and walked to the end of the hall. The door to apartment D had already been propped open in anticipation of his arrival. Sterling knocked a couple times, then pushed the door open.

"I'm out here on the balcony," McGovern called.

Sterling closed the door behind him and walked through the small apartment. A tiny kitchenette had been squeezed between the front door and a coat closet. A bedroom sat off to the left, but the biggest room was straight ahead, facing a wall of windows and the balcony. Sterling took a few minutes to look around the cluttered front room. Every inch of wall space had been covered by framed animal photographs, stuffed birds, and rows of bookcases full of wildlife picture books. Sterling stopped to read several plaques and citations honoring McGovern's commitment to the "protection and preservation of our treasured wildlife." The masculine apartment had been carelessly decorated in muted colors and cozy furniture.

"Glad you could make it, Mr. Bledsoe," McGovern said as Sterling walked through the tall French doors. He wore a button-down blue pinstriped shirt and white cotton trousers held up by bright green suspenders decorated with ducks. His portly abdomen stretched over his waistband, and his short arms hung out from his sides as if they had been stuck on at the last minute and never grew. A charcoal-gray puff of a cat was balled up in a chair next to McGovern's. It lazily swiveled its furry head toward Sterling, its green eyes glowing. After assessing the situation, it buried its head and went back to sleep.

"Thanks for seeing me on such short notice," Sterling said. "I'm doing some research and Zhang told me that you're the most knowledgeable person in the country on what I'm after."

McGovern let out a rolling chuckle that made his drooping jowls quiver. "Xao has a tendency to oversell me. But if that's how a genius describes me, then who the hell am I to disagree? We sponsored Xao many years ago when he was trying to get his start here. 'We' meaning my wife, Madeline, and me. The kids and I lost her a couple of years ago to ovarian cancer. Took her away in less than a year." McGovern's bright blue eyes lost their luster as he looked out over the balcony. Sterling let him have his moment. "Anyway, that's the breaks, I guess," McGovern sighed, still looking off the balcony. "We had fifty-three wonderful years together and nobody can take them away from me."

"Death is hard," Sterling said. "I've recently lost my only brother."

"Were you close?"

The words stung. This was not the direction he wanted to take the conversation. "It's been tough," Sterling said. "In more ways than I ever imagined." He looked across the park, focusing on a tall, redbrick apartment building. All the windows had been dressed with black shutters and each one had a flower box full of bright pink, red, and purple blooms.

"It helps when you have others to lean on," McGovern said. His eyes were much more youthful-looking than the disheveled mane of gray hair snaking down his shoulders. "The children have been wonderful through all of this."

Sterling wondered if Wilson's death would've been more difficult if they had been closer. "Mr. McGovern, I was hoping you could tell me about the Blackbird Project," he said.

"Call me Mack. Everyone else does. And how much time do you have on your hands?"

"As much as you need to tell me everything you know."

McGovern motioned for Sterling to have a seat at the small table. A pitcher of ice water and two glasses sparkled under the sun. McGovern filled Sterling's glass first, then his own, then sat back in his chair. The clanking of the ice cubes awakened the cat and it stood up, looked around slowly, then jumped to the ground. It brushed against Sterling's leg several times, then curled up at his feet.

"That's Jessica," McGovern said. "My wife's cat. She hasn't done too well with strangers since Madeline died, but by the looks of things, I think she likes you. Now what do you know about the Audubon Society?"

"Not much," Sterling said. "I know it's a not-for-profit organization that focuses most of its work on protecting birds and other wildlife. But that's about all I know."

"You're on the right course," Mack said. "Indulge me for a minute. I'm an ex–national president of the Audubon Society, and despite how most people have labeled us, we are not animal rights fanatics. We leave that to the PETA people. We don't commit crimes and violate other people's rights. We simply work to protect birds and other wildlife and the habitats that support them. The society was incorporated back in 1905 and named after the great ornithologist, explorer, and wildlife artist, John James Audubon. Our mission has always been simple and after almost a hundred years, we haven't strayed. Instead, we've only gotten stronger with six hundred thousand members and more than five hundred chapters. If the industrialists and commercial organizations had their way, half of the species we see today would've been extinct a long time ago."

Sterling drank his entire glass of water in one long gulp. The cold liquid felt good going down his parched throat. He didn't mind McGovern taking his time. His reverberating baritone voice was like a sedative, and while the nuts and bolts of animal activism had never interested Sterling in the past, he listened to McGovern attentively.

"Now you ask about the Blackbird Project?" McGovern said. "This is the mother of all programs directly aimed at harming blackbirds and other forms of wildlife in the upper Midwest."

"Zhang told me about the sunflower farmers and their association. But what I want to know is how nasty has this fight gotten?"

"As nasty as a battle like this can get. You have to understand, this isn't the first time they've proposed killing red-wingeds. They've been largely supported by the U.S. Department of Agriculture through one of their divisions, the Animal and Plant Health Inspection Service—APHIS. They're proposing using the avicide DRC-1339 to kill two million birds a year for three years, eliminating 25 percent of the region's blackbird population."

"Hold on for a minute," Sterling said. "I want to make sure I get this right. APHIS is proposing the poisoning of six million birds?"

"Precisely."

"And where's the proof that killing these blackbirds will spare their crops?"

"You're a fast learner, Bledsoe. That's exactly the question we've been asking the last couple of years."

"Then why in the hell are these scientists willing to promote a policy that takes such drastic steps without confirmation the program will work?"

McGovern's laugh startled Jessica, who looked up at her master, then fell back asleep at Sterling's feet. "Because politics are dirty, even when it comes to wildlife. Take a big guess who funds a great deal of APHIS research?"

"You gotta be kidding!"

"That's right. The National Sunflower Association. So if your sugar daddy tells you to jump, what are you going to say?"

"How high?"

"Damn right. So fast you'll jump clean out of your shoes. That's how the game is played."

"This sounds like a stolen script from 60 Minutes."

"Don't turn the channel yet. It gets even better. Basically you have a bunch of frustrated farmers who've tried everything to save their crops and nothing has worked. Killing what they perceive as the enemy sounds good and emotions begin to overtake reason. We have never denied that blackbirds damage sunflower crops. But what they are completely ignoring is that more harm to the crops could actually be caused by killing off the blackbirds. Nature is a peculiar thing. Predator and prey are always in a delicate balance. It's the simple math of ecology. Alter one thing in the food chain and there's the potential of destroying everything. Any farmer worth a bale of hay knows that blackbirds primarily feed on insects, and many of these insects are just as lethal or even more lethal to the crops than the birds. So removing the blackbirds would mean an overgrowth of these insects, which can then lead to greater crop ruination.

"The USDA and the farmers have no answer for our second concern, which is what will be done to protect the other wildlife that remain susceptible to the poison. Our last count found sixty-eight species of nontarget birds living in or near sunflower fields in the spring. Thirty-two of these bird species eat grain, which means they too are likely to be killed by the poisonous bait."

"So has the Blackbird Project taken off yet?"

McGovern shook his head. "I guess you could say they're still taxiing on the runway hoping to get final clearance."

"What's holding them up? You've already said the National Sunflower Association and farmers have powerful friends in Washington. Can't they just get the project rubber-stamped and rolled out?"

"Not exactly. See, we have our friends too." A mischievous grin spread across McGovern's face. "In order for the project to be carried out, permits must be approved by the U.S. Fish and Wildlife Service. Thank God they had enough brains and balls to stop APHIS dead in their tracks. Fish and Wildlife made their position very clear. No reliable proof exists that killing large numbers of blackbirds will save crops. They were also concerned about potential damage to other wildlife inhabiting the area."

Sterling processed the information. "If APHIS is the department mostly charged with handling these issues, then why can't they trump Fish and Wildlife Services?"

"Now you're catching on," McGovern said. "This is where the real politics start digging in. APHIS is part of the Department of Agriculture, whereas Fish and Wildlife is part of the Department of the Interior. The two men who run the separate agencies hate each other beyond words. Our ally is Jonathan Cardi, secretary of DOI. An elitist asshole by the name of Allistor Guyton runs the USDA."

Sterling wrote the names in his book, not that he expected them to be of much help, but he had learned in more than one investigation that the smallest details could be the snag that unraveled the entire story.

McGovern poured himself and Sterling another glass of water and wiped his wet forehead with a perfectly folded handkerchief before sitting back in his chair and looking out at the elaborate flower beds spread throughout the gated park.

"I have one more question," Sterling said. He searched for the right way to ask without revealing his motive. "Do you think this Blackbird Project would have anything to do with the poisoning of blackbirds in other parts of the country?"

McGovern tightened his forehead and drew in a deep breath, holding it as if he were swimming under water. "Tough call," he finally said, letting the words and his breath escape at once. "Blackbirds can be found in other parts of the country, but the major problem has been reported in Minnesota and South and North Dakota. Small farmers in other parts of the country may have their own reason and methods of killing birds damaging their property, but connecting it back to the APHIS project could prove tough."

Sterling mulled over McGovern's words. Not exactly what he was hoping to hear, but at least the door hadn't been completely shut. He had taken enough notes to keep him busy the next twenty-four hours. He stood to leave.

"You never told me what type of research you're working on," McGovern said, rocking himself in his chair until he had enough momentum to stand.

"Right now I'm looking into blackbird populations and how people might be experimenting with means of keeping them under control. From what you've just told me, it seems to be as much a political issue as it is a scientific one."

Jessica stood up with Sterling and stretched her front legs until her stomach fell flush against the floor. After a long yawn that showed the depths of her throat, she brushed against Sterling's leg a couple of more times, then jumped into her chair, curled up, and went back to sleep.

McGovern rested his hands on Sterling's shoulder. Tiny networks of bright red capillaries weaved their way across his bulbous cheeks. "I'm retired now, but I was in the advocacy business for a good forty years," he said. "I've seen and heard a lot, some things I'll never repeat. But let me give you a little advice from my experiences. Despite the good intentions the government says it has for maintaining and restoring agricultural standards, there are a lot of fat, grubby hands digging into this country's rich agricultural stew. What most people don't know is that sunflower seeds and oil could be the gold mine of the future."

"How's that?" Sterling asked uncertainly.

"Because they're experimenting with alternative uses. Farmers are now using the oil as an engine lubricant. Sales could soar into the billions if the growers can develop this type of industrial market. I was talking to one of my old friends out there who's been keeping an eye on the developments. Some of these farmers have already completed a three-year trial with the U.S. Postal Service vehicles using sunflower oil to lubricate their old truck engines. Promising results. Not only did it decrease tailpipe emissions enough to make the Greenies happy, but the engines had less wear than if they had been fed traditional motor oil. I'm telling you, Bledsoe, there's big money in those sunflower crops, and the first one to get everything lined up takes home the biggest slice of the pie. In this business, suspect the least suspicious and, above all, don't trust anyone. Sounds cynical as hell, but when money like this is at stake, very little is what it seems."

40

Sterling waited at the northeast corner of Avenue B and Tenth Street, hiding between two parked vans as he scanned the buildings and sidewalks. He carefully watched the light but constant flow of traffic heading into the pale blue door of the Hotel DeWitt. With any luck, Veronica wouldn't ask how he had come to learn of this less-than-glamorous enterprise.

The Hotel DeWitt and its fluorescent gold wallpapered rooms had been part of a dark chapter in Sterling's life. Years ago, when he was spinning in a turbulent cyclone of depression, he had spent the better part of his nights running a stream of women up the narrow staircases and into the squalid rooms. The only way he could look back now and not hate himself was to remember that he had never purchased the sex. These were women he had met in dark bars full of desperate men and lonely women. It wasn't that he had enjoyed the sex so much as it was that each conquest represented a success, something he badly needed at a point in his life when everything seemed to be going wrong.

The last woman Sterling brought to the DeWitt almost cost him his life. After two bottles of cheap wine turned his mind fuzzy, she let in an accomplice who beat him with a crowbar until he was practically unconscious. All for the mere $78 he had in cash. Thankfully, the receptionist on duty that night had the presence of mind to load him into a cab and direct it to the emergency room of a private hospital on the Upper East Side. That was the last time he had seen the DeWitt.

Sterling scouted the area for forty-five minutes before making his way into the hotel. He pushed through the smoky revolving glass doors and entered the small hallway that had been converted into a lobby with a high, black Formica counter and a lopsided brass chandelier hanging from the ceiling on a knot of copper wire. He walked past the clerk, whose attention was directed at a big box in the corner of the makeshift office, and up the back stairs that led to the two floors of rooms. He tapped three times on door 517, waited a moment, then tapped once. He stood back from the door so that Veronica could clearly make him out through the peephole. The door flew open.

"Thank God you're all right," Veronica said, pulling him in and planting small kisses around his face before landing a wet one on his lips. Her eyes were red and swollen. "I've been sitting here scared to death that something happened to you."

Sterling slammed the door shut with the back of his foot and squeezed her in his arms. He pulled off his hat and threw it onto the made bed. Veronica hadn't even attempted to go to sleep. "It's been a long twenty-four hours," he said. He hugged her tightly, then kissed her again, this time long and hard. They fell back onto the bed, clawing at each other's clothes. Sterling wanted all of her at once. He kissed behind her ears, then worked his tongue down her long neck, forming small, wet circles that made her body twitch underneath him. It felt good to taste her again, to feel the weight of her body pressed against his chest. He opened up her shirt, then tossed it aside, slowly running his hands along the contours of her chest before sliding them down to her narrow waist.

"I missed you," Sterling said between heavy breaths.

"And that's exactly what a girl likes to hear," she said, unclasping his belt buckle and pulling off his pants.

Veronica traced the knots of muscles in his shoulders and washboard abs. Just looking at his naked body was enough to make her quiver.

Sterling lifted her supple body, then pulled back the covers and spread her across the small bed. He paused for a minute to admire her honey-colored skin and the way the curves had formed in all the right places on her slim frame. She smiled as if she knew what he was thinking. Then, unable to resist the temptation any longer, he enjoyed her for the next hour as if he were intent on making up for all of the time they had spent apart.

When they both were dressed again, Sterling walked her to two chairs near the window and took a seat. "A lot has happened and I know you have tons of questions. But I don't know if I have all the answers."

Veronica ran her hand over his slick head. "How about start by telling me why you've shaved your hair off."

Sterling gave one pass over his dome and enjoyed the prickly feeling of the short stubble that scraped the palm of his hand. "They think I killed Wilson, Ronnie. Right now they're spreading all across the city looking for me."

Veronica covered her mouth with her hand. She was trembling. "So this is part of a disguise?"

"It's the best I could come up with on short notice," Sterling said, reaching out to comfort her. "But I'm still open to suggestions."

"I don't understand. Why would they think you'd kill your own brother, and then go up there and be part of the investigation? It just doesn't make any sense."

"It's a long story. The bottom line is someone is trying to set me up for this. Three people are dead right now and whoever killed them must feel like I'm getting too close. What better way to get me off the trail than make it look like I did it? And it's working. Agents from the New York office are fanning out across the city right now searching for me. For us. It's going to get real dicey if I don't come up with some answers soon."

Veronica's head slumped forward. She closed her eyes hard, but that didn't stop the tears from forming in them. "So everyone's looking for you right now? The murderer and the FBI?"

Sterling nodded. "At least until I can put everything together and nail the real killers. I know there's more than just one person behind all of this. I'm making progress, but I need to be out and moving if I'm going to solve these cases. If they pick me up, who knows how everything will play out?"

"Why can't you just sit down and tell them everything you know? It's not like you're a stranger. And you have an alibi. I was with you. Can't you just tell them that?"

Sterling smiled at her innocence and stroked her hair. Looking into her eyes, even as they filled with tears, reminded him how much he had missed falling asleep and waking up with her curled beside him. At that moment he felt the urge to tell her how badly he wanted to love her forever. But there'd be enough time to get into all of that once they had put this behind them. He leaned over and kissed her on both cheeks, then passionately on the lips.

"It's complicated, Ronnie," he said. "When people in my profession smell blood, their only instinct is to hunt until they can actually taste it. Even if it's the blood of their own."

As she held her arms around his neck, he moved the shade and peeked out the window. He didn't like what he saw.

"What is it?" she asked.

He quickly pulled her to the floor and took another glance out the window. Two men in identical dark suits were walking down Tenth Street toward the hotel. He recognized the big one right away—Skip Dumars. Both men already had their weapons drawn. They would be fast on the trigger the minute they spotted him.

"Where's the gun and the money?" he asked.

"In the closet. Why? What's wrong?"

"They tracked me here. I don't know how in the hell they did it. I was sure no one followed me. Did you use your cell phone?"

"No, you told me not to. I just made one call from the room phone."

"Ronnie, I told you—"

"I tried calling your cell, but you didn't answer. I was going crazy not hearing from you. What was I supposed to do?"

Sterling ran to the closet and grabbed the Glock 36, preferring this to the Beretta Tomcat he typically carried because it had a longer barrel and was more accurate at greater distances. He motioned for Veronica to go near the door as he took a position at the window. They were still half a block away and Skip Dumars was leading the charge. He had to stall them.

"Go throw your clothes into a bag," he said. When Veronica had moved across the room, he lifted the window several inches and fired two shots across the street at a rusted car whose windshield had been papered with orange parking tickets. The car was far enough away from the advancing men that they were in no danger of getting hit, but the loud implosion of the windshield scared them enough for them to hit the ground and roll over behind a row of parked cars. He closed the window and grabbed Veronica. They ran the hallway, then down the two flights of steps. Sterling opened the door to the main floor of the hotel and put a finger up to his mouth for her to be quiet. He walked about five feet, then turned down another short hallway. At the end of the hall, he opened a narrow steel door that had been painted to look like it was part of the wall. He pulled a rope handle and a second door split in half, the top part lifting and the bottom half sliding down.

"What is this?" Veronica asked.

"A dumbwaiter. Get in." Sterling pushed her forward, but she resisted. "Dammit, Ronnie, get in. We don't have time to debate." Sterling gave her a big shove into the darkness, then followed her, closing the door and pushing a red button on the side of the elevator shaft. The elevator was slow to start, groaning and screeching as the pulleys and gears clicked into place. He remembered this dumbwaiter from a night when the police raided the hotel. He noticed one of the regulars fleeing from her room, but instead of running for the exit like everyone else, she slipped down the back hall. He gambled and followed her even as she climbed into the dumbwaiter. She showed him the tunnel that led out the back of the building, explaining that in the late thirties the hotel had belonged to a wealthy artist whose staff had used the elevator to serve the weekly parties he held in the mansion. Most of the DeWitt employees didn't even know the dumbwaiter existed, but those like herself who often needed to leave in a hurry and undetected had come to rely on the hidden contraption and the tunnel leading to the back alley.

When they reached the basement, Sterling grabbed Veronica's hand and pulled her through the darkness. Two quick lefts, then he kicked hard and daylight poured in. Police sirens rang off in the distance, and Sterling knew it would be only a matter of minutes before cops had encircled the entire block. He and Veronica were traveling east on Ninth Street, but a platoon of cruisers was heading in their direction. They turned south on Avenue C but were stopped by another cruiser barreling toward them, going up the narrow street in the wrong direction. Then Sterling saw the large blue van marked DREW's UNIFORMS AND CLEANING. A short man with thick, hairy arms was coming out of the East Village Bed and Coffee Shop carrying a large box of dirty uniforms. "Jump in," Sterling shouted, hoisting Veronica into the van first, then jumping in himself. He landed somewhere near her and was immediately assaulted by the smell of grease, stale food, and dried sweat as he buried himself under the mound of filthy uniforms. The driver's hollow whistle grew louder. The siren from the cruiser also seemed to grow louder. A new batch of soiled uniforms landed atop the heap, then the back door slammed shut. The truck's engine started, the scratchy radio blared, and they were moving.

Hidden underneath the uniforms, Sterling couldn't see out the side window, but he kept track of the truck's movements in his head. It stopped after about seventy feet, which meant it had pulled up to the corner of Eighth

Street. The loud wail of sirens was coming from the west, which meant they were driving away from the hotel and the massive manhunt that was under way. Sterling held his breath, wondering if the truck would turn left toward the mayhem or right to their future escape. He cradled his gun just in case he needed to persuade the driver of the turn he needed to make.

The engine revved and the truck leaned to the right. It rolled ahead without stopping for the next several minutes. The sirens had been replaced with honking cars, and Sterling slowly cleared a hole in the uniform heap so that he could see where they were. He saw the back of the driver and almost laughed when he noticed the two phone books the man used to lift himself in the seat. Sterling craned his neck to see out the front window. The truck was traveling north now on Avenue D. They passed a school on the corner of 12th Street, then stopped on 13th Street. Sterling watched as the driver hit the hazard lights, jumped out of the cabin, then opened the side door and grabbed a metal crate for his next pickup. Once the driver had cleared the truck, Sterling quickly tossed aside the uniforms and stood.

"Let's go," he said, burrowing through the uniforms to find Veronica. "He stopped to make another pickup."

Sterling couldn't stop himself from smiling when Veronica's face emerged. She wore the expression of someone who had opened a refrigerator full of spoiled milk and rotten meat.

"You all right?" he asked.

"I smell like shit."

"But shit never looked this pretty."

"Not bad, Romeo. You really know how to lift a girl's spirits."

Sterling checked the door first to make sure the driver wasn't near the truck, then jumped out and caught Veronica as she followed. Two men sharing a smoke at the corner pointed toward them and laughed. Sterling ignored them, grabbed Veronica's bag with one hand and her with the other, then broke out into a jog heading north to 14th Street. Veronica pointed toward the corner where a police van sat double parked outside a Baskin-Robbins ice-cream shop. Sterling waited for the traffic to stop, then moved her into the dense pack of bodies crossing the street. They followed the swarm west along 14th Street until they reached the subway station on First Avenue. They raced down the steps and in seconds disappeared on the crowded L train screeching its way through the dark New York underground.

41

Sterling walked out onto 138th Street and looked left, then right before taking deep gulps of the cool night air. His stomach was full, his body washed, and his clothes replaced with a pair of old jeans and a roomy black sweat jacket. He turned back and looked up at the old scrubbed edifice of the Abyssinian Baptist Church. If there was anyone he could trust to take good care of Veronica, it would be Reverend Briggs, the savvy and popular senior pastor of the famed Harlem church. Sterling considered Reverend Briggs a savior and it had little to do with his starched white pastor's collar. Along with Dr. Lieteau, Reverend Coleman Briggs had pulled him from the steel claws of depression and depravity. The determined minister never gave up on Sterling, visiting him daily in the hospital after the beating at the Hotel DeWitt, then bringing him into his own home once he was well enough to leave the hospital. Mrs. Briggs, a strong and colorful disciple with a spiritual fervor that rivaled her husband's, nursed Sterling back to physical health, promising him that she wouldn't let him out until he was steady enough on his own two feet not just to walk but to run. Even after that experience, Sterling never became a deeply religious man, but he still found himself making a small sign of the cross in front of the towering granite statue of Christ. He thanked the sacred walls of Abyssinian for once again providing the safety and comfort he desperately needed.

At the corner of Adam Clayton Powell Boulevard, known outside of Harlem as Seventh Avenue, Sterling stopped one of the black gypsy cabs and bargained a fare all the way down to Penn Station. He sat behind the driver, hoping to discourage conversation, but it wasn't until he had delivered several one-word answers that the spirited young Haitian man got the message. He turned on one of the hip-hop stations and sang along as Sterling mapped out a plan.

It was only seven in the evening and he would dedicate the remainder of the night to looking through Wilson's papers. He was counting on something in the e-mails or printed documents that would give him the snag he could pull to unravel a deeper connection between Wilson and Heidi Vorscht. It still bothered him that Wilson had confided in a graduate student yet explicitly told Mandryka they should keep their discoveries a secret until the case report had been finished and published. What was it about Heidi? What was she up to? Vivian Sinclair had said Heidi possessed unbelievable charm, but Sterling now wondered if it was charm or powerful abilities of manipulation.

Sterling had the taxi driver drop him off on Eighth Avenue, a couple of blocks south of Madison Square Garden. He checked the entrance for uniforms or agents, then joined the heavy flow of people walking down into the belly of Penn Station. This was a perfect time for him to slip in as the last of the evening rush hour commuters filled the station, waiting under the big board for the announcement of their gates. He looked into the faces of the exhausted men and women lugging briefcases and bags, some of them chomping on pretzels because it would be too late to eat dinner by the time they arrived home in the suburbs. Sterling made his way down the east corridor of the station, avoiding the National Guard booth before slipping into the locker hallway. He inserted the key into the locker, grabbed the box, then headed with all the others rushing to the subway lines. He pulled down his skullcap before passing through the subway turnstile and waited just seconds on the elevated platform before jumping onto the uptown 9 train.

Riding the cramped, dirty subway for the third time in one day made Sterling long for his Porsche. He wondered if they had already impounded it, claiming they were searching for clues but mostly trying to irritate him, knowing how careful he was with it. The thought of Skip Dumars gripping the steering wheel nauseated him. By now they had turned both of his apartments, the one down in Virginia and the one here in the city, upside down looking for evidence. Dumars probably had been thrilled searching through his personal belongings. Sterling prayed that they hadn't found his psychiatry bills.

The train made numerous local stops before Sterling exited at 116th Street/Columbia University. Just inside the school's gate, he found a campus phone and asked the operator for Bettie Hill, Department of Adolescent Psychology.

Bettie was one of Sterling's old flings, but unlike his others, their relationship had dissolved amicably and both had walked away feeling fulfilled. They had spent one hot, lustful summer together, but both knew that it would never amount to anything more than that. She was serious about her graduate studies and he was serious about not being serious. Without either of them having to utter the words, they both knew when it was over.

"Extension 2498," the operator came back on. "Can I connect you?"

"Please." Sterling waited as the phone rang. If Bettie wasn't teaching a class, she could almost always be found in her office. Ever the ambitious academic, she had earned her doctorate early and found her way onto the Columbia faculty, where sometimes she taught students twice her age.

"Hill," a woman's voice curtly answered. It was obvious the phone had distracted her from something more important.

"Blinky, it's me." That was the nickname Sterling had given her that summer. It had something to do with a pair of hot-pink shorts she liked to wear.

"Sterling Bledsoe?"

"In the flesh."

"Where in the hell have you been?" She perked up now.

"I've been around," Sterling said. "Same drill. Trying to catch the bad guys and still looking for a rich wife who'll support my golfing addiction when I retire."

"I see you're still delusional. The more things change, the more they stay the same." That had always been one of his lines.

"And how are you, Blinky? Let me guess. Right now you're hunched over a bunch of term papers marking them up in red."

"About right. Semester's over in a month and I'm way behind. Vacation can't come fast enough. So to what do I owe the pleasure? I'm sure you're not calling to talk about my teaching woes."

"I'll cut to the chase, Blinky. I need your help. And I need it right away."

"Uh-oh. The last time I helped you I found myself on my back looking up at the stars in Central Park."

"You enjoyed it just as much as I did."

"Never said I didn't. I just fell behind an entire summer's worth of research."

Sterling thought about that first night. They had met in front of Butler Library. She was on her way to the movies, alone, and he was looking for Fayweather Hall. He asked her for directions and after a short exchange, neither made it to their planned destination. He remembered how her hair had been tucked under a Yankees cap, and she'd worn just enough lipstick to make him want to kiss her for days.

"No directions this time," Sterling laughed. "I need to borrow your computer for a little while."

The request surprised her. "My computer? For what?"

"I have some disks here with documents I need to print out. But I need to do it soon."

"How soon?"

"Right now."

"Doesn't the FBI provide you guys with basic computer equipment?"

It was a fair question. "It's not that simple," Sterling said. "I don't need just your computer and printer. I also need your discretion."

"Discretion? Sterling, are you in some kind of trouble?"

"Not exactly. Just a temporary jam. Don't worry, everything will be worked out in a couple of days. So will you help an old friend?"

"I don't know, Sterling. I still have twenty papers sitting on my desk that need to be graded by tomorrow morning."

"I promise I'll be quick." There was a long pause. Sterling knew she was struggling not to say yes.

"Do you remember how to find my office?" she said, relenting.

"How could I ever forget?"

You didn't say you had all of that to print." Bettie Hill stood with her hands on her hips looking down at the box of disks. "That could take all night."

"I'll be done in a couple of hours," Sterling said. He planted a long kiss on her cheek before pushing his way past her to the computer. A meditation candle burning on the corner of her desk made the room smell like jasmine. In typical fashion everything was in perfect order, including the pens on her desk, which had been arranged on the glass top with all the caps lined up in the same direction.

"Are you gonna at least tell me what's going on?"

"I can't." Sterling inserted the first disk into the drive tower and moved the mouse on the screen, clicking the documents ready to be printed.

"Is helping you going to get me in trouble?" Bettie was now seated across the desk. It had been five years since they'd last seen each other, but to Sterling she seemed unchanged. The black rectangular glasses and long ponytail made her look more like a schoolgirl than a professor. He looked away from her, knowing how easy it would be to get distracted.

"Blinky, I'd never involve you in my cases in a way that would get you in trouble," he said. "That's why I won't share with you the details of what I'm doing. We have to agree that you won't ask any questions related to this. That way you can't be held accountable for something you don't know."

Bettie grabbed the papers off her desk and began marking them, occasionally looking up as Sterling hammered away at the keys and sent the printer into overdrive. In the next two hours she changed the toner cartridge once and reloaded the paper tray four times. She attempted to keep her mind focused on her work, but couldn't stop herself from looking up at the computer screen and wondering why Sterling was printing out so many e-mails. But she knew well enough not to ask any questions.

Sterling moved methodically through the disks, printing out the e-mails and at the same time scanning the screen for any correspondence that had Heidi Vorscht's name on it. He was down to the last disk and hadn't yet seen her name in the address line or in the body of a message. Then he realized that he had been looking for the wrong name. The computer had arranged the sender and recipient names in alphabetical order. The name now flashing on his screen brought him back to the conversation he had had with Kanti. It read simply: WOGAN.

42

Sterling found an empty table in the corner of the fifth floor of Columbia's Butler Library. He slung his jacket over the back of a chair, then arranged the e-mails by sender. The largest packet turned out to be from Wogan. The first fifty were standard, no different than what other students might have sent. Though Vorscht was a graduate student in the school of engineering, she seemed sincere in her interest in Wilson's research. She mentioned how she had always been intrigued by matters of wildlife and while her mother shared her interests, she had insisted that if Heidi were to be taken seriously and earn a decent living, she needed a degree in one of the hard sciences. Sterling analyzed the e-mails not only for their content but also for their tone. The exchanges had been cordial at first, but then they took on a personal character. Heidi mentioned that she was lonely living in Mrs. Potter's big farmhouse and was having trouble making friends. All of the other students wanted to talk about engineering or their research, and she wanted to talk about movies and music. Wilson reacted like any concerned faculty member would, suggesting she visit the student activities center or participate in some of the intramural sports that were also open to graduate students. At the height of their correspondence, there had been as many as two or three e-mails a day. But then they suddenly stopped.

Sterling checked the dates and counted the e-mails. Over a span of two months, Heidi and Wilson had exchanged over two hundred e-mails, excessive by any standards, but more so considering she wasn't even one of his students.

The next e-mail didn't come for several more months. It was addressed as usual to "PB," for Professor Bledsoe:

How is your investigation going? I've been doing some research on my own, but don't worry, I haven't mentioned you or your discovery. I think this is a problem in other parts of the Upper Valley. I've been in touch with someone who knows of a blackbird problem in another area in the mountains. I'll let you know what I find. I miss our talks. Hope to see you soon.

HV

Sterling reread the note several times. This was the first mention of the blackbirds. He picked apart every sentence, breaking it down to each word. He searched for Wilson's reply.

The same date, several hours later, almost nine o'clock that night.

HV,

I'd very much like to hear what you've learned about the birds. I think it's better to discuss this in person rather than blitzmail. I found another fifty this past week, all of them looking the same, no physical evidence of what might have killed them. At first I thought these deaths could be some strange coincidence or freak of nature, but I'm now convinced these deaths are purposeful. I've enlisted the help of Professor Mandryka to help me sort through all of this. Your continued privacy in this matter is essential as we've already discussed. I really look forward to seeing you soon. I miss our chats.

PB

Sterling detected an urgency in Wilson's desire not only regarding the birds but regarding Vorscht herself. There was an unmistakable feeling of attachment in the letter's closing. Sterling wondered if Mandryka knew about Vorscht.

Heidi's next e-mail arrived a couple of days later.

PB,

Thanks for taking me on your walk this morning. I've lived on this property for almost two years and never realized how close I was to such environmental perfection. The innocence of the wildlife in these vast mountains reminds me of the walks I took with my mother as a little girl. For hours, we'd discover flowers and animals and play games naming them. Finding those dead birds this morning made me realize how cruel and arrogant man can be. Sometimes I'm ashamed for our people. Seeing those birds has convinced me that evil is lurking in these great mountains. I want to help you figure this out. You can definitely trust me. And thanks for listening to me ramble this morning about my loneliness. You are a sweet man.

> HV

Wilson's response was brief, echoing her pleasure in their walk that morning and expressing his willingness to see her any time that afternoon to discuss the birds. He had an hourlong grant meeting to attend at three o'clock, but after that he'd be free for the rest of the day.

Sterling continued to read through the e-mails, tracking Heidi and Wilson's conversations about the birds but also recognizing the increasingly affectionate tones in their messages. Nothing explicit, but it was there. Some of the e-mails had nothing to do with the birds, but spoke of movies they'd seen or books they'd read. They e-mailed at all hours, late at night, first thing in the morning. Sometimes they rambled, at other times they were brief.

Sterling found an e-mail that Heidi sent at 1:30 AM.

> PB,
> Thank you.
> HV

Sterling turned away from the e-mail and looked down the empty aisle, almost afraid that someone else had read the message. A strange combination of sadness, anger, and confusion swirled in his chest, and he rubbed his eyes hard as if that would erase the words on the page. But he looked down again and read what she had written, then whispered to himself so that he would believe what his mind already knew—Wilson had had an affair. Only two words, but it all started to make sense. Kelton had recalled the many closed-door visits. And now it was clear why Heidi had spent so much time in the lab when she served no official research capacity like the other students. Sterling played back the image of that picture. She stood next to Wilson, her hand resting on his shoulder, almost as if daring the world to discover that they were lovers.

Sterling checked the date of the e-mail. Less than three weeks ago, only two days before Wilson was murdered. He looked for Wilson's response. There wasn't one. That was the last e-mail either of them had written to each other.

An overhead bell rang briefly, startling Sterling. He looked at his watch. Eleven thirty. The library would be closing in half an hour. A student bounced down the aisles, pushing in chairs, reshelving volumes that had been left on tables. In a voice that could only be meant to annoy, she reminded everyone that it was time to check out any books they planned on taking home overnight.

Sterling dug back into the e-mails. He scanned them quickly, casting aside the mundane correspondence—appointments with students, collegial banter with other faculty. Even in e-mails, Wilson came across as thoroughly self-confident, at times writing with a flash of levity and biting sarcasm that Sterling had never appreciated.

Sterling noticed patterns to the correspondence. Those Wilson seemed most familiar with, such as Yuri Mandryka, were addressed by the initials of their first and last names—YM. Only when he wanted to maintain a formal tone did he sign off "Professor Bledsoe"; otherwise, it was simply PB. Almost everyone called him Professor, and some of his students would send him chain e-mail jokes, which surprisingly, instead of deleting, he'd send on to others.

The e-mails also demonstrated Wilson's willingness to do anything to help his students. They were like his children, and even when he needed to reprimand a student for not completing an assignment or for turning in a poorly written project, he did it in a way calculated not to embarrass or upset them. With the finesse and cheerful encouragement of a skilled coach, he not only pointed out their shortcomings but gave equal attention to what they did well.

Sterling reread the correspondence between Wilson and Mandryka. In the early part of last year, Wilson made his first inquiry of Mandryka, seeking counsel in the study of blackbirds. His e-mail was vague, but his tone was serious. Over the span of five months, the two exchanged as many as fifty e-mails, but they wrote almost in code. Only once did Sterling actually mention the blackbird deaths, and when Mandryka sent back detailed information about the anatomy of the birds, Sterling suggested they speak in person. After that, the trail went cold. The last month of e-mail exchanges never mentioned blackbirds or death or any of their suspicions.

Sterling then tackled a series of e-mails from President Mortimer. The first twenty, brief and formal, held no surprises. They were perfunctory, an invitation to a meeting of the president's advisory council, a reminder that one of the department chairs was to be feted at a luncheon at the faculty club. Occasionally Mortimer would include a line at the end of his short missives asking about Kay, but his words were as flat in print as they were when spoken. The rest of the e-mails weren't sent by Mortimer, but by his office staff. The typical presidential spam mail, announcing the appointment of a new professor, or a spirited bulletin rolling out yet another program to enhance the continued excellence of the Dartmouth tradition.

Sterling turned to a fresh page in his book and jotted notes, trying to fill in some of the holes. Suddenly, he winced from the high-pitched, screeching sound of metal on tile. He looked up to find the library warden staring in his direction. She looked like a softball player, wide shoulders, dirty-blond hair pulled back into a ponytail, her shirt and jeans oversized despite her large frame. She was transfixed not on him but on something near his table. Her mouth was open as if she were about to speak. He followed the direction of her stare and looked at his jacket. She still stood there. He leaned over and pulled out the chair, then he saw what had paralyzed her. The Glock was in full view. He quickly closed the jacket, but by the time he looked up, she had disappeared down one of the aisles.

Sterling knew he had to get out of there in a hurry. He quickly went to work stacking the e-mails in chronological order, but was distracted by the jingling of keys echoing from the other end of the hall. He looked up and saw the library warden pointing in his direction, talking to two rent-a-cops in matching gray uniforms. One of them spoke into his radio, while the other gripped his club. They picked up their pace as Sterling threw the e-mails into the box and grabbed his coat. He ran down an aisle and flung open the door to the back stairwell. Practically jumping an entire flight of stairs, he turned to descend the next flight when he heard loud footsteps charging up from several floors below. Radio transmissions echoed up the stairwell as well. He made out the words "gun" and "careful."

The door above him opened and he heard the library warden's voice.

Sterling turned back and entered the fourth floor. He ran through a small passageway that led to a more desolate part of the library housing small offices and intersecting rows of tall, dusty bookshelves. He spotted an exit sign and ran down the dark, narrow aisles. Two quick lefts and along a short hallway and he was in another stairwell. He took the steps two, three at a time, the adrenaline rushing too fast in his arteries for him to feel the burn in his muscles. He jumped the last five steps and banged his way against an emergency exit door whose alarm screamed as the crisp night air welcomed him.

He looked right toward the sirens and flashing lights that had strangled the corner of Broadway and 114th Street. Officers ran through the gates on the west side of the campus, screaming into their radios, their guns drawn. Sterling ran in the opposite direction, toward Amsterdam Avenue. He dodged the cars as he ran against the green light and behind St. Luke's Hospital. Two medics were lifting an old woman from the back of an ambulance. She had all sorts of wires and tubes connected to her emaciated body. Sterling ran as hard as he could while carrying a box and wearing stiff new boots. At the end of the block he jumped a small fence and landed in a dark, deserted park, the wail of sirens dying away behind him.

He slowed to a jog, keeping himself in the shadows rather than the dimly lit walkways. A cluster of homeless people had constructed a small village of cardboard-box houses along the paths. He could hear them roll from one uncomfortable position to another. He even heard the plaintive cry of a hungry baby and a woman's sleepy voice begging for quiet.

This was not the kind of park where children picked flowers and chased bright balloons. Used condoms and cracked syringes littered the uncut grass. The glass of broken beer bottles formed a dangerous trail that sparkled under the flickering lamps. Sterling kept his hand near his pocket, making it easier to draw the gun if the need arose.

He finally made it out of the park and onto Manhattan Avenue, where he quickly hailed a battered gypsy cab cruising the neighborhood for fares. He gave the address for Abyssinian, then fell back into the seat and tried to catch his breath. His heart pounded against his chest and his thigh muscles were cramped in tiny knots. He cursed himself for being so careless with the gun. If they hadn't identified him yet, it wouldn't be long before they checked the security cameras and got a confirmation.

Sterling paid the cab as it pulled up to Abyssinian, but before scaling the back stairwell he got a sudden idea. It was a long shot, but with time running out, at least worth a try. He went to the corner pay phone and punched in the home number of ex–field office director Agent Martin Gilden.

"Hello." It was an old woman's voice, weak and full of sleep.

"Professor Gilden, please," Sterling said. He had always called him Professor, even after he joined the Bureau.

"He's sleeping right now," the old woman said. "Is it possible you can call back in the morning?"

"I'm sorry to call this late, ma'am, but can you tell him that it's Agent Sterling Bledsoe? I'm sure he'll take my call."

There was a pause at the other end. "Hold on."

Sterling heard shuffling in the background, then a voice he hadn't heard in almost ten years. "Bledsoe, my boy. Don't you have any clocks in your damn house?"

"Apologies, Professor, but I wouldn't be calling you if it wasn't an emergency."

Sterling could hear muffling over the phone, then Gilden say, "Don't worry, hon, go on back to bed." Gilden must've waited for her to leave before speaking. "Are you all right?" he whispered.

Sterling blew out a long breath. "Under the circumstances, yes."

"What's the problem?"

"I need your help on a case."

"A case? Bledsoe, I haven't worked a case in twenty years."

"I know that, sir, but it was you who told me, 'Once in the Bureau, always in the Bureau.' I need that to be true right now and in a bad way."

Gilden released a long, pensive sigh through the receiver. "Give me a minute. I need to go downstairs and change phones."

Sterling waited for Gilden, knowing that with Director Murphy's approval on the massive manhunt to capture him, this could be one of his last chances to get some information from inside. He had thought about calling a couple of agents with whom he had developed a friendship over the years, but decided against it. It was too much of a gamble for an active to risk going into the shitter to help save Sterling's ass. The Bureau was still a stagnant cesspool of politics, even when it came to helping another agent who had put his life on the line countless times.

"What case has you in a snare?" Gilden was back on the phone. He sounded more like his old self, in control.

"My brother's."

"Wilson?"

"He's been murdered."

Sterling knew the words had hit Gilden like a cannonball to the gut. Men in the Bureau were accustomed to murders and deaths, but when it involved one of their own, the news was always difficult to hear.

"I had just read somewhere that he won a major science award," Gilden said. "That couldn't've been more than a couple of months ago. What happened?"

Sterling hesitated at first, worried that bringing Gilden in could also land him in a heap of trouble, but with Skip Dumars on the hunt and the agency looking to contain collateral damage, it was this or nothing. He started from the beginning when Kay had called and told him that Wilson was missing. He laid everything out for Gilden, who like any good agent spent most of his time listening, only asking questions when he needed clarification. Sterling brought Gilden up to the final e-mail between Wilson and Heidi, then did something he had never done except with Dr. Lieteau. He told Gilden about his strained relationship with Wilson and how as a child he had harbored so much animosity toward his older brother that he couldn't even stand to hear the mention of his name. He explained how most of his life had been focused on stepping out of Wilson's shadow and proving to himself that he had his own talents.

Gilden let him pour out this last part without the slightest interruption, and when Sterling fell silent Gilden asked the question that brought a smile of relief to Sterling's face. "What can I do to help you catch these sonsabitches?"

"I don't want to jeopardize you, Professor."

"Don't be silly. I know how these things work when there's a fix against you on the inside. Besides, what can they do to me? I'm not active. My pension is protected. And most of them don't even know I'm still alive."

Sterling could feel Gilden's energy. "I need help with Vorscht," Sterling said. "It blows me away to say this, but it's obvious that my brother had an affair with her. I don't know if he ever planned on leaving Kay or if he found himself trapped in something he couldn't get out of, but I get the feeling from Vorscht's last e-mail that things were becoming one-sided. I think that Wilson was trying to end it. Whatever it was, he must've fallen for her pretty hard."

"Sterling, your brother wouldn't be the first professor to have an affair with a student. That doesn't seem to be enough to get him murdered."

Sterling agreed. He had already ruled that out as a single motive. But he still felt the affair and the blackbirds and Wilson's research formed some kind of messy triangle.

"There was something more than just an affair," Sterling said. "Every time I get a break in this case, it leads back to her. She was everywhere."

"So you want me to run a background on her?"

"That's what I was thinking. It's too risky right now for me to call anyone inside for help. If you dig deep enough, I'm sure you'll find something."

"Spell her name for me."

"V-O-R-S-C-H-T."

"You know her mother's name?"

"No."

"How about where they're from?"

Sterling flipped back to the pages from his conversation with Nel Potter at the farmhouse. "The woman she lived with said that she came from Stuttgart."

"Does she have any other name?"

"Well, the local Native American tribe called her Wogan, but other than that I think everyone else just called her Heidi."

"How do I reach you if I find something?"

Sterling gave him the number of the Abyssinian Baptist Church. "Ask for Reverend or Mrs. Briggs. But if they aren't available, don't leave any messages. Keep trying them. One of them will be there some time during the day."

"Give me at least twenty-four hours," Gilden said. He would need to call on his few remaining contacts in the Bundeskriminalamt, or BKA—the German equivalent of the FBI.

43

Sterling knew he had a long day of research ahead of him, but before he burrowed into the computer, he needed to secure some untraceable means of communication. He stopped by Jerry's Den on 125th Street and quickly found out from the barber who had cut his hair yesterday where he could pick up a burner—an illegal cell phone that has no listed owner with the phone company, thus making it impossible to trace to its user. Fifty dollars and thirty minutes later, Sterling made his first call to Windsor McGovern.

"Yeah," McGovern answered, his voice swallowed by the strains of a scratchy record in the background.

"It's Sterling Bledsoe, Mack. I hope I'm not disturbing you."

"Hold on," McGovern yelled into Sterling's ear. The music suddenly disappeared. "That's better," he said, now out of breath. "How's the research coming?"

"Pretty well," Sterling said. "I just have a couple of questions I didn't think of before."

"You wanna stop by this morning?"

He knew McGovern was looking for company. Nothing could be lonelier than living in that apartment full of memories of his wife. Sterling wouldn't have minded paying the old man a visit, but today he had to make every minute count.

"We can do this over the phone if you don't mind," Sterling said. "It really shouldn't take too long."

"If that's what you'd like," McGovern said. His disappointment was evident. "I'm ready when you are."

Sterling flipped the pages in his book. "You told me they used something called DRC-1339," Sterling said, reading from his notes. "What kind of toxin is that?"

"It's what we call an avicide," McGovern explained. "Just like pesticides are toxins that kill insects, avicides are toxins that kill birds. DRC-1339 isn't anything new. It was developed back in the early 1960s in a collaboration between the Denver Wildlife Research Center and the Ralston Purina Company. They registered two products—Starlicide Technical and 1% Starlicide Pellets. The major goal at the time was to control the starling bird populations in animal feedlots, thus the name Starlicide."

"Hold on, Mack," Sterling said, running his pen quickly across the pages of his black book. "Did you say the Purina Company, like the cat food?"

"You heard me right. They make that cat chow my little Jessica hates with a passion."

"So this Starlicide is the same stuff APHIS is now proposing to kill the six million birds?"

"Not exactly. Back in the sixties, APHIS was called the ADC—Animal Damage Control. Because Purina had the patent, ADC had to ask their permission to register a 98 percent concentrate that was much more powerful than the pellets. They were having lots of special bird problems and everyone just figured they could kill more by making the old stuff stronger. And bingo, they had a solution."

The poison Mandryka had detected could be a variant of the DRC-1339, but that seemed too damn easy. Maybe the answer had to do with their killing mechanisms. Related toxins might have different names, but could still kill their victims in a similar manner.

"Do you know how this DRC-1339 works?" Sterling asked.

McGovern let out a loud grunt. "It's been a while since I read up on the stuff. But if my memory serves me right, one particle of the treated bait is sufficient to kill a blackbird. The more bait it eats, the faster it dies."

"How fast?"

"Depends on how much it eats. Probably anywhere from three to fifty hours."

Sterling flipped back in the book to his conversation with Mandryka. He had guessed the birds died within a matter of hours to a couple of days, depending upon how much and the concentration of the poison they had ingested.

"How does it kill them?"

"Shuts down their organs and gradually kills them from uremic poisoning."

"Uremia?"

"That's right. The poison is absorbed into the bloodstream and impairs the liver and kidneys. The kidneys start to shut down to the point they can't get rid of the body's waste products, causing these toxic chemicals to build up in the blood to a lethal level. At first the birds drink tons of water—instinctively trying to dilute the accumulating toxins. Then they stop drinking altogether. About four hours before they die, they stop eating and become listless and inactive. We shot a video of the process to show the world how cruel this poisoning was. The birds just sit there with their feathers ruffled the way they do in cold weather. They look like they're dozing off. Just before they run out of steam, their breathing increases and becomes more difficult. They slide into a coma and die."

Not what Sterling was looking for. Mandryka had said the blackbirds he examined died from electrical abnormalities in the heart, much different than uremia and kidney/liver failure. He quickly ran over the notes he had taken with Mandryka, then he thought of something.

"Can you find traces of the DRC-1339 in the blood?" he asked McGovern.

"Absolutely," McGovern said. "A few years back a small group of farmers experimented with DRC. Our guys just stumbled on the carcasses and brought them back to the lab. A little blood work and bingo—they could tell right away what had killed them."

"That's it!" Sterling said, circling a line of text in his book. He remembered that Mandryka had told him not all of the birds had the bufalin toxin in their bodies. And even in those in which he had found the bufalin, it had been in different stages of degradation. It made perfect sense. The longer the birds had been dead, the more likely the bufalin compound had already broken down in their bodies, making it undetectable in the blood when it was examined. Sterling ran his finger over Mandryka's words. *It's a perfect poison. It does its dirty work in a matter of hours, then quietly degrades and disappears.*

"What are you hollering about?" McGovern asked.

Sterling had forgotton that McGovern was even on the phone. "Uh . . . nothing. I was thinking about something else I had heard about the birds. Thanks a lot for your help, Mack."

"That's all?"

"At least for now. You've been a big help."

"Any time. But the next time you want to talk, stop by. Jess doesn't care for many visitors, but she took a liking to you."

"Tell her I'm flattered," Sterling laughed, before disconnecting the line. He sat and stared at Mandryka's quote. The poisons were chemically different, but still related. Someone was testing a new toxin, but they were doing it far enough from the battleground in the upper Midwest so that no one would notice what they were working on. Halfway across the country, in the wilds of Vermont, who would ever find these dead birds, or better yet, who would think to investigate even if they did find them? Sterling could've kicked himself for looking at the problem all wrong. Wilson had been a target, but only because by finding the dead birds he had unknowingly crossed someone's path. The question that still needed to be answered was, whose?

44

Sterling hailed a gypsy cab and directed the driver to yet another school, this time to City College, a sprawling collection of neo-Gothic buildings set on thirty-five acres of greenery between Convent and Amsterdam Avenues and stretching from 131st to 141st Streets.

Riding up the steep hill of Amsterdam Avenue and past the caged, graffiti-scarred storefronts of the St. Nicholas neighborhood, one couldn't confuse City College with Dartmouth. The crowded surrounding streets were rumbling with signs of imminent danger. Teeth-baring pit bulls strained at their leashes while their masters gathered under the scarce shade, sipping from brown bags, their unbuttoned shirts exposing the shiny chrome handles of guns jammed into their waistbands.

Sterling walked quickly, keeping his attention directed on the school's towering buildings, then entered on the east side of the campus and passed under the stone arcade in the center of the quadrangle. The sense of struggle was pervasive even within the safety of the school grounds. The nearly twelve thousand students who crisscrossed campus weren't trust-fund babies bearing prominent names. Almost half of them had been born abroad, and those born in New York weren't strangers to the hardships of a tough city life.

With a knapsack slung over his shoulder, a pair of stonewashed denims, and the burner in his hand, Sterling was all but anonymous as he made his way to the V-shaped North Academic Center. He rode the long escalators to the second floor and entered the Morris Raphael Cohen Library. He flashed his Hunter College ID to the young clerk. She waved him through without so much as a turn of her head.

Sterling knew the library well, having spent several weeks many years back using some of its prized research materials on human anatomy. The library had changed little except for the worn-out circles in the thin red carpet and the new signs pointing to the online catalogs in the reference section. Sterling walked down the long aisles of disorganized bookshelves and exposed beams until he found a relatively secluded workstation.

As he placed his knapsack down, he thought about his own computers. He was certain Skip and the other agents had already confiscated every piece of hardware in his Hunter College office and both of his apartments. Sterling knew the procedure all too well. Some computer geek in the IT lab was already running through his hard drive recording everything from how many times the computer had been turned on to the addresses of the websites Sterling had most recently visited.

Sterling moved the mouse and scanned the long list of databases before clicking on the LexisNexis icon. He typed in the name Wallace Mortimer, then waited for the search engine to respond. When it did, it offered far too many sites for Sterling to review. He clicked back to the home page and reentered another search item. This time, Wallace Alexander Mortimer III. Much better. The computer spit back a little more than a hundred hits and ranked them by relevance. Sterling made one more revision to the search, typing in the words Dartmouth College next to Mortimer's name. In seconds he had narrowed the results to seventy hits, most with high relevancy ratings. He hit the print button and read through some of the headlines as he waited for the printer to finish. Most of the articles were in either academic journals or business magazines. The Associated Press had carried some of the stories, as did the *New York Times*.

However great the urgency, Sterling was not ready for the next exhausting round of research. He packed the articles in his knapsack, exited the library, and crossed Convent Avenue to a quiet courtyard in front of the administration building. As much as he hated Skip Dumars, it still bothered him that he had been forced to fire his gun to buy himself some time. There was no doubt in his mind that Skip would have taken full advantage of the incident, overplaying what had actually transpired and sending inflammatory words up the flagpole that Sterling had tried to kill him. Another excuse for Murphy to believe the ridiculous theory that he had killed Wilson and Heidi and Harry Frumpton.

Sterling took a seat on a concrete ledge facing the expansive stone building of Shepard Hall. Small groups of undergraduates lugged their heavy nylon knapsacks, most of them chatting away on cell phones with blinking antennae. Sterling felt old when he thought about how primitive technology had been when he was in college. They had had only one pay phone on each floor and the line could be up to an hour just to make a five-minute call home.

He watched an old couple feed bread bits to the squirrels. With his cane and disheveled whiskers, the man reminded Sterling of Mandryka. It had been more than forty-eight hours since they last spoke, and Sterling now grew concerned. Mandryka had agreed to call within twenty-four hours. Sterling pulled out the burner.

Sterling dialed his cell number and once his voice recording came on, he pressed a series of numbers that put him into the phone's voice mail. He had two messages. The first was from Director Murphy warning him that he was making a big mistake and assuring him things could be worked out if he just turned himself in. Sterling smirked and deleted the message. He knew the embarrassment and political fallout of a rogue agent on the run. His ass had already been fried. Now they just needed to produce him in handcuffs to parade in front of the news cameras. Sterling pressed the number key for the next message. He didn't recognize the voice. "Mr. Bledsoe, this is Amy Rimsdale from the Dartmouth-Hitchcock Medical Center in Hanover. I'm the social worker assigned to Professor Mandryka. He wanted me to call and tell you that despite the accident, he's really fine. He'll be with us for at least a few days of observation." She ended the message with her office number.

Reciting the number so as not to lose it, Sterling disconnected from his voice mail and called Rimsdale. Her answering machine picked up. He cursed at the phone, then pressed 0 for the operator and asked to be connected to Yuri Mandryka's room.

A woman answered. "Professor Mandryka's room." Her voice was tight, her tone impatient.

"Who's this?" Sterling asked.

"Gloria Edson. His nurse. How can I help you?"

"I need to speak to him."

"He's taking a nap right now. Who's calling, please?"

It was too risky to give his real name. "His nephew, Stanley. I just received word about the accident and I'd really like to talk to him."

There was a pause on the other end. "Are you coming to visit him?"

"If I need to, but I'm on the other side of the country. I'd really like to talk to him now if that's possible."

"He needs his sleep," she insisted. "He hasn't been sleeping well. Can you call back in an hour or so? Or if you leave your number, I'll see to it that he gives you a call when he wakes."

That wasn't good enough. Sterling needed to find out what happened, but he had to be careful not to push too hard. "I'm on my morning break," he said. "Only fifteen minutes and the clock is ticking. Now would be best for me. Boss isn't too crazy about me making long-distance calls on company dime and time." Sterling heard her suck her teeth in frustration.

"Hold on, please."

Sterling listened as she called Mandryka's name. They had a brief exchange, then she was back on. "Okay, but please don't make it too long. He really needs to get some sleep. He was shaken up pretty badly in the accident."

Sterling heard Mandryka ask the nurse to close the door behind her. A few seconds went by before he spoke. "Nephew Stanley, you there?" Good old Mandryka.

"Yup. What the hell happened?"

"I don't remember much. It happened so fast. I left home a few hours after we spoke. I waited till almost daybreak because my driving isn't too good at night. I was heading down Interstate 91, considering all you had told me about there being some connection between the murders. I was trying to remember if Wilson had ever mentioned this Heidi person, when all of a sudden I felt a hard jolt from behind. It startled me, and I looked in the rearview mirror and saw the headlights of a truck. The last thing I remember was losing control of the car and skidding across the road."

"How do you feel now?"

"Like someone took a battering ram to my head. And this Edson gal doesn't want to give me too many painkillers for fear it'll clog me up down low. They said I had a subdural hematoma. Bleeding on the brain. My doctor, a young guy who just moved here from one of the Boston hospitals, said given the condition they found my car in, I was lucky to even be alive. I asked to see the pictures, but no one will show them to me."

"Where did they find the car?"

"Trapped between some trees in a ravine. The social worker, cute little girl named Amy, said the trees saved my life. If they hadn't been there, I would've kept going."

"Yuri, I want you to think back to what you saw before the accident."

"The problem is, I didn't see much."

"I know, but you said you saw the headlights. Did you by chance see if there was someone in the passenger seat?"

There was a pause on the other end. "I can't say for sure," Mandryka said. "It all happened so fast."

"How about the color of the truck?"

"Nope. Too dark. Anyway, the headlights blinded me."

"Had you seen the truck before it hit you?"

"That's the strange thing. I never saw it. There's not much traffic on those roads that early in the morning. I was the only car in the southbound lane."

Sterling already knew this wasn't an accident. The truck had purposely hit Mandryka, and when he drove off into the ravine, they had left him for dead.

"Let me ask you this. Before the accident, did any trucks pass you in the northbound lane? Take your time and really think hard about this."

Mandryka's response was immediate. "Just one."

"Did you get a good look at who was driving?"

"No, but there were two of them."

"Did you catch the make of the truck?"

"I'm not sure. I'm not too good with car models and such. But I remember it was an old pickup with flimsy wood railings in the back."

Sterling remembered what Miles Borwind, the manager at the Grand Union, had said. Wood railings to keep cargo from falling out. There was only one conclusion to make—the killers were still closing the circle on everyone who knew about those dead blackbirds. Sterling wondered if Kanti was still alive.

"What's your prognosis?" Sterling asked.

"Good, according to my doctor. A couple of more days and they'll know if they have to go in and drain the blood off my brain. My left elbow was broken in two places, but they've already set it and put it in a cast." Mandryka released a hacking cough. "Enough about me," he said, winded. "I'll survive. What about you? Any progress?"

"I'm inching closer," Sterling said. "Just trying to tie some things to-gether. I had one question that I thought you might be able to help me with."

"Shoot."

"How well do you know President Mortimer?"

"We're not close, if that's what you're asking. He's always been pretty standoffish."

"I know he inherited a lot of family money, but I was just wondering if you knew of any of his commercial interests."

Mandryka cleared his throat before speaking. "I think the story has it that his great-grandfather made a bundle in the stock market, then after turning the fortune over several times, he left a lot of his money to char-ity."

It wasn't the answer Sterling had hoped for. "Thanks, Yuri," he said. "Remember what we talked about before. You're still a target. It wouldn't hurt if you could stay in there a couple of extra days while I try to wrap this up."

"If I don't die from the mush they serve around here."

They shared their first laugh since they had met at Wilson's memorial service. "Stay well. I'll check on you in a couple of days."

Sterling dialed the inside line to the pit.

"Officer Hanlon here."

"Hanlon, it's Bledsoe." Sterling gave him a moment to register the name before continuing. "Put a couple of men on Yuri Mandryka's door at the hospital."

"What the hell are you talking about? With all that's happened, you're calling about some old professor?"

"He's not just an old professor, he's the next target of the killers. Don't ask me any questions, 'cause I'm not answering. That was no accident a cou-ple of days ago. Whoever killed Wilson and Vorscht were also trying to kill Mandryka."

"Why the hell should I believe you?"

"Because I'm recording this conversation. If the old man dies, his blood will be on your hands."

Sterling hung up before Hanlon could answer.

45

Sterling returned to Cohen Library, this time staking out a table on the fourth floor in the desolate archives section. A couple of students flipped through old volumes, but with no windows, dim lighting, and no computers to check e-mail, people visited this area of the library only when absolutely necessary.

He spread the printouts across the table, arranging them in the same order of relevance as the Factiva search engine had. He read through all the notes he had written on Mortimer, then he picked up the first article.

For three uninterrupted hours, he read every word of every article. Most of the stories were duplicates, announcing Mortimer's initial appointment to the presidency by the board of directors or describing his widely lauded programs that distinguished the school from other top-tier universities. Serena and her work in the Romance languages were mentioned in some of the articles. But other than the academic announcements, little else caught Sterling's eye.

He got up for a stretch and walked near the windows on the opposite end of the floor and looked out over the campus. Night had fallen and the lights illuminating the old buildings made them look like medieval castles minus the moat and charging knights.

Sterling's thoughts shifted to Wilson. He never would have suspected his brother of having an affair, but in a strange way, he was relieved to discover that Wilson hadn't been so perfect after all. He wished again that he and his brother had had the time to really get to know each other.

Sterling felt the sting of impending tears and pulled himself away from the window and back to the table. His sadness flashed to anger. He was angry at himself for letting Wilson down, angry at the cowards who murdered him when he had so much more living to do. Sterling attacked the remaining articles, recharged and committed to finding something, anything that would give him insight into what went wrong that night.

An hour later, he found it.

The article had appeared in *Forbes*. Unlike most of the other stories, it was a feature, focusing on transgenerational philanthropy. It covered the usual suspects—the Vanderbilts, Rockefellers, and Fords. Then there were the Mortimers, whose name was not as well recognized as those of the others but whose generosity was equally impressive. Sterling read the article because it traced the Mortimers' wealth back to the great-grandfather, Spencer Mortimer, who had had to borrow money to pay for his education and started the family's long tradition at Dartmouth. After graduation, he went on, as Mandryka had said, to make his fortune on Wall Street. He was a great speculator, finally striking it big when he traded heavily in railroad stocks in the 1860s. His philanthropy was also impressive, because, unlike the others, he started with nothing but still willed half his estate to charities upon his death. The senior Mortimer had also been a man of integrity, honoring a promise he had made to himself that if he ever made it big, he'd give back big too. He bequeathed the school half of his estate upon his death, endowing a professorial chair in the name of his wife of sixty years and providing enough money to break ground on a new business school, which he insisted be named after a classmate who had been killed in the Spanish-American War.

The great-grandfather not only understood how to make money but understood that it was a lot easier to lose it. He willed the other half of his estate to a family trust and loaded it with stipulations that guaranteed that no single family member could squander the fortune he had spent a lifetime building. The article was critical of Spencer's son, Wallace A. Mortimer Sr., who was evidently something of a playboy, wasting his riches on fancy cars and beautiful women. He had gone to Dartmouth College, but no one was fooled as to how he had gotten in, especially after his father gave the school's endowment a healthy boost.

The article quickly dispatched of Wallace Jr., but dwelt extensively on the current heir, the III, who had his great-grandfather's business acumen as well as an academic flair. He had been commonly referred to as the wealthy academic, a title, his friends had said, he secretly enjoyed. In the ten years since he had taken managerial control of the family trust, he not only had doubled their portfolio but had purchased the Sunny Fields Company, which annually beat financial projections to the satisfaction of corporate raiders who offered the family twice what they had paid for the company.

Sterling read the next line and felt his breath catch in his throat. He read it three more times before the air finally escaped his opened mouth.

> The Sunny Fields Company has acquired numerous small and large farms in the Dakotas, quietly becoming the largest supplier of sunflower products in the country.

The snag. Right there in black and white. Sterling's hands trembled as he read the rest of the article. The Sunny Fields Company had become one of only a few Fortune 500 companies that was still privately owned. While Wallace A. Mortimer III didn't oversee the day-to-day operations of the company, he kept a close eye from his academic perch at Dartmouth, often calling his managers to Hanover to deliver company updates or review the complicated financials. The last paragraph was a gold mine:

> Unexpected damage to some of the crop caused the company's profits to flatten in the past year, but Mortimer is confident that its highly skilled team of agricultural scientists will soon have a solution that will once again send the company profits soaring.

46

Sterling stuffed the articles in his knapsack, then rushed out into the breezy night. He punched in Reverend Briggs's private number and waited.

"Evening," Reverend Briggs answered. His voice was relaxed, as if he had been reading Scripture.

"Reverend, it's Sterling."

"Your ears must've been burning. I just mentioned your name."

"Really?"

"A gentleman called about half an hour ago looking for you."

"Did he leave his name?"

"No. Just said to tell you that he called and you'd know what he was calling about."

Sterling knew it was Gilden. He was the only one who had the number. "Everything all right up there?" Sterling asked.

"Other than the hunger pains shooting through my stomach? Another peaceful night, thanks be to God."

"Is Veronica okay?"

"She's just fine. She and Delthia are back in the kitchen fussing over a pot roast."

Sterling smiled at the thought of Veronica in the kitchen. They had been dating for almost two years and she hadn't even fixed him a slice of toast. But to her credit, she'd be the first to admit that cooking wasn't one of her strengths. "Tell Veronica I'm okay and thinking about her."

"She's gonna make an honest man out of you yet, Sterling," Reverend Briggs chuckled. "Just mark my words."

Sterling hung up the phone wondering if marriage really was in their future. The telling sign, his father had always said, was when you enjoyed a woman's company beyond her talents under the sheets. And with Veronica, Sterling had found this to be true. What he most appreciated about her was how low-maintenance she was for a woman who was so damn gorgeous. As long as she had her lazy Sunday mornings of cuddling and mindless television surfing, she never uttered a word about how little time they spent together. Sterling figured if that didn't make him an honest man, nothing would.

He dialed Gilden's number. This time Gilden picked up the phone.

"Professor, it's me," Sterling said. "I just got your message."

"We need to talk."

"Good or bad?"

"Interesting. I have some papers here you might want to see. Do you want to come by tomorrow morning?"

It was only eight o'clock. Depending on when the next Metro North train was leaving 125th Street, he could be in Croton Falls in about an hour. "If you don't mind, how about tonight?"

Gilden didn't mind.

"I'll be on the next train," Sterling said.

O ne Hundred and Twenty-fifth Street in Harlem stretches all the way from the East River in Upper Manhattan to the Hudson River on the West Side. Flooded with cars and loud music and vibrant people during the day, 125th Street quickly transforms into a dark, empty passageway at night, a place where people venture only if they truly belong. Sterling moved easier in this part of the city where his color, his clean-shaven head, and his young urban attire made him inconspicuous. He exited the gypsy cab at the corner of Park and 125th and hurried into the newly renovated train station. He joined the line of passengers waiting in front of the only open ticket window, his eyes slowly scanning the room. Suddenly he stiffened. Two uniforms, a Latino and a black, were chatting up two young women whose skin-tight minis and midriff-revealing tank tops left little to the imagination. The men were leaning against the wall, their hats resting in the bend of their arms, one taking down what was probably a phone number.

Sterling quickly turned his head and watched them out of the corner of his eye. He could tell by the patches on their sleeves that they were part of the MTA force, most likely rookies from the look of their shoes and heavily starched uniforms.

Sterling thought about slipping out the door, but he badly needed to see what Gilden had found. He convinced himself that way up in Harlem, in a small train-station lobby, no one would recognize him.

"Sir, you're next." The woman behind him was pointing to the now vacant window.

Sterling pulled his cap down over his forehead and stepped to the counter. An old man with reading glasses dangling around his neck and a gray Afro that had been perfectly trimmed into an even dome slumped on a stool behind the bulletproof window. Sterling asked for a round-trip ticket to Croton Falls and slipped a twenty through the slot. The old man took the money, but kept his eyes trained on Sterling. He frowned as he punched the buttons of the ticket machine. Sterling looked away nonchalantly, but when his eyes met the bulletin board adjacent to the window, his heart froze in mid-beat. He looked into his own face, sketched in black and white, shaved head and all. The artist had done a commendable job, even getting the wayward patch of hair in the middle of his left eyebrow.

Sterling cut his eyes to the officers. They were still working the girls. One of them looked in his direction, but only momentarily. Sterling turned back to the sketch. The Bureau had listed everything except his mother's maiden name. A loud throat clearing snapped him to attention. The ticket-counter agent slid his ticket under the window. His face had relaxed and his eyes fell. He knew.

Sterling tilted his head to one side and hiked his shoulders in a give-me-a-break gesture.

The old man closed and opened his eyes slowly, then nodded almost imperceptibly. "Have a good night," he said, before looking at the next customer.

Sterling wanted to plead his innocence and explain how it had all been a mistake. There was an entire story not printed on that bulletin board about an innocent man brutally murdered in the cold mountains of Vermont and how his brother was being set up to take the fall. But he didn't have to. The old man already understood.

"Thank you," Sterling said, slipping the ticket in his jacket pocket and turning to the staircase at the opposite end of the lobby. He found a bench at the far end of the elevated platform, feet from the tracks, but close to an exit stairwell just in case the old man had a change of heart. As he looked out over 125th Street at the crumbling Harlem tenements and buildings, he knew the old man would remain committed.

Sterling had dozed off, only to be awakened by the loud screech of steel wheels grinding to a stop. The train had been packed with suburban commuters when he boarded it at 125th Street, but now the cars were practically empty. Sterling grabbed his knapsack and followed a small line of carbon-copy suits exiting onto the barren platform. He stopped under a flickering fluorescent light and looked across the parking lot for Gilden. Volvo station wagons and BMW SUVs waited on the receiving side of the platform steps, their occupants—wives and children—waving to the returning breadwinners, back from another exhausting day in the city.

Sterling finally noticed the flashing headlights in the corner of the lot. They belonged to a black Yukon with tinted windows.

The truck had pulled around by the time Sterling made it across the bridge.

"I barely recognized you," Gilden said, when Sterling had closed the door and they had pulled into the line of other expensive vehicles exiting the lot. "You look like a student."

"I wouldn't mind being one right about now," Sterling said. "A lot of people are after me, and if I don't figure this out . . ." Sterling slid his hand across his neck in a death sign.

The two rode mostly in silence. Sterling caught glimpses of the former agent, his skin sagging underneath his chin, his fingers long and swollen in the knuckles from arthritis. His slicked-back hair was gray now, but his eyes, when he glanced at Sterling, still burned with strength and determination. A few minutes later, Gilden passed through the open gates of a grassy park. He turned off his headlights and flicked on the fog lights. He drove about a mile up a narrow path and pulled the truck next to a pond. A layer of mist crouched over the water. The deep, throaty calls of the bullfrogs and the loud, pulsing sounds of katydids breached the frozen darkness.

Gilden turned off the fog lights so that they were in complete darkness. Then he switched off the engine.

"This Heidi Vorscht had some serious baggage," Gilden opened. "Not your typical graduate student."

"I've gathered that by now," Sterling said. "She's got her fingerprints throughout this entire case."

"She'd also had some rather good fortune lately."

"Why's that?"

"For a poor graduate student she was sitting on quite a pile of money."

"If she had so much money, then why was she serving as a live-in for an old woman in the Upper Valley?"

"Maybe because the money is new."

"How new?"

"It started coming in three months ago."

"She hit the lottery or something?"

"Or something. This is what my guys told me. Heidi's mother, Elga Vorscht, works as a secretary in the history department at the University of Stuttgart. Heidi's father was killed in a random robbery gone bad many years ago. They didn't collect much on his life insurance, and most of their finances have come from the mother's job at the university. A few months ago, wires started hitting the mother's account. Big wires. A hundred thousand at a clip. The mother then turned the money around into Heidi's account, keeping a little spending change for herself."

"Drug money?"

Gilden shook his head. "I don't think so." He turned on a reading light and reached into the backseat, pulling out a thick folder. The silence in the car was broken only by the cacophony of singing insects and pond critters calling into the empty night.

"Here's all the documentation," Gilden said, handing the folder to Sterling. "Most of the faxes are legible enough to make the case."

"So who's sending her the money?" Sterling asked.

Gilden nodded to the folder in Sterling's hand. Sterling opened it and pulled out the first batch of papers. Sitting on top were photocopies of several electronic transfer receipts in the amount of $100,000 per transaction. Sterling didn't recognize the signature at the bottom of the forms, but his jaw went slack when he spotted the name of the authorizing account. The Sunny Fields Company.

Sterling needed sleep. Lots of it. It was well past midnight when he dragged himself up the back steps to the parsonage. His room was tucked away in the corner of the house, which meant he could enter without waking the others. More than anything, he needed to be alone with his thoughts. This was how he always felt after pulling the snag on a long, complicated case—the deep ache in his muscles and joints could only be relieved by the darkness of sleep. He opened the back door and walked by the kitchen. He spotted a wrapped plate of food on the table, but was too exhausted to even think about eating. He opened the door to his room, eased the knapsack onto the bed, and rolled his neck in slow circles to release the cramps knotting his muscles. He removed the Glock 36 from his waistband, turned on the safety, and set it on the dresser.

He opened the window a little because he liked to sleep with the air blowing over his face. He propped the pillows and pulled back the covers.

"Don't move, Bledsoe." The man's voice was quiet, but firm.

The streetlight cast a long shadow against the wall. But next to that shadow he spotted the man's silhouette. He was sitting in a chair against the wall, his left hand jammed in his pocket, his right hand resting on the table.

"Sit on the bed and don't make a move for your gun," the man said. "You even blink and I'll empty a round in your ass."

Sterling thought he recognized the voice, but his mind was oddly sluggish. The day had been long and hard and now this. He sat on the bed.

"Put your hands in front where I can see them and close them together."

Sterling obeyed. He was vulnerable. He thought about Veronica and the Briggses and wondered if they had been harmed.

The light flicked on. Sterling stared across the room at Agent Lonnie Brusco. A silver-nosed Ruger P97DAO pistol sat on the table next to him. He looked unamused.

"I've been waiting all night for you."

"I didn't do it."

"If I thought you did, my gun would be in my hand, not on the table. But there's still some explaining to do. Let's start with your picture showing up in that e-mail, then assaulting and confining Wiley, and discharging a firearm at another agent. Innocent or not, you're in some deep shit, Bledsoe. Start talking. Fast."

For the next half hour, Sterling ran through everything, starting with the blackbirds in Mandryka's secret basement storage facility to the video Wilson had taken of the carnage in the woods. He took Brusco through the picture on Mortimer's desk and the picture of Wilson's lab group with Heidi prominently positioned next to Wilson. Sterling left out the part about the affair, not sure yet what role it had played in the murders. But he did explain the message Ahote had given him and the meeting he held with Kanti in the mountains. Sterling wrapped it up with what had happened since he left Hanover and the papers that showed the Sunny Fields Company had made hefty payments into Heidi's mother's accounts.

Brusco listened to the entire story without so much as clearing his throat. Then he spoke. "It all makes sense," he said. "But it's still circumstantial. A group of high-priced lawyers will puncture enough holes in it to leave any jury doubtful."

"I'm almost there," Sterling said. "Today gave me the motive. Now I just need a little more time to collect the hard evidence."

Brusco looked away. Sterling knew he was uncertain. There was trust chiseled into his face, but sometimes that trust came hard.

"Forty-eight hours," Brusco said. "Tie this thing together and we never had this conversation."

Sterling's shoulders slumped in relief. "That's all I need," he said. "And when I put the noose around these sonsabitches, your name will go right next to mine."

Brusco waved him off, then replaced the gun in his shoulder holster. He stood up and walked to the door.

"How did you find me, anyway?" Sterling asked.

"Frumpton."

"He's dead."

"I know. I found an old phone book of his in the cottage. He had a bunch of numbers listed for you. This was the only one we didn't already have."

It made sense to Sterling. When Reverend Briggs had taken him in after the beating at the Hotel DeWitt, Harry was the only person in the Bureau whom Sterling had contacted, because he needed someone on the inside to cover for him while he was on the mend.

"This means a lot to me," Sterling said.

Brusco swung the door open. "Just don't make a fool of me, Bledsoe. I got two kids on their way to college. I need this fuckin' job."

47

Sterling raced down the steps of Penn Station. With the train departing in only half an hour, he didn't have a minute to spare. The main concourse was a sea of moving bodies and colors, each person in more of a rush than the next. Sterling allowed himself to be swallowed in the commotion. He quickly walked behind the big board, avoiding the small police depot in the northern corridor. Finding an empty ticket machine, he pulled out the credit card Reverend Briggs had loaned him. Several buttons later he had purchased a one-way ticket to Savannah, Georgia.

The train was called the Silver Meteor and it was perfect for the mission. Sterling had memorized most of the route: quick stops in Newark and Trenton, New Jersey, then Philadelphia, Delaware, Maryland, D.C., and a few other stops on the way to Savannah. The long train ride and frequent stations would make it difficult for them to nail down his location.

With the ticket safely in his possession, Sterling bought a newspaper, a small roll of tape, and a pair of scissors. He got into line at the boarding gate and moved with the crowd as the conductor lowered the chain. A quick flash of his ticket and he descended the long escalators to the dark tracks. He looked at his watch.

While most of the commuters filed to the front of the train, Sterling headed to the back for one of the unreserved coach cars. He hurried past the café, then two cars down locked himself in the bathroom. Time was slipping by. He pulled out his old cell phone and turned it on for the first time since coming to New York. Seven minutes before departure. He started counting down in his head. He pulled out a small piece of paper from his pocket and punched in the 800 number. It belonged to a cut-rate pharmacy that sold everything from ginkgo biloba to Viagra, all promised at an unbeatable discount. He already forgot the name of the city, but he remembered their headquarters was somewhere in Oklahoma.

Sterling checked his watch again as he waited for the call to go through. Five minutes. After eight rings, he heard the recording. A woman's voice slowly took callers through a long list of options. She paused after each choice, then continued if there was no response. When none of the choices had been selected, the loop started all over again. Sterling had done a test run the previous night. For five hours she ran through the menu of choices again and again and again.

Three minutes before the departure whistle. Suddenly a tap on the door. He quickly flushed the toilet and waited for the water to stop before calling out, "Just a few seconds." By the time he finished in the bathroom and stepped out the door, the train's engines were slowly coming to life.

He's hot," Special Agent Glazer screamed as the monitors in the truck sprang to life. The others were in various positions of repose, but jumped into action when those words bounced off the walls. "And he initiated the call."

Skip Dumars barreled his way down the aisle, pushing aside anything that stood in his way. He yanked a pair of headphones off the table and adjusted them to his wide head. "What's the number?" he grumbled. He was in a nasty mood, much worse than his normal disagreeable state. He'd had his ass chewed out and handed back to him when Washington learned they had bungled the capture at the Hotel DeWitt. Find Bledsoe or get used to pushing files in the office had been the thinly veiled threat. Murph and his contingent had even flown up from headquarters to deliver the message in person.

"We'll have a match in forty-five seconds," Walsh replied, running her fingers across the keyboard.

Three monitors had been arranged on a small table in this portable command center. Three agents from IT—Glazer, Walsh, and Perkins—operated the computers. Everyone else had lined up behind Dumars's bulk as if sneaking into a peep show.

"Is the tracker ready?" Dumars barked to Perkins, the youngest of the agents, who looked like he still belonged on a college campus. No one bothered with his name, instead simply calling him Freshman.

"It's up and running," Freshman answered. He moved the cursor across a complicated screen. A colorful global map with the longitude and latitude lines covering the earth's sphere slowly rotated until North America was centered in the monitor. A few more clicks of the mouse and the zoom brought the United States into sharp focus.

"This is going to take some time," Walsh said. She sat in the middle. "It's an 800 number." The number combinations spun on the monitor. A couple of minutes later, all ten digits had locked into place.

"Call it," Dumars ordered.

The dial tone erupted over the speakerphone and everyone waited out the ringer. The recording for the One-Stop Pharmacy came on, prompting them to make their choices.

"He's moving, sir," Freshman said. Everyone shifted their attention to the rotating map. A blinking red light represented the signal source.

"Where is he?" Dumars asked.

Freshman typed in a string of numbers and the map rotated to the East Coast. Seconds later, the state of New York filled the screen.

"He's in Manhattan," Freshman said. "But he's moving." The red light slowly moved across the screen.

"Give me a direction," Dumars demanded. His nostrils flared and thick veins popped out of his bulging neck. He looked like a bull ready to charge.

"Southwest."

"Is he still connected?"

"Yup," Walsh answered.

Dumars turned to an agent in the back of the truck. "Call over and put the damn choppers on standby."

"Both of them?" the agent asked.

"Damn right. We'll run his ass down from the air. Let NYPD know we have a make on him and get them moving on ground support. He's not getting away from me this time."

"He's moving really fast, sir," Freshman reported. He typed a series of commands and waited for the computer to respond. "At least forty miles per hour. And he's not making any stops. He must be in a car."

The woman's recorded voice from the pharmacy continued to prompt them for their selection.

"Cut that goddamn thing off," Dumars yelled. "How long has he been connected, Walsh?"

"Seven minutes," she said, her long fingers expertly working the keys. "We need him at least for another three before we get the permanent lock."

The new intelligence division of the FBI had developed a state-of-the-art wireless tracking system like no other in the world. With the quiet cooperation of the phone companies and device manufacturers, they had come up with a program that allowed them to track a cell phone location even after the call had been disconnected. Using a special cellular wavelength, once the satellite locks on to the phone long enough, it then opens a wireless tracking connection by sending small bursts of signals to a chip embedded in the phone. The chip returns a signal that allows the global positioning software to track the phone's location within five city blocks. The satellite could only establish a location lock after the connection has been live for at least ten minutes. They kept their eyes glued to the clock.

"Uh-oh," Freshman mumbled. "The signal has some diffraction. Something is making it spread. Some kind of interference." He punched in a series of numbers that changed the color and map rotation. "I can't say for sure, but the pattern looks like it might be water."

"What the hell is he doing?" Dumars thought aloud. "He has to know we're on to him. And why is he traveling south?"

"Ten minutes confirmed," Walsh said. "Satellite has the lock. He's ours."

"Stay on him," Dumars said. He ripped the headphones off and threw them to the table. "I'm going in the air."

Dumars and two other agents bolted from the back of the truck and jumped into an unmarked sedan. They switched on the sirens and flashed the lights in the grill. The choppers were on the East Side helipad. If traffic wasn't too bad, they'd be there in fifteen minutes.

48

High winds and poor visibility kept Dumars and the other agents grounded for another hour before they got the clearance to take to the sky. They stayed in constant communication with the command center back in the truck and learned that Sterling's call lasted for almost half an hour before the line was disconnected. Freshman had tracked the phone from Newark to Trenton, then when the phone went dead, the satellite located the signal in the northern suburbs of Philadelphia. Police departments from New York City all the way down the East Coast were put on alert. A fugitive agent might be on his way through their jurisdiction and their help would certainly be needed.

Dumars and the other agents peered down from the chopper, following an electronic computer grid they carried on board and the wave of flashing cruisers snaking through the streets below. Unsure how long the chase would continue, they ordered two more helicopters to be refueled and waiting in Philadelphia. Then the transmission from one of the ground cars came across the radio. Bledsoe was on board an Amtrak train heading south. There might be enough time to surround the train in Philadelphia, but the station was busy and extra manpower would be needed for better crowd control. Dumars thought quickly and ordered everyone to step down. He gave the orders to run the train through the Philadelphia station without stopping, then alerted the team in Wilmington to begin making the necessary preparations to apprehend Bledsoe once the train pulled to a stop. The Wilmington station was smaller, in a more remote area, and much easier to blockade. Equally important, it would give Dumars enough time to get into position and be the one to snap on the handcuffs.

Another cell phone rang and one of the agents announced the director.

"We've locked in on him, sir," Dumars said. He rounded the edge in his voice.

"Where is he?"

"On a southbound Amtrak train in Philly. We'll be apprehending him at the Wilmington stop."

"How much support do you have from the locals?"

"Everyone's on board. City, state, and transit in all jurisdictions have been coordinated. They know what we're dealing with."

"We need him," the director growled. "Alive. This is not the time for heroes or egos to get in the way of the mission. Remember, he's still one of our own."

"And what if he resists?"

"Do whatever it takes to stop him, but keep him alive and protect the other passengers. We don't need this to blow up in our faces."

There was a long pause.

"Do I make myself clear, Dumars?"

"As a bell."

Dumars looked at the chaos below. An army of flashing lights raced down both lanes of the highway, keeping pace with the speeding train. It was already turning into a spectacle. Drivers of parked cars stood outside their vehicles, pointing at the train and the blur of whirling cruisers. Less than half a mile away, a local news chopper buzzed in a holding pattern. The ground command center continued to inform Dumars of the satellite readings. A look of intense satisfaction flattened some of the deep lines in Dumars's hardened scowl. He knew the cameras would raise the stakes and he was prepared. Every major network would report the capture on the evening news, and the morning papers across the country would carry it as a front-page headline. If that didn't make him a household name, the trial certainly would.

As the train steadily made its way toward Wilmington, Dumars picked up a pair of binoculars and looked into the distance. He could make out parts of the terminal building through the trees, ablaze in a sea of flashing lights. As he had expected and hoped, several news vans were parked alongside the tracks, their satellite poles reaching into the sky. He placed a call to the Wilmington police chief and explained in excruciating detail how he wanted the capture to proceed. Everyone was to move on his command, with the safety of the innocent passengers receiving the highest priority. He would allow one television camera and one still photographer on the train, but they were only to film on his signal.

Dumars ran a stiff hand through his salt-and-pepper hair until it fell back into a helmet. He'd been waiting a long time for this moment, a chance to nail Bledsoe and at the same time give his own career a much needed boost. Several field directorships would become available next year because of early retirements, and this high-profile capture might be exactly what he needed to get his name bumped up the list of potential successors.

The train slowed as it entered the perimeter of the station's wooded property. Uniformed officers, many with their guns drawn, lined the tracks in a two-hundred-yard, elbow-to-elbow show of force that impressed even Dumars. The pilot landed the chopper in an area that had been cleared in the parking lot. The conductor had been extensively briefed on the plan. All the doors were to be kept locked until Dumars and the other agents appeared at the door of the first car, where they would enter the train and work their way car by car until Bledsoe had been located. Freshman called in again and confirmed that the signal had stopped and the satellite tracking matched the coordinates of the station. Bledsoe was definitely on the train.

The two photographers had already been selected and stood ready to join Dumars and his team of agents. A tall, gangly man in ripped jeans and a stained T-shirt already had his camera slung over his shoulder. Next to him, a young, petite woman with eager bright blue eyes and golden-blond hair stuffed several rolls of film into her fanny pack and waited patiently for instructions.

"He's armed and dangerous," Dumars said to the gathering. The sense of urgency in his voice seemed rehearsed. "I want two lead agents, myself, then two trailers." He pointed at the photojournalists. "You two on last. For your own safety. And don't roll any film till I give you the go-ahead. Is everyone clear?" His words were met with a chorus of "yups" and head nods. Dumars pulled out his own gun and plodded his way through the empty station as stranded passengers stood behind police barricades, pointing and yapping into cell phones. Moments later the team was on the platform swarming with barking dogs and a rainbow of uniforms. They made their way to the first car and radioed for the door to be opened.

The leads boarded first—two young, athletic agents who looked like they spent way too much time curling dumbbells. Dumars followed with the trailers behind him, then the photographers. Many of the passengers were standing in the aisle trying to exit the train, confused and scared. The agents calmly asked everyone to remain seated and quiet as they methodically carried out their search. A group of nuns had their heads bowed in prayer, gripping their rosary beads and making the sign of the cross. The beating sounds of footsteps could be heard walking along the roof as the officers outside staked their positions.

They searched each car, under the seats, behind the luggage compartments, but no sign of Sterling. Dumars called Freshman.

"Are you still getting his signal?" Dumars asked.

"It's still strong and not moving."

They searched the café car and the small outside standing areas between the cars. Dumars took out the electronic grid, pulled out the antenna, and called the command center. "Position us," he demanded.

Seconds later the response was clear. "You're less than thirty feet away."

"He's in the rear car," Dumars radioed to the team outside. "We're going to enter the car now. Remember, no one fires unless I give the command."

They entered the last car slowly, their guns drawn. Four passengers returned fearful stares: a woman with a small child, an old man sitting by himself, and a young woman wearing a college sweatshirt. The lead agents motioned for them to stand and walk toward the door, which they did quietly and slowly with the trailing agents escorting them to the adjacent car. When the car was empty, the team moved slowly down the aisle calling Sterling's name, offering him a peaceful resolution. No response. They walked the entire length of the car and stopped at the rest room. Dumars gave the photographers the signal before the lead agents tapped on the door. When it went unanswered, they tested the handle and discovered it was unlocked. On Dumars's count they stood back and kicked the door wide open. Nothing.

Dumars pulled out the electronic grid and called command. "Position us!" he barked.

"Can't you see him? You're only two feet away."

Dumars snapped shut the phone and walked to the paper-towel dispenser. He punched the lid with the side of his fist and watched as it flipped open.

He stood there for a brief moment, then clawed at the paper towels until he uncovered a sleeve of newspaper that had been taped to the back wall of the dispenser. The camera's flash popped just as Dumars unwrapped his grand capture—the cell phone of Special Agent Sterling Bledsoe.

Sterling pulled the silver Lexus SC 430 convertible into the parking lot of the Mountaineers Motel on Route 10A in Lebanon, just fifteen minutes from the Dartmouth campus. He knew that the hard evidence needed to nail Mortimer and his accomplices was somewhere in these mountains. His instincts told him that he had probably seen it a hundred times earlier in the investigation, but had simply overlooked it. Though it was risky, he needed to be back where it all happened, breathing the air and taking another look at the crime scene. With the Mustang burned out in an abandoned lot in New Jersey and his Carrera sitting somewhere in an FBI garage, Reverend Briggs had once again come to the rescue. His oldest daughter was off on spring break, and he had let Sterling borrow her car.

Sterling kept the baseball cap he had bought pulled over his eyes and registered with the old woman behind the counter. She wore a hearing aid in each ear and her glasses were thick enough to be bulletproof. The chances of her recognizing him and sounding an alarm were between none and none. He requested lodging in the back of the short strip of rooms, telling her he needed as much quiet as possible for all the reading he had to do. She offered him a pair of foam earplugs, which he politely declined, but he asked her to make sure no one disturbed him until the morning.

Sterling parked around the back, completely out of view from the road. He quickly unloaded all of the papers and his two guns into the room. After a shower and a couple of granola bars he had snatched from the lobby vending machine, he went to work. First came a phone call to Special Agent Mickey Strahan in surveillance.

"Talk to me," Strahan said when he picked up. That's how he always answered his phone. He was probably sitting at his desk in Quantico. He always had his cell phone nearby, hoping the next call would be an invitation to a round of golf.

"Stray, it's me," Sterling said. "You alone?"

"No, there are lots of papers around my desk."

Sterling got the message. "I need you to get outside where no one can hear you."

"Hold on," Stray said. "Let me run out to the car. I think I left that box of papers in my trunk."

Sterling heard a chair scraping against tile, footsteps, and then a series of doors open and close. The sound of rustling wind came through the receiver and he knew Strahan had made it outside.

"What the hell are you doing, Doc?" Strahan was the only one at the Bureau who called him that. Strahan reasoned that anyone who had put up with the school bullshit long enough to earn a Ph.D. at the very least deserved to be called by his proper title. Even if he worked as an agent.

"I need your help in a big way."

"You need more than my help," Strahan said. "From what I'm hearing, Murph is gonna fry your ass if the New York boys don't kill you first. What the hell kind of mess have you gotten yourself into now?"

"It's all bullshit," Sterling said. "I don't know what kind of lies you've heard, but I'm clean. Somebody's setting me up."

There was only silence on the other end.

"What the hell, Stray!" Sterling yelled into the phone. "Don't leave me hanging out here like this. They've gotten to you, too?"

"Easy, Doc. Of course I don't believe you did this. At least most of it. But shooting at Dumars is gonna take a lot of explaining to the people upstairs."

Sterling sighed. His temples were vibrating. He searched his bag for the bottle of Tylenol Extra Strength. "Okay, that was true, but not what people are probably making it out to be. If I wanted to kill Dumars, I could've. He was fifty yards away from me. He was coming after me and I needed some time. So I fired at a car window across the street to stall him. That's it. Anything else you've heard is total bullshit. The body count is climbing. Only three dead right now because the fourth person survived. I need your help. I wouldn't get you involved in something like this, Stray, if I wasn't so sure I was being set up by some powerful people."

"I don't know what I can do," Stray said. "It's not like giving you a goddamn mulligan on the first tee or letting you take a drop without a stroke penalty. We're talking some serious shit. They're piling a list of charges on you a mile long. The only thing they haven't done is put you on *America's Most Wanted*."

"None of those charges will wash if I can get a little more time to piece this together. What I need from you isn't complicated and won't take much of your time."

"What is it?"

"Phone records. I think whoever's behind this might've left a phone trail."

Stray blew out a long breath and Sterling knew he was torn. Stray was one of those fiercely loyal types—he'd dive in front of a bullet for a friend without thinking twice. He was an ex–college football player who would have been a star in the NFL had he not blown out both knees and ripped a disk in his back. Instead of tossing around quarterbacks and slamming helmets, he spent most of his days slumming in surveillance. But like most ex-jocks who once thought golf was for pansies, he was now in love with the manicured fairways where he could take out his aggression on the tiny white balls that at times reduced his raucous laughter to frustrated whimpers.

"I don't know, Doc," he said. "Maybe you should come clean with the boys upstairs and lay out what you have. If they get to you before you get to them, who knows what will happen in the field?"

Sterling knew Strahan was right. The Bureau had a way of handling their internal problems in a much more permanent and less civil way than they did the crimes of ordinary citizens. Big politics were always at work, especially when there was the potential that the Bureau's image could be compromised. Fairness in these matters was merely an afterthought.

"I gotta take my chances, Stray. All I need you to do is check some phone records. Nothing more, nothing less."

Sterling heard that same infamous low groan that Strahan had let out countless times on the golf course when negotiating a difficult shot. More often than not when the shot was completed, the groan turned into a string of expletives.

"I wouldn't do this for anyone else but you, Doc," Strahan relented. "What's the number?"

Sterling gave him Wilson's home number. "I need to know all the incoming and outgoing calls on March twenty-third."

"Just that day?"

"That's it. The numbers and the times of the calls."

"Give me a few hours. I have to finish writing this open report. Records is climbing up my ass. Where are you right now? Aw, forget it. That was a stupid question. Call my cell in a few hours."

"I owe you one, partner."

"Yeah. Just dig yourself out of this hole so I can take out my long irons when you get back and kick your ass on the course."

"Too bad your swing isn't as good as your imagination."

Sterling pored over the Mortimer articles. He wasn't sure what he was looking for, but he felt that if he just looked long enough, he'd find it staring right at him. The cramped, moldy room was exactly what you'd expect for $79.99 a night with a bottle of White Mountains water included. The back rooms were the quietest, mostly because they didn't have windows. So Sterling occasionally opened the door to get some fresh air circulating. Darkness had started to fall, which meant soon he could move around the small town with less chance of being noticed. The Lexus was still there, hidden underneath a large pine. It wasn't a bad little ride, definitely a woman's sports car. It must've set Reverend back a little, which made Sterling laugh. As tough as Reverend Briggs tried to be, he was a pussycat when it came to his children. Sterling closed the door and went back to the bed where he had laid everything out, including a replica of the time line they had constructed in the pit.

He reviewed his notes from Windsor McGovern. Something Mack had said was bothering him, but he couldn't put a finger on it. He looked over the Mortimer papers a third time.

Then he stopped.

He picked up the article from *Forbes* and focused on the third paragraph. It was only one sentence, but a sentence that wrapped a smile around Sterling's face.

President Wallace Mortimer has made lasting friends with his college roommates, Cooper who went on to build a computer software empire, and Allistor Guyton, Secretary of the Department of Agriculture.

Sterling flipped through the pages of his black book so quickly that he almost ripped out an entire section. He stopped at the first conversation with McGovern. He had written several questions, but it was the last one that jumped off the page. Why was APHIS so dead set on poisoning the blackbirds when it had no hard proof it would save crops? Now the pieces fit together perfectly. APHIS was largely funded by the National Sunflower Association but was also part of the USDA from which it ultimately took its orders. McGovern had mentioned that the head of the USDA was Allistor Guyton, who turns out to be a close friend of Wallace A. Mortimer III, the managerial beneficiary of the Mortimer Family Trust, which not so coincidentally owned the largest sunflower company in the country. Sterling shook his head. Just as he had suspected all along, the answer had been there right in front of him, scattered in bits and pieces.

Sterling dialed the Dartmouth College operator.

"Carlos Sandoza," he said, wondering why all operators had that nasal voice.

"One moment, please."

It wasn't Carlos who answered. "He's not here right now," the man said. Sterling assumed he was a roommate. He had a similar Bronx accent.

"Do you know where he is?"

"Grubbin' at Shabazz. Who's this?"

"I'm calling about a job he applied for. It's pretty important I speak with him as soon as possible. Does he have a cell phone?"

Sterling wrote down the number. "Thanks a lot." He dialed Sandoza's cell. It rang four times, then kicked into voice mail. Sterling tried again. This time it stopped on the second ring.

"What up?" It was Sandoza, still full of attitude.

"Carlos, it's Sterling Bledsoe."

"Professor's brother?"

"Yeah. I need to ask you a couple of questions."

"We already talked."

"I know, but I thought of one thing I forgot to ask you."

"Shoot."

"Did President Mortimer walk Professor Bledsoe to his car?"

"Not to his car, just to the porch."

"Did Mortimer go back inside once Wilson had pulled off?"

"Hmm. After a few minutes."

"Not right away?"

"No. He stood outside and lit a cigar. He smoked a little, then pulled out his cell phone and walked around to the side of the house."

"Are you certain?"

"Positive. I thought it was strange he'd be making a call when he had all those people partying inside."

"Did he make the call or did someone call him?"

Sandoza took his time before answering. "I'm not sure. I was too far away to hear the phone ring. If it did ring."

Sterling paced through the tiny room, trying to keep up with the thoughts speeding through his mind. "How long did he talk?"

"Not too long. Maybe a few minutes, not much more. I was getting into another car when he walked back inside."

"Thanks, Carlos. You've been a big help."

"I don't know what I did, but sure."

Sterling dialed Strahan's cell. It was time for confirmation.

"Got it?" Sterling asked.

"What phone are you on?" Strahan said. "A different number showed up from the last time you called."

"Let's just call it a borrowed phone." These burners were a work of genius, Sterling thought. Worth a lot more than the $50 the dealers charged.

"Hold on. I'm in the car. Let me pull over." The radio fell silent and Sterling could hear the rustling of papers. "You have a pen?"

"Yup."

"There were four incoming calls that day," Sterling checked off the numbers in his book as Strahan read them. Two came from Wilson's phone, matching the times Kay had said he called home. Sterling already knew that. The third call came from the Norwich Police Department, while the fourth number matched the Hanover Police Department.

"Are you sure there were only four incoming?" Sterling said. "No cell phones?"

"March twenty-third, right?"

"Yup."

"Then that's it."

Sterling exhaled slowly. Not what he wanted to hear. He figured Mortimer had placed a call to Kay. He wasn't sure why he thought that, but now the theory had just been blown to hell.

"What about the outgoing?" Sterling asked.

"Five going out." Once again Strahan read the numbers and times and Sterling followed along in his book. The second and third were to Wilson's cell phone. The fourth and fifth calls had been placed to the Norwich Police Department and the Hanover Police. But the first call didn't match any numbers in Sterling's book.

"You sure about that first one?" Sterling asked.

"Positive. These logs are straight from the phone company's computers." Strahan repeated the number to be sure.

Sterling lowered his head and massaged the tangled muscles in the back of his neck. Every time he thought he found an opening, it suddenly closed. "That's it, I guess," he resigned. "Thanks for your help, Stray."

"Wherever you are, Doc, be careful. I was talking with someone in the New York office about another case. Dumars is all over your ass. He's out for blood."

"Yeah, I'm not surprised." Sterling smiled to himself, thinking how foolish Dumars must be looking. "Don't worry, Stray. When I wrap this baby up, I'll give you a couple of strokes on the golf course for all your efforts."

"Fuck you, Doc."

"Ah, the eternal ingrate."

No sooner had Sterling hung up the phone than he dialed the unmatched number. He wasn't sure what he'd say to whoever answered it, but he'd grown so good at lying lately it didn't matter. Voice mail picked up immediately. Sterling was astonished when he heard the recording. He looked down at the time Strahan said the call went out. It was only seconds after Wilson's first call home. Kay had placed a call to Wallace A. Mortimer III.

49

 terling had worked out almost everything. Wilson stumbles upon
the blackbirds on one of his night scouts. He doesn't grow suspicious until he starts finding groups of carcasses, and that's when he enlists
the help of his mentor, Yuri Mandryka. Wilson knows that Mandryka can be
trusted to keep things quiet and even to help figure out what killed the birds.
Somehow Heidi and Wilson meet and begin a friendship, with her expressing
an interest in the environment and wildlife. She accompanies Wilson on
some of his scouts and he confides what he has found on the Potter farm.

 Heidi and Wilson begin to have an affair, and at some point she decides
to take him to meet Kanti, who has also found dead blackbirds on his property.

 Mandryka knows that Wilson is writing a case report on the birds, but
it's unlikely that Heidi and Kanti are initially aware of his intentions to
publish his findings. Kanti does, however, know that Wilson put a call in
to an agency in Washington and was waiting for a response.

 Mortimer's Sunny Fields Company is behind the poisoning of the birds
for obvious reasons. The heavily wooded mountains of Vermont are a perfect place to test a new avicide out of sight of the watchful eyes of the Fish
and Wildlife Service. Mortimer enlists the help of his old college roommate, Allistor Guyton, at the Department of Agriculture, parent of APHIS.
Not surprisingly, APHIS decides to push the Blackbird Project despite
protests from environmentalists and wildlife experts.

 Then comes the night of the big party and the perfect opportunity to kill
Wilson. Kay is home nursing a virus and preparing Wilson's favorite meal.
Wilson leaves the president's mansion and starts driving home. Wilson
places his first call to Kay at a little after seven and tells her that he's on his

way. Kay calls Mortimer, who answers his cell and walks around to the side of the house to take the call. Mortimer calls the two men in the truck, who are already in position on River Road. He informs them that Wilson will be coming over the bridge soon. They pretend to have truck problems when Wilson passes, and once he stops, they chase him into the woods and brutally murder him.

Heidi is next on the list. She knows all the players, but most important, she knows about the birds. Heidi confronts Mortimer, which results in a payoff of half a million dollars. Somehow Serena Mortimer finds out about Heidi and the extortion, which explains the animosity the two women had for each other. Heidi is a liability in every way. The same guys who kill Wilson also kill her, dumping her remains behind the Grand Union once the store has closed.

Now there are still three people alive who know about the blackbirds—Mandryka, Kanti, and Bigfoot. Sterling finally convinces Mandryka to duck out of town for a few days until everything blows over. It's no coincidence that as he's heading up to his cabin, a truck runs him off the road and into a ditch, the driver leaving him for dead. Mandryka describes the same truck that Miles Borwind had seen after he closed the store. The killer, not knowing that Mandryka has survived, assumes two people are left—Kanti and Bigfoot. They haven't been killed already, but they are next on the list. Sterling turned to a fresh page and wrote the questions that still lingered. Why did Kay call Mortimer on his cell after Wilson called her? How did his own face get on that last e-mail that Harry sent? And what did Wilson do with the blackbird papers?

Sterling dialed Sean Kelton's home number. Sean's wife answered the phone.

"Is Sean home?"

"No, he's not. May I ask who's calling?"

"Professor Nelson from the biology department. I wanted to ask him about a grant proposal my lab is working on. Do you know when he might be home?"

"Not for a couple of hours. At least."

"That long, huh?"

"Yeah, he's over at the medical school library pulling some research papers. But if you want to leave your number, I can have him give you a call when he gets home. He should be back before eleven."

"That's all right," Sterling said. "I'm probably turning in early tonight. I'll just try him tomorrow or reach him on blitzmail."

Sterling disconnected the line, grabbed his keys, and jammed a round in his Glock before slipping it into a belt clip holster in the back waistband of his pants. Just to be sure, he also loaded the Beretta and strapped it in his right ankle holster. With his most recent discoveries he probably had enough to steer the investigation in the right direction, but he needed more than that if he was going to nail Mortimer. He needed some luck and a little help from Wilson.

The concrete fortress of the Dana Biomedical Sciences Library stood menacingly at the northern end of the circular entrance to the medical school. Unlike the undergraduate libraries, it saw little traffic. It was a library for the serious medical scientists, mostly graduate students and the occasional premed undergrad who came by to study and rub elbows with their medical idols. Sterling avoided the circular drive, instead pulling the Lexus into a small empty lot around the back. Two students sat on a picnic table bench in the shadows of the library, one playing the guitar, the other accompanying on a tinny harmonica. A golden retriever looked up at both of them with a long expression on his face as if he had a million other things he'd rather be doing.

Sterling entered through the back door and walked down the short hallway of closed offices and laboratories. Whereas the undergraduate libraries had been staffed with security guards and ID checkers, the medical school surprisingly remained open for students or the public to come and go without restrictions. Sterling moved slowly through the first floor, walking down the aisles and peering into the cubicles as if looking for a vacant desk. He had to be careful with Kelton, so a quiet approach would be critical. By now the Dartmouth Security team and Wiley's men had already warned Kelton to stay away from Sterling and to consider him armed and dangerous.

Sterling finished the sweep of the first floor and went on to the second, walking slowly around the perimeter, trying not to draw attention. The narrow aisles were crammed with students toiling under stacks of texts, taking notes on their laptops or the old-fashioned way, by hand. Sterling knew their pain, having spent the better part of his late twenties stuck in stuffy libraries reading till he couldn't keep his eyes open or writing until the pen had dug a permanent impression into the side of his middle finger. Even now he could hold his finger up to the light and turn it at an angle to remind himself of those late, listless nights when all he wanted was to find a warm bed and sleep for an entire year.

The second floor proved a bust, and as Sterling climbed another set of steps, he grew concerned that Kelton had already left or gone to another library. He had Kelton's cell phone number, but calling it might only scare him off. Right now, the element of surprise was a necessary ally.

Sterling found more of the same on the third floor as he walked along the back wall of classrooms where students were holding group study. In one room, they were taking notes from a video recording of a class lecture. Sterling heard the professor's monotone voice repeat "mesoderm," "endoderm," and "ectoderm." An embryology course, Sterling thought to himself.

At the end of the hall, he looked through the door window of the last classroom, ready to climb one more flight of stairs. The room appeared to be empty. Then he saw the sweatshirt. Big Red. Cornell. For a second Sterling wondered why the Ivies were so damn stuck on colors. Why couldn't they find an animal mascot like the normal colleges? The Crimson, Big Green, Old Blue. Sterling pressed his face to the window. No one there. He backed down the hall and found a seat at an empty desk. He could see the door from where he now sat.

Sterling waited a few minutes, then he heard the elevator door open and the sound of sneakers squeaking in the hallway. Then he saw that mop of burnt-orange hair. Sean Kelton, carrying a small brown bag, opened the door to the classroom and closed it behind him. Sterling got up, paused briefly to make sure no one joined him, then quickly walked to the room and entered.

When Kelton looked up and met Sterling's eyes, his already colorless cheeks went from pale to a ghostly white.

"Take it easy, Sean," Sterling said. "I'm just here to ask you a couple of questions."

Kelton nodded slowly, his paralyzed jaws unable to close his mouth. He was grasping his pen so tightly that the skin over his knuckles seemed like it was going to rip.

"I know you've probably heard a lot of bad things about me the last couple of days, but they're all lies," Sterling said. "I did not kill my brother or Heidi Vorscht or anyone else for that matter. I'm being set up, Sean, and the real killer is out there. Do you understand what I'm saying?"

Kelton nodded his head up and down, seemingly incapable of producing words.

"Now you can still help me catch the killer before anyone else gets hurt." Kelton gave another trancelike nod. "I need you to tell me how the mail gets delivered to the lab."

Kelton's face wrinkled into a frown, merging the freckles across his forehead into a straight line. "The mail?"

"That's right. I need to know how mail is delivered to Wilson's lab."

"It's not," Kelton said, his voice dry. "We pick it up from the mail room."

"Every day?"

Kelton nodded. "Twice a day. Once in the morning and once in the afternoon."

"Where's the mail room?"

"Hinman, over in the Hopkins Center."

"Is it open this time of night?"

"The student boxes are always open, but the lab doesn't have a box. We have to pick it up from the counter."

Sterling thought for a minute. It was about ten o'clock. The counter would definitely be closed by now. But there had to be a door somewhere. If he couldn't pick the lock, maybe he could borrow his old friend Otto Winter from the troubleshooter's office. There was probably a smoother plan, but he needed to get into that mail center tonight.

"When's the last time someone went to pick up Wilson's mail?"

Kelton shook his orange mess from side to side. "It's probably been weeks. The lab hasn't been opened since . . ."

"I understand," Sterling said. Neither one of them wanted to hear the words again. "I'm not sure what you're thinking right now, Sean, but I need you to be rational. If I were the killer, I wouldn't be sitting here talking to you so civilly."

Sterling pulled out his gun and waved it so Kelton could get the full effect.

"I could've shot you a long time ago and been well on my way out of town. You have to believe that."

Kelton's eyes were fixed hypnotically on the shiny black gun.

"So I need you to do me a big favor and keep this conversation we've had between us. Don't even tell your wife that you saw me here tonight." Sterling returned the gun to his holster, breaking Kelton's trance. "There are some big and important people caught up in all of this and you can't trust anyone. Understand?"

"Yeah."

"Wilson thanks you," Sterling said. He startled Kelton by taking his hand and shaking it. Then he was out and down the back stairs.

50

The front entrance of the Hop was a blur of students, even at this late hour. A small pack of dogs chased each other in circles. Two Dartmouth Security cruisers idled in front of the building and Sterling thought he recognized one of the officers but couldn't be sure in the darkness. He drove far enough that they couldn't see him, then jumped out of the Lexus and walked through one of the open doors on the side of the building. Two men were delivering what looked like boxes of paper.

A student pointed Sterling downstairs to the basement, where he found a series of bright, deserted corridors. He made two right turns before entering a dark, open area with several walls of small combination mailboxes. The lights burned on as he walked near the mailboxes and activated the motion sensors. Sterling approached the center, where the walls converged into a vortex. A sign giving the counter hours had been posted on the double doors.

A quick look at the doors and Sterling knew he was in luck. This type of lock was the easiest to pick because of the small strip of open space between the doors. Any kind of laminated or hard plastic card would do the trick.

Sterling had it within seconds and immediately began his search for Wilson's mail. The office was in shambles, with mail circulars and envelope bundles scattered everywhere. A mound of oversized boxes had been stacked along the entire back wall with return addresses as far away as China and New Zealand. Looking at the laundry tubs stuffed with postcards and envelopes, he better appreciated the unsung miracles of the U.S. Postal Service.

Sterling next raided a series of wall cabinets, expecting to find more mail, but instead discovering shelves of tape, markers, rubber bands, and other supplies. He stopped suddenly. It sounded like someone was outside. He crept close to the door and listened. A few minutes passed and there was only silence. He went back to his search, raking through the tall laundry tubs, hoping to spot Wilson's name.

Then he noticed the shelves under the front counter. Two rows of plastic U.S. Postal Service bins had been lined up along its length. Sterling's heart kicked into high gear as he pulled the bins out one by one and inspected their contents. So far so good—most of the mail had been marked for the administrative offices and department heads, which meant Wilson's mail would likely be there. And it was. Wilson's name had been written in heavy marker. The bin had been stuffed with so much mail that it barely fit underneath the bottom shelf. He slid it out into the center of the room and cleared a large circle of floor space before turning the bin on its side.

Small letters, scientific journals, sports memorabilia magazines—they all fell into a collapsing heap. There must have been a couple of hundred pieces of mail, but Sterling was looking for a specific package. He put the small envelopes and magazines off to the side, then methodically inspected the packages and larger envelopes.

That's when he found it.

Kelton had said it. *And Professor was very specific about how he wanted us to deliver our drafts. When we were done, we would copy a version onto a diskette and leave that on his desk along with a printed version. We'd also e-mail him a copy. Then as a final precaution, we'd go to the post office and mail him a copy.* Never demand of others what you don't demand of yourself. Wilson had followed the same routine and sent a copy of the paper to himself.

Sterling just stood there, unable to move his eyes past the title: "The Blackbird Papers."

"You did it, Wilson," he whispered. He pushed the other mail aside and took a seat in the middle of the floor.

The manuscript read more like a mystery novel than it did a scientific case report. Wilson began by detailing one of his morning nature scouts when he discovered the carcasses of two blackbirds. He was drawn to the birds because the death seemed fresh, and unlike the other dead animals he had found in the woods, these bodies were intact, untouched by scavengers, almost as if predators had purposely avoided the feast. For the next several pages, Wilson enumerated the birds he discovered, the times he found them, and their various stages of decomposition.

Wilson then dedicated an entire section to Mandryka's laboratory work and the conclusion they had drawn that too many birds had died for it to be a mere coincidence. They searched for an environmental cause, which they isolated in blood samples taken from the dead birds. Bufalin toxin was the active ingredient, but it had been combined with a novel protein that caused the entire molecule to degrade and disappear from the blood, leaving only a chemical trace if caught in time.

Then Sterling read something he hadn't heard before. Wilson reported on a series of suspicious deaths that he had reviewed in the Dartmouth-Hitchcock medical records. Over the last two years, ten people in the Upper Valley had died from "suspicious natural causes." Only a handful of those cases had actually reached the county medical examiner's table, but a finding that either the ME had ignored or thought insignificant was that each of the corpses had an enlarged heart. The most alarming case was an otherwise healthy twenty-one-year-old woman who worked as a hiking guide. She woke up one morning, got into the shower, and dropped dead. Her body was found two days later with the water still running. Her heart, just like the others, not only showed enlargement, but a damaged electrical system, similar to what Mandryka had discovered in the blackbirds. Wilson dug even further and found that all of the "suspicious death" victims lived on property that shared the same water system running through the back of the Potter farm. The toxin had contaminated their well water.

Wilson had saved the best for last. He explained how during one of his night scouts he stumbled on an empty metal canister buried underneath a heap of fallen branches and dead leaves. On the bottom of the concave cylinder, he found the company's stamp: Sunny Fields Company. Wilson had contacted a chemist friend at Harvard and asked him to examine the canister and see if he could analyze the liquid residue. The tests confirmed what he had already expected. Highly concentrated bufalin toxin.

Sterling read the acknowledgments and paused over the name Yuri Mandryka. He placed the manuscript back in the envelope, slid it inside his jacket, and turned off the lights before closing the door. He picked up his cell phone and dialed FBI headquarters and asked to be connected to the cell phone of Agent Lonnie Brusco. A few moments later and the phone was ringing.

"Brusco."

"In before forty-eight hours," Sterling said.

"Are you ready?"

"All the pieces are in place." Sterling started walking down the dark hall, but didn't notice the motion sensors hadn't activated the lights.

"Where are you?" Brusco wanted to know.

"Hanover. I'm heading to the pit." Sterling turned the corner and walked toward the exit sign in front of the dark stairwell. He opened the door, but jumped when he felt something hard digging into his back.

"Put the phone down, Mr. Bledsoe." The voice was deep and uncompromising. "Slowly."

Sterling held the phone with his fingertips and slid it in his front pocket, then raised both hands above his head. The pressure in his back felt like it was going to snap a rib.

"Now slowly put your hands behind your back and put your wrists together."

Sterling obeyed, hoping this would snuff the intense fire burning in his back. Cold metal handcuffs pinched the skin of his wrists, followed by the loud snap of sliding locks. He almost lost his balance as a powerful shove spun him around. He froze when he looked up into the meaty face of the giant mound of flesh towering over him. Bigfoot. No shawl or headband or turquoise-studded vest. Instead, he wore a khaki two-piece suit with a white shirt spread open almost to his shoulders to accommodate his massive neck.

"We need to take a little ride," Bigfoot said, shoving the barrel of the gun so hard into Sterling's chest that he doubled over in pain. "You've been quite a busy man."

51

They rode in silence, except for Sterling's futile attempts at extracting an explanation from the stoic Bigfoot. "Kanti has your answers" was all that Bigfoot was willing to say as the small car strained up the steep mountains and rattled over the rocky dirt roads. Sterling sat crammed in the passenger seat, shoulder to shoulder with Bigfoot, his leg knocking into the stick each time the gear needed to be shifted. He thought about his options but they were limited. His feet were free, but space was so tight in the car, he'd never be able to reposition himself to get a good kick at Bigfoot or the steering wheel. Besides, what would that accomplish other than sending the car plunging down the side of the mountain or provoking a pummeling from the much larger man.

Sterling looked out into the darkness and read aloud the few signs they passed along the deserted road. Bigfoot shot Sterling a menacing look, expressing his displeasure in a low grumble that started deep in his enormous girth and got caught somewhere in the middle of his tree trunk of a neck. Sterling spotted the deer crossing signs, the same they had passed on his first trek to Kanti's house. Then it dawned on him as if a shade had been lifted in his brain. He had his answer. Kanti and Bigfoot were the last two names on the list of those who had known about the blackbirds. Last man standing held all the secrets. Sterling cursed himself for not figuring it out sooner. It all made perfect sense, the way they had enticed him with the message from Ahote and her refusal to answer his questions that afternoon when they spoke behind Mortimer's mansion. Was she part of the plan or had she truly just been the messenger?

Sterling thought of her hypnotic eyes, the color of the waves in the ocean. Strong and unforgiving. He prayed like hell that she had not been a part of all of this, but it only made sense if she had. She worked for Mortimer and worshipped with Kanti. Sterling shook his head. He should've asked more questions, done more investigating. But he was so taken by Kanti's noble presence and the stories and his calling the blackbirds from the sky. Could someone like that be caught up in such a devious and murderous plan?

Bigfoot turned the car onto a small path of tall grass and low-lying shrubs. Two other cars were parked in the clearing, but it was too dark for Sterling to make them out. Bigfoot killed the engine, then lifted himself out of the small car and thundered around to the passenger side, opening Sterling's door and ejecting him from the car like a parent snatching up a disobedient toddler. The thought of running off into the darkness occurred to him, but any escape plans Sterling might have been hatching disappeared the minute he felt the barrel of Bigfoot's gun burrowing once again between his shoulder blades.

Sterling followed the narrow path, stumbling over the rocks as the tree branches and thorns sliced through the sleeves of his jacket. They emerged from the thicket of heavy brush and stepped onto the soft grass of the open lawn. Every light in the house burned through the windows, giving it a strange, partylike atmosphere. Any minute he expected the band to start playing and the balloons to start flying. Then he stopped. He suddenly realized that he was marching to his death. He wondered if a more glorious end to his life would be attempting to run rather than simply walking to his slaughter.

"Keep it moving," Bigfoot grumbled. He pushed the gun so deep in Sterling's back that Sterling thought if his hands were free, he could feel the nose of the barrel poking out of his chest.

Sterling stumbled forward a couple of steps, then regained his footing and walked toward the house. The door opened just as his foot struck the top step. He looked into the cold, unflinching eyes of Kanti, who greeted him with an almost imperceptible nod of the head. Kanti said something to Bigfoot in a foreign tongue, then motioned for Sterling to enter the adjacent room. Sterling wasn't surprised by the two men seated next to each other against the far wall. They had been in that same position when he first met them, their heads leaning toward each other, speaking in low tones. Mortimer was dressed for a day at the races, with his forest green blazer and a gold ascot that looked like it had taken someone hours to fold it just so. The orange flames from the burning fire bounced off of Chief Gaylor's hairless dome as if it were a video screen. He wore a black windbreaker and plaid pants, perfect for a round of golf at the club.

"So the gang's all here," Sterling said, looking into the faces of his brother's killers. "I'm glad I could make it before the champagne is gone."

He felt a hard shove in the middle of his back and tumbled onto the sofa.

"It didn't have to come to this," Mortimer said. The same condescending tone, his chin slightly elevated. "We never intended for anyone to get hurt."

"Because you never intended for anyone to find those blackbirds," Sterling said. Kanti took a seat, but Bigfoot remained standing with the gun aimed at Sterling.

"I would've done anything for someone other than Wilson to have stumbled upon this," Mortimer said. "Not that I expect you to believe me, but I was very fond of your brother and the tremendous service he gave to the school."

"But not fond enough to spare his life," Sterling said.

Mortimer let the words pass. His expression remained flat. "We wouldn't be sitting here right now if you had just listened to us."

"The WLA was set up perfectly to take the hit." It was Gaylor this time. His big, doughy ears twitched like a clown's when he spoke.

"It was too damn easy," Sterling said, adjusting himself on the couch until he found a more comfortable position. "Those rednecks had no more interest in my brother than that bear's claw sitting over there on the mantelpiece."

There was silence as wood popped in the fireplace.

"Now that we're all gathered around the campfire, maybe I can get some answers to a few of my questions," Sterling said.

"Like?" Mortimer said.

"How did you first know that Wilson had discovered the dead birds?"

Mortimer picked up a coffee mug from the end table next to him and took a long drink. "Kanti and I have been working on this for some time," he said. "I explained to him why we needed to control the blackbirds, and he wisely agreed."

Kanti said nothing.

"Because they were damaging crops in the Midwest?" Sterling asked.

"You've done your homework," Mortimer said. "That's right. We needed to find a way to kill some of those damn birds without their deaths getting traced back to us. These were perfect testing grounds, far enough into the woods where no one would notice, away from the Fish and Wildlife Service. What most people don't know is that sunflower seeds will soon be a big business, much bigger than cooking oil. We'll be using it to lubricate automobile engines. It's cheaper and more effective than what's on the market right now. And better for the environment. Kanti and his people saw the importance of protecting sunflowers from these ravaging blackbirds. We compensated them generously, and they helped collect and bury the carcasses. Unfortunately for all of us, Wilson found them."

Sterling digested the words slowly. "So Wilson tells Heidi and she in turn uses it to blackmail you."

"She was a very misguided young woman," Mortimer said. "She played all of us to get what she wanted."

"And how did you manage to get my face in that last e-mail? The one that Harry sent from the lab."

"That was a little more difficult," Mortimer said. "And quite costly." He nodded at Gaylor.

"It was only a matter of time before the lab unscrambled that video and got a clean shot of our man leaving Burke that night," Gaylor picked up. "He had gone in to get the film Professor Bledsoe shot of the dead birds. But we had forgotten about the camera surveillance, and afterward underestimated your team's ability to process a recognizable still photo from it. We knew that e-mail was coming, so we needed someone down in Washington to rearrange things for us. The name is irrelevant, but after we had agreed on a price, he was more than happy to accommodate."

"Does that satisfy your curiosity?" Mortimer asked.

"Just one more thing," Sterling said. "That phone call."

"Which one?"

"The call Kay made to your cell phone. Why was Kay calling you on your cell phone?"

"Because your brother threw away thirty years of my life for a little tramp who never wanted to do anything more than manipulate him like she had everyone else." Sterling turned toward the unlit doorway in the corner of the room. Kay walked out of the shadows and stood defiantly with her arms folded across her chest. She looked tired, as if she had aged ten years in the last couple of weeks. Maybe it was because her hair had been pulled back, but for the first time, Sterling noticed streaks of gray hair along her temples.

"I didn't want to believe it, Kay," Sterling sighed. "I would've accepted any explanation for that call other than this."

"And I didn't want to believe Wilson had betrayed me, betrayed us." Her voice was starting to crack. "I found out about them almost right away. I kept asking myself how he could have done it. I'd been too good to him to be treated like that." She began to cry. "You can't even imagine how much it destroyed me, everything we had built together."

"But murder, Kay? After all those years? Divorce him and take what's yours. But to go along with him being murdered . . ."

Kay wiped her eyes with the backs of her hands. "Look who's talking. You hated your own brother so much that the mention of his name made you physically ill. Don't sit there and preach to me like some saint. Death might be better than the kind of hurt you brought him all those years."

These words stung Sterling. There was no denying how much pain he had caused Wilson through the years. He couldn't help but wonder if Wilson would be alive at that moment had the two of them been on better terms. He looked away from Kay and found himself once again drowning in a sea of what-ifs.

Sterling didn't notice Mortimer nod to Bigfoot.

"Let's go," Bigfoot said, snatching Sterling to his feet. "Time for a little walk."

Sterling knew that all of this had been leading up to something, and now he was going to find out what. He looked at Kay, but she turned her back on him and left the room. Bigfoot shoved him down a short hallway and out the back door. Kanti followed. They walked in the frozen darkness, guided only by the hazy glow of lights from the house. The night calls of the animals filled the air with the sounds of a wild kingdom. Bigfoot shoved him to the edge of the property, then ordered him to stop.

Sterling turned and could barely make out the house off in the distance. He looked down beside him and into a deep hole that had been freshly dug. A shovel stuck out of a mound of wet topsoil.

"One day, they will find me here," Sterling said. "If I figured all this out, so will someone else."

"But they will never find you," Kanti said. "This is protected land, part of the Indian Reservation System. that our people control. Without our permission, they have no rights to search this land. This will be your grave. And it will return you to the earth from which all life is born."

Kanti walked behind Sterling and pulled a key out of his vest. Sterling felt the handcuffs loosen.

"It is dishonorable to kill a man whose body is not free," Kanti said, coming around from behind Sterling. He made a small sign in front of Sterling's face, then returned to Bigfoot's side.

Sterling looked up into the sky, tracing the stars dancing on the black stage of night. He had done this hundreds if not thousands of times as a little boy, allowing his imagination to carry him to distant lands. He thought about Wilson, chased through the woods in these lonely mountains, killed like helpless prey and carved like game fowl. But at least Wilson had gone down with a fight, valiantly struggling to save his life against weapons that his bare hands could never match.

Sterling decided he, too, would fight for his life so that in death he could have honor.

"Let's make this easy," Bigfoot said, almost as if he had read Sterling's mind. "Turn around and kneel. It will be fast."

Sterling looked up into the eyes of the imposing man, searching them for a glimpse of compassion but finding only cold determination. He looked over Bigfoot's shoulders and into the thicket of trees and shrubbery, quickly mapping out the escape route he would try. It was likely he'd be full of lead by the time he reached the dense cover, but if he could get there without too many bullets, he might be able to outrun the enormous man and his ancient leader.

Just as Sterling turned and prepared to run, a shot cracked the still night. He felt a hard thump in his right shoulder that knocked him to the ground. The intense pain came on in seconds, burning him like the jab of a hot poker. A hail of shots rang out and Sterling looked up. He could see Bigfoot's hand jump as the pistol discharged. Bigfoot fired several times, then his body fell backward as a bullet struck his firing arm. He switched the gun to the other hand and returned fire. This time, his leg jerked as a bullet struck his thigh.

Sterling reached down to his ankle holster and pulled out the Beretta. He couldn't lift his shooting arm, so he grabbed the pistol with his left hand and emptied the entire round in Bigfoot's back. Bigfoot fought to remain on his feet as he absorbed the bullets and fell to the ground only after his legs could no longer support his collapsing weight.

As Sterling got to his feet, he realized that Kanti had fled. Sterling ran toward the house, still uncertain who had saved his life.

"You all right, Agent Bledsoe?" Lieutenant Wiley stepped out from the trees, holding his gun firmly, pointing it in the air.

Ahote soon followed. A cacophony of sirens filled the open air and swirling lights cut through the darkness as a platoon of cruisers rushed to the property. Sterling met Wiley and Ahote in the middle of the lawn.

"What took you so damn long, Lieutenant?" Sterling smiled.

"We couldn't find the place at first," Wiley said, winded from all the excitement. "I owe you a big apology, Agent."

"Not necessary," Sterling said, compressing the wounded shoulder with his free hand. "I was beginning to think that this wouldn't work." Sterling pulled the burner out of his jacket pocket. It was still connected to Brusco. "Did I make the forty-eight hours?" he said into the phone.

"By the skin of your teeth," Brusco answered. "Good thinking with keeping the phone line open. We have everything recorded."

"Thanks for believing, Lonnie," Sterling said. "You're a damn good agent."

"We couldn't have done it without her help," Wiley said, pointing to Ahote.

Sterling looked at Ahote. "I owe you my life," he said, bringing her to his chest with his free hand.

She grabbed him tightly, tears spilling down her face. "A lot of this is my fault," she said. "I should've known about this. Instead, I just trusted them."

"Don't be ridiculous," Sterling said. "They had all of us fooled. Except Wilson."

He took out the envelope containing the Blackbird Papers and with his fingers traced the loops and lines of Wilson's handwriting. Sterling had never been one to believe in spirits or the supernatural, but he felt a tingling sensation that started in his fingertips, traveled up his spine, and straightened the small hairs on the back of his neck. His shoulders relaxed and the taut muscles in his back eased in relief. It wasn't too late after all. For the first time he felt connected to a brother he had never known in life, but had come to learn about and even love in death.

52

Even with Veronica at the wheel, the shiny black Porsche wasn't daunted by the steep, rugged climb in the Vermont mountains. Sterling looked out at the familiar, deserted countryside as the wind raced freely through the convertible. His right arm rested in a sling, but his left hand rubbed small patterns along her exposed thigh. The clouds had disappeared and as far as the eye could see there was a soft blanket of light blue sky. Wilson rode along with them in a covered silver urn propped up in the backseat.

Gaylor, Kanti, Bigfoot, and Kay had all accepted plea bargains and been put away in different lockups around the country, serving long sentences despite their deals to cooperate. Mortimer was the only one who got off easy. As the officers rushed into Kanti's house that night, he grabbed Gaylor's gun and fired one fatal shot through his mouth and out the back of his head. Sterling regretted that Mortimer hadn't been forced to suffer the more painful death of public humiliation and scorn.

The actual killers, Horton Crawford and Charlton Gaithers, had been picked up near the Canadian border on a random traffic check. When Crawford's license had been run through the system, the state trooper's computer had flashed an outstanding warrant for his arrest. He later confessed to killing Harry Frumpton in an effort to silence him.

While Sterling was on the run, Dr. Withcott's office had reported to Wiley the laboratory's findings on the saw blade that had broken off in Wilson's chest. Several computer searches later, they had found the store in Ascutney, Vermont, where the blade had been purchased. A combination of receipts and the salesman's memory had identified Horton Crawford as the customer. The impressive length of Crawford's rap sheet suggested that he had bought the blade for something more than carving arts and crafts for the local church fair.

Kay had been stripped of everything she had inherited from the estate, the courts quickly transferring the money, cars, and house to Sterling.

The inside man was identified as Richard West, a low-level investigative specialist who had deposited several large checks in the past several months, all drawn on the Sunny Fields Company account. Among other things, he had doctored Harry's e-mails and the photos to implicate Sterling. He was found dead a couple of days later in the front seat of his car with the garage door closed and the motor running.

Sterling sneaked glances at Veronica. After all they had been through during the last month, he wondered if destiny wasn't sending him a message. She hadn't put any pressure on him, but he could see it in her face, the innocent touches when they were sitting in restaurants or even now as she reached across and ran her hand down the back of his neck. She wanted bigger things for their relationship and this could be the start.

Veronica brought the car around a long curve, and on Sterling's instructions pulled into the same scenic viewing area he had visited by chance a few weeks ago.

"This is it," Sterling said, jumping out and pulling the urn from the backseat. Veronica killed the engine but didn't move. "Come with me," Sterling said.

"Are you sure?"

"Absolutely. I want you to see what Wilson loved so much about these mountains."

Veronica followed Sterling across the road, her hand resting comfortably in the small of his back. They walked up a short flight of steps to reach the viewing platform.

"Isn't this amazing?" Sterling said, nodding toward the open horizon, a kaleidoscope of rich colors and textures.

"It's the most beautiful place I've ever seen," Veronica whispered. "It doesn't even look real."

"Almost what you imagine heaven to be."

They looked out over the side of the mountain and down into the tree-topped terrain of the valley. The jagged white snowcaps stood stoically in the distance. From their perch thousands of feet in the air, the broad

Connecticut River looked like nothing more than a squatter's stream snaking through the rocky quarry. A cackling sound suddenly filled the air, seeming to linger before reluctantly evaporating into the sky. An eagle crested from a nearby tree line, riding the wind in long, lazy arcs. Sterling immediately recognized its white face and tuft of white tail feathers. A bald eagle. As it circled closer, he could make out the hooked bright-yellow beak and feet. Sterling uncapped the urn and pressed close against the railing. He waited for a strong breeze, then slowly emptied the ashes on the back of the wind. Just as Wilson would have wanted.

Acknowledgments

It's interesting how luck and chance happenings can change your life. I've had this story simmering in my head for many years, title and all. But it wasn't until a literary angel by the name of Janet Hill came into my life that this story went from an idea to a reality. Janet is an extremely accomplished editor at Doubleday/Broadway/Harlem Moon. I met her at a gala thanks to one of her authors, E. Lynn Harris, a generous spirit who has selflessly shared with me his wisdoms of the book world. I told Janet about my book idea, and the rest is literary history. Janet introduced me to the incomparable publisher of Doubleday, Steve Rubin, who has supported me from day one and has, over a series of lunches and dinners, shared his publishing genius and vision, which confirmed for me that I was at the right house. Rubes, you're the man, and you know it!

Then came my amazing and tireless editor, Stacy Creamer, who, excuse the cliché, is truly a writer's dream—even if she did go to that school they call Yale. Stacy, thanks for being a magnificent editor and dear friend and making this story sing. You are truly in a class of your own.

I'd be remiss not to mention the rest of the Doubleday crew who have also been terrific: Beth Buschman-Kelly, Stacy's editorial assistant; Bill Thomas, editor-in-chief; Suzanne Herz; Alison Rich; Meredith McGinnis; John Fontana and the rest of the art team for an amazing cover; and the incredible Doubleday sales force.

Thanks to my family—my twin brother, Dana, who is one of the greatest storytellers I know and who has inspired me my entire life to reach for the gold and dream the biggest of dreams. My parents, Rena Cherry and Noy Bustion—I am me only because of the two of you. I hope one day I can accomplish even half of your greatness. My Aunt Lynn, who reads more books than anyone I know and has protected me since I was old enough to get into trouble. My uncles Robert and Johnny—thanks for always being there and making me proud. My grandfather, Robert Cherry Sr.—you will always be the original inspiration, and the lessons and wisdoms you've taught me through life I will one day share with my children.

A very special thanks to my über agent at the William Morris Agency, Jennifer Rudolph Walsh, who I knew when I first met her that she was sheer power, and I soon learned that she could work it like nobody's business. Mary Pender, her ever-helpful and astute assistant, has also been a big help.

My golfing buddies: New York Giant Mike Strahan; the best NFL insider, Jay Glazer; Gene Wolfson; Bob "Brownie" Brown; Ty Williams; and Tony Abrahams. Thanks for tolerating me while I was working on the book. But now that I'm done, get the sticks back out because I'm coming back to the fairways to kick your butts and take your cash!

Special thanks to Harlan Coben. Dude, you're huge! Thanks for showing me the way.

Last but not least, great friends: Jonathan Cardi, Ron Mitchell, and Leon Carter. Thanks to Alex Garfield for my little writing haven. And thanks to all of my teachers who have imparted knowledge and told me I could do whatever I wanted if I worked hard enough. Teachers are the true unsung heroes.